W9-BYR-847

LEGACY

Also by

MOLLY COCHRAN

Poison

The Forever King

Grandmaster

World Without End

The Third Magic

The Broken Sword

LEGACY

MOLLY COCHRAN

A PAULA WISEMAN BOOK

SIMON & SCHUSTER BFYR

NEW YORK   LONDON   TORONTO   SYDNEY   NEW DELHI

SIMON & SCHUSTER BFYR

An imprint of Simon & Schuster Children's Publishing Division
1230 Avenue of the Americas, New York, New York 10020

This book is a work of fiction. Any references to historical events, real people, or real places are used fictitiously. Other names, characters, places, and events are products of the author's imagination, and any resemblance to actual events or places or persons, living or dead, is entirely coincidental.

Copyright © 2011 by Molly C. Murphy
All rights reserved, including the right of reproduction in whole or in part in any form.

SIMON & SCHUSTER BFYR is a trademark of Simon & Schuster, Inc.
For information about special discounts for bulk purchases, please contact Simon & Schuster Special Sales at 1-866-506-1949 or business@simonandschuster.com.
The Simon & Schuster Speakers Bureau can bring authors to your live event. For more information or to book an event, contact the Simon & Schuster Speakers Bureau at 1-866-248-3049 or visit our website at www.simonspeakers.com.
Also available in a SIMON & SCHUSTER BFYR hardcover edition
Book design by Krista Vossen
The text for this book is set in Bodoni.
Manufactured in the United States of America
First SIMON & SCHUSTER BFYR paperback edition December 2012
2 4 6 8 10 9 7 5 3 1

The Library of Congress has cataloged the hardcover edition as follows:
Cochran, Molly.
Legacy / Molly Cochran.
p. cm.
"A Paula Wiseman Book."
Summary: Stuck at a boarding school where her fellow students seem to despise her, Katy soon discovers that Whitfield, Massachusetts, is the place where her mother committed suicide under mysterious circumstances when Katy was a small child, and as dark forces begin to converge on Whitfield, it is up to Katy to unravel her family's many secrets to save the boy she loves and the town itself from destruction.
ISBN 978-1-4424-1739-7 (hc)
[1. Good and evil—Fiction. 2. Supernatural—Fiction. 3. Witches—Fiction. 4. Boarding schools—Fiction. 5. Schools—Fiction. 6. Massachusetts—Fiction.] I. Title.
PZ7.C6394Le 2011
[Fic]—dc23   2011019437
ISBN 978-1-4424-1740-3 (pbk)   ISBN 978-1-4424-1741-0 (eBook)

For Charlotte and Gordon Follett,
who know what love is

CONTENTS

LEGACY

TRANSFIGURATION

I was sixteen years old when I discovered exactly who—and what—I was. Before then, I suppose I wasn't much of anything, just a girl who'd somehow managed to spend most of my life in southern Florida without becoming blonde, athletic, or comfortable with boys.

I'd lived with my father, who did his level best to turn me into the biggest geek in Palm Beach. His main contribution to my discovering myself was to ditch me in a boarding school fifteen hundred miles from everything I knew. *Thanks.*

I brought my hands to my face and tried to warm them with my breath as I waited for the hired car that was to pick me up at Boston's Logan Airport.

I was being sent away because my dad didn't want me anymore.

That's what he always did when he felt uncomfortable about something. He just stopped thinking about it. He'd done that with my mother after she died. And maybe before. By the time

I was old enough to ask questions, he'd already banished her from his memory.

I'd only ever seen one picture of her. It was a sticky, worn photo that I saved from the trash after my dad had tried to throw it out. I reached for the photo in the front pocket of my purse. We had the same eyes. Strange eyes, everyone says, although I don't think they're so weird. I held the picture and waited for the familiar flood of feelings to wash over me. It was like I could feel everything she felt that day—how she was crazy in love with my father. And torn about leaving her family to be with him. And afraid of fire . . .

Beeep beep beeeeep. The blare of a horn tore me from my thoughts. Whitfield Airport Limo had arrived. *Classy*. I slouched into the backseat of the decades-old Crown Vic.

"You ever been to Whitfield before, Miss?"

"Huh?" I looked up to see the driver's eyes in the rearview mirror. They were a piercing blue beneath wild, shaggy white brows. He looked as if he'd spent the past fifty years facing down nor'easters. "Whitfield," he repeated. "Guess it'll take a little getting used to, after New York City."

"I'm not from New York," I said glumly. "My father got a job there."

The skin around the old man's eyes crinkled into a kind smile. "So you're heading out on your own, is it?"

I turned away. I wasn't heading out on my own. I was being discarded. There was a difference.

"But you could look at it that way, couldn't you?"

My head snapped up in irritation. "Excuse me?

"Whitfield may not seem like a very exciting place at first,

but you'd be surprised at how much we've got going on here."
He winked.

Right, I thought. Whitfield, Massachusetts, the fun capital
of the western hemisphere.

"Have you heard of Wonderland?" he asked.

"Yeah, I've heard of it." Wonderland was only the biggest
retail chain in the world. My dad's loathsome girlfriend was
their VP of Public Relations. I heard *nothing but* Wonderland
at home.

"We're going to be getting a new one in town," he said as if
I were a child and he was holding out a puppy.

"That's a thrill," I said. As if every podunk town in America
didn't have a Wonderland. Or a Kmart, Wal-Mart, or, more
likely, all three.

He laughed. "I thought everybody loved Wonderland," he
said. "Least, that's what their commercials tell us."

"I'm not much of a shopper," I said.

"And then, we've got the fog," he went on cheerfully,
undeterred by my obvious hostility toward his hometown.

"Fog?" I couldn't believe he was telling me that watching
fog counted as an activity, second only to shopping at discount
department stores in terms of excitement.

"Our fog's been in every edition of Ripley's *Believe It or Not*
since 1929, when Mr. Ripley started writing it."

He was looking at me expectantly in the rearview mirror, so I
took the bait. "What's so special about it?" I asked with a sigh.

"Depends on what you call special." He chuckled. "But it's
unusual, that's for sure. Only comes to one spot, in a place we
call the Meadow, right in the middle of Old Town. It shows up

eight times a year, like clockwork, and always in time for the first day of school. You're going to Ainsworth School, aren't you?"

I took the packet the school had sent me out of my jacket pocket. "Yes, Ainsworth," I said, reading the return address.

"Forget the name?" He was grinning broadly.

"I guess," I said, confused now. So he wasn't joking. They really did watch the fog come in.

"The public schools are already open. But Ainsworth has a tradition. It waits for the fog."

Perfect. I was entrusting my education to an institution that based its academic schedule, as well as its entertainment, on weather phenomena.

"We're coming into Whitfield's Old Town now," the driver said.

Old was right. Whitfield was a village straight out of Nathaniel Hawthorne, with rows of meticulously maintained stone buildings and three-story frame houses with candles in the windows. The town square was lined with quaint-looking shops selling books and tools and kitchen wares; a combination candy store and café called Choco-Latte; two rustic-but-tasteful eateries; and a storefront with APOTHECARY written across the window.

"The town was founded in 1691 by colonists who'd had it with the Puritans," he announced as if he were a tour guide. "Run off from Salem to the wild tidal waters here, off Whitfield Bay. If you squint, maybe you can see Shaw Island off to your right."

"Er . . ." I interrupted. "Is the school nearby?"

"Coming right up to it," he said. "By the way, that's the Meadow." He nodded toward the left.

I gasped out loud. Ripley had been right—it was one of the

strangest things I'd ever seen, acres of vacant land blanketed by dense fog at least two feet deep, right in the middle of the village square.

"Why is it only in that one place?" I asked.

"If you figure that out, you'll be the first," he said, grinning. "Like I said, Whitfield's more interesting than you might think."

The car stopped in front of a grim-looking building with a discreet sign above the doorway reading, AINSWORTH PREPARATORY SCHOOL, FOUNDED 1691.

"I guess this is the place," I said, as I got out of the car. The driver got my bag from the trunk. I tried to give him a tip, but he refused.

"Not from our own," he said.

"Um, thanks," I replied.

He tipped his hat. "Good luck to you, Miss Ainsworth," he said as he got back in behind the wheel.

"I'm not—" I began, but he was already driving away.

Oh, well. It didn't make any difference. Hell was hell. Whatever they called you there didn't matter much. I picked up my bag and headed toward the doorway.

The wind was high, and smelled like the sea. September was only half over, but this far north, the air was already chilly. I pulled my jacket more tightly around me. It was the heaviest piece of clothing I'd ever owned, but on that blustery New England afternoon it was about as warm as a sheet of wax paper.

I stood there for a moment, blinking away tears as I took in the depressing façade of that dreary brick building. At that moment I felt more cold, lost, and alone than I ever had in my life.

"Welcome home," I whispered before letting myself in.

INITIATION

Inside, I stood at the bottom of an enormous stairway whose white marble steps were so worn with use that they appeared to bow in the middle.

"Gar," I grunted as my suitcase thumped over the mountainous flight, echoing hollowly through the empty halls. The building was a lot bigger than it looked from the outside. "Anyone here?"

"Indeed," a woman's voice called. I looked around. There was no one on the stairway except me. Then she popped up from behind the railing at the top of the stairs with a tinkling laugh.

She looked like a fairy, slim and slight, with big eyes and a chiseled nose.

"Welcome," she said, darting toward me with the quick, quirky motions of a hummingbird. She was young and friendly looking, even though she wore her hair in an old-ladyish bun. "I am Penelope Bean, assistant to the headmistress. You may call me Miss P, if you like." She smiled. "And you are Serenity?"

"I go by Katy," I said quickly.

"Katy?" Miss P mused.

"Yes. Katy Jessevar."

"Jesse—" She looked puzzled. "But you're Serenity Katherine Ainsworth, aren't you?"

"Excuse me?" My father had said something about my ancestors founding the school, but I thought he said they were my mother's relations, not his.

"Well, no matter," Miss P went on. "Come with me." She led me toward an old-fashioned door made of oak and old glass with the word OFFICE printed in an arc on it. "By the way, perhaps you've noticed that the school year starts much later here at Ainsworth than at most other institutions."

"Er . . . That's okay with me," I said stupidly.

"We begin each year on September twenty-first to commemorate the opening of the school—which was founded by your ancestor, Serenity Ainsworth. The townspeople here in Whitfield tend to keep old customs. To balance things out, however, our classes also continue later than other schools— until June twenty-first."

I nodded.

"Well, then," she said brightly. "Let's take care of your paperwork, and then I'll show you around."

Every room at Ainsworth was a little different from every other, whether it was the configuration of the walls, or the view from the large, wavy-paned windows, or the polished wooden floors.

"Here is our chapel," Miss P said, pointing out a plain but

restful room with wooden pews and fresh flowers on a stand. "And over here is the library." This was the first room I'd been in that was inhabited. A lot of students were in here, lounging on the overstuffed chairs or reading at the study tables.

"Students," Miss P announced, "I'd like you to meet our new enrollee, Miss Katy Ains—" She broke off. "I'm so sorry."

"Jessevar," I reminded her.

"Yes, of course." She blushed. "Katy Jessevar, everyone."

It was the moment I'd been dreading, when I'd be introduced as the new kid and everyone would look me over. A few people smiled. Two or three held up their hands in greeting. A few girls huddled around the September issue of *Vogue* looked up momentarily to examine me inch by inch, assessing how much I'd paid for my jeans, rolling their eyes at my Converse sneakers.

Then I saw him. Tall and lean, with honey-colored hair that flopped in a wave over deep-set, intense eyes. His arms were crossed over his chest, and he was staring at me. I felt my cheeks burning. Working up my courage, I smiled.

The boy kept staring. He raised his chin a fraction, and I saw now that his smoky eyes weren't friendly. Not even a little bit.

"Ainsworth," he hissed. He said it softly, but I heard it. Afterward, the only sound in the room was the crackle of the fire.

"Would you like to stay in here for a while, Katy?" Miss P asked.

She might as well have asked if I'd wanted to sit on a lit firecracker. "No," I said, probably too quickly. "I . . . I mean, I think I ought to see the rest of the place first."

"Of course. What was I thinking? We haven't even been to the dorms yet." She smiled. "Katy will see you all again at dinner. I trust you'll invite her to sit with you."

Someone laughed. Not a good sign. Miss P put her hand on my back to show me out. As we left, I saw her glare at the boy in the corner. He glared right back.

Once we were outside the library, a hum of whispers followed us.

"She shouldn't be allowed to come here," someone snarled.

"Are you going to be the one to stop her?" another voice countered. "Or do you want to keep both your nuts?"

Some girls giggled at that, while others shushed him.

"She didn't look so bad."

"She looked like an Ainsworth," someone else said. I recognized the voice. It was him.

I inhaled sharply. *Ainsworth.* That was what the driver of the car that had picked me up at the airport had called me. The same name. The name of the school.

I turned to Miss P. "Why . . ." I began, feeling my cheeks redden. "Why are they—"

Before I could get the rest of the words out, she touched my shoulder. "Don't worry about things you can't control," she said softly.

Then she smiled at me so sweetly that I almost believed her.

The closer we got to the dorms, the more students I saw. Fortunately, Miss P didn't introduce me to any of them. "Forgive me, but I'm running a little short on time, and I want to get you settled into your room."

"My room?" I was expecting an orphanage-type ward with

twenty cots lined up next to each other, like the drawings in the *Madeline* books.

"At Ainsworth, all the rooms are singles," she said. We turned down a short hallway and into a vacant space, where she turned on the light. "Here it is, Katy," she said, opening a pair of wooden shutters over a window with a tiny stained glass panel at the top.

I was stunned. Outside was a breathtaking view of a lake with a weeping willow on the far bank. Nearby was a small rowboat shaded by big trees whose leaves were beginning to color. It was like a scene from a postcard.

"The change of seasons is lovely here," Miss P said wistfully. "You'll be able to see it all."

The only items inside the room were a small dresser, a desk, and a bed covered by a down comforter. "I understand you have no bedding with you, so that will be provided," she said. "You may decorate it however you like, so long as you damage no surfaces. However, the décor must be reasonably tasteful and inoffensive to the common sensibility."

"I understand," I said.

"The lavatory and showers are shared, and you'll find them down the hall to the right. Mealtimes are at seven in the morning, twelve noon, and six in the evening, in the main dining room."

I nodded.

"Speaking of meals, all new students are invited to lunch tomorrow at Hattie's Kitchen. Have you heard of it?"

I shook my head.

"Then you're in for a treat," she said, smiling. "Hattie's is a little restaurant in the Meadow."

"The Meadow? Is that the place that's covered in fog?"

"Exactly. Whitfield's claim to fame."

"I didn't see a building on it."

"Probably because of the fog. And it's not even very dense yet. Once the fog really rolls in, no one will see Hattie's at all." She laughed. "But we all know where it is. It's a charming place, and Hattie herself is as much a part of the school community as we are. We like to say that at Hattie's you always get what you need." Her eyes sparkled. "Well, if you don't have any questions, I'll leave you to unpack." She nodded and started to walk away, but something was sticking in my mind.

"Um, Miss P?"

She turned toward me. "Yes, dear?"

"I was wondering . . . about my name. Everyone here seems to think it's Ainsworth."

She smiled. "It's a natural mistake, Katy. You see, the Ainsworth women traditionally keep their names. It's their husbands who change theirs."

"What?"

"It's not so strange, really. The Japanese used to do it regularly, to maintain a family line."

"The women never change their names?"

"Not if their name is Ainsworth. But clearly that's not the case with you, so we'll just forget it, shall we?"

"Okay," I mumbled.

"And by the way, your legal name, Serenity, . . ."

"Ugh."

" . . . is one that is very well respected here."

"Oh. Sorry."

"Serenity Ainsworth founded our school. She was a teacher

in England, and taught the children of Whitfield as soon as the land here was settled. She was, by all accounts, an extraordinary woman."

"I see."

She smiled again. "We'll still call you Katy, though."

I relaxed. "Thanks."

CHAPTER

•

THREE

 EMPRESS

As soon as she was gone, I fell back on the bed, exhausted. I hadn't slept much during the past three weeks. Or the past three months, really.

I turned my head to look out the window. A breeze was sending ripples over the lake. Somewhere a woodpecker was *klok-klok-klok*ing like crazy, and from far away I could smell the salt air of the ocean. I closed my eyes. Strangely, I felt safer in this room where I'd been for approximately seven minutes than I had for almost as long as I could remember. Oh, I knew I'd probably have a hard time fitting in with the other students—nothing new there—but things like that didn't rattle me anymore.

Not after Madam Mim.

Her name was Madison Lee Mimson or, as I'd dubbed her, Mad Madam Mim, after a crazy sorceress in an animated Disney movie. But she was worse than a cartoon monster.

She was Grendel. Mim was the Beast, the Creature from the Black Lagoon, Godzilla, Mothra, Lex Luthor, Saruman. The motherlode of horrors. And the number one reason I was stuck in Whitfield, Massachusetts, for the foreseeable future.

As a VP of public relations for Wonderland, Mim represented "the interests of Wonderland" up and down the East Coast. I'll never know exactly how she met my father, but within days they were shacked up and some weeks later, Dad and I were on our way to New York to start our "new lives." After years of teaching at a series of small Florida colleges, Dad had gotten an assistant professorship gig at Columbia. Major strings must have been pulled for that. And where there were major strings, there was Mim doing the pulling. It was during the plane ride up that Dad decided to let me in on his plans for my future.

"We . . . that is, *I've* found a school for you, Katherine." Dad looked serious.

Something in his voice made me shiver. He wouldn't make eye contact. "Where is it?" I asked quietly, carefully.

He cleared his throat. "It's a . . . it's a boarding school, Katherine."

"A boarding school?" I squeaked. "Where?"

"It's a fine place, really—"

"But why do I have to live there? How far away is it from you? And *her*."

A long moment passed. Too long. "It's in Whitfield, Massachusetts," he said finally. He looked out the window.

"I see," I said.

"Let me explain." He put his hand over mine. I yanked it away. "There are some things I've never told you, Katherine. About your mother. And her family."

My mother? He had never spoken a word about her. I inclined my head slightly, listening, though I wouldn't look at him. "Go ahead," I whispered.

"Agatha—your mother—er, went to school at Ainsworth. That's the name of the school where you'll be going. Her family founded it, in fact." He smiled. "Which is why they're willing to accept you at no charge."

I felt my jaw clench. "Are you telling me—" my voice caught, "—that you're dumping me in some Dickensian institution in fricking Massachusetts BECAUSE IT'S *FREE?*"

The people in the row next to us turned to stare.

"Katherine—"

"Excuse me," I said, and went to the restroom, where I spent the rest of the flight.

Mim was waiting for us at her Sutton Place apartment. She was blonder than she'd been in Florida, and dressed in a silk-and-lace camisole and jeans, trying to look like the teenager in the family.

"Hi, Kathy," she bubbled.

"Katy."

"Riiiight. So, nice to see you."

She showed us around the apartment, pointing out all the tacky, expensive details that were supposed to impress us.

"And here's where *you'll* sleep, Kay-Kay," Mim said cheerily, gesturing inside a leather-appointed office strewn with papers. "The couch is really comfy."

"Kay-Kay will be fine here," I said dully. I went inside and closed the door.

That night I tried to sleep, but it was a losing battle. This was supposed to be the quietest address in Manhattan, but it still sounded like a jet runway to me. And the leather couch I was lying on was covered with buttons that stabbed into my flesh like pokers. I spent most of the night reading through Mim's work memos, which was how I found out that Wonderland Corp. was considering opening a store in Whitfield, Massachusetts.

So I knew whose idea this really was.

Who does she think she is? I kicked over a pile of papers. I was so furious I couldn't see straight. *It's my father! My life!* I shoved the files littering Mim's desk on the floor. Papers were whirling around the room everywhere. Still I wasn't satisfied. I felt all the anger I'd been penning in about Mim, Dad, school bubble up from the very center of my being until it was shooting out my hands, my fingertips, my eyes. I concentrated on her papers until they swirled into a cone, very attractive, very neat, like the funnel of a tornado. Then, when they were all in motion, I pushed them with my mind out onto the street.

Bite me, Wonderland.

"Why couldn't you?" I heard Mim saying. She had two voices, I'd learned: The throaty, sexy blonde voice she used with my father, and her Wonderland voice, the sound of corporate fingernails against a blackboard. It was demanding. It was confrontational. And it carried.

It was the Wonderland voice I was hearing now. I opened the door a crack.

"You had every chance to explain things on the plane."

"Keep it down, please. She's asleep."

"You've been protecting her far too long, Harrison."

"She doesn't have to know everything."

"Is it better that she find out from the other students?"

"It was a long time ago, Madison. My guess is, no one will even remember."

"Not remember? It was all over the national news! For the past ten years, Wonderland has been paying through the nose for that woman's insanity, and that girl—"

"Her name is Katherine."

"Then *Katherine*"—she spat out my name as if it were an insect that had flown into her mouth—"had better be prepared with a believable story."

"You mean *your* story," Dad put in sharply. "The story your staff wrote to make Wonderland seem like a superhero fighting against a demonically possessed woman."

My breath caught. Who were they talking about?

"It's for her own good, Harrison. If she appears sweet and humble, everything will go easily. With that angelic face, she can carry it off. It can work, a win-win situation all around. We're saying, yes, her mother may have been criminally insane—"

What?

"But things are different now, thanks to—"

"Wonderland," Dad said cynically.

"Thanks to the forgiving community of Whitfield," Mim finished. "And Wonderland." She giggled.

I pushed. Their door slammed open.

"What was that?" Mim asked.

Dad appeared in the doorway down the hall, wearing a silk robe. "What are you doing awake?" he asked, annoyed.

"'Criminally insane'? 'Demonically possessed'?"

He stared at me for a moment, looking scared at first, and

then defeated. Without answering, he closed the door.

We never discussed it again. Dad started teaching at Columbia, Mim worked sixteen hours a day, and I stayed in "Kay-Kay's" room. Three weeks later, a taxi picked me up and took me to LaGuardia Airport.

That was how easy it was for Mim to take my dad from me.

Slowly I sat up and keyed in his cell phone number. The phone rang for a long time before his voicemail message came on.

"This is Dr. Harrison Jessevar. Please leave your name and number and the reason for your call."

"Hi, Dad," I said. "I got here safely." I hesitated. There must have been something else to say. There must have been, but I couldn't figure out what it was. "Bye," I whispered.

Mim took him, but I guess he hadn't been hanging on very tight to begin with.

Chapter

•

Four

 CAKES & ALE

The first thing I saw when I woke up the next morning was a pair of cardinals perched on my windowsill. Behind them, the water on the lake looked pink in the dawn light. Even my memories of yesterday's debacle in the school library had receded somewhat after a decent night's sleep in a place other than Madam Mim's home office.

That afternoon I walked through the fog, which was thicker than it had been the day before, to a little building that looked as if the Seven Dwarfs might have lived there, with sloping, rounded eaves, stucco walls, and windows with hundreds of little square panes separated by black leading. Over the Romanesque door was a sign in rounded script: HATTIE'S KITCHEN.

Inside, it was everything Miss P said it would be, charming without the self-conscious cuteness of places with names like Ye Olde Pubbe. The wooden chairs were big and sturdy and comfortable, four to a table. The windows looked out on every side except for the one facing the street so that, like the school, it gave the sense that the place was in the country, not in a town at all.

I was seated at a table against a wall with two other students, a girl named Verity Lloyd who wore striped tights and a beret, and a boy with white-blond hair that looked as if it had been electrified.

"Cheswick," he said, formally extending his hand to me.

"Uh . . . is that your first name?" I asked.

He nodded crisply. "Cheswick Fortescu."

That figures, I thought. I wasn't going to bring it up with these two, but from what I'd seen, the student body at Ainsworth seemed to be divided into two distinct groups. There were the typical boarding school types, rich kids with cool clothes and names like Muffy. But the second group was totally different—not just different from the Muffies, but different from any kids I'd ever met.

They were definitely geeky, but not public-school geeky. For one thing there were a lot of them, at least half of the student body. Most were local. Some stayed at the school even though their families lived right in town.

But there weren't a million varieties of geeks like there had been at Las Palmas where the halls teemed with Emo kids wearing black eye makeup and tight pants; techno geeks; audiophiles; the Anime freaks; goths; theater nerds; and the kids who wrote poetry and listened to groups like Coldplay and Starsailor, the types I called the QMSes, or Quivering Masses of Sensitivity.

None of these would describe the geek faction at Ainsworth. They were, rather, *confident* geeks, if there is such a thing.

Kids who dressed exactly how they felt and were proud of it, who didn't hate school, or their parents, or even the village they lived in. These were hard-core townies, unapologetic and united. A *tribe* of geeks.

Not that I was part of that tribe. So far, no one except Miss P and Cheswick Fortescu had even said hello to me.

"Have you ever been here before?" Verity asked me.

"No." I looked around. At the table next to us a couple in their twenties was arguing. They were so truly angry with each other that I could almost see sparks flying out of their mouths. "Did anyone get a menu?"

Cheswick laughed, his dandelion-puff hair bouncing. "Nobody gets a menu here," he said. "You just get what you need."

"And you never know what that's going to be," came a deep woman's voice from behind my shoulder.

With a gasp I turned around to see a beautiful middle-aged black woman standing over me. She was very tall, with gorgeous silver-streaked hair that looked as if it had never been cut. Pushed back behind her ears, it hung in dreadlocks to below her waist, interrupted only by a pair of big gold hoop earrings.

"Well, looky here," she said, grinning at me. "An Ainsworth."

Again. *Seriously?*

"Actually—"

"And a beauty, too!" Her eyes widened. "Could you be little Serenity, all grown up?"

I felt myself melting with embarrassment, while making a mental note to complain to Miss P for blabbing about students' personal details.

"My name's Katy. Katy Jessevar."

"Katy Jessevar," she repeated slowly. Then she burst into peals of loud laughter. "Trying to be someone else," she said. "Why? Don't you like who you are?"

I didn't know what to say. I wished the sky would open up and hurl me into another dimension.

"Don't be afraid," she said, touching my cheek. Her hands were rough and bony and warm. "You don't even know who you are yet, but I do. Your eyes tell me everything."

I smiled wanly. She laughed again. So did the others at my table.

The woman chatted with the two of them for a while before moving on to the other new students, but when she passed by on her way to the kitchen, she gave me a big wink.

"That's Hattie," Cheswick said.

"I figured." I folded my hands so that no one would see how they were shaking.

"It's always a little scary the first time you meet her," Verity said kindly. "My parents said I cried."

"Yeah, I can see that as a possibility," I conceded.

"Hey, over there." Cheswick was gesturing with his chin toward another table, where an old man was sitting alone, eating soup and biscuits.

"What is it?" Verity whispered.

"Look what just came in the door."

It was a dog, a spotted little fellow with a jaunty walk and a big canine grin. It made its way directly to the old man and sat down next to him.

The old gent took a while to notice the dog, but when he

did his wizened face broke into a broad, toothless smile. "And who might you be, sir?" he asked in the too-loud way of people who are hard of hearing.

"Woof!" the dog barked in answer, jumping up onto the chair opposite. The man howled with delight. At that moment, a server placed a bowl of kibble in front of the dog, who gobbled it up with gusto. It was a very weird sight, the old man and the dog sitting across the table from each other like old friends playing cards.

"He got what he needed," Cheswick said.

"They both did," Verity added.

"Are dogs allowed in here?" I asked, knowing instantly how lame I sounded.

They laughed. "Everything's allowed here," Cheswick whispered conspiratorially.

The fighting couple was served cake. Within minutes they were eating off each other's forks and playing footsie under the table.

"Everyone gets what they want?" I asked.

"What they *need*," Verity corrected, accepting a platter of tofu from the waitress with a sigh. "I just wish I liked tofu."

Cheswick hit the jackpot with a cheeseburger and fries. I was eyeing it longingly when my meal came—a tuna fish sandwich.

"Isn't it fabulous?" Verity asked, scarfing down her tofu. "Mine is."

"It's okay." I mean, tuna's tuna. It's not like it turned into the nectar of the gods or anything.

I was trying not to drool as Cheswick inhaled his cheeseburger when my foot came across something on the floor. It was a book, a blank book filled with handwriting. I looked at the first page. *Peter Shaw*, it read. *#412.*

"Do you know this person?" I asked.

"Sure," Verity said between mouthfuls. "He's one of us."

"Would you take this to him?"

"Just give it to Hattie," she said.

Since I'd finished my sandwich—it was disappointingly small, with the crusts cut off—I excused myself and took the book into the kitchen, where a staggering number of different platters lined every surface. Hattie was hovering over them all, adding a radish here, a cheese crisp there. In the background, loud reggae music made it seem as if the dishes were all dancing along, moving of their own accord.

"Um, ma'am," I mumbled, way too low for her to hear me.

"Yes!" she answered, whirling around to face me. "Ah, the girl with the false name," she said. "You were not happy with your meal, then?"

"No," I said. "I mean, yes. It was fine. I like tuna."

She laughed. "Good. Do you think you could make such a sandwich yourself?"

I blinked. It was a strange question. "I guess so," I said. "I used to cook for my dad. I can make a few things."

"Good, good."

"Er . . ." I held out the book to her. "This was under my table. It says it belongs to Peter Shaw."

"Ah, Peter, yes. You can take it to him."

I hesitated.

"He's in room 412."

"Yes, I saw that—"

24

"Fine. I'll speak to Miss P about you. Come back soon!" She blew me a kiss.

I stumbled out, not sure exactly what had transpired. Verity and Cheswick were waiting by the door for me. "She told me to give it to this guy Peter," I said. "So if you're going to see him . . ." I held the book aloft, hoping one of them would take it from me.

"She told *you* to give it to him," Verity said.

"All right, all right." Jeez, I thought, what sticklers. I was still resentful over the cheeseburger.

I left the two of them at the gym—they were both runners— promising I'd see them at dinner, then began the long trek to room 412, which naturally was at the very end of the last hall on the fourth floor of the most distant wing of the school. No wonder Verity and Cheswick had refused to help. I hoped Peter Shaw, whoever he was, would appreciate the effort I was making to return his stupid notebook.

I knocked. As soon as the door cracked open, I knew exactly who would be there: Of course, with my luck, of *course* it would be—and it was—the nasty boy from the library.

That's great, I thought as his scowling face came into view. *Just great.*

"I found this at Hattie's Kitchen," I said, holding out the book. "She told me—"

"Thank you," he said coldly. He took the book from me and then, in the same motion, pushed the door so that it would close in my face.

"Hey," I said, pushing it open again. "What the hell's going on with you?"

"I don't know what you're talking about," he said.

"No?" I coughed slightly, hoping to produce a few molecules of saliva. "Well, maybe we can start with that name you and your buddies keep calling me."

He took a step backward, looking as if he were totally surprised. "What, Ainsworth?"

"That's it. Look, whoever you think I am—"

"I *know* who you are, all right?" he bristled. "Even if you pretend you don't."

"I'm not pretending anything. And I've never met you in my life."

He frowned. Two spots of pink appeared on his face beneath the smoky gray of his eyes. "Whatever," he said. "Are we done here?"

We weren't, but I felt the corners of my lips quivering, and I didn't trust my voice. It was just so *unfair*. I hadn't done anything except exist.

"I'll take that as a yes," he said. "Now, if you'll excuse me, Miss *Jessevar*, I'll say good-bye. Have a nice day." He closed the door.

"You, too, jerkface," I muttered.

CHAPTER

·

FIVE

 ALCHEMY

The world is full of horrible people, I thought philosophically. After all, I'd lived with two of them.

My dad finally acknowledged my phone call. He didn't call me back, though. He sent me an email.

> Congratulations on beginning your new school
> term. Never use the phrase "In conclusion."
> HJ

Miss you too, Dad.

Still, it was the first day of classes, so I wasn't going to let anything upset me. Dweeby as it sounds, I always enjoyed the start of a school year, probably because I was usually the best student in every class.

And who knew? I might even make some friends. If I avoided the library, I reasoned, I'd probably never have to see Peter "Sunshine" Shaw again.

Until my first class. There he was, his long limbs folded into one of the antiquated desks, scowling at me from behind the sociology textbook, *Communities in Transition,* as I walked into the classroom.

He was in my algebra class too. Also European history. Wherever I went, it seemed, I was subjected to his snarling if painfully attractive visage. I was beginning to formulate a new philosophical thought: *Contrary to historical belief, horrible people often look really good.*

There was simply no justice.

During the next few weeks I tried to eradicate Peter Shaw's hate-filled countenance from my mind by concentrating on my coursework. Ainsworth was academically a lot better than my old school Las Palmas High could ever hope to be. There were electives, for one thing, just like in college.

I got into a course in, of all things, medieval alchemy. I had no idea what that would cover, but I'd done a lot of reading on medieval literature (Dad's specialty), so I thought I'd be okay. The other weird class I got into was called Existentialism in Fiction. That sounded pretty hard for a high school course, but it was the only elective available when I registered. But at least Verity and Cheswick signed up for that one too.

Unfortunately, so did Peter Shaw.

Like I said, no justice.

At first I thought that maybe I was being paranoid about him disliking me. But I wasn't. If he got to class after I did he made a point of sitting as far away from me as possible. And if he got there first he'd make sure to surround himself with people so that I couldn't sit anywhere near him.

As if I would, anyway. I'd been around long enough to know that lying low was usually the key to not having your lunch money stolen, your cell phone thrown in the toilet, or your locker decorated with colorful epithets. The thing was, though, that I didn't think Peter Shaw was one of *those* kids. I mean, granted, having a cute boy practically gag at the sight of me wasn't my favorite fantasy under any circumstance, but it might have been understandable if Peter was the star quarterback or Homecoming King or something.

But he wasn't any of those things. He was, if anything, as far as I could tell, the King of the Geeks, even though he looked more like a movie star or the front man for a rock band. He was tall and thin and had perfect skin and wild, wavy hair the color of dark gold. He had gray eyes and the kind of thick black eyelashes you sometimes see on little kids. He had big hands with long fingers like a pianist's, and a soft voice and an easy laugh.

Not that I paid much attention to him.

Well, okay, I did. But I couldn't help it. He was just very visible, in addition to being very gorgeous. The Muffies were always hanging around his locker or walking with him to class, asking him to help them with their homework. But he didn't seem to gravitate toward that crowd. It was the geeks who surrounded him most of the time, an army of them, protecting him as if he were their god. Any Muffies who wanted a crack at him had to first penetrate the geek lines of defense.

And he wasn't stupid, either. I could tell from the things he said in Existentialism in Fiction that he thought about ideas in a way that most of the guys I knew didn't. Like when the teacher, Mr. Zeller, asked what Sartre meant in *No Exit* when he wrote that hell is other people, Peter said that he thought every kind of suffering came from other people, even if they were people you loved, and that sometimes loving someone caused more pain than hating them.

I could imagine the response if anyone else had said that. But Peter got away with it. No eye-rolling, no snickers, no barking of "loser!" beneath the guise of a cough. Even I didn't write "QMS" on my notebook, because I knew that he wasn't a Quivering Mass of Sensitivity, and he wasn't just talking to be heard.

On the other hand, he'd also said that some people weren't worth going to hell over, at which point all his cronies turned to look at me.

Strangely, though, even though he was the primo geek god in the Ainsworth pantheon, Peter didn't hang with the geeks outside of school. Sometimes I'd see him on the running track with Verity and Cheswick—both definitely in the protective inner circle, as it turned out—and occasionally I'd see him studying in the library (on those occasions I'd leave as soon as possible, before the geek army got around to pushing my books onto the floor or making fart noises around me), but that was about it as far as his social interaction with them went. He rarely showed up for after-school clubs, and never for dinner. Never. And he wasn't picked up by his parents, either. On Fridays the visitors' lounge would be teeming with local kids whose parents had come to take them home or out to dinner, but Peter was never among them. It seems that he just vanished every weekend, the way he vanished every evening.

I thought about asking Verity and Cheswick where he went, but they had closed ranks against me. I'd been in school for nearly four weeks, and still no one was speaking to me. V and C would occasionally grant me a quick hello, as long as they weren't near any of their friends, but if Peter were around, they'd sneer at me along with the rest of them. It was as if he had ordered everyone to shut me out, and they all obeyed.

The worst of it was, I couldn't even say that Peter was just a prick. Because he wasn't. As much as I hated to admit it, he really seemed like a decent person . . . with everyone except me, that is.

CAULDRON

I might have spent the rest of the year feeling sorry for myself if Miss P hadn't offered me an after-school job at Hattie's. I didn't want it at first—it had never been one of my big dreams to be a kitchen grunt—but at least it would take my mind off what a social failure I was at Ainsworth.

"Come in, and welcome!" Hattie looked up from a pile of bright green scallions to smile at me. "So you've come to help me cook?"

The music—it was the Rolling Stones this time—was so loud I could barely hear her. "Yes, ma'am," I shouted.

"Hattie. And I will call you Katy, as you wish."

"Thank you," I said, though I'm sure she didn't hear me over Mick Jagger.

"Wash your hands and put on an apron. There, by the sink."

That's how it started. No application, no time clock. I didn't know how long I was expected to stay, or even if I would get paid. All I knew was that I'd been ordered to work here, and I was in no position to refuse.

"Now," Hattie said, tossing the scallions into a pot. "Are you clean? Good. You can start with tuna."

"Like a sandwich?" I shouted.

"Just like what you had, m'dear. But make it your own way. With love."

Love. Right. I scrambled around the kitchen concocting what I hoped was the perfect sandwich.

"Is this okay?" I asked.

She frowned. "Very pretty," she said, "but where is the love?"

I blinked. "Love?"

"Yes, yes," Hattie said. "After all, the Ainsworth women understand all about love. They have made it into an art." Her brows knitted together. "Now concentrate!"

Totally intimidated, I tried to focus on the sandwich. What did I love about it, I asked myself. It was good bread, okay. And I liked celery, although I couldn't honestly say I *loved* it. I suppose a tuna somewhere had given its life for this sandwich, and I knew a few vegans who could work up tears over that, but still . . .

"No, no, no!" She snatched the plate out of my hands and propelled me toward the swinging doors leading to the dining room. "Come with me."

At 3:30 in the afternoon, the place was still pretty empty. The old man I'd seen during my first visit here was sitting at a corner table across from his dog, who seemed to be communicating with a series of grunts, growls, and some occasional muffled barking. They both appeared to be having a good time, absolutely engrossed in whatever strange conversation they were sharing.

"That's Mr. Haversall and Dingo. They come in every day now," Hattie said. "But *this* is your customer." She led me to a sour-looking man wearing glasses and a pinstripe suit.

"It's about time," he said. He took one look at the sandwich I'd made, and threw down his napkin. "Oh, *please*," he moaned. "You've got to be kidding. A *sandwich*? What sort of scam are you running here? I suppose you're going to charge me as much for that . . . that *snack* as you would for a steak."

"That's right, sir," Hattie said pleasantly.

"Well, I'm not going to eat it."

I looked over at her, appalled. She gave me a wink. "That would be up to you, sir."

"Well. I *never!*" He made a move to stand up, but Hattie stopped him.

"Just hold up one second, before you go," she said. "Katy, take his hand."

"*What?*" the customer and I both shouted at the same time.

"Just do it."

His hand was slippery and wet and clammy, just the way I thought it would be. Gross. Out of sheer obnoxiousness I clamped down on it until he gave up with a disgusted *tsk* and a flutter of pale eyelashes. Hattie was doing the same thing to his other hand, I noticed.

"Isn't this special," he said, his voice dripping with sarcasm.

"Do it now, Katy," Hattie said. "Love."

Love? Yuck. I didn't want to give love to this cretin. I didn't want to give him jack.

"Do it. Clear your mind."

"Just how long is this session going to take?" the man demanded. "I'd like to include it in the police report."

"Oh, brother," I breathed.

"Katy!"

"Okay, okay," I relented. What a stupid job this was turning out to be. "Love, huh?" I took a deep breath.

"Any day now," the man sneered.

I cleared his voice from my mind, along with everything else—the noise in the restaurant, the words I was thinking, even the feelings that were passing through my mind like scarves floating on the wind. Then into this emptiness I envisioned a big red heart that burst open, filling the space with flowers.

Okay, hearts and flowers, I know this was all very corny, but it was the best I could do on the spur of the moment. Anyway, after that I zeroed in on the heart. It was hollow now, showing scenes from the man's life. I watched him being beaten by some impossibly huge man—I guessed it was how whoever-it-was had looked to him when he was small. I saw a young woman laughing at him and pointing at him as if he were a freak. In fact, the word FREAK popped up and bounced around inside the heart like a screen saver. In the next scene, an old sick woman turned her back on him as he tried to put his arms around her. I saw the woman dying, and this man burying his face in his hands, alone in an empty room.

"Oh," I whispered. I was beginning to understand.

And then it happened: My own heart sort of *shivered*, and then it opened up, too, like a flower, and something shiny and warm poured out of it into his.

"You should have had this a long time ago," I said, before I even knew I'd spoken.

The man's hands were cold and trembling. "I don't know what you're talking about," he said, but the harsh words didn't fit his voice, which cracked with uncertainty. He cleared his throat. "Well, I suppose a sandwich wouldn't hurt. You've taken up so much of my time that I'm really . . ." He looked at me with eyes that were filled with sorrow, a dam that had burst. " . . . hungry . . ."

"Take it," I said. "It's what you need."

A slow smile spread across Hattie's face. "We'll leave you to your lunch now," she said, and we all let go of each other's hands.

We were almost back in the kitchen when Hattie poked me in the ribs with her elbow. "Good girl!" she rumbled.

"Wow." I shook my head. "I don't know where that came from."

"No?" Her eyes slid sideways toward me.

"Is that what you put in *my* tuna sandwich?"

She laughed. "Oh, no. You needed something different. Very different."

We both pushed open the swinging doors with our hips at the same time. Hattie moved on; I didn't. The door swung back, nearly knocking me over.

He was there, in the kitchen, standing in front of me with a crate of lettuce in his hands.

Satan.

Well, almost. Peter Shaw. Actually, he didn't look exactly malevolent, only surprised. Maybe as surprised as I was.

"Oh, Peter," Hattie said breezily. "This is our new helper, Katy."

"Kaaaay," crooned a voice from behind him. It was a child, maybe ten or eleven years old, sitting in what looked like an oversized high chair.

Something was wrong with him. His head lolled to one side. His eyes were crossed. His mouth hung open, and a line of drool ran down the side of his chin in a rough red gully. There were a few broken crayons on the tray in front of him, and a piece of paper with a drawing on it.

"Kaaaay," he repeated, thrusting the drawing toward me.

Hattie dabbed at the drool with a tissue and put her arm around him. "That's right, honey," she said, giving the boy a kiss on the top of his head "This is Katy, our new friend. Katy, this is Peter's brother, Eric. He lives here."

At the sound of his name, the boy kicked his legs and clapped his hands together. The drawing fell on the floor. I picked it up. And gasped.

It was a drawing of birds flying over a lake, and might have been drawn by Michelangelo. The water shimmered. The crayon-colored sky looked so real that I could almost feel the wind moving. The birds themselves were magnificent, each tiny creature muscled and feathered, each sparkling, living eye minutely different from all the others.

"This is unbeliev—" I began, but Eric was twisting around in his chair, shrieking and kicking furiously.

Peter grabbed the drawing out of my hands and smoothed it out in front of his brother. "Leave him alone," he said.

I backed away. "I'm sorry," I said. "It's just that he's so . . ."

"Brain damaged?" Peter spat. "But then, you'd know all about that, wouldn't you?"

"I . . . I . . ." I didn't know what to say.

"Hush, Peter," Hattie interrupted. "She doesn't know any such thing. Katy, dear, you go cut six tomatoes into slices, and take out some basil. I'll show you what to do with it in a minute."

I scurried away to the large walk-in fridge, stealing glances at Eric and Peter from behind my shoulder.

"Why *her*?" I heard Peter ask as I retreated.

Hattie didn't answer him.

CHAPTER

·

SEVEN

 SIGILLUM

By the last week in October I was an old hand in Hattie's Kitchen, part of a three-person crew including Hattie, myself, and my new buddy Peter Shaw. Unlikely as it was, Peter and I managed to stay out of each other's way as we knocked ourselves out to prepare for the annual community Halloween party. Apparently it was an old tradition in Whitfield, as well as the anniversary of the opening of Hattie's, so Halloween was a big deal all around. We spent the week before cooking and freezing enough food for at least two hundred people, and that didn't even count the salads and fruit and sauces and desserts that would have to be made fresh. Since there were only sixteen tables in the dining room, I had no idea how we were going to accommodate everyone.

"Oh, don't worry about that," Hattie said, laughing. "There will be plenty of room, you'll see."

I didn't know how that would be possible, but I'd learned not to doubt anything Hattie said.

It hadn't taken long for me to get used to my job. Every day there'd be a new recipe for me to try, usually with some weird component as part of the mix: An antique silver spoon, a handful of rose petals, the branch of a willow tree, a string of glass beads. Even the music she played, I discovered, went into the food. Once Hattie had me cry real tears into a pot of bean soup. That wasn't easy. I don't like to cry. Still, for the sake of the menu, I worked up a few drops.

Also, she was always making me think or concentrate on some emotion or other. "Pick it out of the air," she'd say, as if things like curiosity and courage were just floating on the breeze, waiting to be snatched up and then tossed into a salad like slices of cucumber.

Everything we did in the kitchen seemed to be infused with some sort of strange spirituality. Strange, but good. Nobody ever left Hattie's kitchen feeling sad or mean or wishing they'd never been born.

Not even me.

So I just went along and did whatever she told me. If Hattie wanted a custard full of perseverance, I gave it to her.

Besides, most of these "spells"—that's what I called them, anyway—were variations on the love bomb I'd given the cranky man in his tuna. Crazy as it seemed, love was becoming my specialty.

Sometimes I wondered if what I was doing really was as magical as it seemed. I mean, I wasn't chanting incantations or burning toads' tongues, but I could actually *feel* the love I was putting into that food.

Or I thought I could feel it.

I asked Hattie about it once, if what we did had anything to do with magic.

"There is magic in everything," she said in her low, warm voice. "You just have to be able to see it. And to see it, you must first believe that you will see it."

Getting ready for the Halloween party was so hectic that I hardly had enough time to read my emails or to do any of the other solitary things that my life used to revolve around. It was as if suddenly my whole world got *bigger*. But it was even more than that: It was as if all my senses were becoming heightened. I could smell the fall air in the food I cooked. I could touch the living heart of a pumpkin or a butternut squash. I could taste the very stars in a sprig of carrot tops. I could hear the song of the sea in the oysters that Peter and I shucked open by the hundreds.

We had arrived at an uneasy but workable truce. That wasn't hard, really, since most of what he did was on the outside—pulling up weeds and rotting stalks from the herb garden, driving Hattie's truck to the docks for seafood, bringing in crates of produce from the market, hauling out the garbage. On the occasions when we'd have to work together, we were usually too busy to do much talking, anyway.

And Eric was always there, drawing those fabulous pictures with his crayon stubs on the backs of paper placemats. I'd never met a sweeter kid in my life. He was irresistible. Every time he held out his little stick-arms to me and yelled "Kaaaay!" I melted. I think I got more hugs from him during our first week together than I'd had in my entire life up till then.

And every time was a weird, unique, and wonderful experience. Eric was all elbows and ribs and flailing head. Whenever I'd go near him, he'd get all excited and kick out his skinny legs, usually connecting painfully with some part of my anatomy, while at the same time grabbing me anywhere he could—my hair was a popular spot—and then crush me to him like his favorite teddy bear.

No one had ever held me like that, as if my being with him were simply the greatest pleasure he could imagine. Or maybe I was just projecting.

At first Peter made a big deal about my not going near his brother, but Eric just insisted on bringing me into their circle, and in time Peter backed off a little. It was a strange quartet, Hattie and Eric and Peter and me. Strange, like everything else in Whitfield.

Halloween didn't start out auspiciously. Eric was sick, so Hattie had to divide her time between his room upstairs and the kitchen which, even at ten in the morning, was a complete nuthouse.

"Of course this would happen on the biggest night of the *year*," Hattie muttered as she carried a stack of pie crusts to the side counter. "Katy, we'll need ten pumpkin, four French silk chocolate, two lemon meringues, and two banana creams. Peter, you start on the vegetables. There's a list on the table. I'll get the bread into the oven."

In place of the usual music, all I heard was the clattering of pans as I gathered the ingredients I needed for the pie fillings.

"I need a roll of parchment!" Hattie cried.

"Coming up."I dropped what I was doing and dragged a

stepladder over to the cabinets. Above the canned goods were dozens of industrial-size rolls of foil and plastic wrap, plus smaller oblongs of wax paper, storage bags of various sizes, take-out boxes, doggie bags, and a variety of liquid containers with lids. "We're in luck," I said, spotting the one remaining roll of parchment. "Hey, what's this?"

There was something behind it, stuck in the corner. From my vantage point on the stepladder it resembled a flattened tree, but when I pulled it out I saw that it was a wall hanging of some kind, with a frayed leather cord that had been snapped in two.

Under the dust and grime I could tell it was really a beautiful thing, a miniature garden trellis filled with climbing dried wildflowers. Along the bottom were some tiny pumpkins flanking a wooden sign with "Hattie's Kitchen" painted on it.

"Look at this," I said, scrambling down with it in my hands. "It'll be perfect for tonight. We'd just have to fix the—"

I don't know what I said after that. I felt a rush in my head as if everything was speeding up and slowing down at the same time. When I looked back down I was still holding the wall hanging, but it was perfect. No dust. No dirt. I touched it and turned it over, examining it on all sides. It looked brand new. *But how?*

I lifted it, felt its weight, smelled the fresh green scent of new flowers. The hanging was going to be a gift for Hattie. *My best friend.* I'd made it myself, in honor of Hattie's opening night, October 31, 1994.

1994? That was before I was even born! I pushed. I struggled. I scrambled to make sense of things, but in the end I wasn't strong enough. When I looked down again I realized that the hands holding the wall hanging *weren't mine.* They belonged to someone older than I was, not *old*, but a grown woman.

And I was not Katy Jessevar any longer. I was *her*, this woman with her slender, busy hands, who smelled like roses and wore blue shoes and white stockings. I had made the wall hanging with flowers from the Meadow and miniature pumpkins I'd grown myself, in a window box. I'd drilled holes into the "Hattie's Kitchen" plaque and used wire to hold it in place.

Hattie wouldn't see it, but on the back of the sign I'd drawn the sigils for "Best Efforts" and "Help From Others." I'd wanted to wish her luck, but every witch knew better than to call for something like "Good Fortune." That was a sure way to trip yourself up, because no one really knew what "good" meant. Or "fortune," either. No, Best Efforts was straightforward. Hattie would always give her best effort. And you never knew when you'd need help. My wish for her was that when that time came, someone with a kind heart would step up to lend a hand. I hoped it would be me.

I put clear nail polish on the pumpkins as a finishing touch, then blew on them. Love breath. As I did, I caught sight of my reflection in the mirror on the dresser. It was disturbing. My eyes were as strange as everyone said they were, inside and out, strange eyes that saw farther than I wanted to see.

I wish, I wish . . . but there was no sigil for what I wanted. I wanted a subtraction. *Take away the sight, the gift, the visions, the knowledge. I'll trade them all, gladly, for a life like everyone else's, a normal life spent with no thought of what was coming, no thought of the Darkness, the Darkness and the fire that was its sou . . .*

In the mirror the breath that poured out of me caught fire and spun around me like a dragon's.

I shut my eyes tight. *Not real,* I told myself. I'd had these visions before. They didn't mean anything. But behind that rational, clear thought was another, a voice speaking softly from deep inside, from a place that knew more than my mind could ever know. And that voice said, *Not yet. But soon.*

Oh yes, it was coming. My nightmare vision would darken the whole sky and destroy us all. But who would believe me? Why was I the only one who could see it?

Run! I thought desperately. I could run away, couldn't I? Leave this place, take the people I loved, move far away. . . .

No, no, no. Darkness and fire. That was how my world would end, I knew, and nothing I could do would stop that.

The flames exploded around me. I felt my skin blistering, smelled my charring flesh.

I screamed.

I came to in Peter's arms.

"Katy, Katy!" Hattie was pressing a wet cloth to my face. "What happened, child?"

"I don't know," I said. The parchment and the wall hanging were lying on the floor beside me. "I was bringing this thing to you, and—" I touched it with the tip of my finger. Instantly I felt the fire around me again. I jerked my hand away. "It was as if I was someone else," I explained, bewildered. "A whole other person."

"Never mind," Hattie said. "Did you hit your head?"

"No, I'm fine, except . . ." I pointed to the hanging. "*She* made that. The person I . . . I was. It was for you, I think. She wrote something on the back of the sign."

"Oh?" Hattie chewed her lip as she untwisted the thin wires. There on the back, just where the woman in my—what? Fantasy? Dream?—had drawn them, were two geometric symbols.

"Best Efforts," I remembered.

"Help From Others," she added, her eyes filling.

"They're sigils."

"Yes."

"But how did I know that? I've never even heard that word before. 'Sigil'? What's it even mean?" I heard my voice growing shrill with panic.

"You probably read it somewhere," Peter said. He made it sound as if I was showboating.

"I'm telling the truth!" I shouted.

"Shh." Hattie stroked my hair. "I know you are. What else did you see?"

"Well . . ." I didn't know if I should even mention this part.

"Go on."

"And then the room burned around her," I said quickly. "At least, I—she—imagined it did."

Peter frowned, but said nothing.

"Hey, I don't understand it, either," I said defensively.

"The Darkness," Hattie whispered. "Even then she saw it coming."

"That's what she called it," I blurted, astonished that Hattie would accept what I was saying so easily. "But it wasn't really darkness. It was *fire*. And it was as if she knew . . ."

Peter pushed me onto the floor and moved away from me, a look of suppressed rage on his face.

"Hush up, boy," Hattie spat.

He threw up his hands and stomped back to the vegetable table.

I pulled myself up to a sitting position. "Tell me what's going on," I said, too tired to play any more games.

"I should have known," Hattie said. "The first day you worked here. When you touched that man's hand, you could see his whole life."

"I guess."

"That is your gift, Katy."

I shrugged. "It was more like a game, really—"

"No." Her eyes were stern. "It was never a game."

"But I was concentrating then. It doesn't happen all the time."

"It still happened. And now you touched this—" She smoothed the tips of her fingers over the hanging. "—and you saw the one who fashioned it. You *became* her."

"But how?" I asked. "And why? Why me? Why *her*?" I rubbed my eyes. "I didn't even know her."

Hattie took my hand and exhaled, a long, ragged breath. "Yes, you did," she whispered. "She was your mother."

JUSTICE

An ear-piercing shriek broke the tension. It was Eric. His screaming shook the walls. Peter wanted to go to him, but Hattie insisted that he stay in the kitchen with me.

It was embarrassing. I hadn't meant to make a scene, especially not today. And Peter Shaw and his crappy attitude were the last things I wanted to have around while I was trying to figure out what had happened.

I'd somehow gotten into the head of my *mother*. My dead mother, who my dad and his girlfriend had called criminally insane. And what else? Oh, yes, demonically possessed.

"You're supposed to be making coleslaw," Peter reminded me. I jumped.

I had kind of come to a standstill over the twenty-gallon mixer. The vat was filled with eight heads' worth of sliced, chopped, and marinated cabbage. All I had to add now was mayonnaise, seasoning, lemon juice, and twenty grated carrots. It was some time after carrot number ten that I'd zoned out.

"Yeah," I said. "Sorry."

"Don't know what you're doing here, anyway," he grumbled.

"I was invited to work here," I said, full of bravado.

"You were invited because you're an Ainsworth."

I slammed my fist on the counter. "Doesn't anyone around here listen? My name is—"

"It's Ainsworth," he said quietly. "Whatever you say, whatever you *believe*, you're one of them. What happened today proved that."

I looked at the floor. "I think that was just . . . stress . . ."

He threw up his hands. "*Stress*? You were reading a dead person's thoughts, Katy."

"Hattie said it was a gift."

"Yeah. An evil gift." He picked up the wall hanging from the counter and threw it into the garbage bin.

"How dare you!" I huffed. "My mother made that!"

"Your mother was a psycho!" he spat.

I lunged at him. He grabbed both my wrists and held me at arms' length. "Do you want to know what kind of person your mother was? I'll tell you. When my brother was a baby—a *baby*—she picked him up and threw him against a wall."

I felt the air whoosh out of me.

"I was there. I saw it. So did Hattie. And about a hundred other people."

"You're lying!" I screamed.

"Go to the library and look up the news stories," he said. "Afterward, she walked away like nothing had happened."

My arms felt suddenly too heavy to hold up. Peter dropped them with a look of disgust, as if my skin had dirtied his hands.

"And by the way, your dear old mom was right about the

fire coming for her. She set it herself. Burned down your house while she was inside."

He walked back to the cutting table, picked up his knife, and began attacking a bunch of onions as if he wanted to destroy them. Then he gathered up the skins and roots and dumped them in the garbage, on top of my mother's wall hanging.

The cool October air was a shock to my system as I burst out of Hattie's back kitchen door. Between the wisps of coming fog and the tears streaming down my face I could barely see in front of me, but I didn't care. I wasn't ever going back to the restaurant. Or to school, for that matter.

I had to pull my hair to stop myself from screaming. I coughed for a while, sobbing. And then I started to run. I ran until I could hardly breathe, and after that I walked. If I could have walked off the face of the earth, I would have, but I only made it as far as Old Town.

There was just too much to sort out all at once. *My* house? Peter had said that my mother had set fire to my house. Had I lived here once? Here in Whitfield?

I realized then that I'd been circling the library for an hour. There was no point in putting it off. I knew I wouldn't get a moment of peace until I knew if the terrible things Peter had told me were true.

I didn't know where to start looking in the microfilm files, because I had no idea when everything was supposed to have happened. Peter had said that Eric had been a baby, so I went back ten years in the local paper. While I was going through the headlines for each issue, I tried to remember my own life. It's funny, how little you remember when there's no one to remind you. My father had never spoken a word about my mother. It occurred to me now that maybe he hadn't just forgotten all about our time with her. Maybe he had made a point of keeping that part of our lives carefully blank.

Who was my mother? I didn't remember. That is, I remembered *having* a mother. I remembered *missing* my mother, crying over her every night until I had no more tears left. I imagined her constantly, as an angel, or a movie star, or a pixie on my shoulder, whispering in my ear. But I really had no inkling of what she looked like until I found the photograph that Dad had thrown away. And even though I'd only been a little kid when she died, I'd always felt ashamed that I didn't remember her.

For me, she was just a space, a hole in my heart that was never filled.

After a half hour I found the first story. "Local Woman Attacks Infant, Sets Fire." A bizarre headline. And on the following day, an even stranger one: "Wonderland Scene of Attempted Baby Slaying." Apparently, the "crazed woman who may have been under the influence of hallucinogenic drugs" had tried to kill Eric Shaw in the Home Improvements section of the biggest discount department store in Whitfield. And the third: "Witchcraft May Figure in Ainsworth Infanticide."

By the fourth day permutations of the story were appearing not only in the local press, but also in the Boston and New York papers. By week's end, *Time*, *Newsweek*, and every other national magazine were running pictures of Whitfield ("A New Salem?"); the house on Summer Street that my mother had burned down with herself in it; the desecrated interior of the Wonderland store where the incident had taken place (an amateur photo for which the publication had paid an enormous price showed a stack of two-by-fours stained with Eric's blood); a police mug shot of Hattie Scott, who had been arrested as a possible co-conspirator, but later released; and my mother. There were so many pictures of her: yearbook photos from high school, snapshots from picnics and Christmases and meetings in rooms with flags in the corners. *Where had they all come from?* I wondered. There were no other people in the pictures. Some of the photographs looked as if other figures had once been included, but had been removed. No one had wanted to be associated with her, I guessed.

Then came the secondary stories, many of them clearly public relations pieces about how the Wonderland Corporation had generously assumed all of Eric's medical expenses, even though Wonderland and its subsidiaries were in no way involved in the tragedy.

"Our customers are like our family," announced someone who I imagined was Madam Mim's mentor, "and Wonderland takes care of family." I wondered how long it had taken their Executive Committee to come up with that spontaneous outpouring of concern. Wonderland had gone to great lengths to eradicate the psychological mark left by those bloodstains on its lumber. It had built a $130 million children's neurology center named "Planet Wonderland" alongside Whitfield Memorial Hospital. It was a state-of-the-art medical facility that looked like a theme park decorated in cartoon colors, with play areas on every floor and a toddler-size train in the lobby. Now, ten years after the incident that prompted this corporate altruism, the company was taking the last step in distancing itself from the horror by replacing the current building with another, bigger, brighter Wonderland Megastore on the other side of Whitfield.

The other news sidebar—fortunately, one that didn't amount to much in the press—was about my mother's alleged association with the occult. ("Is Witchcraft Making A Comeback?") None of these stories had any facts in them, and probably wouldn't even have been conceived if Whitfield hadn't been in the heart of Witch Hunt country back in colonial times. The only "evidence" that my mother had been a witch was the word of some New Age store merchant who'd once sold her something called a "scrying mirror."

And yet, in my vision—or whatever that experience I'd had was—she had called herself a witch. She had inscribed magic symbols on the wall hanging, and had witnessed her own future death by fire.

Had my father known? That was the part that sent ice water shooting through my veins. All the stories included the fact that Agatha Ainsworth had had a husband and a six-year-old daughter. The daughter's name was never mentioned, but the husband's was.

It was Harold Ainsworth.

My eyes were burning and my head felt as if it were going to explode. I left the microfilm room, logged onto one of the library's computers, and sent an email to my father, asking a single question:

When did you change your name?

I didn't expect him to answer me, because that was how Dad handled every situation he didn't like. He pretended it didn't exist. But I knew it was true. It explained why everyone thought my name was Ainsworth. Because it *was*. Or had been.

And then, after my mother went insane and tried to kill . . . Eric . . .

Oh, God, I thought, trying to keep my heart from bursting out of my chest. Peter was right. My mother was a psychopath.

And my father, who had changed his name to hers, following an age-old tradition, had changed it again—from Harold to Harrison, from Ainsworth to Jessevar, which is probably what it had been originally—to protect me. He had kept me ignorant all these years because he knew that the truth would have been too hard.

I was the offspring of a monster.

CHAPTER

·

NINE

 SAMHAIN EVE

Outside, it was already getting dark. I was nauseated. Maybe if I sat on the library steps for a while I might get to feeling well enough to . . . What? Set myself on fire?

I buried my face in my hands. It was true, it was all true. That was why no one at school wanted to be my friend. That was why Peter was so disgusted when I'd picked up on my mother's thoughts. And why he wanted me to stay away from Eric. There was no place for me to go anymore. No place at all.

"Get up, Katy. We have to go to Hattie's." I looked up in surprise.

It was Peter. "You left over four hours ago," he said, consulting his watch.

I tried to dry my eyes on my sleeve, but I just couldn't stop crying. After a few minutes, I stopped making the effort.

"That's okay," he said after a while, and sat down beside me. "Here." He handed me a handkerchief. A real handkerchief, not a tissue or a paper napkin from the dining room. I hesitated for a moment, and he offered it to me again. "You can blow your nose in it," he said.

I took it from him. I guess it was clear that I wasn't going to start any conversations. There was nothing more to say. I just wanted him to leave.

He cleared his throat. "Hattie sent me to find you," he said.

Well, you found me, Sherlock, I thought. *So you can buzz off now.*

"It's the busiest night of the year, and Eric's sick. There's a lot to do."

I tried to move away from him, but I was pressed against the railing as it was.

"I'm sorry," he said, so quietly that I could hardly hear him, even though he was six inches away. "About today." He looked at the darkening sky, then down at his feet again. "Look, I understand if you don't want to come back to the restaurant. We'll get by. But I was wrong to tell you those things."

I blew my nose into his handkerchief. "They were true."

"The truth can mean different things to different people," he said.

I stood up. "Whatever," I rasped, and walked away.

I'd gone twelve blocks before realizing I was heading toward Hattie's, but I kept going. However I felt about Peter, or myself, he'd been right about it being the busiest night of the year. There were going to be a zillion people there vying for sixteen tables, Eric was sick, and I'd left a lot of things undone. I owed it to Hattie to go back, if only for this one shift.

The fog was up in the Meadow. It must have come in all at once, while I was in town. Walking into it was like falling into a cloud, dense and moist and so thick that I couldn't see anything at all, and the only thing I could hear was the sound of my own breathing. About halfway to Hattie's, judging from how far I'd walked, I encountered—of all people—Mr. Haversall, the old man who ate lunch every day with his dog. He was wearing a neon pink shirt. The dog wore an illuminated collar.

"Hey, there!" he called to me, waving broadly. "Are ye lost in this pea soup?"

"Hi, Mr. Haversall," I said, hoping I didn't look too teary. "Hi, Dingo."

"Ah, it's one of our own," he said, tipping his cap. "Couldn't see you at first."

"Well, I can sure see you." I gave Dingo a scratch behind his ears.

The old man chuckled. "Ayuh, these here're my docent clothes."

"Docent?" I asked.

"A guide," he said.

"Oh. You're directing people to the party."

He laughed so hard his knee twitched. "No, you goose of a girl! Them as wants to go to the party just has to follow their feet." He raised his eyebrows and spoke in a whisper. "I'm directing them *out* of the Meadow. You know . . ." His rheumy eyes scanned the horizon suspiciously from left to right. " . . . the cowen."

"Cows?" I asked.

He screeched with laughter. "Off with you, Miss Ainsworth! Cows, indeed!" Dingo jumped up and down, barking joyfully. "Tell Miss Hattie to save us a seat!"

"Okay," I said doubtfully, although he had already

disappeared in the fog. For a while I heard Dingo barking in the distance, but before long that, too, fell into silence.

"Follow your feet," I muttered. "What's that supposed to mean? For all I know, I could be walking in a gigantic . . ."

And suddenly there it was. Light and laughter and music, and people everywhere.

"Gracious, girl," Hattie said, grabbing my arm and hauling me into the kitchen. "We need fifteen salads in the next half hour. Start with the crab."

I nodded. "Uh, is Peter—"

"Yes, yes. He beat you by five minutes, and I have a piece of my mind to give both of you," she said, handing me a wooden spoon. "But right now, we all have to get to work."

Somehow we got all the food made. Hattie gave me a black bistro apron to serve in. I guess Peter got one too. I couldn't look at him.

There must have been ten dishes, all different, all for specific guests, on the tray that Hattie helped me hoist onto my shoulder. "Go clockwise, starting with the table in front of the band," she said.

"What band?"

"Just go." She pushed me through the swinging doors.

When I saw the place, it took all of my self-control not to drop the tray. Hattie's postage stamp-sized dining room had somehow transformed into a vast reception hall with nearly a hundred tables illuminated by tall candles and occasional fountains glowing with unearthly light. The view from the windows was of the Meadow, where deer grazed beneath a full moon. Beyond it was the fog, rising like a luminous blue-white hedge.

"How did you do it?" I asked when I came back into the kitchen.

"Glamour," Hattie said, immediately starting to fill the tray with new dishes.

"But the place actually is bigger," I went on doggedly. "It's not just an illusion."

"Everything is an illusion, m'dear," Hattie said. "Good and bad, right and wrong. Life itself. And death. Illusion, all of it."

I swallowed.

"Then again, the dining room would have to be bigger, wouldn't it?" She shrugged as she shook the water out of a bunch of leaf lettuce. "How else would it fit all those people?"

I didn't know how to respond to that. It was the sort of logic only people like Miss P could follow. "Er . . . right," I said. I forced myself to think about nothing except which table was getting which dishes. Anything deeper than that would be dangerous, I knew. *Concentrate on the food. Just concentrate on the food,* I told myself.

Just then, Peter swooshed through the doors. The band's version of "Witch Queen of New Orleans" momentarily swelled. Peter and I avoided each other's eyes as the three of us filled our trays with both hands.

"All the twenty-seven families are here," Hattie said. "Some of them came thousands of miles for this party."

Peter laughed. "Some people will do anything for a free drink."

"Who are the—" I started to ask, but the walls were shaking. Eric was kicking. Even through the din of the music, the kitchen, and the guests' conversation, we could hear him crying.

"Gracious," Hattie said, exasperated. "I was hoping he would stay asleep. I'll have to bring him down here now. Mercy!" She shook her head. "You two go. Hurry, before the food gets cold." She sent us on our way and took off in the other direction, upstairs.

In the dining room, Mr. Haversall waved to me as I passed. He had changed into a tuxedo. Dingo wore a bandana with a skull-and-crossbones motif. There were people of all ages there, from small children to ancient crones towing oxygen tanks. It was like a big wedding, where everybody knows everybody else. There were even some kids from school who were there with their families. They all made a point of joking and talking with Peter. Naturally, none of them spoke to me.

Most of the guests were in costume, some of them very elaborate. There were Elizabethans in ruffs and codpieces, Victorians wearing heavy jewelry over their velvet gowns, a number of medieval Guineveres and Merlins, and a few that were pure fantasy. Verity Lloyd was made up to look like Pippi Longstocking. That wasn't much of a stretch. Cheswick was tricked out in a velvet smoking jacket. I think he was trying for Edward Cullen, although with Cheswick's finger-in-a-light-socket hair, I don't think he quite pulled it off.

When I got back to the kitchen, Hattie was carrying Eric in her arms.

"Kaaaay . . ." He rubbed his eyes and looked as if he were about to burst into tears again.

"Hey, guy," I said, going over to him.

"Don't," Hattie said.

It seemed that Hattie had finally come around to Peter's thinking. "Fine," I said and went back to loading my tray.

We all understood why I couldn't be trusted with Eric, but he didn't, and started wailing.

"Take him into the dining room," Hattie told Peter. "The activity will distract him."

Peter looked nervous. "Are you sure?" he asked. He glanced over at me. "I mean, he's sick."

"It'll be all right. He's coming out of it," Hattie said. "He'll sleep."

While Peter was gone, Hattie and I filled his tray. Her hands worked with tremendous speed and ease, arranging each dish so that it looked as good as it tasted, all the while chatting or singing along with the band's music.

"So this is a family party?" I asked, remembering what she'd said earlier. There was no point in being sullen, and small talk didn't hurt anyone.

"That's right. Everyone in the dining room is a descendent of one of the twenty-seven families who originally settled here," she said while arranging a platter of *brie en croute* with fresh figs. "They were . . . special people. Most of those descendents still live in Old Town."

"Special?"

"Like your mother. Like me."

My skin prickled, as if a cold wind had suddenly blown through the room.

"Like you, Katy," she added.

I swallowed. I think Hattie knew there were a thousand questions I wanted to ask, because she held a finger to my lips.

"Plenty of time for that," she said. "Anyway, those people"—she nodded toward the doors leading to the dining room—"are the only ones who can get into the Meadow in the fog, when it comes. Everyone else is cowen."

"That's the word Mr. Haversall used. He said he was guiding them out of the Meadow."

"That's one of his jobs."

"But why aren't they welcome? The . . . the cowen?"

"What?" Hattie looked irritated. "What a question. Cowen can't stay because they're . . ." She exhaled, searching for the word.

"Not special," I offered.

She smiled. "Just so."

"But what about the school lunch? Wasn't everyone invited?"

"We make an exception on that day," she said. "That was why Mr. Haversall wasn't working then."

"So he's . . . special, too."

Hattie nodded. "The Haversalls are among the twenty-seven families," she said.

Peter burst through the doors. "Where's my tray?"

"Right here," Hattie said, and shooed us out.

Amazingly, the whole dinner went smoothly, and everyone seemed to be in a good mood. The dance floor was packed and the bar was swarming with middle-aged revelers. By nine o'clock, everyone was finished eating. Peter was clearing coffee cups and dessert plates off the tables while I walked around with a pitcher refilling water glasses. Some children were already asleep, including Eric, who sprawled over his high chair like an amoeba.

He was really too big for that chair, and he'd been fidgeting in it so long that his pantleg was all twisted around his knee and his sneaker was dangling off his big toe. Also, I don't want to be disgusting here, but I was pretty sure he'd wet his diaper too. I couldn't do anything about that part, but I thought he'd be more comfortable if I rearranged him in the chair.

Big mistake. As soon as I came near him, his foot shot out and slammed me in the stomach. I was carrying the pitcher at the time, so water sloshed all over me. I thought I heard a few people—probably kids from school—laughing about it, but mostly no one really paid much attention, at least until Eric started screaming and punching the air like he was trying to kill me.

Then Peter appeared from out of nowhere, and shoved me halfway across the room. "Get away from him!" he bellowed.

Everyone looked. Now the kids really were laughing. I could hear them, because no one else was saying anything. Even the band stopped playing except for the trumpet player, who went on for a few lame bars of "The Lonely Bull" by himself before giving up. My only thought was to get back into the kitchen so that I could grab my jacket and get the hell out of that place. Trying to muster the last shreds of my dignity, I pushed my dripping, flattened hair out of my eyes, said "excuse me" to the people standing around me, and hoped my rubber legs would remember how to walk.

I don't think they did. There was a thump that knocked the pitcher into my chest with unbelievable force, and then a fireball—yes, a *fireball*, that's the only way to describe it— seemed to emanate from the pitcher onto the wall right beside Eric's head, where it exploded in flames.

"Fire!" someone shouted, and the whole place burst into pandemonium, with people screaming and crawling over one another to get to the exits as the flames spread with astonishing speed over the wall.

I knew that it was too late for water, even if I'd had some in my pitcher. The only way this thing was going to be quelled was by suffocating it. As soon as that idea came into my head, I pictured a blanket of blue gelatin moving toward the fire, covering it, wetting it down. Then, once I had the picture, I pushed.

Somewhere in a corner of my mind I could see Peter pulling Eric out of the high chair, but it was as if he were in a movie I was watching. I was completely with the blanket, smoothing it over the flames, hearing them sputter and sizzle as they succumbed in a haze of smoke.

It was all over in a minute. The guests who a few moments ago were crazed with panic now just looked sheepish and drained the cocktail glasses they'd hung on to during the melee. A lot of them didn't even seem to notice that anything had gone on at all. Hattie ran into the room and lifted Eric, who was kicking and screaming like a madman, out of his brother's arms.

"What happened here?" she demanded.

Peter nodded toward the charred half-moon on the wall.

"She started it," a girl my age volunteered, pointing at me.

"Go back where you belong!" Hattie snapped.

The girl made a face and, with a flounce of her red hair, stomped off. Hattie just shook her head impatiently and hauled Eric away.

That left Peter and me standing alone and facing each other. I wanted to tell him that I hadn't started the fire, but I doubted that he would believe me.

More than anything I just wanted to go back to my dorm, although I knew that wouldn't be for some time. The place was a wreck after the stampede that had broken out after the fire. There was food all over the floor, lots of broken plates and glasses, and pools of spilled liquid.

"I'll go . . ." My voice came out sounding like Gollum's in *Lord of the Rings*. I cleared my throat. " . . . find a mop," I finished in a whisper.

MAGUS

At school on Monday some of the kids in Peter Shaw's inner circle tried to block my way at the top of the stairs.

"Where're you going, Katy?" The girl who'd accused me at the party stepped forward. I recognized her wavy red hair. Her name was Becca, I think. She'd never spoken to me before. The others—I guess there were around ten of them—slowly gathered around me so that I was surrounded on three sides, with the stairs behind me. I tried to maneuver past them, but the whole group shifted whenever I moved.

"Maybe you don't know how we feel here about people who attack little kids," Becca said.

"While they're sleeping," someone added.

"Or setting fires in a crowded place."

"All our families were there," another voice put in. It was Verity. She looked pained. "You could have killed them all."

"No," I said. "It wasn't—"

"You were the only one there without parents."

I looked around. They were closing in on me. The only way out, it seemed, was down the marble stairway. I backed down one step. Two.

"Did you come here to finish what your mother started?" an earnest-looking boy asked.

"Why couldn't you just leave us alone?"

"What did Eric Shaw ever do to you?"

"Or to your mom?"

"Did you think changing your name would fool anyone?"

"Snake eyes."

Three steps. They moved closer. I shuffled backward, teetering. My books tumbled out of my arms, scattering papers all over the stairs below. I was going to fall, I knew. My arms windmilled. The last thing I saw before I lost my balance was Becca's mouth spread like a toad's into an expression of malicious satisfaction.

Just when I was sure I was going to end up smeared across those white marble stairs, someone ran up behind me and broke my fall.

Peter.

I don't know how he managed to keep his balance with me crashing into him. All I knew was that instead of being dead, I was now lying across his arms, so close to him that I could feel the beating of his heart.

He was looking up at the crowd, his gray eyes incandescent with fury. "Why are you doing this?" he shouted, his voice cracking. "She didn't start that fire, you morons, she put it out!"

My head snapped around. He *knew*?

"And she saved my brother, while the rest of you were running around like a bunch of scared chickens!"

The expressions on the faces of my would-be attackers were more bewildered than menacing now.

"Are you all right?" he asked softly, leaning over me.

I nodded as he set me down and helped me pick up my books and papers. My hands were shaking so badly I could barely move my fingers.

"I'll walk you to class," Peter said. Then, to make a point, he put his arm around me and led me through the phalanx of bodies at the top of the stairs.

The late bell rang, and Becca and the others dispersed. As we approached my classroom Peter and I were alone in the hall. His arm was still around me, even though there was no one to protect me from.

"I guess I owe you big time," I said.

"It's the other way around. I saw what you did Saturday. I should have thanked you then, but I was . . ."

"That's okay," I said.

"And . . . I'm sorry I shoved you. It wasn't what you think. That is . . ." His hands fidgeted uncomfortably. "You didn't do anything wrong. With Eric. I know you like him."

I nodded.

"And the other thing, at the library. I meant that."

I held up my hand. "You didn't have to apologize. I told you, it was the truth."

"And I told *you*—"

"That truth can mean different things to different people."

There was a hint of a smile in his eyes. "You remembered that?"

I felt myself blushing. "I didn't understand what you were talking about then," I admitted. "But I guess it's like how you and Becca both saw what happened Saturday at the party, only you ended up with two different versions of what I did. She thought I started the fire. You thought I stopped it."

"I'm right, she's wrong," he said.

This time it was my turn to laugh. "How do you know?"

"Because you couldn't have created that fireball." There was no humor in his eyes now. "Whoever did that had more chops than you could have come up with."

It took me a moment to absorb what he was saying. "You mean you think someone shot that thing at Eric *deliberately*?"

He shrugged. "There was a lot of energy in the room. Those people . . ."

"The twenty-seven families."

"Yes. Well, they're . . ."

"Special, I know. Hattie's word."

"Right. Special." He chewed his lip and stared at me through narrowed eyes, as if he didn't know how much he wanted to tell me. "I'm just saying you might not want to look too closely at them. At us."

"You? I thought I was the freak here."

"No, you fit right in. The Ainsworths are one of the twenty-seven families, but you didn't grow up here, so you don't really know what's going on. You don't know what can happen to you."

"What's that?" I asked. "What can happen?"

He turned his head away. I could see him wrestling with himself over something. Then he looked at me with his soft gray eyes that seemed to pull me into the center of his soul. "Nothing," he said quietly. "I won't let it."

I felt my stomach flip.

"Will you sit with me at lunch today?"

I think my mouth fell open. I prayed it didn't, but I think it did. His arm was still around me. I could smell his aftershave . . .

"Yoo-hoo there!" Miss P was heading purposefully down the hall toward us, her shoes clacking. "Miss Jessevar!"

I sighed. I figured she was going to yell at us for being in the hall after the late bell. "We—"

"Please go to the visitors' lounge at once," she said. "I'll notify your instructor that you'll be late for class." She cocked her head quizzically at Peter. "Why are you here after the bell, Mr. Shaw?" she asked, but didn't wait for an answer. "Never mind. Just get to wherever you're going. Good day." She clacked away.

Then Peter took my hand. "I'll look for you in the dining room," he said, giving my palm a little squeeze.

My feet felt as if they were dancing as I made my way to the visitors' lounge. In fact, I was so preoccupied with thoughts of Peter (he *squeezed my hand!*) that I didn't realize until I was almost at the door how odd it was that I should have a visitor at all. "Dad?" I asked tentatively at the entrance.

Wrong. Instead there were two women who looked as if they represented the Temperance League.

One was very old, probably close to eighty, and appeared to be dressed in her Halloween party clothes, all lace and black velvet, with high-button boots and a doily-like object that hung across her head like crocheted dog ears.

But it was the other one who held my attention. She was

in her late thirties, I guessed, and though pretty, not very remarkable except for one thing:

She looked exactly like my mother.

The resemblance to the woman I only knew from a photograph was so startling that I felt my breath involuntarily whooshing into my lungs. "Mom?" I whispered.

"Hello, Serenity," the older woman said kindly. "I am Elizabeth Ainsworth, your great-grandmother. And this is your Aunt Agnes."

The younger woman stepped forward, offering her hand. "Your mother Agatha was my twin sister," she said.

She smiled at me with bright green eyes that were gentle and loving and beautiful. Not a monster's eyes, but an angel's. My mother's eyes. My own.

"We've come to tell you about your family," she said.

FAMILIA

Agnes and Elizabeth Ainsworth, my aunt and great-grandmother, lived together in a rambling old house in Old Town, not far from the school.

The doors were open, and workmen were going in and out carrying lumber for wainscoting.

"Watch your step, dear," Mrs. Ainsworth cautioned.

The men all tipped their caps in unison. As soon as they saw me, though, all their tools and wood clattered to the ground.

"Carry on, Jonathan," she ordered, unperturbed. "She's one of us."

"Yes, ma'am." He nodded to me, but his eyes slid immediately toward Agnes as we approached.

She blushed. "Jonathan," she whispered, lowering her eyes.

"Miss Agnes," he whispered in return.

Inside, the rooms seemed to spread out in all directions from a central hallway. Our destination was a parlor with wooden shutters over the windows and a stone fireplace above which hung a large glass-framed piece of needlepoint.

"That was fashioned by a distant ancestor," Mrs. Ainsworth said. "She was very clever with knots. Shortbread?" She held out a plate of cookies while Agnes made tea in the kitchen.

I accepted one, but I couldn't take my eyes from the needlepoint. It was obviously very old, with Ss that looked like Fs, but in perfect condition. There were three lines of text, nonsensical to me, interwoven with flowers and vines:

> In the alban field, the circling mists twist low
>
> Kith and kin draw the Botte on crafted bow.
>
> Arise, great Arrow—swift as sparrow, sprung from below.

"What does that mean?" I asked.

The old woman glanced over her shoulder at it. "It's a spell," she said. "A community spell. Nine families of the twenty-seven have been given these three lines to memorize through eternity. Nine others remember another three, and so on. There are nine lines in all. When all the lines are spoken, the spell is cast."

I swallowed. "Spell?" I croaked.

So she was one of them too. A "special" person.

We stared at one another blankly for a moment. Then Mrs. Ainsworth coughed and fluttered a handkerchief in her hands. "Good gracious, you're not cowen, are you?"

"Of course she isn't," Agnes said, hurrying in with a tray of tea things. "Hattie was quite certain. Nevertheless, Katy is new here. There are many things she doesn't understand."

She poured a cup of tea and handed it to me. "Please don't be alarmed if we seem . . . odd to you. We are an ancient family. Some of our ways may seem quaint."

I nodded. "I'm happy to see you," I said, relying on form so that I wouldn't have to try explaining the jumble of thoughts swirling inside my head. "Until today, I never knew I had any relatives. Any family at all, except for my dad."

Mrs. Ainsworth sniffed. "Your father did not understand our ways," she said. "It is always a mistake for our kind to marry cowen."

"Our kind?" I asked.

"Witches," she said.

"Oh." I looked to Agnes. She'd said it. Actually used the word. "Grandmother, please," Agnes hushed. "That is not a term we should use."

"Not with cowen," Mrs. Ainsworth clarified. "But Serenity surely—"

"She goes by Katy," Agnes said crisply. "And that in itself should tell us that she is not ready to hear—"

Mrs. Ainsworth looked pained. "You were so dear to us." Her teacup rattled in its saucer. "And we've missed you . . . so much . . ." She had to set the cup down and cover her face. This was my great-grandmother, I realized. Batty or not, she was my legacy, my blood. I moved to sit beside her, and she threw her arms around me with a little cry and the soft scent of powder.

"Oh, my precious child," she whispered, her eyes filled with tears. "Do you really not remember us at all?"

"I'm sorry," I said. "I really don't remember ever being here before."

She took my hand. "Darling Katy," she said. "How difficult it must have been for you all these years."

"Perhaps it was better, under the circumstances," Agnes said. "Her father was cowen. She may not have manifested at all." She looked at me curiously. "Or did you?"

"Did . . . did I what?" I stammered.

"Display some unusual ability before you came to Whitfield. Something that you may have felt wasn't quite . . . well, normal."

I inhaled sharply. I'd never told anyone about the pushing before. "Well, sometimes I think I can make things move. Actually, I don't know if I can or not. It's probably just my imagination."

The two women exchanged a glance between them.

"We heard about the party," Agnes said. "And the fire."

"I didn't set the fire," I said stolidly.

"No, of course not."

"I put it out. I pushed. Made something move. Only this time it wasn't a real object. I used a blanket. But the blanket was only in my mind." I shook my head. "I'll bet that sounds completely crazy."

"Not to us, dear," Mrs. Ainsworth said.

Agnes looked stern. "We don't care for that term, either."

"Oh, stop it, Agnes!" The old woman waved her handkerchief agitatedly. "One mustn't say 'witches'. One mustn't say 'crazy'. For heaven's sake, why can't you just let people say what they mean!"

Agnes was silent for a long moment. Finally she said, "Of course, Grandmother. You're right. The name-calling hasn't done us in yet."

"And it won't, as long as we don't let it," Mrs. Ainsworth said stubbornly.

"Is it because of my mother?" I asked. "The name-calling, I mean."

"Only the crazy part," Mrs. Ainsworth said, shifting in her seat. "People have been calling us witches for centuries." She raised her eyebrows. "Ourselves included."

A little puff of air escaped my lips. *Witches.*

Agnes sighed. "All right. I just wanted to avoid shocking Katy." She turned toward me. "You see, among the uninitiated—"

"She means 'ignorant,'" Mrs. Ainsworth interrupted.

" . . . the term 'witch' is sometimes misunderstood. Ordinary people—cowen—often believe that witches are evil, or even worship the devil. We don't really know why this misunderstanding came into being, except—"

"Oh, pooh. Of course we know. Men aren't comfortable with women having power, and the kind of power witches have tends to be inherited through women. Some men can do magic, of course, but far more women. It's in our nature. Even cowen women know when their babies are in distress."

"Nevertheless, in their world, that sort of ability isn't honored. To cowen, power means money, influence, and physical strength. Getting others to do what they want." Agnes sat up straighter. "But our world is different. Our first ancestors were humans with extraordinary abilities: Magicians, shamans, witch doctors, medicine women. Also clairvoyants, psychometrists, teleporters . . . psychics of one stripe or other."

"What's a psychometrist?" I asked.

"Someone who can see into another's life by touching an object belonging to that person."

I sucked in my breath. That was what I'd done at the restaurant, with my mother's wall hanging.

"We know, dear," Mrs. Ainsworth said kindly. "Hattie told us. These episodes will probably occur more and more often. That is why we came to you, despite . . ." Her voice trailed away.

"Your father forbade us to contact you," Agnes said. "He made that very clear when he left Whitfield with you. We are going against his express wishes by speaking with you now. Knowing that, you may leave now or at any time, and we of course will never bother you again."

"But we wanted you to know that you're not alone," Mrs. Ainsworth said, stroking my hair.

"I don't want to leave," I said. "Yet," I added cautiously.

Agnes' lips curved into a slight smile. "At any rate, cowen believe that these special abilities—the sort of thing that you've begun to exhibit—are not gifts, but merely aberrations of normal behavior. Many of them don't believe these abilities even exist at all. Everything to them is a trick, an illusion, a lie."

"Or crazy," Mrs. Ainsworth added.

Agnes didn't say anything to that. The two of them just sat for a moment, absorbed in their own thoughts and, it seemed to me, inexpressibly sad.

"Was she?" I asked. Both women looked at me, their heads turning in unison. "My mother. Was she crazy?"

Neither spoke for a moment. Finally Mrs. Ainsworth said, "We don't know, dear." Her voice cracked. "She was the most gifted witch in Whitfield. Perhaps too gifted. Her abilities may have been too great for her mind to bear. We know it was very hard for her to see some of the things she saw."

"The Darkness," I said. "That's what she called it, 'The Darkness, with fire as its soul.'"

The old woman's face sagged. "We call it the Darkness because we cannot see it. All we see are the results of its power, the evil it spreads." She dabbed at her eyes. "It was, however, well known to your mother. She had been in its presence at a young age."

She took a long, ragged breath. "You tell her, Agnes."

My aunt templed her fingers, thinking carefully before she spoke. "Your mother possessed a most rare and peculiar talent. She was what we call an oracle, one who can see the future. Like all great gifts, it was both a blessing and a curse.

"But to tell you about my sister, I must first tell you about our parents. They were intense, passionate people, a very political couple during very political times. When Agatha and I were fourteen, they visited a remote community of expatriates in Africa. It was supposed to be some kind of people's paradise, where everyone shared things equally, and there wouldn't be any kind of government interference. No taxes, no wars."

"Unfortunately, that didn't turn out to be the case," Mrs. Ainsworth said. "Thank God you had the flu, Agnes."

My mother's twin cleared her throat. "Yes, it was just the three of them, our parents and Agatha. The day after they arrived, gunfire broke out in the compound. Almost everyone was killed."

"My . . . grandparents?" I asked hoarsely.

Agnes nodded. Mrs. Ainsworth covered her eyes with her handkerchief. Her wrinkled hand was trembling like a leaf in the wind. I put my arm around her. "Agatha made it back home, though," she said. "She was never the same, but she came back."

"For the rest of her life, Agatha was obsessed with the Darkness."

"And so, Katy," Mrs. Ainsworth said gently, "we can't really say with any certainty that your mother wasn't . . . mentally incapacitated by this event." She wrung the handkerchief in her hands. "I think it may have been why she married a cowen. To get away from her visions."

"As if she could."

"Then again, the Ainsworth women always marry for love." The old woman smiled. "Whatever demons she battled, dear, your mother did love your father. Very much."

If only he could have loved her back, I thought.

"I believe she planned to move away from Whitfield and raise you as cowen," Agnes said. "Your father was already in the process of changing his name back to what it had been when . . . when the incident happened with the Shaw baby."

"Why did she do it?" Mrs. Ainsworth whispered. Clearly, she had asked herself the same agonizing question for the past ten years. "How could she even think of doing such a thing?"

Agnes shook her head.

"Your father blamed us," Mrs. Ainsworth said. "He said that we'd fostered Agatha's insanity. He'd never believed in witches, you see, and Agatha may have hidden her talents from him at the beginning."

"So of course when she could no longer hide them, he interpreted her abilities as psychosis."

"We tried to keep in touch with you, but all our letters were returned. Also, there was such a fuss made in the news that we thought perhaps he was right to take you away."

Something occurred to me. "You weren't at the Halloween party," I said.

"No." Agnes looked at her hands. "We keep to ourselves these days."

"But Hattie said that all twenty-seven families were represented. Who was there for the Ainsworths?"

They both looked at me then. "Why, you, dear," Mrs. Ainsworth said.

"Oh." I blinked. "Everyone knew from the beginning, then," I said. "Everyone except me."

The old woman clucked. "Shameful," she said. "Keeping you in the dark like that. Naturally, as soon as you'd matriculated at the school, word spread like wildfire. That's why we've made ourselves known to you. After what happened at the restaurant, Hattie thought that . . . well . . ."

"That I'd need a family?" I suggested.

"We're sorry that it's such a notorious family," Mrs. Ainsworth said. "But at least you know that there are two people who care about you."

"And care very much," Agnes added.

My eyes filled. My heart felt as if it would burst. I wasn't alone. I belonged here with these women, and with Hattie Scott, and Eric. And with Peter.

I belonged with them all.

Finally, I belonged.

CHAPTER

•

TWELVE

 SORCIERE

There are all kinds of magic, I've learned. Some is spectacular, and bends your mind just to think about it. But there's other magic, too, quiet magic that maybe you don't even notice unless you're looking for it.

Hattie says that magic, like love, has to be believed to be seen. Once I became willing to see I noticed magic everywhere, in the trees and the wind and the sea, in the way everything changes all the time, but is still beautiful.

Whitfield was full to the brim with magic. My job was full of magic too. Hattie kept me on even after the Halloween rush, teaching me how to make all sorts of soups and stews, mulled cider and hot chocolate, plus whatever exotic things she came up with. Once we made a dish called *yang gobchang-gui* (broiled beef tripe and chitterlings) (!!!), infused with an anti-anxiety spell, for two Korean students who wandered in tense and left mellow.

School, on the other hand, wasn't magical. It was just

common sense not to try reality-bending things in front of the Muffies. But I was doing better there, too. Thanks to Peter, people started opening up to me a little. I rarely had to eat lunch alone anymore. Verity and Cheswick issued a standing invitation for me to run with them on the indoor track after school. I think it was their way of apologizing for wanting to kill me that day.

I visited the relatives a couple of times a week. I even talked them into having dinner at the restaurant a few times. Hattie cooked for them on those occasions, though. I guess they needed more magic than I could come up with.

I grew to understand exactly why my dad had fallen in love with my mother. If Agatha had been anything like Agnes, he'd only have had to listen to her discourse for five minutes on *Le Morte d'Arthur*, and he'd be hooked.

Mrs. Ainsworth tried to teach me tatting, which is lace-making, but all of my efforts came out looking like maps of the Yucatán. So we switched to quilting, where I fared a little better, although my only task was to cut out the little squares. Still, I liked it because it gave me a chance to just sit with her. Everything about her was soft and gentle and cloudlike. I realized that, even when I didn't know she existed, I'd missed her.

She told me I could call her Elizabeth, but that just seemed wrong. And "great-grandmother" was really awkward. Finally I came up with "Gram," which I hoped she wouldn't think was too familiar. One day I tried it, tentatively, as I held up a quilting square.

"How's this . . . Gram?" I swallowed.

She smiled. "It's perfect," she whispered, adding "Katy."

Sometimes a name can mean a lot.

Then there was Peter. Peter, with his beautiful chiseled face and eyes like an angry sea. Peter, who'd caught me in his perfectly muscled arms on a marble staircase. Oh, Peter . . .

Actually, Peter hadn't done anything romantic since that day.

What if he was only being nice when he walked me to class, or joked with me at work, or stayed up with me late nights studying? What if he was just being friendly when he took me to his friends' dorm parties?

Maybe he totally wasn't interested in me at all. Maybe he was gay.

The prospect began to gnaw at me. I wished I knew someone who understood these things. I needed a consultant, but I couldn't think of any girls who might be able to help me. Verity Lloyd was, if anything, even less worldly than I was. The Muffy girls would probably know, but I could just imagine what they'd say if I asked them how to get my pseudo-boyfriend to kiss me.

So I did the unthinkable. I went to my relatives.

Aunt Agnes was standing in the entryway, talking with Jonathan and his crew. I was glad my great-grandmother wasn't around. I loved her, but I wouldn't feel right talking about the possible homosexuality of my boyfriend with an eighty-year-old woman who wore a doily on her head.

As I approached, once again all the lumber and tools fell out of the carpenters' hands onto the ground. It occurred to me that these guys must be the clumsiest workmen in New England.

"It's all right," Agnes said quickly. "Katy's a teleporter."

"Oh, is she now?" Jonathan asked, smiling in surprise, although it was not the degree of surprise I might have expected from a workman hearing that information. Then he lowered his hand to his side and spread his fingers. The fallen hammer shot upward through the air into his waiting palm.

"Me, too," he said cheerfully.

It took me a moment to recover, but as he and his men all summoned their tools in the same manner, I realized that they hadn't actually dropped anything when they'd seen me coming, because they hadn't actually been holding anything in the first place. The materials they'd been working with had been suspended in midair.

"Get me one of those three-inch planks, would you, pretty?" Jonathan asked, gesturing toward a pile of wood.

"Uh, sure," I said, picking one up. They were very thin and light. "Do you want more than one?"

"One'll do. But don't use your hands." He winked at Agnes. "Well, you said she was a witch, didn't you?"

Agnes crossed her arms over her chest. "She doesn't need to prove anything to you, Jonathan."

"Oh, let her." He gave me a smile of encouragement. "Have at it, Katy."

I hesitated. I'd never pushed in front of anyone before. There was the incident at the Halloween party, but the blanket I'd used to put out the fire was imaginary, so no one really saw anything.

Blushing a little, I tried to forget my embarrassment and concentrate on moving the wainscoting. *Up*, I thought, and there it was, easy as pie. Then I pushed it toward Jonathan. It wobbled a little at first, dipping and veering off course once when I looked over at Agnes.

"Hold on to it, Katy," Jonathan whispered. That brought my attention back to the piece of wood. "Right, girl. Put it in this slot here." The wood moved into place with a satisfying *snick*. "There you go," he said, nailing it in. "You'd make a fine carpenter, I'd wager."

I was so pleased with myself that I focused back on the lumber and lifted the whole pile into the air, organizing it into a solid wall before sending it flying over to Jonathan. He laughed out loud and applauded.

"That will do, Katy," Agnes said. "There is no need to show off."

The wood clattered to the floor. "I'm sorry," I said.

"You shouldn't have spoken, Agnes," Jonathan said with quiet authority. He was methodically putting the planks back in place against the wall. "The girl's got a gift."

Two red spots appeared on her cheeks. "Yes," she said. "More than one. Come along, Katy."

Jonathan's hands were full, so he didn't tip his hat, but he acknowledged her leaving with a nod. It was clear to me that they were in love with each other.

I was flushed and thirsty from my unexpected triumph with the wainscoting. Agnes gave me a glass of lemonade and a piece of cheese. "It's important to eat something after doing magic," she said. "Food brings you back."

I knew what she was talking about. While I was pushing, I felt light. Light, and growing lighter by the second. It was almost as if I were disappearing, little by little.

"You are, first and foremost, a human animal," she said. "Not a witch, not a mind, but a physical being. Don't forget that," she said.

"I won't." It seemed to be the perfect introduction to what I wanted to talk about, so I jumped right in. "Actually, that's why I'm here," I said, trying to hide my extreme discomfort. "Because I'm an animal. Er . . ."

She cocked her head.

"That is . . ."

She looked at me as if I were speaking Chinese. I supposed it hadn't been a very good segue, after all.

"Is this about a boy?" she inquired.

Was I so obvious? "No," I lied. "Of course not."

"Who is he?"

"Peter Shaw." So much for my expertise as a dissembler. "Do you think he's gay?"

"Excuse me?"

I considered running, but I knew it wouldn't do any good. One word from Agnes, and Jonathan would trip me up with a floating two-by-four. "Never mind," I mumbled.

"Are you considering him as a love partner?" she asked.

I wished I'd never been born. A *love partner*. Old maid aunts actually thought in terms like that. This was all becoming a horrible dream.

"He's cowen," she said finally.

"No, he's not. He was serving at the Halloween party, same as me. Isn't that the litmus test—getting through the fog in the Meadow?"

"He gets in because of Hattie," she said. "Peter is her ward. Once he's of age, I doubt that he'll ever find his way back."

"But the Shaws are one of the twenty-seven families."

Agnes stiffened. "Not that they'd ever admit it."

"Does that matter? They're the oldest family in Whitfield."

"Not the oldest," Agnes said archly. "Only the richest."

"Does that matter?" I asked, wondering if there was some kind of reverse ratio between wealth and witchcraft.

"Of course not," Gram said, shuffling excitedly into the room. She must have been listening at the door. "There's no need to be bitter, Agnes."

Agnes sniffed. "The Shaws have been denying their magical heritage for more than three hundred years," she said.

"Nevertheless, they are still one of the families."

"Only because their name is in the record," Agnes insisted. "They have no magic."

"But of course they do!" Gram said. "Serenity Ainsworth's own daughter married a Shaw!"

"A Shaw who never changed his name," Agnes muttered.

Gram waved her handkerchief weakly. "Yes. What a pity." She turned to me. "That was Zenobia," she explained. "She was one of twins, also. Zenobia and Zethinia. Our family often produces twins."

"Zethinia fared better, I daresay," Agnes said.

Gram shook her head. "Alas, the Ainsworth women always marry for love."

"Why didn't Mr. Shaw change his name?" I asked.

"Because they have never held to our ways," Aunt Agnes bristled. "They *want* to be cowen."

Gram uttered a little cry at that, as if Agnes had uttered a blasphemy. "Tragic," she whispered.

"From all accounts, Zenobia Ainsworth was an exceptionally talented witch," Agnes said. "I imagine she hoped that, by infusing her magical blood into the Shaw line, she and her husband might produce children with at least a portion of her ability."

"It was she who embroidered the piece above the mantel in this house," Gram said. "It is infused with knot magic."

"Unfortunately, the Shaws did not appreciate the treasure that was Zenobia Ainsworth. In the end, the cowen drove her away."

"Horrid people," Gram agreed.

"Some of the Shaws inherited Zenobia's talent with knots. They became clothing designers, fabric manufacturers, artists who work with string and cloth. Some of them are quite famous today. But none of them live in Whitfield."

"So Peter does have magical blood," I insisted. *And he's also my relative*, I thought, if having a mutual ancestor 350 years ago counts. I decided it didn't.

Agnes sighed. "Actually, Peter is a special case," she said. "His father, Prescott Shaw, left him and his brother Eric in Hattie's care before his death. The Shaw family was shocked by Prescott's decision. They tried all sorts of ploys to get Peter away from Hattie, but Prescott's will was airtight."

"So they disinherited poor Peter," Gram said. "He has no family except Hattie Scott now. And because he's a male . . . " She shook her head.

"What's wrong with him being male?" I asked.

"Well, the Shaw men have never exhibited much magical talent. They're bankers, lawyers, financiers, that sort of thing."

"Also big game hunters, soldiers, aviators and, allegedly, clandestine arms dealers."

"Grandmother, we don't know that."

"Über-cowen," I ventured. Gram nodded.

"So the possibility of Peter's being magical is very remote," Agnes continued, ignoring us. "Although not impossible. He may develop some skills in the next year or so. Hattie's been tutoring him, and she's the best there is."

"The strongest witch in Whitfield," Gram said proudly.

"And she can give him magic?" I asked.

"Goodness, no. No one becomes a witch just because they want to. Some of us, like you, child, are born witches, with talents and abilities that manifest early. Others, with lesser gifts, learn to develop them through teaching and encouragement. But a person with no magical ability is destined to be cowen, even if he comes from one of the twenty-seven magical families."

"So what happens then? To Peter?"

"I'm sure Hattie will succeed," my great-grandmother said encouragingly.

"But what if she doesn't?"

Agnes looked uncomfortable. She cleared her throat. "In that case, Peter will have to accept the life of cowen."

I blinked. "You mean he'll be sent away?"

"Cowen cannot be part of our lives," Agnes said, gently but firmly. "We are too different from them. Those differences may not matter so much in youth, but later, they are nearly irreconcilable."

"But my mother did it," I said. "She married a . . . my dad."

The two women gazed at me balefully. "And look what happened," Gram said. "Zenobia also ended up with an unhappy life. Rather than infusing the Shaw line with magic, the opposite happened. The Shaws treated Zenobia like a pariah. She became known as a witch—the worst thing that can happen to us in cowen society. Her husband grew ashamed of her abilities, and left her. In time, her neighbors turned her in to the authorities. She would surely have been harmed, and maybe even burned at the stake, if she hadn't sought shelter in the Meadow."

"The Meadow?"

"The fog," she explained. "It's a sanctuary. Cowen cannot penetrate it. When witches are inside the fog, we are on another plane. We are invisible to outsiders. That is why the fog appears on each of the eight Wiccan holidays. While we celebrate, we cannot be seen by the mass of men."

"Does Peter know all this?" I asked.

"Of course. Hattie would be quite remiss if she did not prepare him for what may happen. What probably will happen."

"He'll be all alone," I said, mostly to myself.

Gram patted my hand and said, "Try to understand, dear. It wouldn't be good for anyone if you fell in love with Peter Shaw."

"Hattie's seen what's been developing between you, and she's spoken with Peter."

"What?" My hands curled into fists. "I can't believe this!"

"Peter knows he can never have you," she said. "And he's sensible enough not to try." Deliberately, she put her hands over mine and brought them to my sides. "Even if you're not."

CHAPTER

•

THIRTEEN

 BINDING

I cried so hard that night that the next day I looked barely human. All day long people asked me if I was sick, so I said I was. I showed up for Existentialism in Fiction wearing sunglasses. Mr. Zeller didn't say anything. Maybe he thought I was just getting into the existentialist zone or something.

Peter didn't sit near me. And he didn't walk me to work afterward. Just like the beginning of school.

When I arrived for work, he was leaning against the counter, studying a notebook. It was the same one I'd found under the table the first time I'd come to Hattie's.

"Hi, Peter," I said, hanging up my coat. He may have agreed not to have anything to do with me, but I hadn't.

"Aren't you ever going to take off those shades?" he asked.

I didn't want him to see how terrible I looked. "Light sensitivity," I said glibly. "Doctor's orders."

"Okay." I doubt if he believed me. "Katy . . ."

"Mmm?" I picked up a rag and pretended to wipe off the spotlessly clean counter.

"I wanted to walk you to work today."

"It's okay," I whispered. Some things are just too complicated to discuss. "Let it be." I reached for the notebook, which he'd laid on the counter. "Whatcha reading?"

He made a move to hide it from me but, realizing I'd already seen it, made do with an embarrassed shrug. "Binding spells," he said. "Hattie's been trying to teach me. I'm not very good, though."

"It takes practice," I said. Like I'm the big expert giving advice. I wanted to kick myself.

"*You* don't have to practice," he said.

"I don't know any binding spells. I just cook, remember?"

"I think you could do anything."

My heart must have stopped. It was hard for me to carry on any sort of conversation with him while I was looking at him, with his wheat-colored hair falling into his eyes and his lips parting over his perfect white teeth.

I realized that I'd been staring. My neck was getting tired from looking up at him, so I shifted my gaze onto the countertop. It didn't make any difference. He even smelled wonderful.

"Hey," he said softly, touching my chin. I had to look up into his eyes again. It was like falling into a pool of honey. He smiled, an easy, slow grin. "I didn't mean to make you feel uncomfortable," he said.

"No, I . . ." I had to run a finger along the collar of my sweater. "I just . . ."

"Do you even know how good you are?"

I cleared my throat. Four or five times. I didn't want to be *good*. I didn't want to have powers if that meant I couldn't be with him. "Um, why do you want to learn binding spells?" I asked, trying to talk about something besides my alleged talent at witchcraft.

He spread his hands, palms up. "Because they're easy. At least that's what Hattie says. Here, let me try one on you."

"Bind away." I held out my arms, wrists overlapping.

"Take these off first." Before I could object, he removed my sunglasses. Terrific, I thought. Red eyes and no makeup. With my green irises and pallid, northeastern skin, I probably looked like the flag of Italy.

Now he was staring at me. "Witch eyes," he whispered, still smiling. I tried to turn away, but with the gentlest pressure, he stopped me. "Beautiful and strange. One of a kind."

I was trying hard to keep breathing. *Inhale, exhale* . . .

"I can try the spell now," he said.

"The . . ." But my throat had closed in a glottal stop, as if I were speaking some African language. So I just nodded.

He held out my arms, which had taken on the consistency of cooked spaghetti, then took a couple of steps backward and made a face.

"Are you all right?" I finally managed. He'd turned red and was panting.

"I'm concentrating," he said.

"Oh. Sorry."

"Do you feel it?"

"Feel what? Oh, the binding. Yes, I think so." But that was only to be polite. Actually, all I felt was my arms getting tired. "Yes. Definitely." My eyes were closed. I was trying to will myself to feel bound.

When I opened them, though, Peter was standing in front of me with his lips pursed and his hands on his hips. "You're a terrible liar," he said.

I felt crestfallen for him. "I just wanted it to work," I said.

"Yeah, me too. I wish there was an incantation or something, like in books. Just concentrating is . . ."

"Vague, I know."

"You either have it or you don't. And I don't."

"That's not true," I said. "You can develop those abilities. Hattie's a great teacher. She's the strongest witch in Whitfield, and you're practically her son."

He looked at me from under his eyebrows. "You know about me, don't you," he said.

"No! Honestly . . ." But he knew I was lying again. "Okay, yes," I admitted. "Some."

"You know I'm cowen. By next year I'll be thrown out of Old Town."

"I don't know that, and neither do you. What's more, I don't care. I'll never stop . . . being your friend," I said. He had no idea. "No matter what."

"Thanks," he said. "But when the time comes, that won't matter. You'll be in the magic circle, and I won't." He turned away.

"Peter . . ." Just then Hattie walked in with Eric.

He was all excited to see me, kicking and waving a placemat. "Eric has a new drawing for you," Hattie said.

"Kaaay," he said, pressing the paper against my face.

"Thanks, Eric. Well, let's see what we've got," I said. It was the usual. That is to say, a magnificent rendering of birds in flight. This time they were flying in a spiral pattern. It was uncanny, how he could depict every angle of the birds while still conveying a feeling of motion and speed. "Wonderful," I said, tousling his hair. He shrieked in delight.

"Hold him for a minute," Hattie said as she readied his high chair. It was hard to understand. Sometimes she'd act like I was Eric's big sister, allowing me to hold him and feed him. But at other times, she'd order me away from Eric as if I were the Whitfield Slasher.

Hattie handed him to me, and I was engulfed in wild hugs and snuggles.

"The Winter Solstice is right around the corner," Hattie said.

I waited for her to say more. She didn't. "Yay," I said, hoping to sound enthusiastic.

"It won't be busy here. This is a low energy time of year. Since we won't be cooking much, I thought maybe you could use the time to help Peter learn some binding spells." When I didn't answer right away, she added, "I'll pay you the same as if you were working in the kitchen."

"It's not that," I said. "But I don't think I can. I don't know any binding spells. I don't even . . ."

At that moment a huge meat cleaver shot out of a drawer and flew right at Peter's head. I gasped. By the time he turned around, it was headed straight for his right eye.

And then it stopped. Just froze in midflight for a nanosecond before I knocked it away.

"You see, you do know how to do a binding spell," Hattie said.

"Told you," Peter muttered. "You don't even have to practice."

"Excuse me?" I shouted. "Was it my imagination, or did you two not notice that Peter almost became a cubist sculpture?"

Hattie chuckled in that low, maddeningly calm way she had. "Shoot, girl, I knew you weren't about to let pretty Pete get sliced in two."

"But I didn't . . ." I began, but the steam kind of got knocked out of me, because I knew I did. I'd seen the knife coming, and—I don't know, I'd just made it stop.

"Katy will be a great witch one day," Hattie said to Peter. "Learn what you can, and don't be macho about it."

Peter laughed. "I'll try to keep it under control," he said.

As if *control* weren't already his middle name.

It was all very awkward, being Peter's teacher. I was doing this stuff for the first time myself. The problem was, I didn't have to learn how to do these spells. They just seemed to happen. So I had to dissect every move, every thought, and hope that my analysis was correct.

In the beginning I tried variations of Hattie's knife trick, pushing things like books and cabbages toward him, but Peter was so inept at magic that everything ended up smacking him on the head. I felt terrible about that. So I tried another tack, using inanimate objects as targets.

"Just wrap a cord around this tomato," I instructed. One time I actually saw the bindings, so I knew he had some potential. They were little tendrils of thoughts or intentions or something that oozed out of Peter's eyes and fingers and forehead and wrapped weakly around the big beefsteak tomato we were using.

"Make it tighter," I said.

"I don't know how."

"Concentrate!" Sometimes it was so frustrating. There wasn't really anything to it *except* concentrating. It wasn't even about thinking. "Just focus," I said, and then, without meaning to, *I* focused. That was always the problem. I couldn't teach by showing him how to do something, because then I'd end up doing it for him, like with the tomato. As soon as I started to focus, my own binding threads snapped taut around Peter's, and the tomato disintegrated, squirting pulp all over both of us.

"Sorry," I said, wiping tomato out of my eyes. "Hey, maybe that was you."

"Yeah. Right." He tipped his head. Juice poured out of his ear. We both laughed.

"You're getting better, though," I said. "I saw the strings."

"Did you?"

I looked at him. "Didn't you?"

"No."

So I knew where to begin. Since we both had passes to leave the school grounds, I took him to the Meadow at night. The place was so full of magic to begin with that anything magical done there was magnified.

First I set up a gallon jar of mayonnaise about twenty feet away. It was white, so we could both see it in the moonlight. "Now watch me," I said. "I'm going to focus on that mayo jar. Look for strings coming off me."

"Strings?"

"Sort of. You should be able to see them here. Just watch me."

I concentrated on the jar. Almost immediately I could feel

the binding begin. Out of the corner of my eye I could see the threads emanating like wisps of smoke from all over me. It began as a kind of nimbus around me, a sort of full-body halo, and then it went wherever I directed it. I raised my arms so that the energy concentrated in my fingers and poured out of them.

"This is what it's about," I said, marveling at what was happening. "The body. It has to all come out in one place instead of floating away."

"I see it, Katy," Peter said.

"Good. Now you try it. Keep it in your body. Remember that you're a physical being, not a mind. The magic starts in your *cells*."

"Huh?"

"Just do it." I sneaked a peek at Peter. I could see his energy building around him. "That's it," I whispered. In the moonlight it glowed in iridescent colors, as luminous as a comet.

Peter's face was transfigured by the awareness of his own magic. "I'm doing it," he whispered.

"Yes."

Slowly he raised his hands, and the light snaked out of his fingers in ten strong beams. Then he moved toward me. His light merged with mine, creating what looked like a tunnel of starlight, bright enough to be seen by ships at sea.

"I can't believe it," he said.

"Shh," I said. "Don't think. Just be here. With me."

The light intensified, brightening until it was something more than visual. It almost seemed to hum with magic, a low buzz that filled me like warm honey. It was moving out of me, yet coming into me at the same time, and through it all, Peter was with me. Not just beside me, but *there*, in the hum with me, in the honey.

I felt my breath coming faster. The whole Meadow was alight now, the white mayo jar shining like a July moon. My skin was tingling. I felt a thousand times bigger than my body. And Peter was no longer separate from me, but another part of my being, around me. Inside me.

And then his lips were touching mine, soft as roses.

For real. It took me a moment to realize that this wasn't part of the magic, that Peter Shaw really was kissing me, and I was kissing him back.

The glowing jar in the distance exploded, and a fountain of sparkling glass fragments showered the night sky. Our fingers touched, extinguishing the light that had come from them. There was nothing now but the night and the Meadow and Peter and me. I held on to him for my life. My life.

"I'm . . . I'm sorry," he said, pulling away from me. "I have to go."

Go? "Why?" I was so confused. "It's all right."

"No," he said. "We can't do this. Not ever again."

"But . . . the magic . . . You did it. You're not cowen."

"You can't understand," he said. "I should never have let this happen."

"Don't . . ." It was so hard to ask. "Don't you want me?" My hands touched his face. He held one, kissing my palm.

Then he left. Just like that, into the dark.

I looked down at my hands. They glowed faintly, as if remembering the touch of him. I could still feel the heat from his mouth on mine. But he was gone.

CHAPTER
•
FOURTEEN

 YULE

My cell phone rang at five in the morning. It was my dad.

"Are you all right?" I asked.

"Of course. I'm calling from the speakerphone in Madison's London office."

Ah. That must have been why he'd forgotten the six-hour time difference between us, I thought grouchily. "Well, all right, Dad. What's up?"

"Honey, I have great news."

There was a long pause. "Are you talking to me?" I asked finally.

"Of course!" He laughed out loud. "You're not going to believe this, Katherine."

Don't say you're getting married, I thought fervently.

"You're going to join us!"

Another pause. "Wh—what?"

"Madison has agreed to buy you a ticket. Don't worry about missing classes. A week here with me would be worth a semester of school. That is, if medievalism is even taught at Ainsworth."

"Uh . . ."

"I'll have to be at Cambridge for a few days, but Madison would love to take you shopping, or doing whatever women do."

"Um, I don't know, Dad. I'm in the middle of a lot of things here, and—"

"Oh, come on! Where's your sense of spontaneity? You haven't seen us in months."

"Yes. That's why I sent you an email. I have to talk with you."

"About what?"

"About changing your name. I need to know, Dad. People here—"

"You're spoiling everything, Katherine," he growled. "Hold on." Sweet-sounding talk in the background. "Fine, fine," I heard him say before exhaling noisily into the mouthpiece. "Madison would like for you to pick up some things from her office in New York before you come."

"What things?"

"What things," he repeated.

Mim came on the line. "A bottle of nail polish, love. Crucial Fuscial. And a couple of other things. Some pills I forgot to bring. My secretary will get everything from my apartment. Just take a bus into the city and pick them up at the front desk. I'll give you the address."

"You want me to fly to London to bring you a bottle of nail polish?"

"No," she said with exaggerated patience, "I want you to fly to London—*at my expense*—to have a wonderful time. The nail polish doesn't matter at all, really. It just would have been a nice thing for you to do."

"I see. Well, if it really doesn't matter, I think I'll pass."

"Why, you . . ." I could hear her fingernails scraping against the mouthpiece as she passed the phone to my father.

"What's the problem?" he asked wearily.

He was bored. This wouldn't take much longer. "Much as I'd love to see you both, Dad, I think I'd better stay at school and study. I'm having some problems with geometry."

"Is your GPA compromised?" he asked, clearly alarmed. "This semester is going to count in your college applications, you know."

"I know. I think I'll be all right, as long as I take things seriously." He loved that phrase: "take things seriously."

"All right. Got to go, Katherine. Do you need anything?"

"No, Dad."

"See you later, then." Mim was already screeching. It had no doubt been the forgotten pills that had prompted the phone call. Well, now she'd just have to do without them, and Dad might get a chance to see what she was really like.

And I'd get to spend Christmas alone.

I didn't care. That would still be better than being Mim's drug mule.

I checked the clock on my nightstand: 5:09 a.m. Dad and Mim had gotten me so flustered that there was no way I'd be able to fall back asleep anytime soon. *Great.* More time to think about how Peter Shaw kissed me and then ditched me in the Meadow.

It had been the most intimate experience I'd ever had, and I thought he was sharing every moment with me. I felt my eyes filling. I could still feel his soft lips touching me like clouds. Like moonlight.

It hurt, knowing that Peter wouldn't remember the moment the same way I did, but in a horrible sort of way, I was still glad it had happened. I'd taught Peter something that even Hattie hadn't been able to, and I was proud of that. There was something I needed to do.

At around nine in the morning, I knocked on Gram and Agnes's door.

"I've been teaching binding spells to Peter Shaw," I declared by way of greeting.

"We know, dear," Gram said. "Hattie told us. Won't you come in?"

The invitation surprised me. "You're not mad?"

Agnes ushered me in. "Oh, many would say we are quite mad," she said with a quiet chuckle. "But no, we're not angry with you, if that was your question."

"We're proud of you," Gram said. "Using magic to help others is the whole point of living in a magical community."

"But you said I shouldn't be with Peter."

"That's not true," Agnes objected. "We said that Peter would know better than to be with *you*."

I was blushing furiously. "Because of Hattie? Or you? Something one of you told him?"

"No, dear," Gram said.

End of sentence. No matter how I sliced it, Peter just wasn't that into me, and even my great-grandmother knew it. "All right," I said with a sigh. That didn't change anything. I'd said what I came to say. "I'll be going now. Have a nice holiday."

Then I noticed the fireplace. Hanging beneath the mantel were three stockings, elaborately embroidered and decorated with appliquéd holly leaves and ivy. The one in the middle had my name on it, KATY, in big red letters. "You made me a stocking?"

Gram smiled. "For your first Christmas." Her voice cracked. "Except for the name. I changed that yesterday."

"Every year since you left Whitfield, we've hung it up, hoping you'd come back," Agnes said.

I threw my arms around them. Even Peter's rejection didn't hurt so much anymore.

"Won't you stay with us for a while?" Gram asked.

"As long as you'll have me," I said.

Hattie was right. The solstice—Yule to the witches—was a quiet time. Gram and Agnes and I went into the woods and cut down a little tree, which we decorated with real beeswax candles. We put candles in all the windows, too, and made garlands of ivy and holly to wind around the stair railings and doorways. In the evenings, we'd sit around the fire while my great-grandmother told stories or Agnes played the piano. She was very good, although she played with an almost embarrassing passion. Sometimes Gram twanged along on her dulcimer, which generally didn't improve the music, but added a homespun touch. During the days, we'd all cook together or go walking through town. Sometimes I'd hang out with Jonathan and he'd teach me about carpentry. Or I'd walk alone through the woods. Anything to avoid running into Peter. Or thinking about him, although I didn't manage that very well.

It's true what they say about time being a great healer. I

wasn't over Peter—I didn't think I ever really would be—but the edges of the wound I felt in my heart weren't so raw anymore. And inside that wound was still the memory of his kiss. Nothing would ever take that away. Sometimes just the thought of his touch would be enough to make me feel weak. The memory was so powerful, so immediate, that it was as if I were right back in the Meadow with him, holding him, being held.

One day Gram, Agnes, and I went to Hattie's to bake pies for the local nursing home. I could just imagine what that was like, an old folks' home for witches. Miss P showed up too. Even though Miss P was a few years younger than my aunt, the two of them got along famously.

I was stirring pastry cream in the twenty-gallon mixer when Peter came into the kitchen.

I stopped breathing.

"Excuse me," he said. He was heading toward Hattie when he saw me.

In that instant time ceased to exist. His eyes, gray and deep and full of a pain I didn't understand, searched inside mine until they found my soul. And I gave it to him, there, across the noisy, bright kitchen.

I'm yours, it called to him.

You're mine, his called back. *From the beginning, you were meant to be mine.*

"Peter!" Hattie shouted. "What do you want?"

"It . . . it's Eric," he stammered. "I think he needs his medicine."

"I'll be right up," Hattie said, wiping her hands on her apron.

The spell was broken. Spell? Who was I kidding? That was nothing but wishful thinking.

I'm yours. Geez, how corny could you get? I went back to stirring my pastry cream.

"Peter!" Hattie called again. When I looked up, a strong brown arm was snaking around the door, grabbing Peter's shirt and yanking him out of the room.

He was still looking at me.

The kitchen was weirdly quiet. "What?" I snapped crankily, irritated at the nosy women who were so interested in my nonexistent love life that they'd all dropped what they were doing and stood gawking at me.

Wishful thinking. That was all it was.

On the night of the Winter Solstice we lit all the candles in the windows and on the tree, too. They filled the room with warm, flickering light. Sitting on an old horsehair sofa between my aunt and my great-grandmother, with no television or recorded music in the background, I felt as if I'd been transported back in time.

"Yule teaches us a great lesson," Gram said. "It is the darkest time of the year, with the shortest day and the longest night."

"Mmm," I murmured as noncommittally as I could.

"It means that things have gotten as bad as they can," Agnes said. "One tick after the moment of darkest night, the light begins to grow."

"We call it the birth of the infant light," the old woman said. "Another word for hope."

I sat up straighter. Hope, yes. No matter how bad things were, hope was possible. Maybe even with Peter. "I'll try to remember that," I said.

"Very good. Now, shall we try a cone of power?" Gram asked. "And then perhaps a cup of tea?"

"A cone of what?"

"We'll make a wish," she said.

"For power?"

"For whatever you'd like, dear," she said.

"Like world peace." That seemed like a safe bet.

The two of them looked at one another. "Certainly, dear, if that is what you want. Or power, if—"

"No, no," I amended quickly. "I didn't mean—that is, world peace would be fine."

"It doesn't have to be an unselfish wish," Agnes said.

I was confused. "But then . . . well, it wouldn't be *good*, would it?"

"Do we always have to be good?" That sounded strange, coming from an 80-something-year-old woman.

"Grandmother!" Agnes admonished. "She means, Katy, that it's all right to be kind to yourself. Always doing for others is a sure path to resentment."

I'd never thought of things in quite that way before. Yes, I could be kind to myself, I supposed. Now, what did I want?

Peter's face came to mind. His beautiful face, his soft lips . . .

No, not *that*. I couldn't wish for *that*.

World peace. That was safer.

We held hands. Agnes began a sort of wordless chant, a low singing sound deep in her throat. Then Gram joined her, her own voice high and warbly, sounding a lot like Glinda, the Good Witch of the North in *The Wizard of Oz*. I almost laughed out loud. Then both of them squeezed my hands and I realized that they were waiting for me to chant, too.

I panicked. What was I supposed to say? Or worse yet, *sing*?

I decided just to hum. Humming for world peace was okay. *Hmm. Hmmm.*

The air in the space between us began to vibrate, then to move in a circle like a tornado in reverse. It rose slowly off the ground, tapering to a point as it grew.

I've done this, I thought. It was how I'd arranged Mim's papers in her apartment before I'd pushed them out the window. That had been pretty juvenile, I had to admit. My thoughts at the time hadn't exactly been on world peace.

Which I really should have been concentrating on now. World peace. Yes.

Only something kept getting in the way. Try as I might to see ethnically diverse hands clasping one another in friendship across an ocean, all I could really see was . . .

Peter. Peter's eyes, filled with the suffering of a thousand years . . . Peter . . . oh, Peter . . .

The cone whirled, almost too strong for our arms to contain it. I felt my hair flying out behind me. My breath came in ragged gasps. *Peter, my love, my true, my only love . . .*

With an audible *whoosh* the energy in the cone shot through the ceiling. Crap, I thought. What a time to be daydreaming. "World Pete!" I shouted. "I mean *peach*! That is . . . "

Agnes held up her hand for me to be quiet. I hung my head.

Afterward, everything was still. "What were you saying, Katy?" she asked, raising her eyebrows.

"Peace," I whispered. I knew I'd probably blown the whole spell. "I ruined it, didn't I," I said.

Gram straightened her doily, which had gone askew during

the proceedings and now hung over one eye. "No one ever knows if a spell will work or not," she said. "We just send out our intentions, and hope for the best."

I felt bad. Even my intentions had gotten screwed up. There would be no world peace now, thanks to me.

"What did you wish for, dear?" she asked Agnes.

"That's no one's business but mine."

"That means it was about Jonathan," Gram said with a wicked grin. "Although you needn't waste a spell on that. Anyone can see he couldn't be more crazy about you."

"I know nothing of the kind," Agnes said, walking away. Her hair had fallen out of its usual neat chignon and hung in pretty tendrils around her face. She was fanning herself with the electric bill as she left the room.

"The Ainsworth women are famous for their love spells," Gram said. "We are artists in the field."

"Is . . . is that what you wished for, then?" I asked, not sure if I wanted to hear the answer.

"Me? Oh, good heavens, no. I wished that blasted Wonderland didn't get built on the Meadow. I wished hard, too."

"The Meadow?" I asked, shocked. "Is that where it's supposed to be built?"

"I'm afraid so."

"But . . . but . . ."

"It doesn't bear thinking about," she said, closing her eyes to the prospect. "Although I've heard they're very close to an agreement with Jeremiah Shaw."

"Who?"

"Naturally, a cowen Shaw would own the deed."

"He owns no such thing," Agnes said, coming back into

the room with three glasses of apple cider and a plate of sandwiches. "Everyone knows that the Meadow has been public land since Whitfield was founded."

"Nevertheless, the Shaws have paid the taxes on it." The old woman shook her head. "We always said it was a waste of money, paying taxes on property they didn't own. We never thought that even a Shaw would try to *sell* it."

"Or buy it," Agnes added. "Only something as soulless as the Wonderland Corporation would even think of disregarding the Meadow's magic."

"Madam Mim," I said.

"Who?"

"The soulless something at the heart of Wonderland," I said. "My father's girlfriend."

No one spoke for a while. Finally Gram said, "Well, maybe the negotiations won't go through. The Meadow has strong magic."

Aunt Agnes took my stocking from its place over the fireplace and brought it to me. "I don't know," she said. "There are some forces even magic can't stop, and Wonderland may be one of them."

We exchanged gifts. I gave Agnes some tortoiseshell hair combs that I'd bought in an antique store with my earnings from Hattie's. For Gram, I had a big box of English toffees I'd made at night while she was asleep. I'd cooked them using sugar and butter and vanilla, then cooled them and cut them and coated them with the best dark chocolate I could find. Then I'd put them in a pretty box that I covered with handmade paper and silk ribbon. I think she liked them.

In my stocking were two treasures. From Agnes, a handwritten book of spells on a level I'd never known about before.

"Time travel?" I asked, reading through the table of contents.

"Very advanced," Agnes said gravely. "You won't be able to perform any of these for years, but they're worth looking at, all the same."

"Thank you," I said. And I meant it.

I loved Whitfield.

My great-grandmother gave me a brooch that had belonged to Serenity Ainsworth. It was a carved ivory cameo on a background of reddish stone.

"Carnelian," Gram said. "It is the stone of warriors, for that was what Serenity was, in her own way. She was not cowed by adversity, nor influenced by the opinions of others. She was your namesake, and I hope that you make of your life as much as she made of hers."

"Thank . . . " I was having a hard time pulling off the thick plastic that encased it.

"I had it shrink wrapped," Agnes added. "We know about your psychometric abilities. That was why we changed all the furniture in your mother's room. You may not be ready to explore Serenity's inner being so late in the evening."

"Oh. Yes," I said, "that was thoughtful. I'll choose the right time to . . . explore."

By then, the fire was dimming to embers, and the candles were guttering. Agnes passed around the glasses of cider she'd brought in, then raised her own glass in a toast.

"To world peach," she said.

CHAPTER
•
FIFTEEN

 IMBOLC

The next big witch holiday was Imbolc, a.k.a. Groundhog Day. I know, you wouldn't think that Groundhog Day was a cause for celebration, but in the magical community, it is a huge deal.

Back in the day, before the birth of Punxsutawney Phil, the men of the village would gather together on February second to take someone's pet snake and put it in a hole in the ground. Then they'd hang around chewing the fat and drinking tankards of ale until the snake came out again.

When the snake found its way out of the hole, it either turned around and crawled back underground, meaning that six more weeks of winter were on the way, or else it slithered away to freedom, in which case the village elders had to chase it through the woods and put it back into its cage until next year.

Personally, my theory is that most of the time the snake got away, but the elders (who had probably chewed more fat and drunk more ale than they should to be in prime snake-chasing condition) lied and said more winter was coming, because any fool would have known that spring wasn't about to burst forth on February 2. This annual ritual was known as *Imbolc,* possibly because "Snake Day" would have sounded sketchy, even then.

No one bothered with the snake thing anymore, although judging from the noises coming from the local bars, I think the tradition of drinking ale in the morning was still in force. It was all symbolic, anyway. In some weird Celtic language, Imbolc means "in the belly," as in the beginning of the beginning. It's the *I-think-we-might-make-it-after-all* moment when spring starts to become an actual possibility.

As a major holiday Imbolc is entitled to fog. That is, Fog. The Meadow was covered in it, the tour buses marveled at it, and lost cowen were graciously led out of it by Mr. Haversall and the trusty Dingo. But the witches just stomped through it until they reached the plane of magic.

For the occasion, the Meadow was transformed (as it turned out, by Hattie, who was Whitfield's current high priestess for ceremonial events) into a gigantic labyrinth. Not a maze, mind you, but a winding kind of meditative path, where everyone takes a minute—actually, an hour or so—to figure out their lives.

I stayed overnight with the Ainsworths so that we could get an early start. Did I say *early*? I was shaken awake at an obscene hour, before there were even streaks of dark blue mixed in with the black of night.

"Why? *Why?*" I'd begged to know as I was being dragged out of bed by my cheerfully sadistic relatives.

"So that you can get to school on time afterward," Agnes said.

Gram opened my window, letting in a blast of arctic air. "Bracing," she said, taking a deep breath. "Dress warmly, Katy."

New Englanders were extraterrestrials.

To my astonishment, there were actually a few people ahead of us. Wanted to beat the big rush, I guess.

"Now, this is a silent walking meditation," Gram warned me, as if she was worried that I would start clapping and shouting "Amen."

Frankly, in my opinion, Imbolc was one of the least interesting of the witch holidays. I mean, you'd have to have an even tamer life than I did to get a charge out of waiting for spring in the beginning of February.

"Go on," Agnes said, nudging me forward behind my great-grandmother. I supposed there was finally enough space between the first labyrinth walkers and us that no one would bother anyone else's meditating. It all seemed silly to me, anyway.

But at least it was a chance for me to get out of my dorm room, where I'd been going stir crazy. I'd been laid off at Hattie's due to inclement weather, which was apparently the climatic condition for every day from mid-January to mid-March. I didn't mind, though. It would have been hard to work with Peter every day. I kept my feelings in my heart, where the wound was still open, but bearable. I'd learned long ago that almost anything was bearable if you kept it secret enough.

"AHHHHHH!" Someone from the group in the labyrinth in front of us screamed. Instantly all my thoughts flew out of my head. Agnes pushed past me and ran up ahead. I followed her.

When we reached them the group was gathered around a dead crow on the path. Nearby, an elderly man had his arm around a distraught woman while some other people looked on with expressions of horror.

Agnes stopped in her tracks when she saw it. And Gram, when she finally caught up, nearly fainted.

"It's . . . it's a bird," I said quietly. Agnes pinched me to be quiet.

"We should go," Agnes said. Then she picked up the thing by its wings, and we walked out of the labyrinth the same way we'd come.

Once we were back home, Agnes and I buried it in the woods while Gram walked through the house with a bundle of burning sage. Call me callous, but it seemed like a lot of trouble to go to for a bird, especially one that wasn't even anyone's pet. Then when Jonathan showed up for work, Agnes made him go over to the Meadow to make sure there weren't any other dead birds lying around.

"There's bound to be talk as it is," she said. "Quite a few people saw it."

He sighed. "They'll be calling it an omen, then," he said. "But I'll do what I can. Say my dog killed it or something."

After he left I walked along beside Agnes back to the house. She looked thoughtful. "Dead birds have a special meaning for us here. They're harbingers."

I was trying to understand what she was saying. "Harbingers? Of, like . . . doom?"

"Of the Darkness," she said. "For a witch, it is the worst thing there is. Once the Darkness comes, the whole world changes, and nothing is ever the same again."

"What?" I said, coming to a standstill. Aunt Agnes wasn't prone to exaggeration. "The whole *world*?"

She looked at me for a moment, assessing my ability to handle this kind of news, I guess. "The Black Death. The Great Depression. The San Francisco earthquake. The influenza epidemic of 1918. Those are just a few examples."

I ventured a guess. "The Burning Times?"

Her head snapped sharply toward me. "You know about that?"

"It's in every American history book," I said.

"Oh. Of course. I suppose we're ridiculously sensitive about that here."

"Understandable," I said. "I read somewhere that as many as nine million people were killed as witches."

"Over the span of three hundred years throughout Europe and England and their colonies. There are no figures for the killings in Asia and Africa, although we are certain they occurred."

"And you think the Darkness was responsible for that?"

She looked at me levelly. "We know this, Katy."

"But . . . but how? The Darkness isn't even a real thing, is it?"

"Oh, it's real, all right. But it's not a thing. It's a force. It works through people."

"Cowen, according to Gram," I said.

"It starts there. Cowen are easy to influence. They don't tolerate adversity well, and their wills are weak. It doesn't take much to make them turn evil—lack of money, addiction, even a failed relationship is sometimes enough for them to turn their backs on decency and reason. And they almost never recognize that they're evil, so they can't stop. They just keep blaming someone or something else for what's happening, while their destructive impulses run rampant. And the whole time they have no clue that it's the Darkness at work."

"But witches aren't like that?"

"Less so. But we're human. We're susceptible, too, especially if someone close to us has been infected. And if that happens . . ." She shook her head. "Well, it's a terrible thing."

"Is that why you don't marry outside the twenty-seven families? Because you don't want cowen to bring the Darkness into Old Town?"

"Exactly. We've learned this through experience. There have been incidents that we don't want to repeat."

"Like what?"

She was silent for a moment. "You're not ready to learn about those things yet," she said.

"That's not fair, Agnes," I countered.

She smiled. "You're just is too young to be hearing that kind of history. But you ought to know the harbingers, if only so you understand why we're scared silly by the sight of a dead bird."

"It did seem like kind of an overreaction," I admitted. "Are you afraid of all dead birds?" I asked. "Even if they die of old age?"

She laughed. "No. But this one was dead in the labyrinth. That will be taken as a sign. Now everyone will be waiting for the second harbinger."

"Which is?"

"Sinkholes," Agnes said.

"What?" I couldn't help smiling. "But they're everywhere, aren't they?"

"So are birds."

She had me there.

"Do you see? It's hard to tell fact from baseless fear. That's why people here panic so easily."

We'd arrived back at the house. I wiped my feet on the mat outside the kitchen door. "But witches should be able to tell the difference, shouldn't they?" I asked.

"Some can. We're all different. Serenity Ainsworth was the first to notice the progression. First the birds, then the sinkholes. So when the sinkholes don't appear, the panic usually subsides. Unless . . ."

"Oh!" It was Gram, sounding as if someone had put a whoopee cushion on her pew in church. Shocked, distressed, disgusted.

Agnes pushed me aside. "Unless what?" I insisted, but she ignored me.

"What is it, Grandmother?" she asked.

Gram was holding a copy of the *Whitfield Sentinel*. "This," she said with supreme disdain. She rotated the newspaper so that the front page faced us. The banner headline across the top read:

Wonderland a Go: 300+ Jobs Expected

Beneath it was a picture of a man identified as Jeremiah Shaw, who greatly resembled the mummified remains of Pharaoh Ramses II. With him was—who else? Madison Mimson, spokesperson for Wonderland USA.

✛

That day—the school didn't close for witch holidays—
Ainsworth Prep was buzzing with the news about Wonderland,
clearly separating the cowen from the witches. Hence: "My
mom's already been offered a job in the legal department,"
versus: "Grandma says that without the Meadow, we might as
well all move to Boston."

It was the central discussion in social studies. We talked
about the rise of corporations in American history. Naturally,
Wonderland was the day's topic in Existentialism in Fiction.

All I knew was that Mad Madam Mim was coming to
Whitfield. I got an email from her:

> Can't wait to see you, Kathy. Be sure to tell
> all your friends about Wonderland's fabulous
> spring fashions! Coupons attached, good at all
> participating outlets. Print and clip!

Very personal. Not to mention the fact that, hello, this
was February in Massachusetts, with weather more suited to
mukluks than spring fashions.

And speaking of muck, that was almost certainly going to
be the composition of my world once Madison Lee Mimson
moved into it. I didn't want her going to my father with any
juicy tidbits about me. Like that I was way thick with his
in-laws, whom he thought were out of my life forever and,
incidentally, were also card-carrying witches.

*Oh, and BTW, Dad, I myself am telekinetic, pick up on the
thoughts of dead people, and work for the high priestess of the village.*

Yeah, that would go over great.

So far Imbolc hadn't turned out to be the funfest it was cracked up to be, but there was one more ritual before the day ended, and I was looking forward to it.

Before I left the relatives to go to school, they gave me a funny-looking cross made of intricately woven stalks of wheat. "This is a Cross of Brigid, named for the ancient goddess of fire," Gram said. "Sleep with this under your pillow tonight, and you'll dream of the man you're to marry."

So I was ready. Not that I believed in things like that. But I wanted to dream about someone besides Peter, for a change. I needed to stop thinking about him. I needed to move on. It would have been better for me to just cut ties. Spare my heart. The problem was, I just didn't know how to live without loving him.

So of course I dreamed about Peter.

He was sitting backward on a wooden-backed chair, naked from the waist up. His lean, well-muscled chest glistened with sweat, but the skin of his back was striped with a series of long, bleeding cuts, as if he'd been whipped.

His arms lay crossed along the top of the chair, and on them he rested his head. Impossibly fatigued, his smoky eyes were narrowed to slits beneath the fall of his sweat-matted hair, and his lips were bruised and swollen.

"Please stop," he begged, barely able to speak.

I didn't see anyone else in the room with him, but there must have been someone, because Peter appeared to be scared to death.

"Please," he begged again. "Just leave me alone. Leave me . . ."

Then his back arched and his head snapped back. A scream began in his throat, but he cut it off with a tremendous effort of will. His beautiful face was contorted in agony. He bit his lip until it bled, nearly crazy with the need to keep silent through the pain.

This time I heard his skin tearing.

"No!" I shouted, lurching bolt upright in my bed. I blinked. My heart was pounding, my throat dry with panic. My breathing was wild and shallow, like a trapped animal.

I looked out the window of my room. Outside, a full moon shone on the lake, reflecting beautiful colors on the ice.

It's okay, I told myself. *Just a bad dream.*

I turned on the light, put on headphones, and loaded my "favorites" playlist to clear my head. Then I remembered the Cross of Brigid under my pillow, and tossed it into the wastebasket. Stupid superstition.

I looked around, as if to reassure myself that I was really awake, because I didn't ever want to go back into that dream. This was my room, check, fully real. My wicker nightstand with my mother's photograph in a white ceramic frame. And on the walls, a series of Eric's amazing drawings of birds in flight.

Once again I sat up with a jolt, this time tearing the headphones off. The music sounded tinny, spilling out onto my bed. Then slowly, my hands shaking, I walked over to Eric's latest drawing and took it off the wall. There was something there, something I hadn't noticed before. I held it under my study lamp to be sure.

Oh, God, I thought. In the corner, beneath the swirling pattern of the flying birds, was a stationary object.

How had I missed it? There was so much *motion* in the drawing. Each bird was moving, its muscles flexed, its wings riding the wind, a part of the flock that also moved as if it were another creature in itself, swooping, whirling, soaring . . .

Except for the one in the corner, inert, still, in such sharp contrast to all the life in the rest of the picture.

A dead bird.

CHAPTER

•

SIXTEEN

 THE DARKNESS

It was hard for me to ask Peter to meet me, but I had to know what he thought about the drawings, since he knew Eric better than anyone.

As it turned out, he hadn't seen the dead birds either, until we went over all of the drawings with a magnifying glass. There were dead birds in all of them, including the one he'd given me on my first day of work. Some were falling out of the sky. Others were lying on the surface of a lake or stream, or were folded up like rags on the side of a hill.

"Did he always draw birds?" I asked.

"No. That's just been the past few months. He used to draw whatever he saw. Me. Hattie. The bars of his crib. The drawings were always good, but not like the birds. It was as if something was freed inside him when he started drawing them."

I took a deep breath. "Could he have been trying to warn us?"

Peter ran his hands through his hair. "But how is that even

possible?" he whispered, almost to himself. "I don't know how he can draw the way he does. He's never seen a bird up close, except for the chicken carcasses Hattie cooks."

Peter had been getting thinner lately, and so pale that his lips seemed to be nearly red in contrast to his fair skin. I wanted to ask him if he felt all right, but things were still awkward between us.

"Are there more?" I asked. "Recent ones, that is."

"Yes. A lot." He brought another bunch of them into the kitchen and we went over them, too. It was the same, dead birds everywhere.

There was one difference, though. In the newer drawings, another feature appeared on the terrain beneath the birds. There were indentations on the land, almost like the dimples left in rising dough when you poked your fingers into it. Each one was exquisitely shaded, so that you could almost feel the texture of those pockmarked hills.

"Could those be sinkholes?" I asked. "The second harbinger?"

He blinked. "So you know about that."

"A little. Agnes told me about the birds. I kind of thought she was kidding about the sinkholes, though. I mean, it seems almost silly."

"It's not silly if your house collapses into one," Peter said.

"I know, you're right. But why sinkholes?" I thought about it a moment. "Why birds, for that matter?"

He shrugged. "Maybe it's because the one is above the earth and the other beneath it. Magic is all about the earth and the seasons and the elements."

"The elements? Like hydrogen?"

He chuckled. "No, like earth, air, fire, and water," he said. "It's strange to be with someone who wasn't raised by witches."

He put his hand over mine. I was so shocked that I just stared at it as if it were an alien creature crawling over my metacarpals. The next second he pulled it away.

Again, as if nothing had ever happened.

"I have work to do," he said, moving toward the walk-in fridge.

"Hold it, Peter," I said. He was running away again, and I couldn't stop him, but there was something I had to find out first. "Are there other harbingers?"

He looked surprised. "Yes, two. Fire and rain."

"Earth, air, fire, and water," I said.

"Witches use them to perform magic. But sometimes the elements get perverted. That's when we know that something big has gone really wrong. We call that the Darkness."

The Darkness. Somehow, everything that had to do with magic in Whitfield eventually involved those two words.

In March a sinkhole appeared in the Meadow.

The witches went wild. On the day it happened, there had been several incidents of sinkholes appearing in backyards all around Whitfield, but no one paid much attention, except for the people in whose yards the sinkholes appeared. They were, after all, a geological feature of most of the state, caused by collapsing limestone deposits.

There was a feature on one of the Boston TV news stations speculating that buried tree stumps might have been the cause of this recent rash of disasters. "The stumps rot, and the earth caves in on the place where they used to be," a geologist from the State Department of Environmental Protection explained. He didn't mention why all the sinkholes would appear on the same day, but he did say it wasn't at all surprising.

But the *Meadow*! That was not in the news. Wonderland, the new owner of the property, managed to keep all mention of a sinkhole on the site of its new store out of the media. Of course, a tarp cover and a few distracting signs (ELECTRICAL HAZARD, HIGH VOLTAGE, KEEP OUT! DANGER) weren't enough to fool the witches. Too many Old Town residents had seen the hole before the tarp went over it.

Hattie's Kitchen remained closed until further notice, along with most of the other businesses in Old Town. Attendance at school dropped. People boarded up their houses. They knew what was coming.

Maybe it was better to be cowen, I thought. Normal people never knew when the worst-case scenario was going to come true. Sometimes they didn't even know when it was happening.

All I knew was that, if what was coming was going to be on a par with the Black Death, I wasn't planning to sit on my thumbs and watch while it destroyed the world. Whatever the Darkness was, I was going to find out everything I could about it. And then, idiotic as it sounded, I was going to do my damndest to fight it.

I went to the only place I could think of to find answers. Peter's room.

"I'm busy," he said.

"No, you're not." I took a deep breath to steady myself. "Look," I said, "I know you feel weird around me, but I need for you to tell me about the Darkness."

He tried to push me out. "I don't know any more about that than anyone else in Old Town. Ask them. Ask your family."

"They don't want me to know."

"Then I don't either."

"What do you care? Just tell me what you know. Anything."

His eyes scanned the corners of the room, searching for an excuse to get rid of me.

"Please, Peter," I begged. "I'll return the favor someday, I promise."

He relented. "Come in, Katy," he said, standing aside.

Call this Darkness 101, or Everything Peter Shaw Knows Or Is Willing To Tell About The Darkness.

First of all, the Darkness isn't a name. It's more of a description in place of a name. No one knows exactly what the Darkness is, which is what makes it so frightening. But though it is unknown, the Darkness did have an origin that people, *my* people, the witches of Whitfield, have remembered through hundreds of generations.

Peter says he pictures the source of the Darkness as a kind of black cloud the size of a basketball, fuzzy around the edges, from which leak a bunch of thin, snaking tendrils, like invisible wisps of smoke. Before humans came along, these wisps just dissipated into the air like gas bubbles from a tar pit, but with the advent of people—that is, weak, venal, greedy creatures who do not follow natural laws or respect the great forces—the wisps turned into something like tentacles, bigger, thicker, longer, and more powerful than ever. And with every evil brought forth by the humans, the tentacles grew until they slithered out of their hosts like branches of a tree, connecting and coalescing with one another to become even stronger, and darker, and more dangerous.

Now into this mix came the witches. They, too, were human beings, but from the beginning, witches were different. Fortunately for them, they were also useful to the others, the cowen. Some of them may have been clairvoyant, meaning they could see things that weren't in front of their faces— say, a neighboring tribe heading toward the village wearing warpaint—or telekinetic, like Jonathan the teleporting carpenter or myself. Some may have been healers, people of great value in those days when most people didn't live past thirty; or, in rare instances, even oracular (being able to foretell the future like my mother), which I'm told is extremely unusual, even though there have always been lots of fakes who claim they can. The witches were called all sorts of things— magicians, shamans, witch doctors, wise women, *strega*, *inyanga*, *tsukimono-suji*—whatever name they were given to distinguish them from ordinary people. But they all had one thing in common: They knew things the others didn't.

In time, the story goes, the Darkness became dense enough for some of the witches to see it, but by that time it was already too late to stop it. It moved quickly from one person to another, feeding on human fear and anger, expanding in certain weaker personalities to take over their minds entirely. The witches saw this. Another thing they saw was that the Darkness, as opposed to other, lesser kinds of evil, seemed to know what it was doing. When an infected person died, the Darkness leapt out of that person and into the nearest human body. This meant that, under the right circumstances, perfectly good, strong, intelligent people could be infected as easily as those who were weak, foolish, or naturally prone toward vile behavior. It could, in fact, affect *anyone*.

Even witches.

Now this was a very bad thing, because witches have power. Picture someone—me, say—who can move objects with my mind, going all Gothic and running wild in a knife store. And that isn't even a very powerful skill, as far as magic goes. That is why the twenty-seven families are, even today, so fanatical about keeping the No Cowen rule. Cowen get infected by the Darkness easily. They almost invite it, with their ego trips and lust for dominance. It's not that witches are better people, really. But they have *real* power, so they don't have to lord anything over anyone else, or act like money is what makes them important, or use sex to get what they want, or do any of the other crazy things that cowen do. It makes a difference. Witches don't run scared.

That is, except around dead birds and sinkholes and fires and floods.

XENOGLOSSIA

"Historically, the Middle Ages was, for witches, anyway, the Hour of the Darkness," Peter said.

"In those days, a witch was anyone who was different from them. Eventually, it also came to mean anyone who the person in charge didn't like. In 1484, the most powerful person in the western world, Pope Innocent VIII, declared open season on witches, sending out large teams of hit men to burn old ladies and grab their property. The sad thing was, most of the women they tortured weren't even witches."

"Cowen wouldn't even know what those creeps were up to," I said. "At least witches had the harbingers to warn them." I looked at him. "Or did they?"

"Of course. At least they did after Serenity Ainsworth pointed them out."

"Serenity . . . Hey, wait a second," I said before running out of the room.

Actually, it takes a lot longer than a second to run from Peter's dorm to mine and back again. By the time I returned, panting and wheezing from my Olympic-level sprint, he was lying stretched out on his bed, his notebook propped on his knees.

"Hey, Peter, can you—"

"Hold it," he said, shooting five fingers at me. That is when you put your thumb over your four fingernails and then flick all your fingers in the direction of someone or something. It helps to concentrate your energy. Anyway, Peter shot five fingers in what I guessed was supposed to be a binding spell, but it only produced a lot of sticky filaments.

"Ewww." I felt as if I'd walked into a giant spiderweb.

"Oh, sorry," he said, jumping out of bed to help clear away the gooey strings. "I meant to immobilize you."

"Well, you got as far as grossing me out," I complained.

"I see. Would you call that a start?"

I laughed. "I should have pretended it worked," I said.

"But of course. Isn't that what girls are supposed to do?"

"I'll remember next time."

"Seriously, though, I'm getting better," he said.

"Seriously, you are."

"I've just never been able to get to the level I reached when you were with me." He blushed. "I guess that was you."

"It was the Meadow," I said quietly. "Magic happens easily there." I looked away. Some things were better forgotten. I only wished I could forget them.

When I looked back, his eyes, deep and gray and troubled as the winter sea, met mine. I wanted to ask him what he was thinking, what he was feeling, why, why, why . . . But instead, I fished the little plastic-coated cameo out of my pocket. It was what I'd gone to retrieve, after all.

"This was Serenity's," I said. "My great-grandmother gave it to me for Christmas."

He picked it up. "Why is it sealed like that?"

"Because of what I might pick up."

He looked puzzled for a moment, then understood. "Oh, her . . . vibes."

"I just did it the once. But if you're willing to stay with me, I could open this now."

He pulled back slightly. "Are you going to start screaming again?"

"Well . . ." Suddenly it didn't seem like such a great idea. "I don't know. I guess I might." I started to put the thing back in my pocket, but Peter put his hand over mine.

"What I meant was, if you're willing to trust me, I'll look out for you," he said. "I'll try to make sure you don't . . ."

" . . . act stupid," I finished.

"I was going to say, 'get hurt.'"

"Oh." There was such a tenderness in his eyes. And a sadness . . .

"Katy . . ."

I broke away from him. "Got scissors?" I asked, tearing at the plastic with my teeth. Anything to avoid the *I-really-like-you-as-a-friend* talk.

Peter fumbled in his desk drawer, but it was too late. The cameo was free. Its smooth edges felt cool, then warm. Suddenly the room was spinning. I felt a rush in my head. Then the room was gone. Peter was gone. Katy was gone. And Serenity was there. I felt light and floaty, as if I was hovering above her. There was this powerful draw, like her mind was absorbing me. This time, though, I wasn't surprised by the pull. I was prepared. I could feel my namesake drawing me into her secrets until I knew everything . . .

I was thirty-two years old when I came to Massachusetts aboard the Valiant Marie *with my husband Venerable Dalton-Ainsworth and our twin daughters Zenobia and Zethinia. I had known some of the twenty-seven families on board before we'd set sail. A number of them had been witches in London. Others were from Suffolk or Surrey, and some from as far away as Edinburgh and Cardiff. We had planned for years to come across the sea together and start a community of our own kind in a place where we hoped we might be safe from the legacy of the Papal Bull.*

But one of the families, the Lyttels, was not meant to enjoy that future, for they had boarded the Valiant Marie *already infected by the Darkness.*

It had come through an adolescent son who had celebrated his last night in London by lying with a Cheapside tart who died of pox in his arms an hour after their assignation. Sorely fearful, the boy left her in the hay-strewn stall in the alleyway where she'd brought him, and ran home to his family without speaking a word.

Now, those of us who have seen the Darkness know that it is released through death; and upon the death of its host, it will spring into the next closest body, whether that body be willing to receive it or no. Thus the boy, who had been christened Charles Carter Matthew Lyttel, brought the Darkness with him, along with the pox, to the New World.

Young Charles Lyttel was dead before the Valiant Marie *ever made landfall, and the rest of the family lay in a state of* vile sickness of mind and body, until such a time as it became evident to some among us that the mother, my friend Dorothea Stanton Lyttel, was herself the current host of the Darkness.

At first we did nought but keep them all at a distance, a condition to which the Lyttels themselves agreed readily, as they knew well what contamination this pox could spread over all the twenty-seven families in Salem as well as through all the cowen already established there. But when it became known to all that the Darkness was at work as well, some insisted on the fire.

I cautioned against it, as I am loathe to take the life of any human person, most particularly those of my own persuasion, but within days we saw the sea birds lying dead in a line along the shore.

Then came the sinking of the earth in more than twenty places within our settlement alone, and then the fire, caused by lightning during a storm, that made the whole forest to burn day after day, despite the rain which did not cease to fall. Then at last appeared the fourth omen, and no one could deny its import: 'Twas flood, the wild tide that did engulf our roadways and drowned our animals that we had need of for milk and meat.

Four tragedies of earth, air, fire, and water. All saw it, all knew, for these were the Harbingers, the Four Evils of the Darkness, come to claim us as prey. I could protest no longer, for now we were all in danger from the narrow-eyed cowen.

On a cold night in November, long past the rites of Samhain, the killing fire was lit in a clearing made deep into the dense wood. We did not wish for our act to be known to the populace of Salem; as it was, we knew we could not ourselves remain under any conditions after this dread event.

Under cloak of night, Dorothea Lyttel was led to the stake. The course in this matter is clear: The one who harbors the Darkness must die by fire, as fire is at the heart of the Darkness. This is known to us from the earliest teachings.

Alas, it was pitiable indeed to see Mr. Lyttel lead his children away to some place unknown, to live amongst cowen. Not one in that family accused us in anger, though the small children wept, for even Dorothea knew what must be done. As to the rest, we repaired each of us as far from that horror as we could, so as to be distant from the Darkness when it passed out of the expiring body. It was thus that brave Dorothea Lyttel herself lit the fire that would take her life, and uttered not a cry. But around her, hidden in the wood, the families wept one and all, small child or aged crone, for we all knew how most dreadful our lot had become, to give up one of our own to the Darknesss in order to save our community.

This was indeed a day of woe. Soon afterward, the cowen of Salem found the burned remains of Dorothea Lyttel and took sport in tormenting all manner of women, threatening them also with the stake and the fire, for the Darkness had found its way deep into their hearts long before we had ever come.

As for our community, we all walked the distance to a far meadow, which years later we would name White Field, and there we would one day hide from the Darkness and the evil it had brought.

"Katy." Peter was wiping my face with something soft. "Katy, it's time to come back."

I came to slowly. He was cradling me in his arms like a baby. "Where . . . what . . ." I was beginning to remember what

I was doing there. "The Darkness." Tears began to course down my face. Peter sopped them up with what I realized was a wet handkerchief. "Do you always carry those?" I asked, so tired I was barely able to move my lips.

He looked at the white square. "Yes," he said with a gentle smile.

"Did I scream?"

"No, but you were speaking in a strange way. Were you Serenity Ainsworth?"

"I think I was," I said. "Where's the brooch?"

He picked it up off the table behind him. "I'll give it back to your family, if you'd like," he said.

"No. I want to keep it. This was easier than the last time. Not so shocking. Although . . ." My eyes were streaming again.

"I know what you saw, Katy," he said. "You were talking the whole time."

"*They burned their own kind*," I said, wanting to disbelieve it. But I couldn't. I'd seen it with my own—well, with Serenity's—eyes.

"They thought it was the only way to destroy the Darkness."

"But once the cowen got the idea, they just used it to propagate the Darkness, not to dispel it. Do you see? The Darkness *used* it. So it couldn't be the solution. The burning was just another part of the problem."

He shook his head. "But what else could they have done? Let the Darkness infect everyone in Salem?"

"Didn't it anyway?" I said. That was why Serenity and the others left for Whitfield. Even though the American colonists didn't burn their witches, Serenity knew that Salem was already a lost cause. "I wonder what happened to the Lyttels," I mused.

"Their descendents are probably still around, either living as solitary witches or thinking they're crazy. There are a lot of people like that out there among the cowen," he said.

"But who replaced them? To maintain the twenty-seven families?"

Peter smiled. "The Shaws," he said. "Zenobia Ainsworth married Henry Shaw. . ."

" . . . who didn't change his name," I said.

"You got it."

I stood up slowly, groaning with the effort. I felt as if I'd just been through ten rounds of mud wrestling. "I have to go," I said. "Thanks for helping me . . . with everything." I was too tired to be articulate.

I picked up the brooch, gasped, dropped it, then picked it up again. Images of Dorothea Lyttel with her hair on fire came to mind. I forced the image out of my thoughts.

"Leave it," Peter said. "I'll wrap it up for you so you won't have to touch it."

"No, I need to get used to it." I fingered the brooch. Random images. I shut them out one at a time. "This is a new skill for me. If I'm going to use it, I've got to learn to control it." I held it to my forehead. *No images*, I commanded silently, and whatever was inside me obeyed. It was just a brooch again.

I stumbled on my way to the door. Peter caught me. "I'll walk you back to your room," he offered.

With my arm slung around his shoulders like a drunk, we meandered around the maze of hallways until we reached my dorm.

"I guess this is me," I said. He was staring at me. "Is something the matter, Peter?" I asked.

He blinked and looked around, flustered. "No, no," he said, "of course not. Please." He gestured toward my door.

"What is it?" I persisted. I'd known him long enough to recognize the familiar look of anguish in those gray eyes.

He blinked again. Swallowed. "Well. It's nothing, really. Just . . . well, nothing . . ."

"Peter!"

"Oh, it's only . . ." He took a deep breath. "I . . . I was just wondering if . . ."

I was struggling to stifle a yawn.

"Well, I was wondering if you thought it was true," he managed finally. "About the Darkness, that is. That the only way to destroy it is to burn the person alive."

I thought about it as much as my feeble and exhausted brain would allow. "No, of course not," I said. "That would be horrible."

"Yes," he whispered.

"I wouldn't worry too much about it, though," I said, trying to sound reassuring. "No one in Whitfield's infected with the Darkness, as far as I know."

"Yes, right." He nodded mechanically.

"Even if it did happen, which it won't, remember that we're living in a town full of very smart witches. One of them would figure something out."

He nodded again and tried to smile, although it didn't look very convincing.

"Anyway, there have only been two harbingers. Birds and sinkholes. Pah. They might not count for anything."

"Of course." He opened my door for me. "Good night," he said.

He turned away before I could say anything else. Not that I had much else to offer. I knew Peter was worried. I was too. Everyone in Old Town knew something was coming, and I doubted if anyone among those very smart witches had the slightest idea what to do about it.

CHAPTER
·
EIGHTEEN

OSTARA

I suppose it was Mim's idea.

Because of the sudden appearance of the sinkhole in the Meadow, groundbreaking for the new Wonderland store had to be delayed while a team of geologists studied the hole, tested the ground with sonar and X-rays, analyzed the groundwater, and determined how much weight the underlying limestone would support.

But instead of leaving the site covered with tarps and HIGH VOLTAGE signs, someone—and it had to have been Mim, because that was her job—had the area transformed overnight into a kid's Easter fantasy. I hated to admit it, but it was a brilliant save.

There were trees in pots with plastic oranges hanging from them, enormous tubs of fresh flowers that were replaced every morning, and live rabbits in an elaborate pen constructed to look like a Beatrix Potter-inspired English cottage. Directly over the sinkhole was a six-foot-tall Easter Bunny in a heated pavilion, seated on a throne of resinous carrots and cabbages with WONDERLAND stamped in parti-colored pastels across the top, ready to pose for pictures that came with coupons good for 10 percent off any child's portrait taken in Wonderland's in-store photo studio.

The geologists came at night, after all the rabbits had been stashed in cages and returned to the pet store, and the Easter Bunny's throne hauled aside to reveal the gaping maw of the sinkhole beneath.

This was only in one corner of the Meadow, the corner farthest away from Hattie's Kitchen, and was set off by a charming white picket fence and a huge silk banner announcing the First (and last, since the Meadow would be covered by concrete as soon as construction started) Annual Wonderland Easter Egg Hunt, featuring a petting zoo, craft fair, pony rides, and a drawing for five hundred dollars in Wonderland merchandise, redeemable at the store's grand opening.

This whole spectacle occurred during the Vernal Equinox, which is a witch holiday, but fortunately a minor one. Most of the Old Town residents just stayed away, but some diehards brought flowers to Hattie's Kitchen, which had been out of business since the meadow was sold to Wonderland, and placed them by the restaurant's closed doors. It was a funereal sight.

Dad had been pestering me to come to New York, and since it was spring break, I didn't have much reason to refuse.

Mim wasn't at the Sutton Place apartment when I arrived, so Dad and I had some time alone.

"How's school going, Katy?"

"Good."

"Are you keeping your grades up?"

"Yes."

"Making new friends?"

"Uh huh." It was awkward. There was so much I couldn't bring up. Agnes and Gram, witchcraft, Peter . . . none of those seemed like good topics for conversation with Dad. It was going to be a *very* long weekend. But finally I touched on something I thought he might be interested in.

"I'm writing a paper on medieval magic boxes," I said. "They're—"

"Bottes," he said, taking off his glasses.

"You know about them?" I asked.

"I'm a medievalist, Katherine," he reminded me. "But I'm surprised you do."

"I . . . er, found a reference to them online and got interested," I fudged. I wasn't about to out my Medieval Alchemy teacher, Mrs. Thwacket, over a conversational nugget. "Do you think they ever existed?"

"Oh, yes, certainly. Of course bottes weren't really magic. They were mechanical devices, masterpieces of engineering, with drawers within drawers and false backs and bottoms and secret shelves and panels that opened only in a certain order to reveal still more compartments. To your average medieval denizen, it would have seemed miraculous."

"But they were supposed to be repositories for magical tools. Precious artifacts. Dangerous spells. Things like that."

"Spells?" He sat upright, his face alight. "Where on earth did you read that? Some New Age woo woo website?" He laughed aloud. "Really, Katherine."

I had decided to go up to my room—as far as I was concerned, the conversation was over—when Mim crashed in, loaded as usual with parcels and shopping bags.

"Darling," she breathed, planting a big wet one square on Dad's lips. It was, I must say, repulsive in the extreme. Harrison and Madison: Their names even rhymed.

She opened her eyes in mid–tongue kiss to stare at me. Then she must have remembered who I was, because she instantly turned on a flood of manufactured enthusiasm.

"Kathy!" she gushed, running over to me stiff-legged, as if she were a doll with non-bendable arms extended. I think it was supposed to be an imitation of what she had imagined to be spontaneous joy.

"Madison," I responded, holding out my arms to stop her before she engulfed me in her robotic embrace.

"Well!" she exclaimed with her usual breathless cheer as I fended her off. "How's school? Oh, help me with these things, Harrison. They're color swatches for the Whitfield house."

Boing. The Whitfield house. As in *living* there. I'd known the time was coming; I'd just hoped that something like an alternate reality would intervene and make it not be so.

"When are you coming?" I asked woodenly.

"Soon. The place is a shambles. Wallpaper, with *borders.* Country everything. A horror. Darling, what do you think of mustard for the living room?"

"Aromatic," he said, although she wasn't listening.

"So how did you like my talk?" Mim went on, pulling out huge collections of fabric samples. She was referring to an all-school assembly she'd arranged to lecture about Wonderland's good works. "At the school," she elucidated in a tone that demanded an answer.

"Oh. Great. I think a lot of people are considering careers

in retail." Although this may have been true, I had no idea of the impact of her presentation, because I'd spent the hour in the nurse's office. I just didn't want to have to listen to Mad Madam Mim converting my clueless peers to the gospel according to Wonderland. Actually, most of my peers were in the infirmary with me, trying to convince Nurse Thompson (cowen) that a stomach flu was raging through the school. Only the Muffies were subjected to Mim's exhortations to join the Wonderland family. Since they were already a lost cause, I didn't care if they followed in her venal footsteps.

"Yes, that talk usually goes over well," she said, rummaging in her pocketbook and emerging with a cigarette and a shiny gold lighter.

"I thought you quit smoking," Dad said. That was one—maybe the only one—good thing about my father. He thought smoking was disgusting.

"Bear with me, darling," she said, exhaling a putrid plume of blue. "A new store brings tremendous pressure. I'll quit once Whitfield opens."

"Until the next time," he muttered. She ignored him.

"Get dressed, Kathy," she said. "We're having dinner at Cibo. You have no idea what I went through to get a reservation."

"Would you mind calling me Katy?" I asked.

She looked blank. "But why should I call you that? It's not your name."

"Neither is Kathy."

She blew smoke into my face. "Just be glad I'm not calling you Serenity," she said, then laughed so uproariously that she began to cough.

✛

My outfit didn't please Mim.

"You look like a waiter."

I glanced down at my black pants and shirt, thinking that maybe they would be enough to get me out of this forced celebration, but no dice.

"Well, you don't have time to change," she sighed. "You'll just have to go as you are." Dad had on a new suit, I noticed, and a pink op-art tie he would never have chosen for himself.

The restaurant was very crowded, and we had to wait for our table. Looking around at all the people in Cibo, groomed and gorgeous as show dogs on display, each one vying for attention by showing off their possessions—in Mim's case, my father—I was suddenly bored by the grayness of it all. I looked at my dad, feeling a surge of pity and longing.

My dad had sacrificed everything he'd had to keep me safe after his world fell apart. If he really hadn't cared about me, he could have made a new life for himself and left the horror of what had happened in Whitfield *and me* behind him forever.

But he hadn't. That counted, no matter how frustrated and angry I got. Love counted.

I leaned over and kissed his cheek. It surprised him. For a moment, his whole face lit up. His mouth opened in the kind of stunned delight you usually only see in little children. I didn't know it would mean so much to him.

"God, that took long enough," Mim said as we were ushered to our table. "I could eat a horse." She pushed the menu aside. "But I'll have a salad."

Dad and I exchanged a look. It meant nothing except that

across the ever-widening distance of our two universes, we still loved each other.

Mim consumed her salad, plus the lion's share of three bottles of wine. By the time the bill came, she was extremely happy.

"I'll miss you, Pierre," she said to our waiter, clasping his hand. She also slipped him a fat roll of bills and, I think, her business card. "I'll be leaving for Buttcrack, Nowhere, next week."

The waiter clucked sympathetically. Dad looked appalled.

"Do you mean Whitfield, Massachusetts?" I asked, deadpan.

"Site of the next big Wonderland!" she shouted, raising her fist in the air. She tripped over her feet as she rose. Dad put his arm around her. She fumbled in her bag for a cigarette that dangled from her lower lip as we left.

"Yeah, Wonderland," Mim said, lighting up as she slid into the backseat of the taxi.

"No smoking," the driver said.

Mim took a drag, then tossed the cigarette out the window, but not before filling the cab with smoke.

"You should see the place where it's going," Mim went on. "Big old field, right in the middle of town. Waste of prime real estate, absolutely. It's not even a park. No benches, nothing. Waste." She flailed her arms in the air, striking every available surface, including my father and me. "But the worst part— the absolute *worst*—was getting rid of that voodoo queen who lives there. You know the one I mean?"

My heart felt as if it had exploded in my chest.

"Man! I mean, *Mon!*" She cackled. "I thought she was going to put the jambalaya curse on me when I told her to get out."

"Hattie?" I squeaked. "You evicted Hattie Scott?"

Mim's face contorted into a belligerent mask. "She was living there illegally, for God's sake. And for God knows how many generations."

"Did you at least pay her?" Dad asked.

"To get off land that she never paid a dime for? Get real. Hey." She slapped the back of the cab driver's head with her pocketbook. "Slow down. We're almost there."

The taxi screeched to a halt and the driver turned around, furious. "Look, lady, you don't hit me, understand? You hit me, I'm gonna call the cops right here, I don't care—"

"Oh, shut up," she said, throwing a bunch of bills at him. Dad got out and ran over to Mim's side of the car so that he could open the door for her. She spilled out of the seat like Jell-O in a silver fox coat.

"Sorry," I said to the driver. It didn't do any good, though. He was still pissed off, even though he was covered in money. I would have been, too.

I left the next morning, prematurely. I wanted to talk to Hattie. And my relatives. And Peter.

My father didn't look me in the eye when I said good-bye. I understood. He knew what he was, what he'd become.

"See you, Dad," I said. He nodded. He was wearing a Dior golf shirt.

"I'll come up for the summer," he said.

"If I let you," Mim joked.

Sort of.

SANGOMA

The kitchen equipment at Hattie's was gone, leaving big stained areas on the floor where the oven, sinks, refrigerator, and dishwasher had been.

"She gave it all to the school," Peter said. "Miss P's got everything in the maintenance shed."

"I can't believe it," I said. "Hattie's Kitchen, closing for good."

"Closed and demolished," Hattie said, coming down the stairs from her apartment.

She looked tired and thin. The mischievous smile that had always played round the edges of her mouth was gone, replaced by deep furrows. "Will you come in for a cup of tea, Katy?" she offered.

I'd never been upstairs before. She'd decorated the place with a strange but beautiful combination of New England severity and Caribbean whimsy. The ceiling was painted to resemble a blue sky. The doorways were strung with tiny shells that clacked when someone walked through. Some of Eric's toys were strewn on the floor amid the piles of boxes that were already sealed and stacked.

"Where will you be moving?" I asked Peter as Hattie was getting the tea ready.

"We've rented a house near New Town," he said. "It's cheaper there."

"I've been here a long time," Hattie said, returning with a tray. "In 1989 I came back to Whitfield from St. Croix with my skin and next to nothing else . . ." She shook her head slowly, looking into a distance that was hers alone. "That was Hurricane Hugo," she said with a sigh. "That devil wind blew the roof off my house, then reached in and took my boy Dando into the air like he was a stick doll. Where he landed, no one knew. Might still be flying in the thin air, for all that."

I was stunned. "You had a son?" I stammered.

"And a husband. After the hurricane moved on, he went into Christiansted to help pull out people trapped in fallen buildings. He was shot by a looter," she said calmly. She sipped her tea. "So this thing, this Wonderland . . . This is nothing."

I could feel the air fairly crackle with her unspoken emotion.

I drank my tea quickly. "But this place is yours," I said at last. "Gram says it's always been in your family."

"For more than three hundred years. I just don't have a document to prove it."

"I don't suppose the Historical Society was any help," I said.

"Oh, the Historical Society doesn't know squat," she said, dismissing the organization with a wave of her hand.

"We don't even need a Historical Society in Old Town," Peter added. "Everyone here's still living in the past."

We all laughed at that, so loud that Eric woke up in the next room and started to wail.

"Oh, me and my big mouth," Hattie said. "Now, you two keep it down." She got up and left the room.

"I never knew Hattie had a son," I whispered.

Peter nodded. "She doesn't talk about him much," he said. "She grew up here, right in this house. But she met this guy in college. He was from the Caribbean—"

"I'll thank you not to be telling my life story like it was your property, Mr. Shaw," Hattie broke in, leaning against the doorjamb.

"Oh. Sorry, Hattie." Peter blushed.

She gave him a sour look. "Was there anything special you were planning to tell our guest about me?"

"No, ma'am."

She shifted her guilt-inducing gaze toward me. "And was there anything special you wanted to know about me? Because if there is, I am the person you should be asking, not him."

"Yes, ma'am," I said. I know I should have let it go at that, but I couldn't stop myself. "Actually, there is something," I said.

Hattie took a step into the room, her arms folded across her chest. "Yes?" The look on her face was that of a dare. A double-dog dare.

I swallowed. "I was just wondering how you could be forced to leave a place where everyone knows your family has lived for so long. I mean, if there was a deed, it would be hundreds of years old. There must be a way around that."

She sighed. "No, honey," she said, "I'm afraid there isn't. It's just the law. If you got no deed, you got no land. The Shaws have been paying taxes on it, so that makes it theirs. Probably some smart lawyer somewhere along the line came up with the idea to pay those taxes. And the Shaws always had more money than God, anyway, so they never missed that money. Turned out to be a good plan."

"For them," Peter said.

Hattie sat down heavily. "That's a fact. When I came back here after the hurricane, old Jeremiah Shaw came round to tell me I had to pay him rent to stay here. I said my family's been here since before the Constitution, same as his, but old Shaw, he must have been weaned on a pickle, not a spark of nothing in him. He said he'd have to charge me rent because he paid the taxes." She picked up her voluminous hair and hoisted it over the back of her chair like a curtain.

"So you paid him."

"I did. And that made me a tenant in the eyes of the law. Oh, it worked out fine for all this while. Jeremiah didn't mind when I opened the restaurant here. And to be fair, he never even raised my rent. But when he sold the property, it meant I had to close down and clear out." She smiled ruefully. "Didn't even come here himself to tell me. Wonderland sent some stone-hearted hussy with a piece of paper and a fancy pen."

Now it was my turn to blush. Mim strikes again.

"She offered me twenty-five hundred dollars if I promised not to give any interviews to the press." She guffawed. "Imagine that!"

"Did you take it?"

"Not exactly." The corners of her mouth were starting to

dance again. "The interview was cut short when a tarantula crawled out of her pretty blonde hair and down her pretty pink nose."

The three of us roared with laughter until Hattie shushed us.

"Well, anyway, the upshot of it all," Hattie said, wiping her eyes on the hem of her apron, "is that we've got to get out of here, and fast. So get these boxes moved over by the door, Peter. And be quick about it."

We both got to work on the boxes. "Wouldn't want to interfere with the big Wonderland Egg Hunt," he muttered.

When we were done, I leaned against an empty bookcase, thinking. "Are you sure there ever was a deed?" I asked.

He held out his hands in a *got me* gesture. "There probably was," he said. "Even in colonial times, people kept accounts about property ownership."

"And that deed, if it exists at all, would be in the name of Shaw?"

"That's what old Jeremiah claims," Hattie said.

"But we don't know which Shaw, right?"

Peter screwed up his face. "What are you getting at?"

But Hattie understood. She stood as still as a statue, her mind zinging along the same lines as mine.

"Who is Jeremiah in relation to you, Peter?"

"My great-uncle, I think." He thought about it. "No, my great-grandfather's brother. Would that be a great-great-uncle?"

"I don't know. Was your great-grandfather older than Jeremiah?"

"Oh, yeah. Much. They had different mothers. I could check, but I'm pretty sure Jeremiah was younger by more than twenty years."

"So, as the oldest son, your great-grandfather would have inherited the property, not Jeremiah, right? He, then your grandfather, then your father, then you."

Peter's eyes widened. "Oh, I get it," he said. "You think I might own the Meadow." He chuckled. "I wish that were true. Unfortunately, there's one little hitch. The Shaws disinherited me."

"Jeremiah Shaw disinherited you," Hattie broke in. "But your father left you and Eric everything he owned."

"Whoa. My father wasn't the big moneymaker in the Shaw family. 'Everything he owned' comes down to two houses, and Hattie sold one to pay Eric's medical bills."

"That doesn't matter," I said. "If the deed belongs to you . . ."

Suddenly he got it. "I could stop Wonderland."

The room rang with the silence.

Hattie was the one to break it. "Useless talk," she said flatly. "Prescott Shaw spent a lot of time preparing his will. If the Meadow was yours to inherit, that will would have said so."

Peter frowned. "But he may not have even thought about it," he said. "No one ever imagined the Meadow would be sold. The deed might still be in the house." He turned to me. "The one that's still in my name. We didn't put it up for sale because we didn't want cowen to move in."

"It's in Old Town?"

"Right on Front Street," Peter said.

"Now, stop getting all excited over the house," Hattie said. "It's unlikely that there's anything of value there besides the furniture. Prescott never even lived in that old place. No one has, for decades."

"He kept it up, though. That was in his will—"

"Oh, no, you don't." Hattie shook an angry finger at him. "Don't you even think about going there. If that place isn't condemned, it ought to be."

Eric screamed again. Hattie clucked in exasperation. "Katy, sweetie, I surely do appreciate your company, but we've got a lot to do here."

"I understand," I said. "I'll be going."

"Thanks for stopping by."

"I'll help you move when the time comes," I said. I turned to Peter. "Walk me to my bike?"

"My pleasure," he said.

"Peter!" It was Hattie.

"Just a second, okay?" He motioned for me to wait.

He took longer than I'd thought. I was about to let myself out when Peter came back into the living room. Eric was still screaming. He opened the door and led me out, signaling me to keep quiet.

Outside, he took a folded-up piece of paper from his pocket. "Eric just drew this," he said, unfolding the paper.

It was a mass of color, brilliant oranges and reds and yellows, so real I could almost feel the flames they depicted.

"Fire," I said needlessly. "The third harbinger."

"Are you surprised?" he asked.

"Not really."

"Me neither."

I folded up the drawing and gave it back to him. "Do you think the deed might be in that old house you were talking about?"

"It might," he said. "It'd be worth a look, anyway."

"Where is it?"

He gestured with his chin. "I'll show you."

Two streets away he pointed out a huge if rickety-looking Victorian mansion with a wraparound porch and a widow's walk surrounding the upper story. "It was built in 1802," Peter said. "When my great-grandfather died, he left houses to all his children. My grandfather inherited this one. He died in the Vietnam War. My father never lived here, but he liked this place. He'd come for a few days now and then. Or so people tell me. Anyway, since he died, it's been kept up by lawyers. No one's even allowed inside, except for the maintenance people."

I was amazed. "Are you telling me that no one's lived here since your great-grandfather?"

"He may not have, either," Peter said with a smile. "The Shaws own a lot of houses. This one's pretty much a throwaway."

"Is there anything in it?"

"Everything, I think. I mean, the furniture and things have never been catalogued or auctioned. I used to break in and hang out inside. It's fitted with an alarm system, but I've got a key to turn it off." He shrugged. "Sometimes I just like to be alone."

I clutched his arm. "Then the deed might be there."

"That's what I was thinking. But Hattie said . . ."

"She doesn't have to know."

"She'll know if we find it," he reasoned.

"We can worry about that after we find it," I said.

MALEFICIUM

Peter and I met at 8 a.m. on the Saturday before Easter, telling our respective keepers that we were checking out the big Wonderland spring extravaganza. I felt disloyal telling that to Gram, but the Wonderland site was the only place where we knew Hattie and my relatives wouldn't set foot. So they wouldn't know that we weren't there.

The Shaw mansion on Front Street wasn't anything like the haunted house vision I'd conjured. Apparently a team of bonded cleaners came once a month to polish the wood and vacuum the rugs. Ditto the exterminator. Twice a year the place was gone over by a building inspector to make sure the electricity and plumbing were in order and to check the roof. So much for Hattie's worries about the place being unsafe.

It was almost weird how clean the place was, considering the last time anyone lived there was over sixty years ago.

"It looks like it's in better shape than it is," Peter said. "Hattie considered selling it to a funeral home once, but they rejected it because the plumbing was too ancient. I don't know how much it costs just to keep it standing."

"Why hasn't someone torn it down, then?"

"Historical landmark," Peter said.

Walking through the rooms of the house, it was hard to keep my mind on the task at hand. It was like visiting a museum, or some European castle. All the furniture was antique and beautiful. There were rolltop desks, hideaway tables, bookcases with secret doors that opened into other rooms, porcelain sinks with some long-departed Shaw's initials fired into them, massive mirrored armoires, and a lot of pieces whose name or function I could not fathom.

"This is a dower chest," Peter explained, opening a long, elaborately carved piece. "It's to carry a bride's dowry."

"Guess the Shaws got their share of those," I said. We went through the chest carefully. Inside were bolts of silk, stained by time despite the care taken to preserve them.

We likewise went through a linen press, hunting cabinet, several gaming tables, a prayer chair, a gigantic black carved display case called a Shibayanna, a smoking stand (still containing a tin of tobacco), and a bedside potty (fortunately empty), plus any number of buffets, servers, cupboards, jewelry cabinets, highboys, dressers, vanities, and bureaus.

It was nearly three in the afternoon by the time we reached the top floor of the house.

"These would have been servants' quarters," Peter said. "I doubt we'll find any valuable papers here."

"Well, we might as well look, anyway," I insisted, even though I knew he was probably right.

I'd known it was a long shot from the beginning. Beyond a

long shot, really. But I was still disappointed because finding the deed in Peter's house was the only thing I could think of to save Hattie's home.

The furniture on this floor was very different from what we'd seen in the rest of the house. Here were narrow metal beds, utilitarian bathrooms, and unadorned fireplaces. There were only a few plain wooden pieces here, things designed for servants with few personal possessions.

"Look at this," I said, pointing out a little chest of drawers. "It must have been for a children's room originally."

"Maybe. Some items were made small as space savers, though. They were called miniatures. I think this is one. You see, it's really two chests, side by side, connected by a clasp or something here in the back . . ." He reached behind it to manipulate a mechanism. With a loud click, something fell into place, and Peter swung the two chests apart so that they were now back to back.

I wasn't impressed. "Cute, but what's the point of it?" I sneered. "I mean, it doesn't save any more space in either position." I opened one of the drawers. It fell out into my hands.

Peter took it. "It is pretty useless, I admit," he said. "Look at this drawer. It's only about ten inches deep."

I reached into the space where the drawer had been. "Maybe there's something else here . . ." There was. Something snapped. With an embarrassing squeal, I jumped backward.

The chest separated again, this time horizontally.

Carefully Peter pushed the sides apart. By now the piece had expanded considerably. He went to the other side, removed the drawer, and popped the mechanism behind it. Again it opened, revealing other drawers, each one smaller than the previous ones, until we were looking at tiny spaces just big enough for a pair of earrings.

"Can you believe this?" he said in astonishment.

"It's a botte," I whispered.

"A what?"

"A magic box." Again, disappointment nibbled at me. "Only it's not really magic. It's mechanical." Just like Dad said it would be.

"This is probably the most valuable thing in the house," he said. "I wonder why it was put up here."

I took out the bottom drawer. "Because of this," I said, feeling my heart start to thud. Beneath the drawer was a hidden compartment cut into the floor. "It was used to hide things." I reached inside, and felt the rustling of fine, thin tissue. "There's something here," I said, feeling as if I were going to jump out of my skin.

"Do you need help?" he asked. "Or a flashlight?"

I shook my head. Whatever was in there was bulky, but not heavy. I pulled out what looked like a wad of gorgeous handmade paper, and laid it on the floor beside me.

"Could it be documents?" Peter asked, touching the bundle gingerly.

Slowly I unwrapped it. First the paper, then the layer of fabric beneath it, exposing a long roll of something that smelled faintly of cedar. I unrolled it, holding my breath.

It was a baby blanket.

"A blanket?" Peter asked.

The treasure I'd unwrapped so painstakingly was a beautifully preserved linen quilt inscribed with embroidered words grown faint with time.

I felt as if the last train had just left town. There wasn't anywhere else to look.

"What's it say?" he asked, squinting at the embroidery.

I read it aloud as best I could:

The wise and Crafty know rightly where to look.
O Word! Spring forth from out thy secret nook.
Feree Ferraugh diten al blosun na tibuk.

"Kind of an odd thing to put on a baby blanket," he said.

"No lie." I felt in the pockets of my jeans. "Do you have a cell phone?" I asked. He handed it to me, and I took a picture of the blanket. "Who knows," I said. "Maybe that's what deeds looked like back then."

Peter didn't answer. He knew I was grasping at straws.

I rooted around in the compartment to see if there was anything else inside it. There wasn't. I sighed. "I guess it was precious to someone," I said, running my hands over the blanket. It made me think about Hattie and her terrible story. It had been as if a door in her memory had accidentally popped open, revealing a room that had been locked and sealed for decades, a pharaonic tomb of a memory in which a little boy named Dando blew away on the wind and never returned. "She's already been through so much," I said. "I wanted to help her keep her house."

"It'll be all right," Peter said. "Things will be tight without the restaurant, but we'll . . ." Frowning, he walked toward the window that overlooked the widow's walk. "I smell something," he said.

Now that he mentioned it, I did too. Something was burning.

"Oh, no."

I jumped up. "What is it?"

Just then, an enormous tongue of flame shot out of the fireplace and into the middle of the room.

I screamed.

Maybe it was my imagination, because I only saw it for a split second, but the fire that came into the room seemed somehow *solid*, as if it had a skin around it like a living thing. And worse—and this is the part that's so hard to believe that I didn't even mention it to the police afterward—*it had a face*.

Yes.

A horrific face, a demon's face, looking right at me.

"Peter!" I gasped.

"Stay with me," he said, taking my hand. As we made our way down the back stairs, he opened up his cell phone. "The house we're in is on fire," he told the 911 operator, giving the address.

"Did you see it?" I asked, stumbling down the darkened stairs.

"Don't talk." He pushed me along.

The smoke was thick in the stairway. I pulled up the neck of my shirt to cover my nose and mouth, all the while remembering the fire and its vicious eyes staring at me.

"I think we're at the second floor landing," he said, taking me around the waist. "Watch your step."

As he spoke, there was a burst of sudden light as the short cotton curtains over the landing window caught fire, illuminating our surroundings.

It was like a vision of Hell. The smoke lay black and thick as oil, while all around us erupted explosions of fire. Pieces of the ceiling rained down on us; the electrical wiring beneath it sparked and sizzled.

"What's going *on*?" I shrilled, near hysteria. Two minutes before, there was nothing. Now all of a sudden the entire place was an inferno.

"In here," Peter coughed, propelling me through a maze of bedrooms and hallways until we reached the main stairway. It was burning as well, the banisters blazing like pillars of flame. Peter took my hand, and we raced down the stairs. "They're still solid," he said. "All we have to—"

At that moment a ball of fire erupted in front of us, forcing us backward with its heat.

"The library," Peter said. I nearly cried with relief. I remembered that there was an outside door there, leading to a long set of stone steps curving between the first and second floors. We were racing toward it when our way was blocked by a series of whooshing fires that ignited like a row of giant candles—one, two, three, four, five—at unbelievable speed.

We ducked through the nearest doorway into a spacious bathroom covered in tiny blue tiles. A wall of long oval mirrors framed in oak reproduced our reflections many times over. I caught sight of my face, terrified, blackened by smoke. Then, in another instant, the glass shattered and I watched the image of myself blow apart. Flames shot out of the sink and bathtub fixtures like dragon's breath. The tile beneath our feet cracked in crazed lines.

"The floor's going to give," Peter said, yanking the Battenberg lace curtains off the windows and stuffing them around the blazing faucets of the sink. Then he kicked out the glass and hoisted me up onto the wide windowsill. "There's thick ivy all over this outside wall," he told me. "We can climb down, but we have to move fast."

I took a look at the faucets. Already the fabric Peter had put around them was catching fire. Outside, I gauged the distance to the ground. At least twenty feet.

"I'll keep you safe," he said quietly. "I promise." He nodded, and I took that as a signal. I climbed out, my hands shaking so badly that I could barely grasp the ivy. Moving sideways like a crab, trying to slip the toes of my sneakers beneath the strong woody vines, I watched him crawl onto the wall beside me.

"Are you all right?" he asked. I nodded uncertainly. "Good. Just keep your hands on the ivy. We're going to climb down now. I'll be right here beside you the whole time."

"O—o—okay," I stammered. I twisted my fingers around the ivy and took a step down.

"That's it," he said. "It won't be far, but don't look down."

I didn't. I looked up. What I saw was the ivy catching fire as if the leaves were made of paper. Down it came, almost in a perfect line, one burning inch at a time.

"Peter," I croaked. I couldn't believe what I was seeing. It was as if the fire were coming after us. "The ivy . . ."

It began to move faster.

"Get on my back," he commanded, watching the flames speed toward us. "Now, as fast as you can."

I reached over and put my arm around his neck. Then I swung my leg over until he was carrying all my weight. Above, the fire was catching up, only four or five feet away from his hands. Peter moved swiftly, one powerful arm at a time, the muscles of his back tensing and quivering as the heat began to burn his fingers. Once he lost his footing and we both nearly fell, but I grabbed onto some ivy while he found a purchase.

"Get back on," he said.

"I think I can—"

"No, you can't," he said. "Hurry up." I grabbed on to him again and he moved faster, keeping pace with the thing that was following us, staying one step ahead of the fire.

Then, with a *whoosh*, the flames dropped downward like a falling curtain, spilling over Peter's hands.

A soft cry escaped his lips.

"Peter," I whispered. His hands were blistering in the flames, and his whole body trembled with pain. I knew I was slowing him down so much that there was a chance neither of us would survive.

"Hang on," he growled.

He deserved better odds than this. "I can't, Peter," I said, and let go.

I heard the fire trucks coming. When I opened my eyes, Peter was holding me. "Why'd you let go?" he whispered.

I sat up, feeling sore but basically unhurt. I guess I just got the wind knocked out of me. But Peter . . . I took his bloody hands in my own. Just seeing them made my heart hurt. "Are you . . . Are you all right?" I asked.

"I'm fine," he lied. He was looking at the fire that was running down the wall like melting wax, more slowly now, as if it knew we'd escaped. "That's not natural."

"I know," I said, shivering. "Peter, did you see—"

He put his arm around me and pulled me up, wincing. The

fire had reached ground level, and was sizzling its way toward us along the grass. "We have to go," he said.

I was scared. How far was it going to chase us? Because there was no doubt in my mind anymore. The fire was in pursuit, and we were its target.

We had reached the street when the first truck pulled up. With amazing speed the firefighters had the hose off and were spraying water onto the grass.

"What the hell kind of fire is this?" I heard one of them shout over the din of machinery and pumping water.

Another—I guess he was the chief—stopped us. "You the ones who called in?"

"Yes," Peter said.

As the fireman asked us questions, I hung on to Peter as if he were a lifebuoy and I were in the middle of the ocean.

In the distance the house steamed and smoked as the water doused it. With a crack, part of the porch collapsed. One of the chimneys broke off and tumbled along the roof, crashing onto the circular driveway.

It looked, for all the world, as if the house were dying.

CHAPTER

•

TWENTY-ONE

 DJINN

The sky on the day of the official Wonderland groundbreaking ceremony was sunny, but the mood of the Old Town residents in attendance was anything but.

They had given the Meadow a very wide berth, especially since Hattie's Kitchen was torn down. But on this Saturday morning they were out in force. Most of the twenty-seven families, including several who no longer lived in Whitfield, showed up. In fact, aside from the mayor and a few Wonderland officials whose job it was to attend these things, almost all of the people who came to the event were witches.

I was there with Agnes and Gram. It was the first time I'd been allowed out of the house since the Shaw mansion burned down. They wouldn't even let me stay in my dorm room.

I suppose I should have been grateful, though. It could have been a lot worse. As it was, my aunt and great-grandmother and Hattie managed to contain the situation with only the minor consequence of keeping Peter and me under lock and key for the rest of our lives.

Naturally, the police didn't believe us when we told them that the fire had started spontaneously, or that it had spread in the bizarre way that we described, but in the end, it was decided that since there was no evidence of arson, and the burned house technically belonged to Peter, then no charges would be filed.

That did not, however, exempt us from Hattie's wrath. When she came into the police station to claim Peter, I thought the walls were going to burst apart.

"Do you have any idea of the value of the objects in that house?" she demanded.

"I'm sorry," Peter began. "We didn't—"

"No, you do not! You have no idea how many priceless antiques burned to ash because you couldn't see fit to listen to me when I told you to stay away from that place!"

"That's—"

"Don't you talk back to me!" she shouted. I could see the duty officer sinking down in his chair.

"Yes, ma'am."

"I want to know *what* you were doing there after I expressly forbade you to go?"

"We were looking for the deed," I broke in.

"Was I talking to you?" she demanded, turning on me. "Did I ask you to say something?"

"No," I said.

"You placed every house on Front Street, and every family who lives there, in mortal danger."

By now Peter and I knew better than to answer. It was a

good thing, too, because at that moment Gram and Aunt Agnes walked in and stood next to Hattie, all of them glaring at the two of us. It was like being stared down by the three witches from Macbeth—red eyes, vibrating ears, fingers sparking with blue light. The officer on duty didn't seem to notice, but Peter and I could feel the air being sucked out of the room.

"Now I am going to ask you both one question, and one question only, and the answer had better be the truth, because if it isn't, I will find out," Hattie said. "Is that clear?"

I nodded, shook my head, then nodded again.

"Did you in any way cause a fire to break out in the Shaw house?" she asked levelly.

"No, ma'am," Peter said.

"In *any* way," she repeated.

"We did not," I said.

"Neither of you, together or separately?"

"No, Hattie," I said. "The fire just happened. And then it came after us."

"It *came after* you?" the officer scoffed.

"Stay out of this," Hattie snapped. He sank back in his chair.

She stared at Peter and me for a long moment. Finally she inhaled, raised her head, and said, "I believe you."

We both sighed with relief . . . until I got a better look at my relatives. Their bad vibrations were obviously undiminished by Hattie's not-guilty verdict. They are usually very nice people, really, but at that moment I could have sworn that little silver darts were shooting out of their identical eyes. Coronas of dark fury circled their heads.

It was because of Peter, I knew. They hadn't liked the idea

of my seeing him even after he'd proven that he wasn't cowen and had earned the right to stay in Old Town. I don't think they had anything against him personally, but there was some mighty bad feeling against the Shaws in general.

"You will come with us," Aunt Agnes said, after all the paperwork had been gone through. Gram nodded good-bye to the officer, who never moved an inch.

"And you," Hattie said, blocking my way so that I would be sure to hear what she was saying to Peter, "will not see Katy again outside of school. Do you agree?"

Peter looked at me, then back at her. "No," he said.

The police officer rested his head in his hand. I think he really wanted us to leave.

Agnes nudged me. "It's all right, Peter," I said. "It won't be forever."

"Don't hold your breath," Hattie said.

At least I'd been allowed to leave Gram's house occasionally. Peter hadn't even been permitted to attend the Wonderland groundbreaking, which hardly promised to be the social event of the year.

Still, it drew a huge crowd, and the sheer number of attendees lent a festive air to the proceedings. Someone had set up a funnel cake stand, and several hawkers walked around offering soft drinks for two dollars a can. Mabel Bean, who was Miss P's mother, was doing a brisk business selling her famous blueberry cookies from a folding card table. Sharing it was a crafter who made swans out of wheat. All in all, it promised to be a better time than I'd thought.

Except for Mim. At exactly nine a.m., she appeared in the

center of the roped-off area set aside for the groundbreaking. She was wearing a hard hat and a pink Prada suit. In her manicured hands (her nails painted in "Crucial Fuschial") was a shovel.

She was already irritated, I could tell. The shovel, which probably should have been gleaming and new for the occasion, had instead been covered with dried mud and tar and other unspeakable forms of detritus. Also, the handle must have had grease or something on it, because she was dangling it between her index finger and thumb. While the mayor of Whitfield (cowen) was introducing her, she kept shooting threatening looks at the workmen—whom she had undoubtedly offended in some horrific yet typical manner—lined up behind her, their expressions those of perfect innocence.

". . . and here, representing the Wonderland Corporation, is Mizz Madison Mimson!"

She held up one hand, as if to quiet the thunderous cheers of the crowd, although at that point all you could hear were a couple of crickets. "First, I want to thank you all for this terrific turnout," she began, beaming, "because Wonderland isn't just a business, even though it will bring *hundreds* of jobs into Whitfield . . . " (a pause here for more applause that never came). "It's also a—*aggh!*"

Her left foot, shod also in Prada, sank into the ground.

"Sinkhole," someone near me whispered, but a couple of people, including Miss P's mother, shook their heads. A faint smile played at the corners of Mrs. Bean's lips as she bit into one of her cookies.

Mim, however, was not smiling. Leaning heavily on her shovel, she pulled her foot out of the mud with a sucking sound, then went after the shoe that had been left in the muck. She had to dig as far as her elbows to retrieve it.

"It's also a family," she went on doggedly, apparently trying to decide whether or not to put the mud-soaked shoe back on. "And so, without further . . ."

This time I saw it. At least three people shot five fingers at Mim. A moment later, her right foot sank into the ground.

"Where are the geologists?" she demanded. The mayor came over making sympathetic noises while at the same time trying to keep some distance between her and his own impeccable ensemble.

She tried to stick the shovel into the ground—which, naturally, was hard as a rock—to pull her leg out of the muck. Now she was barefoot, covered in mud up to her knees, her pink suit daubed with brown blobs, but undaunted.

"Without further ado . . ."

From my vantage point, everyone in the crowd with the exception of my relatives and Miss P, who was standing some distance away, was pretending to be scratching behind their ears. I could actually see the spells shooting out of their fingers en masse as, with a blood-curdling scream, Mim dropped waist-deep into a churning pool of mud.

"Damn it!" she screeched, flinging away the shovel as if it were a javelin. "What kind of fricking—" At that moment, a toad leaped out of the mud onto her head. Her arms flailed, sloshing mud across her face. Another toad appeared. Then another, until she was surrounded by dozens of croaking amphibians leaping animatedly around her.

"You!" she called to the mayor, who was backing away, his face a mask of horror.

Then from out of the muck slithered a fat eel the size of an anaconda that wound around Mim's waist and worked its way up her torso until it was wrapped around her head like a turban.

"Get this thing off me!" she wailed as the eel settled in. The toads bounced merrily. Big bubbles formed on the surface of the mud and burst, releasing odiferous gases into the air.

A lot of the onlookers had their cell phones held high, taking pictures. The soda vendors made another sweep. Schoolchildren were shooting five fingers willy-nilly, producing things like frog eggs and rabbit droppings and shrieking with delight.

Miss P pushed her way through the crowd. "Mother!" she shouted. Her mom turned to look at her and giggled. Gram hid her mouth behind a lace handkerchief as the mayor retreated out of the Meadow and into a waiting limo.

"You get back here!" Mim screamed at him as the limo sped away. Seething with frustration, she knocked the eel to the ground and grasped it below its head, apparently attempting to strangle it with her bare hands.

She was tough, I'll give her that.

"Go home, Wonderland!" someone in the crowd called. That set off a chorus of jeers and anti-Wonderland epithets as Mim finally released the startled eel and hoisted herself out of the mudhole.

"We don't want your stinking store!" someone else shouted.

I think that must have been the last straw for her. Looking like a *Velociraptor* that had just fought its way out of a tar pit, Mim reared back on her sturdy if filthy legs and bellowed, "Well, you're going to get it whether you want it or not, you low-life jerks!"

The Wonderland executives who, to tell the truth, hadn't offered much help or support from the beginning, looked stricken. One took out a notepad and wrote something down. The construction guys remained in position, chortling.

Then an egg flew over the heads of the crowd and splatted against Mim's forehead.

"Now, that's enough!" The person who spoke was, of all people, Miss P. Even angry, she looked like a cute cartoon version of a mouse. What was weird, though— really weird— was that I'd *heard* her. I saw her when she said it, but she hadn't been standing nearby, and there had been a lot of noise.

What was even more weird was that the crowd dispersed almost immediately after that—so quickly, in fact, that Mim herself was left standing virtually alone in the Meadow, seething, ready to fight anyone who cared to take her on.

I felt sorry for her, not because she was covered in mud, or even because she'd momentarily had the pants scared off her, but because she'd been made aware of how much she was hated.

"Can I help you?" I offered, walking up to her.

"Come to gloat?" she sneered, trying to sweep the egg off her face with a tissue from her pocketbook. "Well, get your fill now, 'cause times are going to change."

I held out a wad of tissues for her. She snatched them out of my hand and tried to wipe off her mud-caked legs. She was blinking a lot. I think she was trying not to cry.

"Katy!" Aunt Agnes called. I looked over my shoulder at her.

"Go," Mim said quietly. "I'll be okay." She held up the filthy tissues. "Thanks for these." She smiled. "Katy."

As I neared the edge of the Meadow, I saw Mim pick up her things and turn on the construction guys. "Get to work!" she snarled, clutching her mud-filled shoes to her chest.

The men laughed. One of them saluted. Then, as they conferred—no doubt about how to proceed, given that a second sinkhole had appeared on the site—Miss P ventured forward, her hands on her slim hips.

I don't know if anyone else saw it or not. Certainly not the construction guys. And most of the people at the groundbreaking (a funny word, considering just how the ground had broken) had already left. But I swear, before my very eyes the mudhole cleared up, drying in concentric circles from the outside in.

It happened in about five seconds. The toads vanished into the shrinking hole, then the eel slithered in, and the place was bone dry again, without so much as a dent in the ground. Mim's shovel lay on top, unused.

When Miss P turned around to leave, I caught her eye. She blushed, embarrassed, and moved past me without a word.

Agnes, who had been talking with Gram, motioned for me to join them.

"It wasn't a sinkhole," I said breathlessly.

"Of course not," Gram said. "That was all a prank."

"A prank that nearly got badly out of hand," Agnes said tartly.

I looked back at the site. The construction guys were gathered in a circle around where the mudhole had been, scratching their heads.

"Did you hear Miss P?" I asked.

"What did she say?"

"I think she said 'That's enough,' or something like that."

"Oh. Yes, of course. Everyone heard her. That's why they left."

"What?" I thought I'd heard wrong. "Are you saying she . . . *commanded* them?"

Agnes and Gram exchanged a glance. Gram nodded once, then cleared her throat. "Penelope Bean is a djinn," she said. "We are fortunate to have her in our community. Djinns are among the rarest of all witches."

"A djinn?" I repeated stupidly. For some reason, the word conjured images of half-naked male genies materializing out of bottles.

"She willed those people to stop tormenting that dreadful woman," she went on, her eyes darting around secretively. "But you mustn't tell anyone. Most of the people who were here don't even know what caused them to leave." She smiled sweetly. "It's better that way, you know."

"Miss P, a djinn," I marveled over tea. "I never would have thought. I mean, she seems so . . . *harmless*."

"That's exactly the sort of person a djinn ought to be," Agnes said. "The ability to bend others' will to one's own can be very dangerous in the wrong hands. People can be easily corrupted by such power."

"When Mabel Bean discovered what her Penelope could do, she enlisted the help of all the most powerful witches in Whitfield to train her."

"Train her for what?"

"Mostly, to use her gift as infrequently as possible," Agnes said. "So try not to speak of it, Katy. Not only does Miss P find public attention extremely unwelcome, but you can imagine how badly she could be misused if her gift were known, especially to cowen."

"Gracious!" Gram fell back in her chair, as if the thought were too much to bear.

I thought about it. I'd heard about djinn, but they were so unusual that I never thought I'd ever even meet one, let alone attend a school where a djinn worked as assistant headmistress. "What happens if . . ." I simply couldn't refer to her as a "djinn" without picturing her in harem pants and a veil and sliding out of a lamp shaped like a neti pot. ". . . if people like Miss P aren't trained?"

"Exactly what you think would happen when people discover that they have complete power over nearly everyone on earth," Agnes said. "They become monsters."

I had a sudden vision of Miss P mind-controlling the Muffies at Ainsworth School so that they all wore sensible shoes and sweatshirts with appliquéd bunnies. "I mean, what do we do with them?"

Gram answered. "We send them away, to live among cowen," she said with a definitive nod. "Serves them right."

"Since they aren't trained, they can't really use their gift effectively, anyway," Agnes said. "But they do very well in the military. Also, unfortunately, in gangs, organized crime, politics, and in many religions. Anything that demands unquestioning obedience. They make excellent leaders, as you may expect. However, it is nearly impossible for them not to be corrupted by the power they are accorded."

"But that won't happen with Penelope Bean," Gram said, recovering herself. "She may not look it, but she is our strongest defense."

"Against what?" I asked.

She opened her mouth to speak, then thought better of it. But Agnes looked straight at me. "Against what we all know is coming," she said.

Chapter

•

Twenty-two

GRIMOIRE

By May, the Meadow had become a moonscape. There were problems at every turn—subterranean boulders the size of automobiles, pockets of natural gas, rainstorms that halted work for hours on end—but the methodical destruction of the spiritual center of our community went on. As my aunt Agnes said, there were some things that even magic couldn't stop, and Wonderland was one of them.

Oh, people tried. Every time I walked past the Meadow I'd see someone shooting five fingers at it, causing a backhoe to break down or a swarm of bees to materialize. Most of the magic was pretty low-level, though. You had to be a witch to live in Old Town, but you didn't have to be a great witch.

Fortunately, the really powerful witches in town weren't particularly worried about Wonderland. Their attitude was that, in the big scheme of things, discount department stores come and go, but magic (that is, the old school, genuine, capital M Magick that created the Meadow in the first place) was forever.

So, despite the presence of bulldozers and the horrible smear that marked the place where the 350-year-old foundation of Hattie's home had been extracted from the ground, on May the second, Beltane, the impenetrable Whitfield fog rolled into the Meadow like clockwork to herald the witches' Rite of Spring.

It was a busy day at the Ainsworths. Agnes and Jonathan were to be handfasted that evening. Handfasting is the witch version of an engagement party. The couple declares themselves to each other. They can use traditional words—this is a very old ritual—or they can make up their own. But whatever they say, it can't include words like *forever* or *till death* or anything like that, because handfasting is not marriage. It lasts for exactly a year and a day. If at the end of that time the couple decide that they really can spend the rest of their lives together, then they marry or, if they're really indecisive, just get handfasted again. If not, they go their separate ways. I think it's a pretty intelligent system, personally. Witches don't divorce nearly as often as cowen.

Gram and I were changing curtains while Agnes got ready for her big night. I don't know why she bothered, since all of the curtains in the house looked the same, anyway. I had been released from house arrest after two weeks and allowed to move back into my dorm room. Unfortunately, Peter hadn't. He hadn't been back in his dorm since before the fire in the Shaw mansion.

A question occurred to me: "Was Serenity Ainsworth a djinn?" I asked.

My great-grandmother appeared to be taken aback. "Good heavens, what an odd question!" she chuckled. "It's like asking if one of your relatives was the king of France. Quite unlikely, I'd say. Why do you ask?"

I waffled. Now that I was finally out of the doghouse, I didn't want to get into trouble again. "It's just that she mentioned something about using her will to keep the settlers at Salem from burning . . . " She was staring at me. ". . . someone. . . "

"Dorothea Lyttel," she said somberly. "You opened the brooch."

"Yes."

"I'm sorry you had to come upon that memory. Serenity had a long life, and so much has been written about it. You might have tuned in at any number of places in it." She dropped the curtain she was carrying and came over to hug me. "Perhaps I shouldn't have given it to you."

"No, it was all right. I think I'm getting better at handling things like that. But I found out something. Something terrible, Gram."

"What was it, dear? Whatever it was, you can tell me."

This was hard. "It was about the witches. I think . . . I think they were the ones who started the Burning Times."

"What? Oh, certainly not. You've misunderstood something, Katy."

"They did it themselves, Gram. They burned their own kind. I—that is, *she* saw it, Serenity. And in the end she approved of it, although it made her feel rotten."

Gram took a handkerchief from her sleeve and dabbed at her face with it. "Very well, then. Now you know the worst of it." She sat down heavily. "There was no other way, child. There *is* no other way. If the Darkness takes any one of us— anyone, no matter how valuable or beloved—that person must be destroyed. Even today."

"By fire."

"Yes, by fire. That is what is written in the *Great Book of Secrets*."

"Excuse me? The great book of . . ."

"Secrets," she repeated. "You've certainly heard of a book of secrets, haven't you?"

180

"Er, no, I can't say I have."

She tutted. "There are so many holes in your education, I don't even know if we can fill them all before you come of age," she said, shaking her head. She took my hand and led me to the sofa. "Every witch has a book of secrets. It's like a recipe book, with spells one has learned and other things— potions, remedies, even keepsakes and stories to share with our descendents. Everything we know and dream about and wonder. Everything, in short, about who we are."

"Like a magical diary?"

"Exactly. So by extension, the *Great Book* . . ."

"Is about Whitfield."

She nodded. "Very good. It contains every spell the community has performed together since Whitfield's founding. It also details every significant news item and biography of those most influential to our world, including Serenity Ainsworth. That, plus our own family's Book of Secrets, would have told us if she were a djinn."

"And that's where it says that witches have to burn themselves at the stake, just because Dorothea Lyttel did?"

"Oh, my dear," Gram said sadly. "The unfortunate Mrs. Lyttel was the only person to have suffered that fate. That is, until much later."

I sighed. "How much later?"

"In 1929," she said. "Seven witches were infected then. The high priestess was pressured to burn them, but she refused."

At least there had been one sensible person in the history of my people, I thought.

"Her compassion did no good, however. Infected people always die anyway, and then the Darkness moves into someone else. In that case, it moved into the high priestess herself."

I gasped. "What did she . . ."

Gram swallowed. "Like Dorothea Lyttel, she lit her own fire. She took her life to save what was left of us." Gram dabbed at her eyes. "She was a very brave woman."

"And the Darkness. . . ."

"The Darkness moved on after that. It had gained so much power through our witches that it went on to destroy the world economy and with it, the lives of millions."

I thought of something that might make a little sense out of things. "Gram, was my mother ever high priestess?" I asked.

She smiled. "No, although it's interesting that you should ask. She was offered, but she turned it down."

"Why?"

She looked at the floor. "She wished to marry outside the community," she said.

"Oh. Right."

"When she . . . moved out of Old Town, Agatha relinquished her right to enter the Meadow."

I nodded in resignation. "I get it," I said. "I just thought that maybe that was why she died the way she did. The burning, I mean. I thought that if she was the high priestess, maybe that was something she did to stop the Darkness."

Gram regarded me sadly. "I wish I could say that was true, Katy," she said. "But even if she had been high priestess, what she did would still have been incomprehensible. Ten years ago there was no indication that the Darkness was anywhere near Whitfield, even among cowen. There were no harbingers, no warnings. No." She sighed. "I'm afraid that the reasons for my granddaughter's actions will never be understood."

CHAPTER

•

TWENTY-THREE

 OLOKUN

At night, all the witches of Whitfield walked through the fog to the center of the Meadow. It was comforting, being in that procession. I felt as if I were a part of something older than written history, something that might never be understood by cowen, but would still remain forever.

On the plane we occupied, none of the earth-moving equipment that littered the area during the day was visible, or even existed. As we neared the clearing that Hattie, as high priestess, had created, the mist thinned until we found ourselves surrounded by lush forest. The deer appeared again, as they had at Halloween, but this time they were accompanied by dappled fawns. The ground, bare clay on the earthly plane, was covered with thick grass and wildflowers here, in this inviolate place where nothing ever changed. No one even died in this realm, but remained among us as spirits. This was where Magic ruled.

The crowd parted and Hattie walked through, wearing a magnificent African *boubou*, a wide-sleeved caftan made of some material that looked like liquid gold, and a necklace of long rectangular stones as blue as a summer lagoon. On her head was a kind of truncated cone, resembling the crown on the famous carved head of Nefertiti. It too was gold, and painted with sigils and other magical symbols.

Displayed thus, she was no longer Hattie Scott, but the high priestess of Whitfield.

As she glided past me, leaving a wake of amber incense behind her, one of the blue stones from her necklace broke loose and fell near where I was standing. When I picked it up I staggered backward, hearing the ocean roar in my ears.

Keep conscious, keep conscious, I willed myself, feeling the overpowering vibrations of the stone in my hand. For a moment I held it out at arm's length, thinking I would return it to Hattie, but she was surrounded.

And I didn't want to give it back. Not yet. The feeling I was getting from the smooth blue stone was delicious, soothing, irresistible. I fell back through the crowd to sit on a moss-covered boulder at the edge of the forest, clutching the stone, breathing in its magic.

The stone was infused with magic, that I knew. Magic and something else. Something that felt almost like music.

Someone was playing the kalimba. It was a simple one, seven tines carved of bamboo. They'd had to leave the larger instruments—the akadina, the kudu horn—back at the village. There had been no time to take anything, even food, when the Europeans had come to take them captive.

A young girl sat on a rock and listened for the spirits to tell her what to do. Ola'ea's teacher had been killed trying to evade capture. That had distracted the whitefaces long enough for her to lead the people of her village to the rain forest.

She was no stranger to the Darkness. It had been growing in that region for nearly two hundred years, since the first Portuguese traders came to take human beings from their homes and sell them as slaves to plantation owners in the Caribbean. But now the Darkness had taken her village, and Ola'ea knew that to fight it, she would need more magic than she had yet learned.

She sat on the rock in the rain forest with the souls of her people weighing heavily upon her heart for three days and three nights without eating or sleeping. Then, on the fourth day, Ola'ea smelled the ocean.

She recognized the scent as the breath of Olokun, goddess of the sea, who was known to other peoples as Kwan Yin or Yemani or Mari. With her sea-voice, Olokun called to Ola'ea, saying, Come with me now, little one, and learn what I have to teach you.

And so, knowing that the goddess must be obeyed, Ola'ea set off on her journey.

After walking for three more days, she arrived at the ocean's shore. "I have come to your home, Olokun!" *she shouted into the waves.* "Where shall I go now?"

To the ships, *the goddess answered.*

"But they will capture and enslave me."

Yes.

This was the first lesson she learned. The lesson of water: Be willing.

Young Ola'ea walked along the shore until she came upon the evil ships that reeked of human sweat and waste, and gave herself up to the whiteface demons who thrust her into the vast stinking hold of the ship along with hundreds of others. The prisoners were given food on the voyage, but Ola'ea ate nothing.

When the ship arrived in Barbados, Ola'ea was so thin that she was considered too weak to work in the fields of the sugar cane plantations owned by the English. But she was also very beautiful, and so was bought to serve the British masters in their house, which was like a cave. It was so large and dark that those who lived inside almost never felt the sun or rain. All of the scents in the place, too, were human, reminding her of the rank odor of the slave ship.

An old man taught her English, which was not like the sibilant water-sounds spoken by the Portuguese slavers or the crisp, clacking earth sounds of her own tongue, but a dry, spitting language, produced at the front of the mouth with no resonance. It was the language of air.

This was how Ola'ea related to all things, through the four elements of nature. Everything she could see, think, know, or dream, could be organized by element: Whatever it was, it was either earth, air, fire, or water. The tangible, solid, physical things were earth. Water was the realm of all things flexible and giving. Air was for creativity and change, and fire . . . fire was destruction. Fire was death, fear, anger, endings. And it, too, had its place.

The old man who had been assigned to teach her English told her to imitate the civilized manners of her betters. "If you are sweet-tempered and helpful, the master will give you an easy life," he said.

"An easy life will teach me nothing," she answered.

"Perhaps the master will take you to his bed," the old man said.

"Then I shall kill him."

The old slave told the mistress of the house that the girl Ola'ea was too wild to be of use indoors.

"Sara!" the English woman called. Sara was the name she had given her.

"My name is Ola'ea," she answered.

The woman slapped her. It was a weak, harmless blow from a useless, indolent body. Ola'ea wondered why the other servants seemed to be so afraid of these people.

She was banished from the house and relegated to the kitchen garden. There she discovered okra and breadfruit, bananas, figs, avocados, and callaloo. From her garden she coaxed ginger, grapefruit, guava, mango, sapodilla, passion fruit, papaya, pigeon peas, plantains, soursop, and star apple; also sunflower seeds, cashews, yams, and christophene. Delicious, gorgeous, fragrant food, earth magic, born of the land. They taught Ola'ea the second lesson of her life: Take your strength from what is offered. The earth was teaching her, making her magic grow along with her vegetables.

Just before the cane harvest during her fourth year on the sugar plantation, Ola'ea once again heard the voice of the sea-goddess Olokun.

Your ship is ready, she said. Ola'ea did not question. She said farewell to her garden, blessing the trees and the ground, then wiped the soil off her hands and headed back toward the ocean.

An overseer saw her leaving the garden and called out to her.
When she failed to answer his call, he ran after her, brandishing
the whip he sometimes used on the field hands.

"I'll teach you something you ain't going to forget anytime
soon," he said, flicking the whip to release its steel tip into the
air. It spun and weaved like a serpent, then shot forward, aimed
squarely between Ola'ea's narrow shoulders.

She heard it, because her time in the garden had taught her
about air. There she had learned the third lesson of nature's
teaching: Everything but the past can be changed.

Ola'ea fixed her sorceress' eyes on the whip and moved
her fingers in a circle. The whip obeyed, curving in the air,
changing direction, doubling back in its graceful dance until
it wound, faster, faster, under the armpit of the screaming
overseer until, with a final click of the steel tip, the man's
arm severed and fell with a gush of pumping blood to the
ground.

He dropped to his knees, his eyes bulging in shock, his mouth
open wide, the sound coming out of it an animal cry. Ola'ea
looked at him, and then at the house where she had sent her
vegetables to be eaten by the weak-armed whitefaces who had
bought her, and she knew what she had to do.

Raising her arms to her sides, she called forth all the anger
that had been stored within her since she had been forced from
her village, and sent it out the tips of her fingers. It crackled
and ignited, shooting sparks. The dry grass caught fire, as did
the trees, the shrubs, the ground plants, the house. The overseer
screamed one last time as his heart cooked in the volcanic
flames of Ola'ea's wrath.

That was the fourth lesson of her journey here to paradise:

Take the bitter with the sweet. *This was a hard lesson, the lesson of fire. Destruction and death were necessary to the wheel of life, and a sorceress must be prepared both to kill, if necessary, and to die.*

Her soul clean now and devoid of hatred, Ola'ea turned away from the flames and walked once more toward the sea. In her wake, the entire plantation burned to the ground, with the exception of the kitchen garden, which fed all the rabbits and birds and goats that came into it seeking shelter.

At the dock, she surveyed the ships at anchor.

That one, said the voice of Olokun.

Ola'ea climbed the gangplank. "'Ere, you," *the ship's boatswain said, grabbing her arm.* "What do you think you're doing aboard this here cargo ship?"

"I must cross the ocean," *she said.* "I will be your cook."

"Cook?" *the man repeated. Just what he needed to make sail.* "You're a cook, you say?"

"I am."

He studied her face. The young woman was strange and beautiful. But a woman. That was the worst part. The men, he knew, must never see her, because she would fill them with fear and lust. "All right, Cook," *he said.* "But you must dress like a man, and sleep alone in the galley. And you must speak to no one."

She nodded her assent. She did not speak another word during the voyage.

Ola'ea fulfilled her part of the bargain, preparing the crew's meals in silence, and sleeping next to the ship's stove. She kept her voluminous hair braided and tied at the top of her head like a cat-o'-nine-tails.

The men, believing her to be the Captain's private slavey boy, did not bother her.

But during the voyage she fell sick. It was, perhaps, the putrid, algae-covered water that she had been forced to drink for lack of any other. She worked as long as she could, but just as she smelled land on the breeze, she slumped to the floor in a fever.

The foretopman found her lying unconscious on the slimy galley deck and summoned the ship's surgeon, who discovered that not only was the cook a woman, but that she was infected with yellow fever. Amid a chorus of curses and oaths, imprecations and sailors' prayers, she was hastily hauled onto the deck and thrown overboard.

If it had not been for the shock of the water against her fevered body, she might never have regained consciousness.

If the month had not been August, she could have frozen in those Atlantic waters.

If she had remained on the ship, she would have docked with it at Shaw Island, where an official of the trading company would have had her jailed as a runaway slave.

But none of this occurred. Hanging on to a plank from a recent wreck, Ola'ea floated past the island and into the warm, shallow waters along the coastline of Whitfield Bay. She was found by Serenity Ainsworth, who was counting dead birds, Cory's shearwaters, fallen by the dozens. And among them, a young woman dressed in men's clothes, with hair like a pirate corsair, skin like teak wood, and the same witch's eyes that Serenity herself saw every time she looked into a glass.

Ola'ea came to in Serenity's arms. "Olokun," she said with great surprise before fainting again.

She had never even entertained the possibility that the goddess of the sea would be an old white woman.

But then, Olokun was full of surprises.

CHAPTER

•

TWENTY-FOUR

 BELTANE

"Katy?" Cheswick passed a hand in front of my face. "Earth calling."

"Are you okay?" Verity looked worried.

"I'm fine," I said numbly. It always took me a while to come out of these psychometric states. In this case, I didn't even know I was going into one, let alone coming out of one. *No images*, I told myself. *No more images.* "I wasn't talking, was I?"

"No," Cheswick said. "You just looked . . . zoned."

Verity looked me levelly in the eye. "Have you been tested for epilepsy?" she asked.

"Verity, I'm fine."

"Okay, okay. We were just trying to get closer to the bonfire, and then we saw you looking weird," Cheswick said. Verity poked him in the ribs. "Well, not weird, exactly, but—"

"It's all right," I said. "Psychometry," I said, holding up the blue stone. "I was picking up on someone's life."

"Awesome," Cheswick said. "I wish I could do that."

"I have an aunt who's a psychometrist," Verity said. "Sometimes she actually *becomes* the person. Especially if they're dead."

"Amazing. Can I?" Cheswick took the stone and closed his eyes. "Nope, nothing," he said, handing it back after a moment. "Say, can you do that, Katy? What Verity said about becoming the person?"

"Sometimes. Not always. I didn't just now. I only kind of saw what was happening. And it took place over a long span of time, four or five years. Sometimes I only get an incident, or just a thought. Once—"

"I think it's almost time for the handfasting." Cheswick said, standing up. "Want to join us? We're going to try to get a spot up front."

"Uh, no thanks," I said, mortified. "I'm fine here."

"Cheswick and I are going to be handfasted next year," Verity said coyly, taking his hand.

"Hey, great," I said. "Congratulations."

"He got me a locket." She moved closer to me so that I could see the heart-shaped pendant dangling from a chain around her neck.

"Have you . . . have you seen Peter?" I asked.

"I think he's still grounded. Sorry." Verity said. Of course everyone knew about the fire in the Shaw mansion and our subsequent punishment, but I'd heard rumors that Peter hadn't been confined to quarters the way I'd thought. I hadn't seen much of him at school, either.

She and Cheswick ran off toward the bonfire, their silhouettes stark against the bright cobalt blue of falling night. The men were carrying slabs of meat out of the bonfire, which was just about at the right level for the ritual. Around it stood the couples, the women with flowers in their hair, the men with belts of vine or with small horns glued to their heads. I stood on the rock I'd been sitting on to get a better look at the proceedings. I could see Agnes, for once unguarded and smiling. I'd never seen her look so pretty. That must have been how my mother looked, I thought.

Then I realized that she could never have been handfasted to my father, because he wouldn't have been able to enter the Meadow. She'd never walked among her people with flowers in her hair, or jumped over the bonfire in a three-thousand-year-old ritual. She could have been high priestess; instead, she'd settled for living among cowen who believed that her people were supernaturally evil, if they believed we existed at all.

She must have loved him so much. So terribly much.

My eyes filled with tears as I watched the couples begin to line up on the far side of the bonfire. The intendeds spoke their true names.

"Lucrezia Penrose," announced the first woman to be handfasted.

"Atherton Bell."

Holding hands, they raced toward the fire and then leapt over it like deer while the crowd roared its approval. A number of men clanked their tankards and drained the contents, a practice they would repeat in honor of each couple until they either lost consciousness or were dragged home.

Agnes and Jonathan were next. He'd given her a ring that morning, even though engagement rings were a cowen practice and not at all necessary for a handfasting. Jonathan had given it to her because it had belonged to his great-great-grandmother, who had had it fashioned into a ring during the Civil War. Before that, it had been the handle of a spoon made by Paul Revere. People in Old Town had deep roots.

"Agnes Ainsworth."

"Jonathan Carr."

Jonathan was a popular guy, and the best carpenter in town. Maybe his coming into the Ainsworth family would help mend the rift between my relatives and the people who still blamed them for what my mother did to Eric Shaw.

But would they ever forgive me?

It was even harder for me to pretend that I was one of the Old Town gang since I'd discovered a new talent I was developing: It seemed that the longer I lived in Whitfield, the more sensitive I was becoming to people's emotional states. Every object I touched had some sort of emotional signature that I could read. Fortunately, most of the time I had to concentrate on the object in order to feel anything.

But *people*—that was something new, another branch of my particular gift that was just beginning to show up. I'd always been able to read people's emotions pretty well, but lately I'd been able to see more deeply into what they were really feeling, even if they couldn't admit it to themselves.

I'd talked with Miss P about it after Becca Fowler tripped me in the hall at school. She'd been all apologetic, helping me retrieve my books and insisting on walking me to the nurse's office, but I knew she'd done it on purpose.

That didn't take any special gift—Becca had been shooting poisonous looks at me ever since the day Peter saved me from falling down the stairs. But what bothered me was what I felt when she took my arm to help me up. It was *anger*, anger of such scope that it was hard for me to feel it, even secondhand.

It went beyond simple jealousy, although that was the first level of the anger in her. Past that was something colder and broader and far more confusing. It was about my mother and my relations, and the Ainsworth women in general. At the moment when I came in contact with her bare skin, her emotions were so strong that I could almost hear the exact words of her thoughts: *You're bringing the Darkness again, the way your people always do.*

"That sounds as if it were part of a collective memory, I'm afraid," Miss P said. "Becca couldn't really help it, if that makes you feel any better."

"She couldn't *help* it?" I asked. "She was practically boiling over." That made me think. "Unless I misread her. Maybe I was just being paranoid because . . ." I was going to say *because of Peter*, but I didn't want to get into that whole complicated relationship, at least not with the assistant headmistress, djinn or not. ". . . because she's not usually friendly to me," I fudged.

"It's always hard to tell the difference between what we really perceive and what we want to see," she said. "It's doubly hard when one is dealing with a psychic gift. How do you know whether it's the gift informing you, or your own desires and fears?"

"Right," I agreed eagerly. "How do you know?"

She shrugged. "I don't know."

Great. A really, really helpful answer, Miss P. So glad I confided in you. "But . . . you said that Becca was involved in some kind of collective memory," I said.

"Yes." She smiled sweetly. I wondered how many people Miss P had driven insane.

"What was that memory?" I prodded.

"That whenever the Darkness comes, the Ainsworth women are somehow involved."

"What? Is that true?"

She held her hands palm-out in front of her. "That is the common talk, Katy," she said. "It would be remiss of me to tell you otherwise. However, it has nothing to do with the truth, which is that the Ainsworths are such an old and direct line that they have, in fact, been involved with *everything* that has occurred in Whitfield ever since—"

"Excuse me, Miss P, but how are they—we—involved with the Darkness?"

"Well, let's see," she said, as if she were reciting the cafeteria lunch menu. "First there was Serenity, of course, who experienced two instances of the Darkness during the span of her long life. The first was when one of her friends . . ."

"Dorothea Lyttel," I put in, hoping to get her moving a little faster.

"Ah, you know about that."

"Serenity didn't want it to happen," I said trying to defend my ancestor.

"Quite. Many of the families, including the Fowlers, felt that Serenity used her considerable influence in the community to delay the inevitable."

"Mrs. Lyttel's murder," I clarified.

Miss P looked at me levelly. "Now, Mrs. Lyttel lit the fire herself, Katy," she said.

She was right. "But how do you know?" I asked. "How do you know all of this?"

She blushed. "Do you know what a Book of Secrets is?" she asked.

"Oh, right," I said. "Mrs. Ainsworth told me about them. And I guess you'd know about everyone, being a . . ." I cleared my throat. Miss P blushed furiously. " . . . school official," I finished lamely.

"For the record, the Beans were on Serenity's side on that matter," she said softly. "That is how I know about the dispute. From my own family's *Book of Secrets*."

"Oh," I said. *And now Katy will attempt to extract her foot from her gigantic mouth.* "Of course."

"The second occasion was, naturally, when she and Ola'ea Olokun created the Meadow to protect the community from the insanity of the Darkness-infested cowen raiders."

"But how could anyone say that was Serenity's fault?" I demanded. "She saved all of Old Town."

"A lot of people felt that the cowen wouldn't have come after them at all if Serenity hadn't been living with Ola'ea."

"They were living together?"

"After her arrival in Whitfield, Ola'ea became a kind of adopted daughter to Serenity, whose own children had grown and married, and who was long since a widow. This didn't sit well with the other settlers, as you may appreciate. They might have accepted Ola'ea as a servant, but not as their equal. However, neither Serenity nor Ola'ea would permit anything other than the truth to be believed. Nor would Ola'ea accept less than equal status in the community."

"So what happened?"

"They remained friends, steadfastly and without excuses. As a result, though, the two of them were obliged to spend many years as outcasts. It says a lot for both of them that when the witch-hunters came, they allowed the whole town into their meadow."

"All the witches, anyway," I said.

"Yes. And because of their good works—the establishment of the school, the creation of the Meadow as a place to celebrate the holidays in the witches' Wheel of the Year—the Ainsworths and Ola'ea's descendents always held a place of prominence in Old Town. But they were never really part of the gang, if you know what I mean. And then there was Constance Ainsworth, who naturally—"

"Constance?"

"A cousin of your great-grandmother's. She was high priestess of the community during another reappearance of the Darkness just before the Great Depression in 1929. She . . . "

"Burned herself at the stake," I finished. "So I'm related to her, too."

"Constance took her life after the Darkness had claimed a number of other women. The families of those women blamed her, as high priestess, for not having acted sooner."

"But she was trying to save them."

"I know," Miss P said kindly. "But they almost couldn't help it, the way Becca Fowler almost couldn't help blaming you for the fear spreading around Old Town now. I say *almost* because people can become bigger than themselves, their habits, their families." She gave me a half-smile that left her eyes sad. "They can, but they rarely do."

"And then there was my mother," I said. "The monster of Whitfield."

She took my hand. A sensation like warm ginger ale spread slowly through me. "Just because we don't understand something doesn't mean it's evil. Or even wrong," she said.

She was trying to be kind, but honestly, how could anyone

who knew what my mother did to Eric Shaw not believe she was evil? "And now here I come, just in time for the Darkness to make its next appearance," I said.

Miss P nodded. "So you understand the fear underlying Becca's anger."

"Are there a lot of people who feel that way about me?" I asked quietly.

She smiled. "There are a lot of people who don't," she said. "Let's see it that way."

"And my . . . this gift . . ."

"Try not to use it," Miss P said, suddenly hard. "For your own sake, for your sanity, don't give in to it, or you'll find it's not a gift at all, but a curse you'll wish you'd never heard of."

Everyone in Old Town expected Eric to die from his head injury. It was as if they were waiting for it to happen, for the tragedy to be complete. And now it seemed that the time was coming, along with the harbingers of the Darkness.

I'd tried to see Eric, but Hattie wouldn't let me. She said that he needed rest and quiet. Maybe she was beginning to feel like the rest of them. Maybe she was afraid that I'd go crazy one day and harm Eric the way my mother did.

I didn't believe that Hattie would turn against me like that, but I had to admit that if she did, no one—probably not even I—could blame her.

As the crowd shouted and applauded for Agnes and Jonathan, I walked toward the woods.

CHAPTER

·

TWENTY-FIVE

 KARAMA

I had thought that Beltane would be fun, but I guess I was just too selfish. All I could see was people in love.

The woods were dank and moist, smelling of moss, tree bark, and rain. A canopy of brilliant stars and a full moon stood out against the silhouetted trees. For a while I could hear the roar of the handfasting celebration, but soon I was in almost complete silence, broken only by the sound of my own footfalls and the occasional hooting of a barn owl.

From between the trees I could see eyes staring at me—foxes, deer, mice—and hear the night songs of insects and frogs. The witches' world is a natural world. We do not fear living things, except for people . . .

Which is what made me stop in my tracks.

I sensed something. Some*one*. A human. I breathed in slowly, silently, listening, extending all my senses outward into the darkness. I'd never been in these woods before, but I had the sense that I was being drawn toward . . . what? A scent? A feeling? I didn't know, but something was calling to me, directing my feet where they took me. The very weight of the air seemed to have changed. It was thicker now, heavy.

No harm. Whoever I was sensing was not waiting to hurt me. But there was sadness there, such profound sadness that I could almost feel my own heart breaking under its terrible burden. I breathed in deeper. The scent was familiar, comforting.

"Peter," I whispered.

From the shadows came his voice: "Katy." He stood up abruptly. He'd been sitting on the bare roots of a tree a few feet away.

I walked over to him. "Why are you here?" I asked. "What's wrong?"

He backed away.

"Peter, I'm—"

"Don't," he said, holding up his hands. He looked at me with the wild eyes of a trapped animal.

"Okay." I stopped where I was. "I guess you're not grounded anymore."

He looked flustered. "I've had to help Hattie settle into the new house," he said, twirling a leaf in his hand.

Oh, yes. Right. So very, very busy. "Sure," I said, trying to sound more neutral than I felt.

"But I needed to get away for a while."

"Yeah, well, I'm sorry if I disturbed you," I said, moving away. "I'll just . . . "

"Please don't go." He crumpled the leaf he was holding and stood facing me, the dappled moonlight illuminating his troubled gray eyes and the smooth skin of his cheek.

I didn't know what to do, so I just stood there, looking at my feet.

"It's Eric," he said finally.

"Is he worse?"

Peter looked at me as if he wanted to tell me something. He sighed and leaned against the tree where he'd been sitting. "Yes," he said. "Much worse."

"Maybe I can do something useful," I said. "I mean, I don't know anything about medicine, but I could sit with him, or change his sheets and things, or even help out around the house while—"

"No!" he shouted. "You're not to come to the house, do you understand?"

He looked so angry that he scared me. "Okay," I whispered in a voice so small I could barely hear myself. "I was just trying to help."

"You can't help!" His voice cracked. He covered his face with one hand. "You can only get hurt."

"What are you talking about?"

He looked around frantically.

"I swear, Peter Shaw, if you run away from me, I'll never talk to you again!"

He sighed, deflated. "That's the smartest thing you've said so far." He took my arm. "Come on, I'll walk you home." At his touch, a feeling like pinpricks shot up my arm and into my chest. I gasped and doubled over.

"Katy?"

"I'm okay," I said, staggering to my feet. I pretended to pick something out of my eye so that I could disconnect from him. The pinpricks disappeared.

"Is something wrong?" he asked.

"I've been picking up . . . well, vibes, I guess you'd say. Feelings, emotional states."

"From people you touch."

"Yes."

"And you're reading me."

"Not exactly. It was just . . ." I couldn't find the words. "Strange," I said.

"You need to be getting home."

"Peter—"

"Get out of my skin, Katy!" he snapped. "You can't do anything for Eric, and you can't do anything for me, do you understand? You have to stay away from us!"

"All right, all right!" I shouted. I put my hands over my face.

For a long time afterward the whole forest seemed to reverberate with the silence. I just stood there, unable to move, feeling as if a knife was stuck into my heart.

"I'm sorry," he said softly. "You scare me, that's all."

"I scare *you*?" I squeaked. "Because I'm a *freak*, is that it?"

"You know that's not what you are." He put his hand over his mouth, as if to contain himself. "You're the best friend I ever had, Katy. But there are things I can't let you know about me."

I felt tears begin to form. "Is that what you're worried about? That I'll read your thoughts or something? That I'll find out all your dirty little secrets and use them against you?"

"No," he said. "I know you wouldn't hurt me. It's what it would do to you."

"You're not making any sense, Peter."

"Then let it go." He turned his back to me. "Just go home and let it go, Katy. Please."

I wiped the tears from my face. "Is it my mother?"

"What? What are you talking about?"

"Because I'm not her," I said bitterly.

He took hold of my shoulders. "Katy, it isn't—"

I flung his hands off me. "Look, I'm going, okay? I hope you'll feel safer now."

"You don't understand," he whispered.

"No, I don't!" I shouted.

He held me again. I tried to push him away, but he wouldn't let go. I slapped his face. He closed his eyes to the blow, but still he held me.

I sobbed.

Slowly he pulled me to him until my face rested against his chest. His heart was thudding, pumping fast, frightened, desperate. A pain deeper than the ocean welled inside me: his pain. *Oh, Peter, why do you keep this to yourself? Let me in. Let me in.*

"Leave me my secrets," he whispered. Then he lifted my chin and kissed me softly, deeply.

He released me for a moment, just long enough to look at me. To truly look at me. I felt as if I had come home.

"I need to let you go," he said, stroking my hair as he pressed me against him. "I need to be strong enough."

"You don't have to let me go," I said. "I want to be with you. Always. Just let me into your life, Peter."

He made a sound—half laugh, half sob—and held me at arms' length. "Coming into my life would be the worst thing that ever happened to you, Katy. Even seeing you like this is more dangerous than I can tell you."

I was confused. "Dangerous how? Are you still afraid for Eric?"

"Afraid for Eric," he repeated slowly.

"Afraid that I'd hurt him," I said. "Because I wouldn't. I couldn't. I know a lot of people here think there's something wrong with me just because of what my mother did, but there isn't, Peter. We're not our parents. You have to believe me."

He stared at me for a moment, then turned away with a mirthless laugh. "You think you're at fault," he said.

"Don't . . . don't you?"

He pulled me to him again, running his fingers through my hair, kissing the top of my head. "You're everything I've always wanted," he said. "I can't let you get hurt. But that's what's going to happen if you stay with me."

"But why, Peter? Who's going to hurt me?"

He wrapped his arms around me. "I am," he said quietly.

"Peter, this isn't—"

"A long time ago I told you that I wouldn't let anything happen to you."

I softened. "I remember," I said. "The day you caught me falling down the stairs."

"I remember it too. And I meant what I said. But the only way I can protect you is to keep away from you."

"Do you expect me to just take your word for something like that? What are you trying to do to me, Peter?"

"I'm trying to save your life," he said. He yanked me close to him. "All right, open up to me, if it's what you want," he rasped. "Open your senses. Feel what's inside me." Then he kissed me again, hard, his lips pressing on mine, his hands pulling on my hair until slowly, like a dam bursting, my fragile emotional membrane ripped open and I was in his mind, inside his skin, burning, gasping, screaming with the horror of it, the pain, *let me go, let me go, stop, please stop stop it stop—*

I screamed. My knees buckled. Peter lowered me to the ground, then took two steps backward so I could see his face.

"That's what it's like to be me," he said.

I curled into a ball on the ground. *Don't give in to it*, Miss P had said. Control the pain. But could Peter control it? Or did he live with this every day? It was the vision I'd had of him, only from the inside. A vision of living hell.

"Who's doing this to you?" I croaked.

"I'll take you home," he said.

CHAPTER

•

TWENTY-SIX

 LITHA

It was the last day of school.

The seniors had already graduated, so the halls felt deserted. Still, there was a lot going on. Finals dragged on until the last hour. I got an A on my paper on magic boxes. I included a drawing of the botte I'd found at the Shaw mansion. Mrs. Thwacket asked me to stay after class to talk to her about it. When I told her that it had burned along with all the other antiques in the house, she looked as if she was going to cry, even though it was only a mechanical botte and not a magic one.

In Existentialism in Fiction, we had a choice of essays. I picked "Perception vs. Reality," which was kind of a crock, because perception pretty much *is* reality, especially for witches, who perceive a lot. I got an A in that, too, even though it was very hard to concentrate with Peter in the room. Every time I looked up, I saw him looking back at me, or looking away, pretending that he hadn't been looking at me, which was what I was doing, too.

Ever since Beltane, he'd taken pains to stay as far away from me as possible. It must be getting easier for him, I thought bitterly.

How could I tell him that I didn't want to stay away from him, whether it was for my own good or not? In the middle of my Perception vs. Reality essay, I wrote this: *How can you explain when bad is somehow good? When bad is somehow the best thing that ever happened?*

After I wrote it, I practically wore out my eraser trying to get rid of it. What was I thinking? Then I started writing like crazy just to cover it up.

But it was true. Being in Peter Shaw's arms was the best thing that had ever happened in my life, and I didn't care what happened next. I wanted to help him stop hurting, but if I couldn't, as he insisted I couldn't, then I wanted to hurt with him. I couldn't stand for him to be alone while whatever demons he faced were eating him alive.

I wanted to help him, *needed* to help, but I just didn't know how. Who could I even trust enough to tell what I knew? Certainly not Agnes or Gram. Like most of the witches in Whitfield, they hated Jeremiah Shaw, and distrusted anyone related to him. Even though Peter was as different from his great-uncle as day from night, they could never see that. And Miss P . . . well, she was sympathetic and open-minded, but frankly, I didn't think she knew much about love. Especially not the kind of love that I was feeling for Peter.

It wasn't enough for me anymore just to be Peter's friend. I wanted to touch him, to have him touch me. I wanted to feel his mouth on mine again, his lips opening me up like a flower. If the pain hadn't knocked me to the ground, I would have stayed there with him forever.

That's how much I wanted him. How much I loved him. Miss P would never understand that.

But Peter did. He understood exactly what I would do, and he wouldn't allow it.

He'd never moved back into his dorm. Whenever I called Hattie's new house, I'd get the answering machine. When he didn't ask me to Spring Fling, the end-of-year dance, I actually went by myself, thinking I might run into him, but he never showed up.

It was humiliating, especially the phone calls, because Hattie wasn't talking to me, either. She couldn't still be angry about the fire at the Shaw house. That was months ago, and besides, she knew we'd been telling the truth. Things must have been very serious with Eric.

Peter had as much as told me, and there were rumors all over Old Town that Eric was dying. No one said anything around Peter, of course, but every witch in Whitfield was waiting for the news that Agatha Ainsworth had finally accomplished what she'd set out to do ten years before. Aunt Agnes warned me outright not to go into any dark alleys.

"Not that the Families will attack you," she said, trying not to worry me.

"But if someone else does, the Families wouldn't help me."

She didn't answer, but I knew that was exactly what she meant. Gram wanted me to move back into her house, but I was probably safer at school than I would be in town, even though the girls in my dorm all seemed to have stopped speaking to me.

Collective memory. Whitfield had a long collective memory.

"Coming to the beach, Katy?" Verity asked after the shouting following the final bell had died down.

"No, I . . ."

"It's a tradition," she said. "Right after the picnic. You knew about that, didn't you?"

The picnic was something I did know about, since it was a school function. Big tables were set up outside of Briggs Chapel, where the final assembly would take place.

Like everything else at Ainsworth, the assembly was a tradition-laden affair consisting mainly of an interminable procession of the faculty, resplendent in a variety of stoles, robes, and headgear, preceded by flag bearers who looked like heralds from the Middle Ages and followed by the Chancel Choir, which sang the school Alma mater while the big pipe organ boomed.

Big chapel assemblies like this were where you could really see the demarcation between the Muffies and the witches. The Muffy girls, seated through no conscious decision on the right side of the chapel, were dressed in Lilly Pulitzer sundresses and strappy high-heeled sandals, while on the other side the witches' clothing ran the gamut from graveyard black to neon colors, from designers like Betsey Johnson or Anna Sui to original designs—kimono wraps or African tops over jeans and boots.

Parents were invited, but usually only the cowen attended. The magical families were all getting ready for the holiday festival that evening in the Meadow. It was Litha, the festival of Midsummer celebrating the summer solstice. The witches in school made jokes about how the last day of school (which always occurred on Litha) really *was* the longest day of the year.

I didn't feel bad that my father wouldn't be around for the

school ceremony, although he could have at least answered the invitation. I mean, *he* didn't know that only the cowen parents took part. He didn't even know what cowen were.

I tried to put it out of my mind. It wasn't a big deal. In the first place, the main point of a Last Day of School celebration was so that parents who'd come a long distance to move their kids out of the dorms would have something to do. The local families—meaning the magical ones—usually waited for the cowen to clear out before tackling their kids' rooms. I'd already asked Jonathan Carr to help me move my stuff in his truck, but he wouldn't be able to make it until after work.

In chapel, fortunately, I ended up with the magical students. We sat by ourselves in the back like adults. It felt good being part of the cool group for once, even though I had to sit next to Becca Fowler, who spent the whole assembly whispering to everyone around her. Except me, of course, but I didn't mind because Peter was on the other side of me.

I don't know how that happened. I was walking into the pew, and he was just there. I think I froze when I saw him, because Becca started poking me and hissing at me to get moving, and then Peter smiled as if he were both embarrassed and pleased to see me.

I knew he wouldn't hold my hand or anything like that in chapel. He'd said he didn't want me in his life, and though I didn't believe that, it would take more than the seating arrangement during assembly to change his mind. But just being near him, touching his clothes, smelling him, was enough. Almost enough.

I didn't even register what anyone was saying. I just tried to be there with Peter, breathing the same air, feeling him being next to me. It was over too soon. He looked at me once more before he left. He wasn't smiling this time, and neither was I. It was just another good-bye.

Afterward, at the end-of-year picnic, everyone was given a styrofoam box containing a chicken salad sandwich and a little bag of chips, plus a cookie.

"So are you coming?" Verity asked.

"Coming where?"

She rolled her eyes. "To the beach. With Cheswick and me." The two of them, like many of the local kids, had arranged to clear out their rooms after the Muffies had vacated. Some of the students were already packed and ready to roll right after chapel. Belinda Freeman, a Muffy and the heiress to the Freeman Jewelry fortune, was on her way to Ecuador, where she would be spending the summer working in the Doctors Without Borders program. Whitney Shannon was going to spend the summer working in a taffy shop on the Maryland shore. Her parents owned a house there, and a bunch of her friends were going to room together. Kendall Ames was going to spend two days in transit to meet his parents, who were both biologists, in Antarctica, where he'd help them tag seals.

It seemed like everyone had interesting things to do. Even Verity and Cheswick got jobs as tour guides at Disney World. I would have to line up something. I could cook, after all, but I knew that wherever I worked, it wouldn't be anything like Hattie's Kitchen. I missed it. Every time I walked past the Meadow, I felt my heart breaking a little more.

"Peter's going," Verity cajoled.

"Huh?"

"To Whitfield Bay. With us. Now."

I looked up. Peter was standing beside Verity. I don't know how long we stood there staring at each other.

I finally spoke. "Are you?" I asked slowly.

His eyes never leaving mine, he answered, "Yes."

"Ouch," Verity said, slipping out from between us. "Too hot for me here."

We barely noticed her leaving. In that expanse of lawn, with people milling around everywhere, there was somehow just the two of us. Nothing else mattered. Nothing else existed.

"I didn't take you to the dance," he said.

"I know," I answered.

"I wanted to."

"But you didn't want to touch me."

He swallowed. "You know that's not true," he said at last, turning away. Breaking the spell.

"Then why do you want to see me now?"

"I want to see you every minute of every day," he whispered, his face so close to mine that I could feel the heat from it. "But it'll be safe to be with you now." He smiled sadly. "At least in a crowd, I'd get to look at you." He reached out to touch my hair, then thought better of it and pulled his hand back slowly.

I snatched it, holding down the sensation that immediately coursed though me.

No image, I told myself. *No pain.* He looked surprised. I wanted to tell him he could touch me, to demand it, beg for it.

But instead, I let go of his hand. "However you want me, I'll take it," I said.

His eyes filled. He turned away and left by another exit.

ZEPHYRUS

I walked by myself to the beach, following a crowd of kids singing bawdy words to the tune of the alma mater. As we wound around the Meadow and through the woods behind it, I recognized the place where I'd met Peter at Beltane. It was different during the day. Cheerful, sunlit, near a well-worn path and a little stream that broadened as we approached the grassy plain above the bay shore, pungent with the scent of the sea.

Straight ahead, a half mile or so out in Whitfield Bay, stood the silhouette of Shaw Island. The quiet, almost desolate isolation of the bay felt like a beautiful gift. The rhythmic lapping of the waves, the breeze, still chilly though it was late May, the stark beauty of the island in the distance with its disused lighthouse, tumbled into rubble after more than three and a half centuries. And through it all, walking along the rocky shore, listening to the low, sad music of the sea, I again felt the pull of something, someone . . .

"Katy." His voice was soft behind me, almost a whisper.

I closed my eyes, trembling, as I felt Peter's strong hands on my shoulders, holding me, wanting me, sending sparks of passion over my skin.

"Phew, whose bright idea was it to come at low tide?" someone shrilled. It was Becca Fowler, with two boys I knew slightly, coming around an outcropping of tall boulders. "What a stink."

Peter's hands slid off me.

"I just thought we were back in your dorm," one of the boys with Becca said.

"Pervert. Where is everyone?" She looked around. "God, Pete, tell me you and the Virgin Queen here aren't the whole party."

"Hey, Shaw, that's your island out there, isn't it?" asked the boy who'd spoken before. His name was Tim Creasy. His father was an advisor to the President, so I assumed he was cowen, but you never know. He was looking through a pair of binoculars that hung around his neck.

"Not anymore," Peter said.

"Peter was *disinherited*," Becca screeched. She leaned in close to me so that no one else would hear her in the wind. "I guess you scholarship kids like to stick together."

"Bad luck, dude," Tim said, oblivious to Becca's sotto voce jibes.

"I suppose it belongs to old Jeremiah now, like everything else," she said.

"A lot of good it does him," the other boy said. I think his name was Porter or Porker or something. He was a beefy, mean-looking kid who'd started at Ainsworth this year, the same as me. "Nobody's even allowed on that island. I heard there was a permanent Coast Guard warning. Anyone who goes out there gets hit with a five thousand dollar fine."

Tim gave Becca what seemed to me like a knowing look.

"Oh, we go out there all the time," she said.

"Really?" I could tell Porker was impressed. He gestured toward two rickety rowboats that had been abandoned on the sand. "In these?"

"Hell, no," Tim said, laughing. "You wouldn't get fifty feet in either one. Why do you think they've been left here?"

"How do you get across the water, then?"

Becca leaned over, as if she were letting the new kid in on a secret. "Why should we tell you?"

Porker spat on the sand. "Why not? What's the big deal? You party out there or something?"

Tim grinned knowingly.

"Okay, I'm cool with that." Porker was practically vibrating with excitement. "So when do we go?"

"Low tide."

"It's low tide now."

"No way, dude," Tim said. "In a couple of hours this basin will drain completely. We'll be able to walk over then."

"No shit!"

"Oh, I just remembered," Becca said. "I won't be able to go tonight. Maybe Katy would like to, though." She looked at me in a friendly, inquiring way.

"I . . . don't . . . " The last thing I wanted to do was to spend the evening with someone named Porker.

"Oh, go ahead," Becca said. "You can round up some of your friends. You too, Pork."

"Very funny," Peter said, crossing his arms over his chest. He turned toward the new kid. "You don't want to go out there. For one thing, you'll get stuck in the mud."

Becca laughed uproariously. "Porker in the mud, get it?" The kid looked at her with an expression that started out as bewilderment but turned quickly into hatred. "Don't worry. Peter would never have let his little pastry chef go to the island."

"Although you were hoping I would, weren't you?" Peter said, visibly angry. "I think Katy and I are going to walk down the beach. See you later." He grabbed my arm by the elbow, shooting emotional arrows in all directions.

Becca shrugged. "Whatever."

Peter didn't say anything for a long time, and I practically had to run to keep up with his long strides.

"So was that a trick?" I asked after we'd gone a couple hundred feet.

"Yeah."

I shrugged. "That's okay. No harm done."

"No, but what if I hadn't been with you?" His gray eyes exactly matched the color of the Atlantic.

I couldn't keep from laughing. "Do you really think I'd go slogging through the mud for a mile just to party with that guy and his friends?"

As he thought about it, Peter's face softened. "I guess that would be pretty unlikely."

"Unless I really needed a drink."

We both laughed. I was just glad to be away from Becca. And I was proud of Peter for looking after me. I slipped my arm around his waist. Then he wrapped his around my shoulders, and we walked together like that for a long time.

"Was he serious?" I asked out of nowhere. "About the Coast Guard warning?"

"There is something like that."

I shook my head. "The Shaws must be powerful people, to get the Coast Guard to protect their privacy."

"Actually, local lore does more to keep people away than the Coast Guard," Peter said. "Haven't you heard about the curse of Shaw Island?"

I punched his arm. "Right. I suppose the ghosts of all those nasty old men walk its shores by night, counting their money."

"Could be. Back in the forties, a couple of frat boys shot themselves on the island. Ever since, people have been saying that the place makes visitors want to kill themselves." He shrugged. "They claim it's part of Ola'ea's curse."

"Ola'ea?" I repeated, startled. "How do you know that name?"

"That's Hattie's ancestor she's always talking about. It seems Ola'ea got royally pissed off at my great-great-whatever, Henry Shaw, when he gave the witch-hunters the okay to turn his wife into Kentucky Fried Sorceress."

"Husband of the year."

"Hey, I come from truly evil stock, Katy."

"And proud of it, I see."

"Damn right. Up until then the island was the main port of call for all the cargo ships from England. The Shaw family fortune was made collecting tolls from all those ships. My uncle's cabin was originally the customs clearinghouse."

"So someone does go out there?"

"Not very often. I went out once or twice with my dad, before I came to live with Hattie. Our family isn't exactly the cookout type, though." He shook his head. "Back in the day when the big ships came to Whitfield, all the cargo had to be rowed ashore. This tidal basin was too shallow for those big clipper ships, even at high tide. And then the rowboats—also owned by Henry Shaw—would have to be paid for separately, while the rowers . . ."

"Employees of Shaw Enterprises, no doubt."

"But of course. The rowers would bring the goods to shore, where there would be a caravan of wagons, also owned by Henry Shaw, which would be loaded by more Shaw employees and taken to a distribution center in Whitfield . . ."

" . . . owned by Henry Shaw," we both said together.

"From there, earmarked items would be transported to other settlements."

"For a small fee to Shaw, of course."

"Of course. The Shaws weren't running any charities, you know."

I shook my head. "No wonder your people are so rich," I said.

"They're not my people," he said, suddenly serious. "Just my name."

"I know."

We found a long, low boulder jutting out of the sand and sat down on it. For a long time we just looked out over the water, not speaking. It was just nice to be there, listening to the ocean together.

"Anyway, Old Henry didn't suffer much from the curse," Peter said. "By then he'd gone into all kinds of other businesses, banking, mostly. But in the end, it did kill him."

"The curse?"

He nodded. "That's what it does."

"It kills you?"

"I told you. You kill yourself."

I leaned back on the rock. "I think you're full of it."

The wind came up, and we fell silent again. This time it was uncomfortable. I could feel him next to me. He was so close. So very, very close . . .

"I'd better be going," Peter said, standing up. "Hattie will be needing me at home."

"Are you sure I can't help?"

"I'm sure."

I nodded. I wasn't going to beg him anymore. It was done, then. I stood up too. "Good-bye, Peter," I said. I walked away without waiting for an answer, back up the shore toward the grass, away from the direction he was headed.

So this is how it ends.

The wind gusted, wild and frightening, blowing my hair around my face. I turned back and saw Peter standing on the shore, watching me. Just watching. I was filled with so much love for him, so much desire and longing and need that I didn't care about what was best for either of us.

I ran down the dunes and into his arms. "Don't go," he whispered covering me with kisses. "Don't leave me."

"I'll never leave you," I promised. "Never."

We held on to each other as if we were prepared to be blown off the earth like Hattie's little boy, taken up by the wind to live forever in the high places. It blew around us furiously, slapping our clothes, pulling at my hair.

Come with me, it sang, *come to the island where living is forbidden, and be part of the air and the sea and the earth and its destruction by fire.*

How can you explain . . .

His lips were on me, so soft, so urgent, willing me closer, sucking softly on my own swollen mouth. I felt him pull me toward him, felt his body straining to touch mine.

. . . when bad is somehow good . . .

His hands were on my face, holding me with a need that was almost pain. I knew, because I felt it too. I opened my mouth, and his tongue touched mine. It felt as if an electric current were passing through me. With a gasp, I opened my lips wider, wanting still more of him, feeling every inch of my skin widening, tingling, offering myself to him.

When bad is somehow . . .

Together we sank to our knees in the sand, kissing each other wildly, hungrily. I unbuttoned his shirt revealing the smooth skin of his chest while he closed his eyes. I closed mine, too, sliding into the sand with his body on top of mine, our mouths red and tender. Then gently, slowly, with the cold rawness of the wind engulfing us, he began to unbutton my blouse.

"Katy," he whispered.

Involuntarily I moaned and arched my back, offering myself, my comfort, to him. I wanted to hold him like this forever, to make whatever was wrong with him right, to heal him with my heart and my body. His kisses were moving from my lips down my neck, and I wanted to stay with him here, in this feeling, this sweet love.

. . . the best thing that ever happened.

"Peter . . ."

"I need to stop now, Katy." His breath came hot and fast.

"No. Don't."

"Yes. Before—"

"Katherine?" The voice was sickeningly familiar. "Is that you?"

"Oh, my God," I said.

"What the HELL are you doing?" my father yelled.

Peter staggered to his feet, pulling me up with him. I began to choke, and then cough spasmodically, frantically grabbing at my clothes, trying to cover myself as I faced Dad standing three feet away from me, with Madam Mim at his side.

"I asked you—"

"Oh, what do you *think* they're doing?" Mim said scornfully. "Grow up."

Dad threw his arms up in the air and let out a roar like a crazed lion. Even Mim took a step backward.

I'd never seen him so furious. His face was covered with red splotches, and the veins in his forehead stood out like rivers.

"Dad . . ."

"For God's sake, get *dressed*!" he rasped, balling his hands into fists. I was certain that he was about to kill me.

Mim covered her mouth with her hand, but her eyes were laughing. For the first time ever, I wished that it could have been Mim with me now instead of Dad. She looked Peter up and down, and seemed to like the down position better.

Meanwhile, I was scrambling to straighten out my clothes, turning around for privacy. "Dad, would you please . . ." I was trying not to cry.

He exhaled noisily and turned away as I fumbled with my buttons. My bra had gone askew too. I couldn't seem to get anything back on right. Finally Mim came over to me and helped adjust my straps and things. Then, to my surprise, she took my hands, which were ice cold and shaking like castanets, between her own for a moment.

"All right," I said when I was finally done. My voice sounded as if I were talking underwater.

The four of us just stood there staring at one another for what seemed like a very long time. Finally my father broke the silence. "Who are you?" he demanded, staring holes into Peter.

"Peter Shaw . . . sir."

"Get out of here, Peter."

"Sir, I want to—"

"I know goddamned well what you want, Peter," Dad said tightly. I closed my eyes, praying for death. "And I want you to go home. NOW."

Peter swallowed. Across a chasm that felt a thousand miles wide, we stared at one another.

"Get moving," Dad said. "Don't make me tell you again."

Peter nodded once. Mim winked at him. With a pained look at me, he turned and loped away.

Now there were three of us standing there like department store mannequins. The wind had died down. The air no longer felt wild, only cold.

"All right, already," Mim said. "This is getting to be boring." At that moment I loved her. "We came to help you move out of your dorm, sweetie."

"I've already arranged for someone—"

"Un-arrange it," my father said, handing me a cell phone.

"Okay," I said, my head bowed. It was one thing to have your friends catch you making out. Getting caught by a teacher was worse by a few hundred percent. But your *father*. I would never be able to look him in the eye again.

He didn't seem any more comfortable than I was. "Sorry we missed your end-of-school ceremony." His eyes narrowed. "Looks like you missed it, too."

"I was there," I said, although I doubt if he heard me.

"You've got your own bedroom," Mim said cheerfully.

"What?"

"At my place. I had it done up in pink ruffles and white wicker."

Oh, good God, no. "Great," I said.

"It's on Oak Street. Are you familiar with it?"

"Um, no," I said. I'd never been on Oak Street, or even heard of it. It was in New Town—the Land of the Dead, as far as I was concerned.

"There's a Starbucks just down the road."

"Wow," I said, trying to muster some enthusiasm. "Terrific."

"But you can forget about going there, because you're grounded," my father said.

As we walked back into Whitfield, I cast a glance over my shoulder toward the town square. The school, the Meadow, the Ainsworth house . . . all the places where I felt comfortable were here in Old Town. But I was leaving, going to live among cowen in a room made up of pink ruffles and white wicker.

On the top floor of Ainsworth school, in the headmistress' office window, stood Miss P watching me. She smiled and gave me a little wave.

I waved back. *Wish me back,* I pleaded silently. *Make them bring me back, djinn.*

But of course she couldn't hear me. No one was going to hear me for a long time.

CHAPTER

•

TWENTY-EIGHT

 HELGARDH

The Land of the Dead. I'd called it right. This was my home now.

I had no phone, no iPod, no TV, no stereo, no laptop. There was a radio in my room, but Dad was writing a book, so I was only allowed to play it at a sound level so low that I practically needed a stethoscope to hear it.

He was there in Mim's house in New Town with me 24/7, writing about medieval troubadours and giving me the fish eye whenever I came downstairs.

Mim had offered to get me a job in one of the Wonderland stores, but I didn't have a driver's license yet, and my father wasn't about to let me get one. I asked him if I could apply at the Starbucks down the street, but he'd only snorted and turned away, as if I'd suggested working as a pole dancer. Then he'd gathered up an armful of the most boring books he could find (which is saying a lot, since basically *all* of Dad's books are dull enough to put bacteria to sleep) and thrust them at me.

"Read these and we'll talk," he said.

I looked at the titles: *Josephine de Beauharnais at Malmaison. Bauhaus: Revolution in Design. A Sailor's Book of Knots.*

"What'll we talk about?" I asked. "Knot tying?"

"I daresay it will be a better use of your time than the activities to which you've evidently become accustomed," he answered blandly. "Though probably not as entertaining."

Silent and seething, I went back up to my room.

He was never going to give me a break. He was even talking about taking me out of Ainsworth School. It was only Mim's intervention (and genuine alarm about having me live with them full time in New York) that had kept him from making the arrangements then and there.

The worst thing was that I wasn't even sure that I'd done anything wrong, not really. I couldn't believe that loving Peter was a bad thing. Even if I was forbidden to see him or talk to him, I dreamed about Peter.

Nearly every night I had the same dream—the one that I first had at Imbolc: Peter sitting in a chair with his shirt off, his back covered with cuts and welts, pleading with someone to stop torturing him. I knew that a psychologist would have said that I was talking myself into a state where I would believe I needed to be with Peter, when really I just wanted to see him again.

And maybe that was true. Miss P had said that it's hard to tell the difference between what we perceive and what we want to perceive, and there was no use denying that I wanted to be with Peter again. All I'd learned from the whole episode was that I loved the touch of Peter's mouth on me.

To pass the time I practiced my skills. Pushing—telekinesis, or teleporting, as the practitioners in Whitfield called it—was fun, and the better at it I got, the more fun it turned out to be. Not only could I *move* items, I could send them sailing around the room, dancing around each other, going wherever I wanted them to.

The psychometry was trickier. First of all, I didn't know where it came from. I could always push; I hadn't even thought of it as much of a gift. But I'd never read anyone's thoughts before I held my mother's wall hanging. And before coming to Whitfield, I certainly hadn't been able to feel anyone's emotions just by physically touching them.

Well, maybe I had. One of the reasons I'd never liked parties was because I'd often felt overwhelmed in the midst of a lot of people. And I'd never been much of a toucher. My father wasn't a touchy-feely type, either, so I didn't think anything was strange about that, but now that I think about it, I just didn't like the baggage that touching people brought. I guess I'd always had certain gifts. It's just that I'd never used them.

Until Peter. For the first time I wanted to touch someone. I wanted to be close to him, to know him. I wanted to feel what he was feeling, think what he was thinking, to touch his skin and his hair and his mouth, and to have him touch me. But even with him the transmission of feeling was too much for me, too overpowering. I had to learn to control the gift so that I only picked up messages from people and objects when I wanted to. So I practiced.

There was a little telephone table in the hallway outside my bedroom with very neutral vibes. It must have come with the house—Mim had put most of the furniture in storage and replaced it, but not all. When I put my hands on the table, I could feel its history: A few screaming fights, a lot of loud kids, an old man who spent months walking back and forth in the hall. The table gave off a fuzzy, sleepy emanation, very low-key, more like a buzz than a sensation. I actually had to strain to feel it, so this was a good piece to practice on.

Over the following days and weeks, I tried it with almost everything in my room. Tapping in, then shutting off the feelings. Most of the stuff was new, so it didn't have any human vibes on it except for those of the decorator who'd placed them there, and those were faint and indifferent. It was vastly different from the Ainsworth house, where every object was so steeped in the emotional past that the place practically glowed with personality.

I knew I'd succeeded when I touched one of my father's books and felt nothing. I'd been avoiding that because I really didn't want to look deeply into Dad's soul. It would have been like him seeing me with Peter on the beach—embarrassing to the point of death, and vaguely horrible in all sorts of ways that I didn't even want to think about. So when I put my hands on *Urban Governance in 12th Century England* and felt nothing, I disengaged with a sense of accomplishment and relief.

I knew I was making progress, and that mastering my skills would keep me sane; letting me feel when I wanted to feel and protecting me when I didn't. But that didn't mean I was happy with my life. That is, if I'd had a life. Which I didn't. Trying not to feel was my principal occupation. Not exactly the thrilling summer I was hoping for.

To make things worse, I was also starving. Mim had decided to go macrobiotic, which meant that all our meals consisted of weird grains like quinoa and millet flavored by seaweed and fermented plums.

"I've lost four pounds," Mim announced proudly. I'd

personally lost fifteen, and was beginning to look anorexic. Dad was looking pretty raggedy too. He normally didn't care much about food one way or the other, but I could tell he was getting to the end of his rope.

One evening, while Mim was rhapsodizing about how *clear* her skin had gotten since implementing her policy of eating nothing that hadn't been prepackaged into cardboard containers at the health food store, Dad was picking desultorily at his seitan and wakame salad.

"What's wrong, Harrison?" Mim asked brightly. She always got perky after her first glass of wine. Apparently, abstinence from alcohol wasn't part of her new healthy lifestyle program. "The seitan's supposed to taste just like turkey."

"I want a steak," Dad demanded truculently.

"Drink your juice, darling. The juicer cost eight hundred dollars."

"The price of the juicer, unfortunately, does not affect the flavor of toadstools," he said quietly, holding up a glass filled with taupe-colored liquid.

"It's reishi mushroom, not toadstool."

"It's shit," he said, balling up his napkin and throwing it on the table. He pushed his chair back with a lot of noise and went upstairs to his office.

Mim waited for him to leave, then opened a drawer in the hutch and pulled out a pack of cigarettes. "Men don't understand the importance of weight loss," she said, blowing out a plume of smoke.

"Er . . . right," I agreed. It was getting to be time for me to finish up my delicious repast and retire to my room before Mim degenerated into drunkenness.

"Well, anyway, I'm kind of glad that you and I can spend some time together without your dad. I'm so busy, I don't usually have much time." She gave a little shrug. "For you, I mean."

"Yes, I got that."

The crazy thing was I could tell she was *trying*. After that horrible groundbreaking, she was actually making an effort to be friends with me.

"So." She burned half an inch or so with a huge drag on her cigarette, then looked for a place to dump the ash. Since Mim didn't admit to smoking ("just one, once in a while, for my nerves"), there were no ashtrays in the house. By the end of the evening her dinner plate was filled with butts swimming in the remains of her meal. "What's shakin', bacon?" she asked, flicking the ash onto the plate without looking at it, so that it would appear to have fallen there accidentally.

"Huh?" I had been too engrossed in the drama of Mim's addictions to pay attention to what she was saying.

"What's going on in your life?" She leaned forward to rest her chin on her hands, half closing her eyes against the smoke.

"Er . . ." I felt my hair standing on end at the prospect of spending girltime with Madame Mim.

"Stop saying 'er'."

"Okay." My gaze wandered toward the stairway and my room, where I had just finished reading *Josephine de Beauharnais at Malmaison*. Nothing awaited me there now except for *Bauhaus: Revolution in Design*. Suddenly, the thought of reading about German furniture in the 1920s seemed irresistible. "I'm reading. A lot. Actually, I'm very busy . . . reading . . ." I trailed off. "All right. I'm not doing very much, Madison," I admitted. "Since I'm not allowed out of the house. Or my room, really." She smiled and nodded at everything I said, as if I were regaling her with tales of my fascinating and totally interesting social life. "Not a lot going on."

She shrugged. "That's what you get for getting caught," she said. "Next time you'll be more careful."

I didn't know if she was serious or not.

"Won't you?"

I swallowed, then nodded slowly.

A slow smile spread across her face. "So who's the guy?"

"Excuse me?"

"*Peter*," she said with a wicked smile.

I bristled. I wasn't about to talk about the love of my life with my father's tacky mistress. "He's a friend from school," I said.

"Friend, right. Listen, girlie, I know you were having a good time on the beach, but you've got to learn when and where to give it up. I mean sand *really scrapes*, you know what I mean?" She poured herself another glass of wine. "Want some?" She raised the bottle along with her eyebrows.

"No, thanks."

"Suit yourself." She put down the bottle with a thud and then drained her glass in one gulp. "They all want the same thing," she said, gesturing broadly with her cigarette. "Not that it's a bad thing." She winked at me.

Winked. There was just no limit to her grossness.

"The trick is to know how much to give them, and what you're going to get in return."

I blinked. "Like . . . money?" I asked, bewildered.

"No, not *money*. Duh." She poured herself another glass, which emptied the bottle, then yanked the second bottle out of the ice bucket. "Unless it's a whole *lot* of money," she added, reconsidering. "No, not even then," she decided. "Marrying money is more trouble than it's worth, in my opinion. There's always a family raising a lot of legal issues." She leaned forward on her elbows. "What you want to look for are intangibles. Advancement. Prestige. Introductions to the right people. You don't want your social life to be a waste of your time."

This was bringing up something I'd been wondering about ever since Dad first brought Mim home. "Er . . ." I began.

"Ah-ah-ah." She held up a finger.

"Sorry. I was just wondering . . ."

"Yes?" She popped the cork on the second bottle with practiced ease and poured out a big glassful.

"Well, if what you say is true, then . . . why are you interested in my father?"

She laughed so hard that she coughed up wine into her napkin. "Jeez, have you seen the size . . . oh." She cleared her throat. "I guess he's just so darn cute," she said.

I nodded. He was that, all right. Cute as a button, and a moron about women.

"And he's terribly intelligent, you know." She lit another cigarette, even though the first one was still burning on the edge of her plate. "None of my friends even know what he's talking about."

"Sounds like fun," I said.

"There you go." She finished her drink. "You know, you're a pretty girl, Kathy . . ."

"Katy."

"See? That's what I'm saying."

"What are you saying?"

"You're a pretty girl, but sometimes you get this attitude. I don't know. Maybe it's going to prep school that does it."

I almost laughed out loud at that. Not only was Ainsworth the least preppy school imaginable, but I didn't even fit in with the uncool kids there, let alone the preppy ones. For most of the past year, my idea of a rocking weekend had been hanging out with my great-grandmother.

"I think I'll clean up the dishes," I said.

"I just wanted you to know the truth."

Oh, yes. Mim the Truth Fairy. "Thanks for enlightening me," I said.

"See? See what I mean? The snottiness."

I took a deep breath. It was time to leave, any way I could. "I'm sorry, Mim. I wasn't trying—"

"What did you call me?"

Gaah. "I don't remember."

"*Mim.* You said, 'Mim'." She poured herself another glass. "As in *Mimson.* That's cute." She smiled fuzzily. "I like it."

I said nothing. There was no point in telling her that I'd named her after a cartoon witch. Especially since I'd grown to like witches.

She stared, grinning beatifically at her reflection in her wine glass for some time. "I never had a nickname," she mused.

I'll bet you had plenty, I thought. *Just none that anyone used in front of you.* "Can I take your plate?" There had to be something in the kitchen that could substitute for an ashtray.

"Don't go," she said, so quietly that at first I thought I'd misunderstood her.

"I beg your pardon?"

"I beg your pardon?" she repeated, mocking me.

I started toward the kitchen, but she grabbed my arm. There was a brief explosion of emotion and a swirl of images—an alcoholic father, an abusive mother, three brothers, and she was never going to wash another dish in her life. Secondhand shoes that squeaked. Having nothing for the collection plate in church. Casting off her family like a pile of dirty clothes, hoping they'd never find her, wanting, wanting . . .

I subdued the messages until they were blank. Her hand on my arm, white and manicured and conveying . . . nothing.

"Your father is a wonderful man," she said woozily.

"Uh," I grunted. It was as noncommittal a response as I could muster.

"He's smart and gentle and sweet."

"Okay." I just wanted to get away.

She yanked at my arm. "No, you don't get it, Kath—Katy. He tries to stay out of your way because he thinks you don't want him in your life."

She had it backward. It was Dad who didn't want me in his life.

"He never got to go to private school. He was the first person in his family to go to college, and he had to fight for that. His people wanted him to drop out of high school and go to work to bring in money. They don't talk to him anymore, did you know that?"

I didn't. Dad had never mentioned his upbringing to me. He never mentioned much of anything about his past. But I was beginning to see that he and Mim had more in common than I'd thought.

"And then he married your mother and had to change his name because of some weird family tradition, and from everything he tells me, the Ainsworths were a bunch of wackos, anyway—"

"They are not!"

"Okay, that was harsh. But you know about your mother, don't you?"

"He can't blame my relatives for what she did."

"He shouldn't, no. But the incident—the publicity from it—almost destroyed him. He couldn't work anywhere in the Northeast, even after he changed his name back to Jessevar. That's why he ended up teaching at a lot of minor colleges in Florida instead of being at a place like Columbia, where he belongs."

"It hurt my aunt and great-grandmother, too," I said. "Hardly anyone will talk to them anymore."

"Yeah, it isn't fair." She lit another cigarette. "I'm not saying it is. I'm only telling you why he acts the way he does."

"Like not giving a crap about me until I do something wrong, and then acting like I'm a criminal?" I was already sorry I'd said so much. I didn't want to have a conversation with her.

"I think there may be something else. The boy, maybe. I don't know. He won't talk about it with me."

I picked up the dishes that I'd put back on the table. "I need to get back to my room," I said.

"Please, Katy." She didn't seem drunk now, or at least not insensate. "There has to be some kind of communication between you two."

"Why? We get along fine the way things are."

"Because he loves you. More than anything in his life. And he thinks he's losing you."

"He has you," I muttered.

"That's not the same. A lover is a measure of what you want to be. But your child lets you know what you are. Everything about Harrison Jessevar is wrapped up in you, Katy. And when he sees you withdrawing, pulling away, trying to find comfort in sex, not fitting in anywhere, never revealing anything about who you really are . . . well, he sees himself, and it hurts him even more than it did the first time around."

For a long moment I just stared at her, the dishes balanced in my left hand, as if she'd been speaking a foreign language. How could this . . . this psychobitch barracuda presume to know *anything* about me? Or my father, for that matter.

"Have another drink," I said, and walked away.

With a little mirthless laugh, she poured the rest of the wine bottle into her glass and sat nursing it, her elbows on the table as if she were at a bar. Within a few minutes, I knew, she'd be in a mean stupor. Fifteen minutes after that, she'd be asleep, if everyone managed to stay out of her way that long.

She flicked her cigarette ash onto the floor. The smoke curled up between her fingers and veiled her face.

As I was climbing the stairs, I heard her BlackBerry ringing.

"Madison Mimson," she said, all business.

CHAPTER

•

TWENTY-NINE

PELE

Dad was sitting at his computer, with three books open on the desk around him, but I don't think he was working. The TV was on, and he was leaning on his fist with his legs stretched out in front of him, watching the news.

"Hi," I said, sliding in.

He looked dyspeptic. "What's the matter?"

"Nothing. Just saying hi."

"Oh." His eyes wandered back to the television.

"Um, I saw a McDonald's down the street when you brought me here . . . those many weeks ago."

He made a noncommittal sound, the way I do when I don't like the direction a conversation is going.

"I could get you a burger."

"I could get it myself."

I tried a weak laugh. "No get-out-of-jail-free card for me, huh?"

He slammed his fist on the desk. "Katherine, you were *necking!*"

God, it never stopped. "So what's the punishment for necking?" I yelled. "Life imprisonment?"

"You've never been appropriately remorseful."

"No, I haven't. You know why? Because being with Peter was the last good day of my life, that's why. If I felt remorseful about anything, it would be—"

"Shh." He waved me down and turned up the volume on the TV remote.

". . . strange goings-on in a place known to locals for its strangeness, thousands of Cory's Shearwater birds have been found dead along the beachfront on Whitfield Bay. Here's Matt Rodriguez with the story."

The camera switched to a view of the bay, nearly at the identical spot where Peter and I had been. A man in a short-sleeved shirt and khakis was walking along the shore, pointing out a ridge made up of large bird carcasses.

"Waste management trucks have been called up to perform the unpleasant task of removing . . ."

"That's happened before," my dad said. "The shearwaters. The last year we were here. Your mother said—"

"It's a harbinger," I finished.

Dad looked at me with an expression that conveyed something like fright. "Are you one of them?" he asked, so softly that I didn't know if he even wanted me to hear him.

I pretended not to.

"And Whitfield's troubles don't end there. In instances that authorities say are unrelated to the dead birds, the town's historic district has been plagued with a rash of arson fires. We have breaking news on one of those fires right now. Channel Nine's Melanie Ott is on the scene. Can you tell us what's happening, Melanie?"

A pretty young woman wearing a pink suit appeared standing before a Rose of Sharon hedge that looked like the one in front of my great-grandmother's house.

"Like the two other fires reported in Whitfield's historic Old Town this past week, this one appears to have been set deliberately. Although our cameras are not permitted to get close enough to show our viewers, several witnesses who claim to have seen the path of the blaze report that the fire does appear to have circled the house. Fire trucks are on the scene now, and damage does not appear to be extensive, although some of the houses here, including this one, have been designated as historic landmarks . . ."

Dad sat up in his chair.

"It's Gram's house," I said. I ran out of his office and down the stairs, making only a brief stop to grab a handful of coins from the change dish in the entryway for the bus.

"Katherine!" my father called.

I didn't stop. He could ground me again later. For now, though, I had to get to Old Town. Since I'd never been free here I had no idea where the bus stop was, but I had a sense of which direction the business district of New Town lay, and I sprinted toward it.

"Katherine, wait." It was my father, pulling up beside me in his car. "Get in. I'll take you."

I didn't know if I wanted him to go with me to my relatives, but it was definitely the quickest way there, and at the moment speed was the most urgent factor. I climbed in and we drove in silence through the development where Mim's house was located and onto the wide thoroughfares flanked by huge commercial establishments that made up most of New Town.

He turned on the radio. To my surprise he didn't tune it to a news station, but to some punk rock music too young for him. That was for my benefit, I guessed. It was a small effort, I know, but something.

"This your car?" I'd guessed it was, since it was a Ford Focus—not something Mim would buy.

He said, "Um,"—that noncommittal sound again—and nodded.

"It's nice," I said.

"Oh?" He seemed surprised, as if he'd expected me to criticize it.

"I like the color."

"Good." He knocked on the dashboard, as if showing me how sturdy the vehicle was. "I got tired of driving Madison's hand-me-downs," he said with a self-deprecating smile.

"It's better to have your own stuff," I agreed.

"Where is she now? By the way, what do you call her?"

"Madam Mim?" I ventured.

He laughed. "That's it."

"She's resting, I think."

The laughter stopped, and the smile behind it slowly disappeared. "Yes. She does a lot of that. But usually at the table."

"That's where I left her."

"She's not there now. Neither is her car." He shrugged. "Alas, a corporate vice president's work is never done."

There was a long uncomfortable silence which I finally broke. "Dad, I know you don't like Mom's relatives," I said. That was so weird, calling her "Mom", as if my mother were someone I knew.

"So they've come after you, have they?" I saw the color rise in his cheeks.

"They're my family, Dad," I said quietly.

"*I'm* your family." He stomped on the gas, and we lurched forward.

The whole area around Town Square was in turmoil. While Dad parked the car, I ran through the gathered crowd, looking for Gram. The TV crews were finishing up, putting their equipment away into two big vans with satellite dishes on top. On the far side of the property an ambulance was parked, its interior light bright against the darkening night. As I passed, I heard snippets of conversation:

". . . lives in New Town with cowen . . ."

". . . I think she's related to that Wonderland woman . . ."

". . . hardly a drop of witch blood in her . . ."

". . . of course you know who her mother was . . ."

". . . hard to believe she'd do this to her own family . . ."

I turned around at that one. Were they saying I'd set this fire? I scanned the faces around me, but no one met my eyes.

Near the side entrance to the house I saw Captain Dryden, the police officer in charge of Old Town, taking notes while he spoke with Aunt Agnes and Gram. The damage to the house didn't look too bad. The fire was already out, and Jonathan was directing a crew of volunteers who'd been helping the firemen. The Ainsworth women might have fallen out of favor in the community, but Jonathan Carr hadn't. When he asked for help, every able-bodied man in Old Town showed up.

"Oh, Katy dear, what a blessing it is to see you," Gram said as I approached.

Captain Dryden must have finished his business with her because he folded up his notebook and moved on.

"Dad drove me over," I said, looking around for him. "He was parking the car, but I couldn't wait for him. What happened?"

Agnes shook her head.

"Harbinger," Gram said, almost in a whisper.

"Perhaps," Agnes said. She looked skeptical.

"What do you . . . " I followed her gaze back to the house. The fire had inscribed a charred circle around its perimeter. "The news report said that the police think it might be arson."

"Oh, surely not," Gram said.

"Natural fires don't burn in a circle, Grandmother."

The old woman squared her shoulders. "They do if they've been set by the Darkness."

"That's ridiculous. Why would the Darkness choose this house?"

"Why would an arsonist?" Gram countered.

"I heard someone in the crowd saying they thought I was the one who set the fire," I put in.

"You!" Gram sounded appalled. "Good grief, what nonsense!"

Just then Jonathan came over, sooty-faced and grinning. "Doesn't look too bad, ladies. Hey there, witchlet, come for the show?" He tousled my hair.

"Can I help, Jonathan?" I asked. "I'll do anything."

"Nah, most of the damage is cosmetic. Nothing a coat of paint and a little airing out won't fix, eh, my girl?"

Agnes blushed despite the seriousness of the situation. "There really isn't any more to be done, Katy."

"But where are you going to stay? I could ask my father—"

"Oh, gracious, no," Gram said. "A number of people have invited us to stay with them. We're not completely friendless, you know." She ruffled her shoulders like a roosting hen.

"You won't have to be gone long," Jonathan said. "In a week, I'll have the place cleaned and smelling like a rose. Fortunately, Mrs. Ainsworth here called the firehouse as soon as it started." He tipped his hat to her.

Gram blushed with pride. "Well, I did make the call, but I'm sure I would have slept through everything if it hadn't been for Katy's friend Peter."

"Peter?" I asked stupidly. "Peter Shaw?"

"He walked through the ring of fire to get me. I'd been dozing at the time, and Agnes was at the grocery . . ."

"Is he here now?"

"Over there, with the paramedics." She pointed to the ambulance. "The flowering pear tree caught fire and part of it fell on us as we were coming out of the house. He used his arm to protect me, poor thing. The medical people told us . . ."

I never heard the rest of what she was saying. Fighting my way through the crowd I finally saw him sitting, shirtless, in the back of the ambulance. A paramedic was wrapping gauze around his forearm.

"Peter," I whispered.

When he looked up at me, he smiled. I must have looked stricken, because he closed his eyes and shook his head.

"Don't freak," he said. "This is no big deal, really."

"He's telling the truth," the paramedic said with a grin. "He's fine. But I've got to have something to do, now that we've been called here."

"Really, Katy, no worries, okay? I got hit by a branch off a tree. A small branch. Mrs. Ainsworth and your aunt are all right."

"I know. I've seen them. How . . ." I looked around. "How did you happen to be here?"

"Hattie sent me out for some things from the drugstore. On my way back I saw the . . ." He glanced at the paramedic, who was obviously trying not to interfere with our conversation while he took care of Peter's arm. " . . . the fire . . ."

"It's made a black ring around the house," I said.

"Crazy, man," the paramedic said, evidently unable to contain himself any longer. "A ring of fire, huh? I heard you talking to the cops."

"Yeah," Peter said. "A ring of fire."

"Could be arson," the man speculated. "If it was a ring, like you say, that could have been some nut with a gasoline can. Ever think about that?"

"I don't know what to think," Peter said, looking at me.

"I hear you. Got enough on your plate with the arm, right?"

Peter smiled. "Really, this is nothing. You shouldn't even have been called out." He reached out with his uninjured arm and took my hand.

"The old lady was worried. This your girlfriend?"

Peter squeezed my hand. "Maybe," he said, teasing. "Want to be my girlfriend, Katy?"

"I'll think about it," I said, filled with happiness.

The paramedic put the last bandage over the gauze. "Okay, you're good," he said. "I just want to check out something before you . . . Whoa." He was leaning over Peter's back. "What'd you do here?"

"Must have gotten scraped by some branches," he said, scrambling to put on his shirt.

"You kidding me? This ain't from no tree." He yanked the shirt back off Peter's arm. "Dude, I got to tell the police about this."

"It doesn't have anything to do with the fire," Peter said.

"Yeah, I know. This wasn't done today. But it's been done a lot."

"What is it?" I asked, craning around behind Peter.

He pushed me away. "It's nothing. Sports injury," he told the paramedic.

"You don't play sports," I said. "Not since your brother—"

"This from your old man?" the paramedic interrupted.

"My father's dead," Peter said. "Look, I told you—"

"You're how old? Seventeen, was it?"

"Peter, please tell me what's wrong!" I shrilled.

They both ignored me.

"You don't have to take this, man. The cops, they can help, I'm telling you," the paramedic said.

"No, you don't understand. No one's responsible. That's the truth."

"Fine, if you say so. But I still have to make a . . . Hey!" He reached past Peter to try to stop me from climbing into the ambulance, but he was too late.

The interior was lit as brightly as an operating room, so there was no mistaking what I saw: Peter's back was covered with deep welts, slash marks, and bruises.

I gasped.

"Katy, please," Peter said miserably.

But I couldn't move. I couldn't even look away.

The wounds were placed exactly where I'd seen them in my nightmares.

It felt as if the whole world had suddenly gone silent. There was the paramedic, his bushy eyebrows raised, pointing at me, his mouth moving. And in the distance, my father, looking lost. Aunt Agnes had spotted him, and looked as if she were deciding whether or not to speak to him.

Then there was Peter, alone with me in this silent shell, meeting my eyes with something like shame.

What are you keeping from me? I wanted to scream. Why couldn't he tell me?

"Katy!" My father's voice cut through the bubble of silence, bringing back all the other noises.

"Honey, I mean it. Get out of the ambulance," the paramedic shouted, pointing at me. Dad was on his way.

"Go," Peter said.

"I love you," I whispered.

I hadn't meant to say that, not there in the ambulance with the paramedic next to us in a crowded, noisy place with my angry father stomping toward me. But it was true. I loved Peter Shaw, and I would love him until the day I died.

I jumped off the back end of the ambulance.

"Thank you," the paramedic said sarcastically as I walked away. Peter didn't say anything.

My father had that *I'm gonna kill that kid* look on his face.

"Dad—" For a horrible moment I was afraid he wouldn't

stop, that he would keep walking until he reached Peter and did something awful to him. I grabbed his arm.

"You came here to see that boy, didn't you?" he accused.

"No. I didn't even—"

"I *saw* you, Katherine."

"He was hurt, Dad. He's the one who discovered the fire."

"The *arson* fire?" Dad asked pointedly. "Isn't that interesting."

He was so beside the point that he wasn't even worth talking to, and I really would have walked away from him if Aunt Agnes hadn't come up to us.

"Hello, Harrison," she said. It was a dutiful greeting, guarded, exploratory.

He took a step backward, clearly astonished. It must have been like looking at my mother all over again. "Agnes," he said formally. "I'm sorry about your misfortune."

"We'll manage."

"I understand you've been . . . looking after my daughter."

The stiffness of the exchange worried me. Dad was lapsing into his stern-professor persona, and Aunt Agnes was every inch the Yankee spinster. "My grandmother and I have done what we could to make Katy's stay in Whitfield a pleasant one," she said.

"That's very kind of you, but I'm sure the school is prepared to provide whatever may be necessary."

"On the contrary, Dr. Jessevar," Agnes said, coloring ever so slightly. "There have been several occasions for which the school has provided neither accommodation nor amusement."

"And exactly what sort of amusement have *you* provided, Miss Ainsworth?"

It was too much. "Stop it, Dad. This isn't—"

"When your opinion becomes necessary, I'll ask for it," he said, his voice rising. He turned back to face Agnes. "Actually, I was thinking of Katherine's indulgence in sexual activities with one of her schoolmates. Is that the sort of amusement you've been accommodating?"

Agnes' face flushed a deep, horrified red.

"Thanks, Dad," I said. "That was swell of you."

"Well, what do you expect? The moment you're out of the house, you immediately fly into the arms of some boy whose major ambition seems to be to relieve himself on you—"

"Shut up!" I screamed, indifferent to the fact that we were in public. "Just because *you're* crude and disgusting and hang out with tramps—"

He slapped me. Slapped me across the face in front of everyone. Total strangers turned to stare at us.

My eyes were so full of tears that I could barely see. When I turned to leave, I bumped right into my great-grandmother, who apparently had just noticed us. I hugged her so fiercely that a little jet of air whooshed out of her mouth. "Gracious, dear," she said, patting my back. "Whatever can be the matter?"

I couldn't answer. I just cried into her lacy chest that smelled of lavender and comfort and home. This was my home, with her and Aunt Agnes and people who were like me. This was where I belonged, and it was crazy to think I could live anywhere else.

"Katherine, we're going home now," my father said.

"I'm not going anywhere with you!" I spat, still hanging on to Gram. "I don't care—"

"Darling!" With her usual impeccable timing, Mim launched herself into my father's arms, her breath reeking of alcohol thinly disguised by mints.

"Go with your father," Gram whispered, gently disentangling my arms from her. "You must."

"Hello, ladies," Mim said brightly. "Tragedy about the fire, isn't it?"

Dad and Aunt Agnes both closed their eyes in exasperation at the same moment.

"Er . . . Katherine and I were about to leave for home," he said.

"I'll go with you," Mim said. "As soon as I meet whoever lives here. It's company policy. When it's a big disaster, Wonderland donates blankets and things, but this doesn't look like much of anything."

Agnes gave her a cold stare. Gram fanned herself with a handkerchief.

"Madison," Dad said softly, "these are the women whose house caught fire."

"Oh, my God, how *terrible*," she gushed, not missing a beat. "It must be horrific to see your life go up in a blaze."

"That was hardly the case," Agnes said, but Mim apparently didn't hear her.

"How can I help? More to the point, how can *Wonderland* help? Of course, we'll provide a hotel room for starters. A caring company doesn't let its neighbors live on the street."

"We were never in danger of that," Gram said drily.

"Do you need blankets? Towels?"

"I assure you, Miss Mimson, we are quite capable of surviving this without the aid of *Wonderland*." Agnes said the store's name as if she were speaking about used condoms. Then she took Gram's arm and led her away. My great-grandmother turned back to look at me, her face sadder than I'd ever seen it.

"Well, how was I to know?" Mim asked belligerently. "This place is like a circus." She gestured broadly at the assembled crowd. "At least I made it here before the news crew left."

"Thank God for that," I said. My father narrowed his eyes at me, but Mim wasn't paying attention.

"You know, the people here are weird," she added in a whisper. "Do you remember that horrible groundbreaking ceremony?" she asked as she put her arm around me. "The whole place was like one big mudhole. I actually lost my shoe in it. Ugh!" Then she laughed, high and tinkling.

Good thing I was already a pariah, since the other most despised individual in Old Town had just put her arm around me. To everyone watching, I was Madam Mim's junior buddy, going off to her lair with her after possibly setting fire to my great-grandmother's home. To make things worse, my father had given my extremely respectable relatives the impression that I was some kind of sweating, rutting harlot before slapping me in public. Worst of all, the person I loved had been beaten so badly that the paramedic wanted to file a police report about it, and I wasn't even allowed to see him.

It had been the worst single hour of my life.

I shrugged off Mim's arm. Instantly she transferred her affections to my father, leaning on his shoulder, clasping his hand as if they were taking a stroll in the park.

"Please, Madison," he muttered, trying to slide her off him.

"Oh, don't be so stuffy. It's good that they see me as human."

He stopped in his tracks, astonished. "Has it ever *possibly* occurred to you that not everything I do, think, feel, or say is about you?"

She let go of his hand. "Well, if you're going to be *that* way about it . . ."

Clenching his jaw, Dad dragged me over to the car, leaving Mim behind on the sidewalk. "Get in," he said, holding open the door.

"What if I don't? Are you going to hit me again?"

He sighed. "Katherine, please . . ." He let the sentence drop.

I looked him in the eye. "I hate you," I said levelly.

He didn't answer for a long time. Finally he said, "I can't help that." Then he got in the driver's side and waited.

CHAPTER

•

THIRTY

 AHRIMAN

Back at Mim's house, I noticed that both wine bottles had been cleared away, and no cigarette butts or ashes were in sight. She could get it together when she needed to. Then I stomped upstairs and slammed the door to my room.

To make things even worse, it was my birthday. Earlier, I kept thinking that Dad was waiting for dinner to say Happy Birthday or give me a card or something, or maybe even that he and Mim were planning to take me out somewhere. In the past, sometimes Dad would take me to a restaurant. Of course, I'd had to remind him for about a week ahead of time that my birthday was coming. I guess I should have reminded him this year.

I started pushing—a calendar, a wicker picture frame, some books. The calendar slapped against the wall, and the books all crashed into each other in midair. But as soon as I could harness my breathing, things got to be more fun.

I tuned the radio to a classical station that was playing the overture to *Carmen*, and began to play. Pushing books was like juggling balls: Three in the air, then four, all twirling in formation. The calendar fanned into a disk, whirring away in a corner. The picture in its frame just kind of zoomed back and forth.

I was so into the whole mini-extravaganza that I almost didn't hear the perfunctory knock before my dad bombed in. I had to drop everything where it was, causing a deafening crash.

"What was that?" he shouted.

"The bed must have hit the wall," I said, turning off the music.

He looked around. There were piles of books on the floor, an overturned chair, two lamps lying on their sides, my wicker mirror and hamper which had been do-si-do-ing around one another, my hairbrush (it had been air-conducting to the music) and a scattering of tissues that had been making patterns in the air. Even the radio itself was buried in one of the pillows on the bed.

"This room is a mess," he said.

"I'll clean it."

He just stood there, looking out of place and uncomfortable. My anger had dissipated with the pushing. "Okay," I said, resigned. "What can I do for you, Dad?"

He cleared off a little spot and sat down on the edge of my bed. "I'm sorry I hit you," he said.

I didn't answer.

"You were rude about Madison."

"Yes, I was." *But truthful.*

"And I was rude about you."

That threw me. "Are you apologizing or something?" I asked.

"Something," he said. "Not apologizing, exactly."

"Oh."

"Except for hitting you. That was wrong. I'm apologizing for that."

"You already did."

"Yes, well . . . But the other . . ."

"You mean my opinion that your girlfriend's a ho?"

He was going to come back at me, but stopped himself. "No. I meant your running off to see that boy."

"I didn't *run off* to see him. He was there, in the ambulance. Peter's my friend, and he was hurt—"

"He's more than a friend, Katy."

I looked out the window. "Okay." Point ceded.

"And you know where that was going, that day on the beach, don't you?"

I sighed loudly. "Look, how long am I going to have to—"

"Let's not have that argument again. He's the brother of the child your mother tried to kill."

"What does that have to do with anything?"

He ran his hand through his hair. "I just don't want you to get hurt," he said.

I bit my lip. "Sure, Dad," I said.

"You don't understand. This town . . . I just want to forget everything that happened here."

"I *have* forgotten," I said.

"Well, I haven't!" He paced. "Look, you may not believe me, but I do care about you, Katherine. Or Katy, whatever you want to be called."

I crossed my arms. "Right. What's-her-name is really broken up about how much you care about her."

With a swat, he sent the radio flying across the room. It smashed against the wall. "I'm not going to tolerate that kind of attitude from you."

I looked at the broken pieces of my radio. It had been pink, like everything else in the room, but designed to look like a retro forties radio. I'd liked it, and now it was destroyed, like everything else that had mattered to me.

"I'm taking you out of that school."

He'd gone right for the big guns. "Please, Dad," I whispered.

"I don't like the direction your life has taken. Those women—"

"Those women are my relatives, Dad." My voice was barely audible, even to myself.

He clenched his jaw. "Believe me, if you knew what they were—"

"I do. It's you who don't know what they are, because you've never given them the chance, the same way you never give anyone—"

"That's enough." He stood up.

"Please, Dad," I begged. "Please don't . . ." I spoke softly, trying not to sound hysterical, trying not to antagonize him. Because really, I wanted to scream and hit him, slap him harder than he'd slapped me. I wanted to tell him that I'd never had anything in my life until I came here, and now that I finally had a reason to wake up in the morning, he was taking it away from me.

I knew I had to bring my feelings under control, but it was hard. In a corner, some of the debris stirred. The cord to the radio snaked out, its plug questing toward my father.

"What's that?" he asked, startled. The plug dropped with a

clink. "A mouse? Good God, Katherine, this room is so filthy, you're drawing vermin. I suppose your dorm room is in the same condition."

"No, Dad. And there are no—"

"You were never slovenly before you came here. You were never antagonistic or defiant. You were certainly never *promiscuous . . .*"

"She was never alive," Mim said from the doorway.

Dad rolled his eyes. "Maybe you'd better take a rest, Madison," he said with undisguised contempt, the way you'd talk to a drunk. The way I'd talked to her after dinner, I realized, suddenly feeling ashamed and bad for her. She'd been trying to help.

"I'm not the one who needs a rest . . . *Harrison*," she said pointedly. "You do. And so does this unending punishment."

Dad squinted his eyes closed, as if someone had just squirted lemon juice in them. "I beg your pardon?" he said slowly. "I was under the impression that I was having a private—repeat *private*—conversation with my daughter."

"Then you were mistaken, darling, because this is my—repeat *my*—house." She crossed her arms over her chest.

"Let me assure you, in that case, that can be quickly remedied—"

"Sit down, Harrison," she commanded.

He sat.

"Katy is your daughter, and you're responsible for her welfare. But this perpetual imprisonment, humiliating her in front of people who are important to her, slapping her in public, and withdrawing her from school are not justifiable consequences for what she's done."

"You don't know what she's done."

"She hurt your feelings. She made new friends. She fell in love. She stopped needing you."

Dad looked outraged.

"She's growing up. Or trying to. And you need to back off."

Slowly, but fast enough so I could see the change, the outrage turned to pure astonishment. I'm sure no one had ever spoken to my father that way.

"As for you," she said, pointing an acrylic fingernail at me, "this room is inexcusable." Her head swiveled toward the corner. "Who broke that radio?"

She looked accusingly at my father. He looked at his nails.

"It cost fifty dollars," she said. "You'll pay me."

Dad nodded, almost imperceptibly. He was always fair about money.

"And you'll clean it up," she said to me.

"Okay," I answered meekly.

"And whether or not she stays in school here is not a decision you'll be making tonight," she said to my father. "So get out of this room, Harrison. You've both said enough for one day. I need a cigarette." Then she opened the door wider and made this subtle but extremely intimidating facial expression that propelled Dad off my bed.

He cleared his throat. "Well, I suppose a little cooling off might be in order," he said. "But the next time I come into this room, it had better be clean, and I mean spotless."

Mim's eyes were the last thing I saw before the door closed behind them both. Eyes that made it perfectly clear who was in charge. Jeez, some people don't even need magic.

I got up and started to straighten up the room. Manually.

I didn't trust myself enough to use magic under the circumstances.

I picked up the pieces of the radio and put them in the wastebasket. I hung the mirror and set up the two fallen lamps. Among last term's textbooks, I discovered Peter's old notebook, with his instructions for the binding spell. I don't know how it ended up with my stuff, but I was glad to have it. It was like having a little bit of him with me.

I finished cleaning my room around midnight. No one came to inspect it. By the time everything was finished, I was so tired that all I could manage was to take off my shoes before I lay down on the bed.

And let myself think about Peter. Peter, sitting in the back of the ambulance, trying to cover the marks on his back. Those terrible marks . . . They'd even scared the paramedic. It was as if he'd been whipped . . . I curled up with his notebook pressed tightly against my chest and slowly drifted off to sleep.

Listen to reason, Peter. You'll find it's the only way. Your father did.

"My father's dead. You killed him."

We? Surely even you must know that isn't true. Your father died of fright. A scared rabbit, dying the same way he'd lived. In fear.

What's going on, I thought from somewhere deep in my mind. Got to wake up, got to wake . . .

Don't you remember? You were six. Old enough to recall. He brought you and your brother to Hattie's after he'd killed your mother . . .

"No! You're a liar! You—"

We have no reason to lie. None at all.

"My mother had cancer."

Yes. But she died of suffocation. A pillow. Painless, really. A favor, just as you'd be doing your brother a favor . . .

Got to wake up. This has to be a nightmare. It has to be.

Peter arching backward. Welts like snakes on his back, drawing blood. He closes his mouth against the pain.

She was dying anyway. The pillow over her face was a mercy.

Peter closes his eyes. He can't bear to look at its face, its eyes shining with mirth.

Yes. A mercy. The boy is an idiot. An inadequate vessel.

Peter stands up, his hands balled into fists.

You know it's true. His mind is worthless. A life not worth living.

"I'll kill you, I swear . . ."

A swift pain in his gut makes him double over.

You can't kill us. You can't even harm us.

Peter bites his own hand to keep himself silent.

But you can kill Eric. It would be a mercy.

"You know nothing." Peter rasps. "You have no form. You have no brain."

We have your brain, Peter. Yours, or anyone else whose thoughts we wish to engage. And we have this form. See? We're smiling.

Peter turns away, disgusted.

Don't you like this body? Then give us another.

Peter winces in pain.

Call for her. We'd rather have Hattie, anyway. No offense, but she's much more powerful than you. You're barely magical at all. And barely a man.

"Then leave me alone."

Now you're offended. We did not mean that you are of no value, Peter. You come from a powerful family. You'll have your own wealth one day. And you're a magician, the first of the Shaws to admit it. You'll do great things, Peter Shaw, and we'll help you. Isn't that tempting? We're not offering you money or influence— you'll acquire those things on your own. But what would you like to do with those things? Feed the hungry? Heal the sick? Bring water to a drought-ravaged country? You can do that, Peter, and more. We will give you everything you need. Free us from this vessel, and we will reward you beyond your wildest dreams.

Peter is still. So, so still. I want to reach him. I want to hold him.

Or do your desires reach elsewhere? You have a fine, strong body. Your little girlfriend certainly thinks so. Tell us her name again?

"No."

That's right, it's Katy. Of course. Would you like us to pay her a visit?

"You can't. You can't leave this room."

You forget, Peter. We can do anything. This aspect of us— this tame being you're talking with—is no more than a fraction of what we are. We are vast beyond your comprehension.

We are the Darkness.

Peter sobs. "Katy," he says, trying to fill his mind with something beautiful. "Katy . . . Katy . . . Katy . . . Katy . . . ."

I woke up breathing hard. Dully, I looked at the notebook still cradled in the crook of my arm. Peter's notebook. Peter's essence, speaking to me.

I staggered out of bed, my sweat-soaked clothes already feeing clammy and cold, and slipped into my sneakers. There was no mistaking: That was not a dream. It was a message.

From the Darkness itself.

Slipping out the back door, I got my bicycle from the garage and headed toward Peter's. I didn't understand exactly what was happening to him, but I knew that whatever it was, he wasn't going to go through it alone anymore.

I found the house without much difficulty. It was a small bungalow in a part of town that probably used to be nicer than it was now. Much of the peeling paint had been covered over by roses, pale pink and yellow and red roses that looked black in the bright moonlight, all climbing up tall trellises that made the house look as if it were caged.

I listened. Peter and whoever was with him were in one of the rooms above the red rose trellis. I laid my bike on the ground and tested the wood. It was strong, sturdy enough to hold my weight.

Gingerly I began climbing the trellis, step by cautious step. The wood creaked with my every movement, but it was too late to turn back. When I'd finally climbed high enough, I pulled myself up until I could see clearly through a corner of the window.

Peter saw me first, I was sure of that. The look on his face was sheer anguish. He wasn't alone.

"Pretend it's us you're killing," came the low purr of the Darkness. "Close your eyes and use a knife. Follow our voice, there's a lad. Then we'll come into you. Easy as that. Easy . . ."

Eric, so odd sitting across from Peter, his legs crossed at the knees, his sticklike arms gesturing elegantly, turned slightly to follow Peter's gaze. "What do we have here?" he asked, his voice so well inflected, his innocent face breaking into a surprised smile.

And then, without another word, he blinked once, and the trellis began to topple over.

Peter shouted, running to the window. I saw him lifting it open as he screamed into the night, saw his wild eyes watching me fall.

And behind him was Eric smiling sweetly.

Just before I struck the ground and lost consciousness, I heard him calling.

"Kaaay! Kaaay!"

Chapter

•

Thirty-one

 TANTRA

I came to twelve hours later in the neuro-intensive care unit of the hospital. The first thing I saw was my great-grandmother's face smiling at me. For a second—or maybe longer, I was pretty groggy—I thought she was an angel. Even now, I think that if I were to die, Gram's face would be the first one I'd want to see on the other side.

"Gram," I croaked.

"Gracious sakes alive!" she exclaimed, reaching for the call button. "My dear, dear Katy." She clasped my hand with both of hers.

The essence that emanated from her was like a drug. Instantly I was bathed in warmth and comfort. My body, which was very sore, even in those first moments of consciousness, seemed to tighten and click into place, as if it were a mechanism that she'd turned on. As she bent toward me I caught the faint scent of lavender in the cotton-candy pouf of her white hair. Her lips touched my forehead, and I caught a second wave of something that felt like cool water washing over me.

"You're . . . you're a healer," I burbled drunkenly.

She kissed her finger and touched it to the end of my nose. "A garden variety talent, but it has its uses," she said as a nurse rushed in.

"Oh. You're awake," the nurse said. "Welcome back!" She took a penlight out of her pocket and shone it into my eyes, then proceeded to do a lot of other annoying tests. I just wanted to bask in Gram's vibes. "Looks good. I'll get Doctor Baddely. She'll want to take a look at you."

Gram smiled reassuringly. "She's one of us," she whispered, glancing at the retreating figure of the nurse. "Your father wanted to have you flown into Boston, but Agnes and I persuaded him to keep you here, in Whitfield General. It's a better place for our kind," she added conspiratorially.

"Dad . . ."

"He's in the waiting room. I'll get him for you, dear. We've been taking turns—"

I grabbed her arm. "Don't go," I pleaded. "Not yet."

She frowned, concerned, and patted my hand. "Certainly, dear," she said. "Is there something wrong?"

I shook my head. I wasn't ready to tell anyone about what I'd seen behind Peter's bedroom window. Gram might not be able to withstand the shock, and anyone else might not believe me. "Is Peter here?"

"He's been waiting all night, even though he's been told that he's not allowed to see you. Only family members are allowed in intensive care, and then only one at a time, and only for fifteen minutes, but he won't leave." She shook her head. "He's a fine boy, Katy. And he loves you so much."

I smiled, although I felt tears leaking out of the corners of my eyes.

"There, dear," Gram said, dabbing at my eyes with a tissue. "You've been through a terrible ordeal, poor thing . . ."

"I need to see Peter."

"Oh, I'm afraid they're very strict—"

"Who's strict, Elizabeth?" The doctor lumbered in. She was a large woman with a loud, hearty voice. "You're looking well, and so is your great-granddaughter." She gave me a big smile as she took a penlight from her pocket. "I'm Doctor Baddely," she said. "Mind if I take a look?"

She began the same procedure the nurse had gone though. "Pupils equal and reactive," she mumbled as she peered into my eyes. "Good eye traction. Would you follow this please, with your eyes? With your head? Can you swallow?"

"I think I'm okay," I said.

"Any headaches?"

I shook my head.

"Blurred vision? Dizziness?"

"No."

She looked at the stitches on the back of my head. "These are coming along well too. Do you remember the accident at all?"

"Yes. I fell off a trellis."

"What were you doing there?" She glanced at my chart. "Serenity?"

"She likes to be called Katy," Gram said.

"Easily corrected." She wrote down my name. "So. What do you remember, Katy?"

"I . . . I was looking through the window," I waffled.

"Hmm. Do you do that sort of thing often?" She was jiggling up and down, trying to suppress a laugh.

"Goodness, no," Gram answered for me.

"I . . . I need to see Peter Shaw," I said. "He's in the waiting room."

"Katy!" Gram admonished, but Dr. Baddely held up a hand for silence.

"Is that your boyfriend?"

"No. I mean, yes, but that's not why I need to see him. That is, it's more important than that."

"Is he the person whose window you were looking through?"

"Yes. I'm not a stalker, though, if that's what you're thinking. I really do need to speak to him. Right away."

"I don't think that's going to be possible, but if you have a message—"

"No. It has to be face-to-face. And it has to be now." Dr. Baddely looked bemused. Gram fanned herself in exasperation. "Please, Doctor. It's urgent. It really is."

She raised an eyebrow. "Is this something the police should know about?" she asked bluntly.

"I'd only need ten minutes," I answered, hoping she wouldn't notice that I hadn't answered at all.

"There are pretty strict rules about visitors on this floor," she said.

"Then I'll go to another floor." I started to climb out of bed, but the doctor pushed me back. "Hold it, Katy." She looked at me like a bull mastiff whose squeak toy I had just stolen. For a long moment we just stayed that way, Dr. Baddely staring at me as if she were preparing to growl; me, cowering and pleading; and my mortified great-grandmother, fanning herself.

"All right," she said at last. "You can see him for five minutes if you have your family's permission." She swiveled toward Gram. "Is that all right with you, Elizabeth?"

My great-grandmother looked stricken. She knew my father would never permit me to see Peter, alone or otherwise.

"Well, *I* have no objection," she waffled.

"And he isn't to touch you, in case you've got some neurological damage," the doctor said.

"Oh, certainly not," Gram agreed.

"Okay. You've got it, then. Ten minutes."

I felt as if I hadn't breathed for the past hour. "Thank you," I said.

"I'll tell the nurse." Dr. Baddely sailed out of the room like a great ship.

"I don't think your father is going to like this," Gram hissed as soon as the doctor was out of earshot. "You should have seen him first."

"I know."

Peter walked in tentatively, hesitantly. "Katy?" he whispered. He stopped short when he saw my great-grandmother. "Mrs. Ainsworth," he said, nodding to her politely.

"I believe I need a drink of water," she said, getting to her feet. "Please remember what the doctor said, Katy. Neurological damage." She tapped her forehead.

"I understand. Thank you."

"Neurological damage?" Peter asked.

"I'm fine. But you're not allowed to touch me, or I might turn into a gibbering idiot."

He stared at me, aghast.

"That was a joke," I explained.

His eyes were anguished. "I'm sorry," he whispered, rushing over to me. He held my face in his hands for a moment, then backed away. "I'm so sorry, Katy."

"I told you, I'm fine." I took his hand. He knelt beside me and kissed it, then let it go, his face a kaleidoscope of warring emotions. "Hey, you weren't the Peeping Tom climbing up the rose trellis," I said. "I did this myself."

He closed his eyes.

"You can't keep doing this to yourself," I whispered.

"It's what I did to *you*," he said. "That first night in the Meadow. I knew even then that it was wrong of me to be around you. To . . . expose you."

"You knew about Eric then?"

"I thought . . . at the Halloween party . . . the fireball."

"*He* sent that?"

"Not him, Katy. Eric couldn't, you know that. He loves you. But I saw it shoot out of him. It was clumsy. The Darkness must not have been able to control Eric's movements very well, since Eric couldn't do it himself."

"The fireball bounced off the pitcher I was carrying."

He nodded. "I saw that. I don't think he—it—was aiming for anything, though. Maybe it didn't even intend for the fireball to manifest, I don't know." He shrugged. "But it would have killed you if you hadn't been holding that pitcher."

"That's how you knew I hadn't sent the fireball," I said, suddenly understanding. "Why you protected me from the kids at school who thought I had."

"I should have left you alone."

"So that I'd have the pleasure of evolving into a stain on the marble staircase? Thanks a lot, Peter."

"So that you wouldn't be in here now," he said. "So that none of this would have touched you."

"Peter, no . . ." I reached for him, but he pulled away from me. "All we can do is to go on from here."

"But it shouldn't be 'we,' don't you see? And it's not going to be. I'm only here to tell you—"

"How long has the Darkness been inside Eric?" I interrupted, exasperated.

"I know it was unforgivable, Katy—"

"How long?"

He exhaled. "Ten years."

"Ten years?"

"I think it happened when my father died," he said slowly. "He brought us to Hattie's that night." He ran his hand through his hair. "I knew before we even got there that something was going to happen. Dad made me promise to take care of my brother. He was just a baby then. Only a few months old. My mother had died the day before, and my dad had spent the whole night with her, the night and most of the next day . . . with her body."

"Oh, my God," I said.

"It didn't seem so bizarre at the time, I guess because I was so young myself. She'd been sick as long as I could remember, and she'd been confined to bed ever since Eric was born. I hate to say it, but I hardly knew her. It didn't seem like she was ever well enough to see me."

He shrugged. "But I remember my father acting strange that night. He was really agitated, scary. After being in Mother's room all day, he came bursting into my bedroom and told me to get dressed, that we were leaving. Then he went into the nursery and took Eric from his crib.

"Then the whole way to Hattie's my father kept repeating that I had to take care of Eric, no matter what happened, and that I had to be brave, because he might not be able to stay with me."

"Where was he going?"

"He didn't say, but looking back, I think he was going to kill himself. On the island, the way Henry Shaw did."

"Henry Shaw, your ancestor? I thought you were kidding about that."

Peter looked at me levelly. "He set himself on fire, Katy."

My hand went to my lips. "Like a . . ."

"Magician, yes." He took a small hand-bound volume from his jeans pocket and handed it to me. "He kept a book of secrets."

"Henry Shaw," I whispered, almost afraid to let the book's vibrations come into me. "I thought he hated witches."

"That's what he said."

"To save himself from the mob?"

Peter held out his hands. "It didn't do him any good. The Darkness got him instead. Henry wrote his last entry after his wife escaped from him and the lynch mob that was chasing her. He left the book for Ola'ea to find. That's how it came into Hattie's possession."

I looked at it. On the first page, in faded, antique-looking script, were the words, "Keep My Secret."

"I hope he at least felt bad about leading the Puritans to his wife," I said, leafing through the diary.

"Bad enough to kill himself," Peter said. "He wasn't really evil, you know. Not in himself. It was the Darkness. It wanted him because he was rich, and because he was magical, whether he admitted to that or not, and because he was married to a powerful witch."

"Do you think that was why he pretended to be cowen?"

Peter shrugged. "He didn't say. He also didn't say how he became infected. Maybe he didn't even know. He might have just been around someone who died. It jumps onto the closest person."

"Like fleas," I said.

"What?"

"Fleas leave a host as soon as its body dies, and then jump onto the closest living thing."

Peter bowed his head. "Except fleas don't kill their host."

"Does the Darkness?"

"In a way." It was hard for Peter to talk, I knew. He licked his lips. His hands were shaking. "I think that my dad killed my mother," he said.

I didn't answer. I remembered what I had heard in the dream that had prompted me to go to Peter's house.

"That's what it—the Darkness—told me. Through Eric, on the night you came. I didn't believe it at first, but I've been thinking about it since then, and it makes sense. She was infected, so the Darkness told him—probably through my mother's own mouth—to kill her. And when he did, it passed into him."

"Just like that," I whispered.

"No," he said somberly. "It wasn't 'just like that.' The Darkness is . . . persuasive. It talks to you, and keeps talking, and won't let you go, until you're so tired and freaked out and beat up that you don't know which way is up anymore . . ." Peter's eyes welled with tears. "And the whole time it sounds so sincere, so *reasonable*, that after a while you start to forget that what it's asking you—telling you—to do is to murder someone you love, and you begin to think that maybe it'll be the Darkness you're killing, and not your wife . . . my mother . . . Eric . . ."

I threw my arms around him as he sobbed into my neck. "It can do anything, Katy. And I've brought it to you."

"No, you haven't. Yesterday was a . . . a fluke. I was at the window, and he—it— managed to push me off. It's not like it could chase me across town. We're safe."

"Not for long, Katy. Every day it gets a stronger hold."

"Does Hattie know?"

"I don't know," he said miserably. "I've tried to keep it from her—"

"For ten years?"

"No, no. The Darkness hasn't manifested until recently. It took ten years for it to be able to use Eric's body and brain. That's probably the only reason nothing horrible has come to Whitfield yet. Eric's too weak to be of much use to the Darkness. That's why it's looking for someone else."

"You."

He nodded.

"Wait a minute, Peter. If your father killed himself—"

"He didn't. I think he was going to. He drew up all the paperwork giving custody of Eric and me over to Hattie, but he never got a chance to leave Hattie's house."

"He died at Hattie's?"

He nodded. "He had a heart attack." He turned away. "Look, you don't want to—"

"Tell me," I said.

Slowly, creakily as an old man, Peter sat down on the visitor's chair and closed his eyes. "I remember every second of that night," he said quietly. "We were all in Hattie's kitchen. Eric was lying in a basket on the kitchen table. Hattie was at the stove, boiling water for tea. My father was holding me by both arms, telling me how I had to look after Eric. He said the rest of the family wouldn't understand, but we'd both be safer with Hattie."

"Were there harbingers?" I asked.

"No. Nothing. The Darkness had no power then. It had slipped into my mother, and then my father, and then . . ." He gave a bitter little laugh. "It's funny, everyone said that Prescott Shaw died of a broken heart. Maybe that was true. All I know is that he was holding me by both shoulders, making me promise to take care of Eric, when all of a sudden he sort of flung his arms out. I didn't know what was going on. He knocked me down. His eyes were bulging and his skin turned dark red, and he kept opening his mouth, but no sound came out. Mostly, I just remember being scared."

He ran his hand through his hair. "And the quiet. I remember that," he said slowly. "It had started to rain, and outside the window, lightning was flashing silently, the way it does before a big storm begins. Everything was so quiet, and yet at the same time so violent.

"My dad sort of spun into Eric's basket on the table and pulled it down with him as he fell full-length on the floor. The basket hit Hattie, and Eric fell out. Hattie tried to catch him, but she couldn't. He kind of bounced into the air, and then he landed on top of my father.

"Then Eric started screaming. And, like that, my father was

274

dead on the floor with this frozen look of horror on his face."

I closed my eyes, trying to erase the image.

"That was how Eric got infected," Peter said.

We looked at each other for a long moment. "You can't keep this to yourself any longer," I said finally.

Peter's gaze shifted toward the open door, his face flushed. "Katy, don't," he pleaded.

"Hattie has to know. They all have to know. This is the Darkness, Peter."

"This is *Eric*!" he spat through clenched teeth, his eyes grown instantly wild with panic.

"Eric's not who put those scars on your back," I said. "Eric's not the one who keeps telling you to kill him."

"I'll never kill him."

"You'll never want to, but I don't think you can hold out against this thing by yourself, Peter. You need *us*. The witches. All of us."

His face fell. "You?" he whispered. "You'd side with them against me?"

"It wouldn't be like that—"

"Oh, no? Do you know what they'll—what *you'll* do? Do you know what Hattie will do? Eric's like her own baby, but she's high priestess, and she'll burn him. *Burn* him, Katy. Because that's how they deal with this."

"Peter, please—"

"I'm begging you, Katy, keep your mouth shut."

"And what will *you* do, then? Allow yourself to be tortured every night?"

"I can handle it."

"No, you *can't*," I said. "How long do you think—"

"I'll be all right," he said, taking my hands in his. "I have a plan."

I flung his hands off me. "What are you thinking about doing?"

"Never mind. Besides," he added with false cheer, "I might not have to do anything. As long as Eric's alive, the Darkness is held captive in his body."

"How long do you think that's going to last?" I demanded baldly. "The harbingers have already started. Fires everywhere, sinkholes, death . . . Something's coming, Peter. It's been coming for ten years, and it's not going to stop now."

"How do you know how the Darkness works?" he snapped. "It hasn't appeared here since 1929. Look, I've been reading about it. A lot of things were done wrong then, and probably at every other time it showed up too. There must be some way to get rid of it without sacrificing Eric. We just have to find it."

"There's no more time, Peter."

"Yes, there is! There is if you'll just keep quiet, give me a chance—"

"Time's up, kids," the nurse announced loudly as she strode into the room. "Sorry, doctor's orders." She checked my eyes again, and the wound on the back of my head. "No promises, but if you ask me, you'll be on a regular floor by tomorrow." She turned to Peter with a smile. "She'll be able to have all the visitors she wants then."

Peter's gaze held mine. I knew he was begging me not to tell anyone what I knew.

"Will you come back tomorrow?" I asked quietly.

He didn't answer.

"Don't do this," I said, my voice breaking.

He took a deep breath. "You're here because of me," he said somberly. "As long as I'm around, you won't be safe." He looked at the nurse and at Gram, who was just coming in. Both women were regarding him with alarm.

"Peter . . ."

"I love you," he said. Then he turned and walked out.

The click of his shoes on the floor as he left was the only sound I could hear. Then silence filled the room, as solid as death.

"Wow," the nurse said at last. "Intense."

Gram cleared her throat. "Now I really do need a drink of water," she said.

I love you.

He loved me. Now that the world was ending.

CHAPTER

•

THIRTY-TWO

 SIX OF SWORDS

My dad walked in looking irritated. Last night seemed like a million years ago, and the things he was so concerned about—my breaking curfew, going to Peter's house, falling off the trellis, ending up in the hospital—seemed so trivial now, compared with what Peter, and ultimately the rest of us, were facing.

"Why did you do it, Katy?" he asked.

"Huh?" For a brief, confused moment, I thought he was referring to the fact that I'd asked to see Peter before him. "There was just something I needed to . . . Oh. You mean why I left the house in the middle of the night."

"Of course that's what I mean," he bristled. He exhaled a long, disappointed breath. "I thought that you and I had come to some sort of *rapprochement*." He seemed genuinely puzzled, even though he'd used a pompous French word with an even more pompous French pronunciation. "After everything that we discussed, why did you go to that boy's house?"

I stared at my hands. I knew I'd let him down. We'd ironed out so many of our problems, and I'd spoiled it all by blatantly disobeying him.

It didn't matter that I'd discovered something important while I was disobeying him, because I couldn't tell Dad about that, anyway. The Darkness wasn't a concept he'd ever understand.

What he did understand was that I'd broken his trust again. I'd blown it.

"I'm sorry," I said quietly.

"I'm afraid that isn't good enough," he said. "You don't belong here, Katy."

"Wake up, Dad," I shouted, nearly pulling the IV out of my arm. "It's the only place I *do* belong."

"I'm not going to listen to this—"

"You've never listened to anything I've said. And taking me away from Whitfield isn't going to accomplish anything. I was away for eleven years, Dad. Eleven years of not knowing who I was or where I belonged. Eleven years of keeping to myself, of never touching anyone, of watching you leave every night and wondering what I'd done to make you not want to be with me, ever—"

"That's not true."

"Was it because you were afraid I'd be like my mother?"

His hands balled into fists, the knuckles white.

"Because I am," I said quietly.

The monitor attached to my heart raced for a couple of minutes, but then decelerated, beeping in a regular rhythm. Outside my door, the bustling hospital corridor was filled with noise and motion, but the two of us, my father and I, remained apart from everything, removed even from time and space, trying to find our way to each other.

Then, slowly, his fists opened. The color returned to them. I heard him breathe again. "I guess I've always known it." His voice was raspy, as if he hadn't spoken in days. "You can move things," he said.

I nodded. "I can read objects, too. And people. By touching them."

He recoiled. It was subtle and momentary, but there was no mistaking the disgust on his face. Touching has never been something the Jessevars were very good at.

"But it's voluntary," I added quickly. "I won't read you unless I make an effort to."

"That's good to know," he muttered.

"We're all different. All the Whitfield witches, I mean."

He winced at the word. I knew he would, but I wasn't going to hide anything anymore.

"How . . . how are you different?" he asked meekly, his fingers toying nervously with the bedcovers. "What can the other . . . witches . . . do?"

I felt a surge of happiness. He had used the word! He was trying. Really trying.

"Well, some can see things that are happening a long way away," I said, cataloging. "Some can make thoughts materialize into matter. There's djinn here—a woman who can bend people's wills. She's very careful, though, very well trained."

"Is Whitfield the only place in the world like this?"

"I don't think so. I've heard about other witch communities. They're not publicized, though."

"No, I imagine not," he said, subdued.

I hesitated for a moment before going on. I wasn't sure he'd want to hear what I was about to say.

"Mother had a very special gift," I said, plunging in.

He looked up at me.

"She could see the future."

He folded his arms over his chest. "No one can predict the future, Katherine." He looked down. "Katy."

"Not in specifics. There's the butterfly effect, where changing one small action can result in a completely different outcome."

"Exactly."

"But there are some forces that can't be stopped. Natural forces, benevolent forces, even forces of evil."

His face colored. "The Darkness," he said, as if he were speaking a foul word.

"She told you about the Darkness?"

"There's no such thing, Katy. No documentation whatever—"

"There's plenty of documentation, Dad," I interrupted. "Every family in Whitfield has a record of everything that's gone on here for the past three hundred years, and many go back a lot farther than—"

"Well, it doesn't exist in the *real* world," he insisted.

"Which one is that?" I shot back.

"The one that would have kept my wife alive!" He buried his face in his hands.

Whoa. I wasn't expecting that.

"Dad?" I ventured, inching my hand toward him.

"The things she saw . . . or thought she saw . . . Either she was crazy, or she was looking into a future I didn't want any part of. You should have heard her, Katy! It was impossible to live with that . . . with that *horror* . . ."

"Is that what she saw?" I asked gently. "Horror?"

"She wouldn't tell me for a long time. But then she began to unravel. All she talked about was the Darkness. And burning. Fire, fire. She was obsessed with fire. I just didn't know what to do, Katy. I thought that if we left this place, changed our names . . ."

"Became normal," I said dully.

"Yes." He looked at me with a defensiveness that was almost belligerent. "I thought it might work. Get her away from these people, and their fairy tales about some mumbo-jumbo comic-book bogeyman. The Darkness! Who in their right mind . . ." He sighed. "She could have had a normal life. She could have—"

"She was an *oracle*, Dad," I whispered. "She saw things that no one else could. And once you see something, even if it's something no one besides you believes exists, you can't unsee it. It's like taking back knowledge. You just can't do it."

I managed to touch him then, just a brush against his fingers. For a moment he stiffened, as if a jolt of electricity had run through him. But then he softened, I could see it on his face. He turned toward me and his hand felt like it melted over mine. "Oh, Katy," he said. "In some ways, she was the sanest person I knew."

"What?" I hadn't believed he would ever speak those words. That anyone would. My mother was not only insane; she was criminally, famously insane. "Why do you say that?" I asked hesitantly.

He stood up and walked to the window, then placed both

hands on it as if it were a wall. "I knew what she was," he said. "How could anyone not know? She was so utterly different from everyone else on the face of the earth." He turned to face me. "She was incredibly beautiful, Katy. Her eyes changed color with her mood, from this brilliant emerald to Caribbean blue, to dark green. Like yours."

"You noticed?"

"It used to hurt me to look at you, because you reminded me so much of her. It's funny, Agnes is her twin, but you actually look more like her than Agnes does. She lacks a special quality your mother had that lent her a . . . a *radiance* that was unearthly." He sighed. "I loved her so much," he whispered.

I was confused. "Then why . . . why didn't you believe her?" I asked.

He waited a long time to answer. "Because I couldn't," he said finally. "I had no place here. I could never belong here."

"And she couldn't belong anywhere else."

"That was my mistake," he said. "I thought she could. But the incident at Wonderland changed everything. Everything."

"Did she ever tell you why she did it?"

"No." He turned back to the window. "I'd left by then."

"You left her?"

"I gave her a choice. Her family—you and me—or Whitfield. I thought it would be an easy decision. When it wasn't, I left and took you with me."

"And she didn't follow you?"

"No. Instead, she went to Wonderland, tried to kill the Shaw baby, and then set herself on fire."

Something stirred inside me. "Set herself . . ." *Kaboom.* There it was. Why hadn't I seen it before? "Oh, my God," I said.

"I'm sorry. I thought you knew."

"I did. It was just—"

"Every day of my life since then, I've wondered if things might have been different. If I hadn't made her choose, if I hadn't taken her daughter away from her . . ."

"No, Dad," I said quietly. "It wasn't you."

He looked at me quizzically.

It wasn't him. It had never been him. It had always been about Eric, and the Darkness, and what my mother knew.

"Dad, I have to stay in Whitfield," I blurted.

"What?"

"I have to stay."

He blinked. "I don't think that's for you to decide."

"I know you don't want me to, and that you don't approve of Peter, or Mrs. Ainsworth, or any of the others, but I'm telling you that I have to stay here."

"You're telling me?"

I hesitated. "I'm sorry, but yes."

A long moment. Eternally long. And then he sighed. "Where do you want to stay?"

"At my great-grandmother's, until school starts again."

"Starting when?"

"I want to be there now, Dad."

"Is it because of that boy?" he asked. "Is that why you want to stay?"

"Partly." There was no use in lying anymore. I couldn't tell him about Eric and the Darkness, but I wanted to be as honest as I could. "It's everything—the school, Gram, Aunt Agnes, Miss P . . ." The words just came tumbling out, all the things I'd wanted to tell him for so long, but never had the chance to.

"There's Verity and Cheswick . . . and Hattie. I had a job with her for a while. I learned to cook. Did I tell you about that? But now they've torn down her restaurant and her house so that a new Wonderland can be built on the Meadow, when no one in Old Town even wants the stupid thing, anyway." I gathered my courage and took a breath, "It's my world. I *belong* here, Dad. I know who I am now. And no matter what happens, I don't want to be anywhere else."

I didn't realize it, but I guess I must have been crying, because all of a sudden my father swooped down and cradled me in his long, strong arms and hugged me so fiercely that I almost couldn't breathe. And then, for the first time ever, I *felt* him opening up to me, allowing me to see into his deepest heart.

In that heart he loved me. Truly, absolutely, eternally.

"I love you, Dad," I said.

"I love you, too, Katy."

"I know."

He took out a handkerchief—he always used real cloth handkerchiefs, like Peter—and dabbed my eyes with it.

"I'm a doofus," I said.

"Me too." He wiped his own face with the handkerchief. "We are both . . . is '*doofi*' a word?"

I laughed though I was still crying. "I guess." I squeezed his hand. After a moment, I said, "I'm sixteen now. "

He looked surprised at first, and then really upset. "Oh, baby, I'm sorry," he said. "Your birthday. It was yesterday, wasn't it. God, I'm a screwup."

"It's okay. But I was thinking that maybe my punishment's gone on long enough." I gave him my sweetest smile. "Being un-grounded would be a great birthday present."

He exhaled roughly. "I'm going to give you a better present than that."

"Dad, you don't—"

"I'm leaving town," he said.

"What?"

"I need to get back to New York. And I think things would be easier for you with the Ainsworths." He looked sheepish. "Also, Madison and I are taking a little break."

"Ouch," I said.

"To be truthful, there's much less 'ouch' without her."

"Not a big surprise," I said. "But are you sure?"

"Yes, Katy," he said. "I'll come visit. As a tourist." He kissed my cheek. "I want you to have your world."

"But you won't . . ."

"Abandon you? No." He stood up and tucked me into the hospital bed, pulling the blanket up around my chin. "Never, never, my darling girl."

CHAPTER

•

THIRTY-THREE

 LAMMAS

They moved me out of intensive care the next day. Gram was waiting in my new room when the nurse wheeled me in.

"We're trying to get you out as soon as we can, dear," she said.

"I can't wait to go home."

"Neither can we. Your Aunt Agnes and Jonathan send their love," Gram said. "They're at the Lammas festival, but I didn't want to go."

"Why not?" Lammas was sort of like Thanksgiving, except that it was held at the beginning of August. There was always lots of food and decorations made of grains in honor of the wheat and corn harvests.

She made a cryptic gesture. "I doubt it will be the same," she said. "Without Hattie."

"Why wouldn't Hattie be there?" I asked, alarmed.

"She hasn't been well," she said. "No one's seen her around Old Town or elsewhere."

Hattie knew about Eric. She had to. The Darkness had spread its horror and dread from little Eric to Peter, and now to Hattie. And to me.

I wanted so much to confide in my great-grandmother. But I'd promised Peter that I wouldn't say anything. I'd promised.

"She's resigned as high priestess," Gram said. "Livia Fowler will replace her at the ritual." She gave a little snort.

"Livia Fowler?" I repeated, hoping I'd heard wrong.

"Yes. She has a daughter at your school."

"Becca," I sighed. "The Fowlers hate our family, you know. Miss P told me."

"Well, 'hate' might be rather too strong a word," she said.

"The Fowlers think that the Ainsworth women are responsible for every instance of the Darkness."

"Is that so?" she asked calmly. She didn't seem even slightly put out. "Well, they're a clannish lot."

"Worse than that! I've heard that the Fowlers have their own private army of thugs who'll beat up anyone they don't like."

"Nonsense. Mr. Fowler is the coach of some community sporting team. Football, or baseball, one of those things," she said with a dismissive wave. "That's why there are always young men at their house. Good gracious, how easily rumors start!"

"Still, doesn't it bother you, even a little?" Just the thought of a private army headed by Livia Fowler was making my stomach churn.

"Bother? No, dear. Sciatica bothers me. Indigestion bothers me. Bunions, arthritis, irregularity . . . These are things that bother me. The opinion of the Fowlers, however, has nothing to do with me. Or with you."

"Gram," I began, feeling as if I were sliding off a cliff, "if the Darkness were to infect one of us . . ."

"Yes?" She was arranging herself in the visitor's chair, leafing through a copy of *Quilting* magazine. "Oh, look. They're already showing pumpkin prints."

"Fine. Well, if that happened, how long would it take to show?"

She brought the page closer to her face. "I think jack-o'-lanterns are far too scary for baby blankets, don't you?"

"Gram . . ."

"Show what? Oh, the Darkness? I don't know. As long as it likes, I imagine." She tittered. "I don't mean to be flippant, dear. But it's true. The Darkness can manifest quickly, or it can take years to reveal itself."

"And during those years, no one would know anything? There wouldn't be any harbingers?"

"The harbingers have always signaled imminent danger." Suddenly she put down the magazine, her face stricken. "Oh, dear, all these goings-on have frightened you, haven't they, dear?" She stood up and fluttered around me.

"No, I'm all right, really. I just wanted to know."

"Well, you are still new to our ways. Perhaps you don't understand why we're concerned about something beyond the sinkholes and fires. Granted, they're certainly bad enough."

"Uh . . . yes," I waffled. "This thing, the Darkness . . . People act like it has a mind of its own . . . as if it were a person."

"But it does, Katy. It has its own intelligence. It uses the minds of its victims—and don't forget, they are *all* victims—but behind those minds, those personalities, the Darkness follows its own agenda."

"So it could be inside a person for a long time without anyone even knowing it?"

"Indeed, yes. There have even been instances of the Darkness infecting children, although one can hardly bear thinking about that."

"But if that were to happen . . ."

"Gracious, you mean a child?"

"Hypothetically. There would be something we could do, wouldn't there? I mean besides the . . ."

She raised troubled eyes to me. "The burning?" she finished. The words sounded sticky.

I nodded. "Given that it's a child, there must be exceptions—"

"There is no other solution," she said. "The infected ones, once found, must be destroyed." Her voice was no more than a whisper. "I wish there were some other way." She clapped her hands together, and a bright smile transformed her face. "But we don't have to worry about things like that, do we?"

"Maybe there is another way," I persisted. "Maybe it just hasn't been found yet. A spell, or an incantation . . ."

She thought for a moment. "Well, there is the 'Song of Unmaking'—"

"Say what?" I felt my pulse quicken. "The song of un-what?-ing?"

"Unmaking. It's a spell for dispelling the Darkness."

"Oh," I said, deflated. "The burning spell."

"Wellll . . ." She stretched out the word. "That's how it's always been interpreted."

I blinked. "You mean it might have been interpreted wrong? For all these centuries?"

She looked thoughtful. "It may have been centuries, but it has actually never been used."

"What?"

She shrugged.

"What about Dorothea Lyttel? Or Constance Ainsworth, back in 1929?"

"Both those women set the fires that killed them *themselves*."

"Like my mother," I whispered.

She nodded. "It is what has been done since the beginning of time."

"But the spell—"

"The song is ambiguous. It has been studied ever since Hattie's ancestor Ola'ea wrote it, but no one knows for certain what it means."

"Aren't the instructions clear?"

"Spells don't have instructions, dear. It's all a matter of interpretation. At first, anyway. After the first time, it's called tradition. Anyway, it can only be found in the *Great Book of Secrets*, which is very difficult to get to. The whole community has to take part in order to open it. I know, because we were almost called upon to perform the opening spell in 1955, when floods in the area . . . Well, never mind that."

"The *Great* . . ." I got it. "You mean the book of secrets for Whitfield, collectively."

"Quite. Everything about us is in that book. Every spell we've evoked. Everything we know. Every bit of information and lore that any of the original twenty-seven families brought with them from England. If it is known, if it has *ever* been known by any witch in Whitfield or her ancestors, it is recorded in the *Great Book*."

"Must be a pretty big book," I said lamely.

Gram clucked. "Of course, it has no real size, until it is called up. And it can only be accessed by magic."

"Then we have to look there," I said.

"But why, dear? Do you have some question?"

I stared at her for a moment. "Er . . . if anything comes up, that is. That would be the thing to do."

"Yes, certainly."

I finally got my walking papers that afternoon, after Dr. Baddely put me through the usual tests. Gram had signed all the papers and we were on the elevator when a couple of candy stripers from my school got on, so excited that they were actually squealing.

"Can you believe it?" one of them chirped.

"It's horrible. The most horrible thing I ever heard."

These were Muffies. That was how they talked all the time. Everything was the worst, the most fabulous, the most absolutely heinous, the most devastatingly awesome. They never even noticed me, of course. I just counted the seconds until the elevator door would open, so I could get away from them. *One, two . . .*

"How'd he do it?"

"Razor. He's in the emergency room now."

"It doesn't make any sense. He was the cutest guy in school."

No he isn't. Peter is. Three, four . . .

"I heard he was in some kind of trouble with the police."

"Not him. His mother was."

Muffled Muffy laughter. "That's not his mother! She's black, duh."

Five . . . Oh no oh no oh no . . .

"Oh, right. Didn't she run that restaurant or something? The one on the corner?"

"It got torn down."

"Yeah. The geeks all went there."

"That's it." Heavy sigh. "I guess you never know when somebody's going to flip out."

"Peter!" I screamed as the doors opened. I shoved past the candy stripers, nearly knocking one of them over.

I ran to the emergency room. In the waiting area, two policemen were questioning an emaciated old black woman. They were flanking her on either side like two stone monoliths beside a gnarled old tree. It took me a moment to recognize the woman, but when I did, it felt as if my heart had fallen out of my chest. "Hattie!" I called. Her gaze, tired and vacant, wandered toward mine.

"Is he alive?" I demanded. I knew it wasn't the right time or place to be questioning her, but I had to know. One of the policemen turned to glare at me.

"Yes," Hattie answered, nodding almost imperceptibly. Her voice was weak and trembling.

Relief flooded through me like warm butter. "I've got to see him," I said, heading toward the double doors that led to the treatment area.

"You can't go in there, miss," the receptionist said.

I ignored her, banging through the doors like a crazed bull. "Peter!" I shouted.

Cloth screens sectioned off patients into makeshift rooms. I ran from one to the next, calling Peter's name. And then I found him, his wrists bandaged, tubes going into his nose, two

IVs in his arms, a bag of blood hanging near his head.

"Peter?" I tried to be quiet, though I felt like screaming at the top of my lungs.

His eyes opened, and he looked alarmed. I fell down on my knees beside him. "Peter, why? Why?" I moaned. Hot tears were streaming down my face.

"Forgive me," he whispered. He made a motion with his fingers. I clasped them with my own.

"Was this your plan?" I coughed. "Your stupid *plan*? To kill yourself?"

"No," he rasped. "But it was the only way."

"Who is that?" someone behind me asked.

Footsteps approached me from behind, and another voice spoke. "Miss, I don't know how you got in here, but you're going to have to wait in the reception area," the voice said.

"It didn't work, anyway," Peter said, so softly I could barely hear him. "Eric didn't like it. He started screaming. Then Hattie came. She saw and called the ambulance."

"Peter, we have to tell, we have to tell everybody."

"No—"

"Get her out of here." Someone grabbed my arm. I threw it off.

"Call security."

"There's a way, Peter," I insisted. "*The Great Book of Secrets*. Gram said—"

"It doesn't matter what she said. No one's going to help us."

"Let's go," a third voice boomed behind me. This one grabbed me firmly under my armpits and yanked me to a standing position. I finally looked at him, seeing a uniform. Hospital security, probably.

"You're wrong, Peter. We'll find a way together."

"Katy, please . . ."

The guard shoved me across the length of the emergency room and through the double doors into the waiting area. "You have parents?" he boomed, finally letting go of me.

"I'm here with her," Gram said, jogging toward us, her handkerchief waving agitatedly.

"She's not permitted beyond those doors, ma'am," the guard said.

"I know, officer. I'll be responsible for her."

"Don't let it happen again," he warned, lumbering away.

"Good heavens, child," she whispered, looking around at the people occupying the chairs in the waiting room. "What on earth were you thinking?"

I was tired of hiding. She had to know. Everyone had to, now. "It's trying to kill Peter," I said.

Nearby, one of the officers with Hattie turned around. Since my foray into the forbidden area of the treatment rooms, Dr. Baddely had joined them. She was looking at me, too.

For a moment I wavered between keeping Peter's secret and trying to help him. Then the two policemen prodded Hattie, and the three of them moved slowly toward the exit. Dr. Baddely stepped away.

They were taking Hattie! To lock her up, to charge her with whatever had happened to Peter. "No!" I shouted. "Hattie, tell them!"

She looked at me with rueful, terrified eyes.

"It's not her," I screamed. "It's the Darkness!"

A dozen heads swiveled to face me.

"Tell them, Hattie! We can find a solution together. Tell them about Eric!"

Hattie slumped in a faint into the arms of one of the officers.

"We're getting out of here," Gram said, propelling me past the police and through the automatic glass exit doors. "Now."

I looked back. Everyone was staring, but the person I noticed most was Dr. Baddely. Her eyes were piercing through me like lasers.

She was a witch, too, then. She knew exactly what I was talking about.

By nightfall, I realized, every witch in Whitfield would know.

"I . . . I had to say something," I tried to explain. "We need to work together, the whole community. We can do the spell of Unmaking, like you—"

"Oh, be quiet!" my great-grandmother snapped.

"But you said—"

"I said there was no way to protect the child!" She shoved me forward, away from the hospital, as if trying to outrun the inevitable.

She said nothing more, but as we made our way through the twisted streets of Old Town, the realization of what I had done came crashing down on me.

I had just condemned a ten-year-old boy to death by fire.

ASTRAL PROJECTION

Penelope Bean's ancestral home looked sort of like Hawthorne's House of the Seven Gables, although it was more like the House of the Hundred and Seven Gables. Gram and I came in through the side door, the former servants' entrance, which was down a flight of steps from the street. The door opened into an enormous kitchen with a gigantic cast iron stove that made the one in Hattie's Kitchen seem positively modern, two gleaming zinc counters, and a table large enough to seat twelve. Then we climbed up a long staircase into a foyer lined with palm trees in big brass planters. Agnes was waiting for us.

"I heard you come in," she said, taking Gram by the elbow. My great-grandmother was wheezing from the exertion of climbing the stairs. "Why didn't you use the front door?" Agnes asked.

"I didn't want anyone to see us come here."

"Oh?"

"It was my fault," I said. "I thought I was helping. The police had Hattie, and Peter almost died, even though he said he had a plan, and I thought that if everyone knew about the Darkness, then we could all work together and do something . . ."

"Stop, stop, stop," Agnes said. "Come in and sit down, both of you."

"I shouldn't have said anything," I lamented as we walked into an old-fashioned parlor filled with heavy dark furniture and oval portraits on the walls.

"It's a little late to come to that realization," Gram said acidly. "Half the people in that waiting room were witches."

"Grandmother, please." Agnes held up a hand. "Now tell me, Katy. Everything."

"Hattie's in trouble," I began. "The police think she's been beating Peter."

Trying not to trip over my words I told her about the marks on Peter's back, what the paramedic had said on the night of the fire at Ainsworth House, the dream I'd had that had made me bicycle over to Hattie's place, and what I'd seen when I climbed the trellis and looked inside Peter's room.

"It was Eric," I finished. "For the past ten years, the Darkness has been living inside that little boy."

"Ten . . ."

"Yes. That was what my mother saw on the last day of her life."

"She tried to kill Eric because she knew he was infected?"

"Yes. She tried, and thought she had. That's why she went home and set herself on fire," I said.

"But the boy lived."

"Barely," Gram said. "I'm sure Agatha didn't even consider that possibility. After what she did to him, little Eric had so many handicaps that the Darkness couldn't even manifest through him."

"That's why it wants Peter," I told them. "Every night for months—ever since it learned to speak through Eric—it's been trying to get Peter to kill his brother so that the Darkness can come into Peter. It keeps saying that Peter will be a better *vessel*."

"Well, it's getting stronger now. What did it do to put Peter in the hospital?" Agnes asked.

"I don't know. Peter said it was the only way, whatever that meant." Suddenly the thought of Peter lying on that cot with the thick bandages on his wrists was just overwhelming. I felt my shoulders start to shake. "Maybe he just got tired . . ." I said, too upset to finish.

Gram put her arm around me. "There, there," she said. "He's all right now, and there's no reason to think—"

"Peter told me not to say anything to anyone, because he's convinced that none of you will lift a finger to help him or Eric."

"It's not like that, Katy," Agnes said. "Of course we want to help them. Every witch in Old Town thinks of Eric Shaw as her own child. But if this is the Darkness—and I hope to Hecate that you're mistaken about this—then we have to consider the safety and survival of the community first."

"But there must be a way to take the Darkness out of Eric without killing him!" I insisted.

"The method is clear—"

"Maybe there's another method!" I shouted. "Maybe there's a way no one has found yet. Just because something isn't four hundred years old doesn't mean it won't work."

"Do you think that no one has ever considered what you're proposing? How many of the witches who've been infected by the Darkness throughout our history do you suppose had families, friends, loved ones who would give up their own lives if that could save them from burning? I'll tell you how many, Katy. All of them.

"No one with even the slightest degree of decency wants to see another being burned to death. Not a cat, not a bug. The problem is that no one has found another way, despite centuries of searching. In the end, the community has always had to resort to the burning. And no one, *no one*, has liked it."

"But what about the 'Spell of Unmaking'?" I asked.

"Song," Gram said. "The 'Song of Unmaking'. It has to be sung."

"It's very obscure."

"Well, what does it say?"

She cocked her head, thinking. "Let's see . . ."

> *Through Love's unbreaking tie*
> *Unmake the Darkness, do not die*
> *No death shall come, good soul, to thee,*
> *For by the Sacred Fire set thou free.*

"At one time I could recite the whole spell," she said. "Anyway, no one knows why she even wrote it, since the solution—burning—is what we'd been doing for millennia."

"But . . . the *sacred* fire. Maybe that's different."

She shrugged. "Some scholars have conjectured that Ola'ea was writing from a Christian perspective, seeing physical death as the pathway to eternal life, although . . ."

"Agnes, I think Hattie needs our help rather urgently," Gram interrupted.

"Ah, yes. And Peter, too, I imagine?"

"Under the circumstances, most certainly."

"What about Peter?" I asked.

"Leave things to me." Agnes stood up and walked over to a high-backed velvet wing chair in a darkened corner.

"Er . . ." Gram rose. "Perhaps I should give Katy our gift now."

"That would be prudent," Agnes said, gathering her skirts around her and sitting down. She templed her index fingers and brought them between her eyebrows. I wondered if she had a headache.

Then one of the oddest things I'd ever seen happened in front of my eyes. In the silent room I heard a low buzz begin to emanate from the corner where Agnes was sitting. Then she began to fade out, as if she were an electronically produced image with static interrupting the transmission.

Gram must have seen me gawking. "Agnes has an unusual talent," she said, pitching her voice low so as not to disturb her granddaughter, who was now blinking in and out of sight. "She is an astral traveler. She can journey long distances without the aid of vehicles . . . or even legs." She chuckled at her little joke.

My eyes were transfixed on the wing chair, which was now empty. "You mean she's . . . she's just gone?"

"Not exactly. That is, her subtle body is still in the chair. Try not to sit on it."

I swallowed. "Does she . . . does she do this often?"

"Oh my, yes. Every day, in fact, when she goes to work."

"Aunt Agnes works?"

"Why, of course, dear. The Ainsworths have never been layabouts. Even I do my part by volunteering at the hospital." She straightened her shoulders. "And I'm eighty-three."

"No, I didn't mean . . . Er, what does she do? In her job, I mean."

"She teaches ethnobotany at Stanford University," she said proudly.

"Stanford?" I was stunned. "In California?"

"Oh, it doesn't matter how far away the destination is," Gram said. "It's a much more efficient method than travel by broomstick, wouldn't you say?" She started to laugh, but then held up a finger. "Shhh." She squinted for a moment, as if listening to something. "Ah, yes. Agnes is with Penelope Bean now," she said.

"Miss P? How do you know?"

"She's sending me a message."

I blinked. "A message? You mean a *telepathic* message?"

"Very minor talent," she said, blushing. "Receiving messages. Anyone can do it, really, with a little study."

"Why is Agnes with Miss P?"

"I have no idea," she said. "But that's what she's telling me. Hmm." She nodded decisively. "Righto, I almost forgot." She walked over to a little table and opened the central drawer in it. "There's something else she wants me to do," she said, rummaging through the drawer. "It concerns you. Ah, yes, here it is." She pulled out a stick.

That's what it was, a wooden stick about ten inches long. "This is for you," she said, handing it to me with a flourish. "A birthday gift from Agnes and me."

"Um . . . thanks," I said dubiously. "Is it a hair ornament?"

Her eyes widened in horror. "Good gracious, child, how did you manage all those years? It's a *wand*, Katy."

"A wand? A magic wand?" Images of Hogwarts came to mind. "Terrificus Splenderosa," I said, twirling the stick. Nothing happened.

Gram clucked. "How disrespectful!" she muttered. "A wand is not a toy. In fact, it would be quite premature for you to have one at all, if it weren't for these extraordinary circumstances. Needless to say it should only be used in case of dire emergency."

I examined the tip. Plain wood. "Is there a phoenix feather inside?" I asked, shaking it.

"Don't be ridiculous. It's just rowan wood, since your birthday occurs in August, the Druidic month represented by the rowan tree."

"How does it work?"

"The way all magic works," she said, snatching the wand out of my hand. "In fact, it does nothing on its own. All a wand does is to focus your intention, which is what creates magic in the first place." She pointed it at one of the Beans' family portraits hanging on the wall, a prune-faced old woman wearing a blue satin gown and a three-foot-tall white wig. "Know what effect you wish to achieve, and focus all your attention and will on it." As she spoke, the sour-looking woman in the portrait produced a wide, gap-toothed grin and crossed her eyes.

"That's wonderful!" I exclaimed, running up to the painting. As I drew closer, though, the woman's expression returned to its former haughty somberness.

"Minor, minor," Gram said. "Anyone can create an illusion." She handed the wand back to me. "Not a bad wand, though."

"Thank you," I said, stroking the thing with my finger.

"Just make sure that what you focus on is what you really want, and not what you think you *ought* to want."

"World peach," I said, remembering the first time I attempted magic.

"Precisely. Be very clear in your mind. Then, once you are clear, you may use the wand. But be careful with it. I cannot stress that enough. So much can go wrong."

I toyed with it awkwardly. It's hard to be casual about wielding a magic wand.

"You'll have to sew a wand pocket into your clothes," Gram said. "Meanwhile, just keep it in your sleeve." She showed me how to press it between my shoulder and my elbow. Now I understood why I'd never seen witches wearing tank tops.

I twirled the wand between my fingers. "How can I use this to see Peter?" I asked. I knew I was grasping at straws, but I couldn't help myself. "Or at least communicate with him?"

Gram put her hands on her hips, annoyed. "You can't," she said. "You can only do what you would normally do, only more so. In the instance you're describing, that would mean more of nothing."

"Just asking," I said, replacing the wand in my sleeve. I didn't mean to seem ungrateful or rude, but I was hoping that something . . . anything . . . would help me get to him. I needed to know that he was all right. And if he wasn't . . . Well, I couldn't think about that. He would be fine. He would have to be.

And I needed to see him. More than I wanted to take my next breath, I wanted to be with him.

"Oh, here you go." Gram cocked her head to the side. "Were you thinking about Peter?"

My jaw dropped. "How . . . how . . ."

She burst out laughing. "That wasn't telepathy, just observation," she said, holding her sides. "When are you *not* thinking about him?" She waved her handkerchief, guffawing.

"Very hilarious," I said.

"What *was* telepathy, however, was Agnes' message to me. Peter is fine."

"Huh?"

"Agnes is with him now. She says he's weak, but out of all danger. They've given him two pints of blood already."

"Have her tell him that I'm here. That I—"

"Yes, yes. She knows, dear." She straightened up, her eyes clear. "The wheels are in motion," she said.

"What wheels?"

"The wheels of fate," she said ominously. "From now on we're all just going to have to do what we have to do."

"What's that mean?" I demanded, alarmed. "No one's going to get burned, right? Nothing like that."

"I truly hope not, dear. But one never knows what one will be called upon to endure."

"No. Wait. That can't be an option. We have to think—"

"We'd best get your things from New Town and bring them back here while we have the chance," she said. "Come along, Katy. I'll drive you."

Gram's car was a dove gray 1956 four-door Cadillac Sedan de Ville with butter soft burgundy leather seats and enough chrome to coat New Jersey.

"Goodness me, I hope I can remember how to operate this," she said as the Caddy lurched out of the garage. "Agnes drove it here."

"How long has it been since you've driven?" I asked.

"Oh, it wasn't that long ago," she said. "1985, I think." The mailman eyed us warily as we approached. "Yes, that was it. I recall it was the festival of Mabon . . ."

We came so close to the mailman that his buttons scraped against the passenger side window. He uttered a little shriek as we passed.

"Er . . . I think you're hitting that guy, Gram," I pointed out.

"Hattie and I were baking bread for the festival . . . Good heavens! What on earth is he doing there?" She lay on the horn. After we sailed past him, I watched through the side view mirror as he sat down on the curb, the contents of his mailbag scattered around him.

That was just the beginning. The drive to Mim's house on Oak Street was the longest three miles I've ever traveled. Apparently Gram had learned to drive at the local amusement park's Dodge 'Em Cars pavilion. She would floor the gas pedal to drive fifty feet, only to slam on the brake at the next stop sign. Then she would gun the engine again, even if there was a car in front of her. By the time we got to Mim's, the odor of burnt rubber lay thick around the car. The beautiful whitewall tires were still smoking as I let myself in the house.

My dad had already moved out. Not that you could see any difference on the ground floor—that was still as sterile and unlived-in as ever—but the little room he'd used as his office had been cleared out. On a bookshelf, along with some scraps of paper and a rubber band, was a small framed photograph of Dad and Mim standing in front of Big Ben in London. It must have been windy that day, because Mim's blonde hair was blowing around her face. It made her look kind of like an angel, surrounded by a nimbus of golden light. Dad looked happy, too.

Looking at the picture, I felt a wave of sadness and guilt. I remembered that trip. Dad had called me, boring me with facts about Westminster Abbey or something. Mim had invited me to join them, on condition that I bring along her nail polish. I'd refused.

I'd begrudged them their happiness together because they hadn't included me, even though I hadn't wanted to be with them in the first place. And now their time was over, I wished I'd been less of a pain to them. I wished I'd given them more of a chance to enjoy each other while they could.

I packed up my few possessions pretty quickly, putting the London photo in the bag with my laptop, phone, and iPod, which Dad had left for me in my room. There was something else there too. Beside my electronics was an 1898 edition of *Beowulf*, translated by William Morris. Inside it was a slip of paper with a message from Dad. *Dear Katy,* it read, *I'm sorry I missed your birthday.*

The book had been one of my father's most prized possessions. He wouldn't have parted with it for anything or anybody.

Except me.

Tenderly I placed it in my bag. Then, on a loose piece of paper, I wrote a quick note to Mim. It said, *Thank you—IOU Big time.* I signed it with the smiley emoticon. ☺. I figured that was about as sentimental a gesture as she could stand.

CHAPTER

•

THIRTY-FIVE

 TERRA

It was twilight, and the stark shadows made the buildings around the square look ominous with a surreal, comic-book feel as we drove back into Old Town.

Gram's driving had not improved perceptibly since we'd left the Bean house. She continued to jackrabbit from stop sign to traffic light, terrorizing passersby as we went. As we bulleted past the school, I was starting to relax a little. I hadn't really believed we would make it back without an accident, and our safety was an unexpected surprise.

That good feeling lasted about ten seconds. Then, with no warning at all, my great-grandmother screeched to a halt in the middle of the street. Since cars made in 1956 didn't come equipped with seat belts, I would have crashed through the windshield if I hadn't thrown my hands, palms out, in front of me.

"Merciful Athena," she hushed, gazing upward.

I followed her line of sight to the easternmost corner of the school, the science wing, which seemed to be weaving. Before

Gram could shut off the engine, I was out of the car. I felt a faint vibration under my feet. That was all it was, nothing like an earthquake or anything, just a vague buzz radiating out from the ground near the school.

And then, in another second, it seemed, the earth just opened up and the whole corner of the building started to tumble into the rapidly expanding hole.

"Katy!" I heard Gram scream from inside the car. It was Sunday, so there weren't many people on the street—only me and Gram in her car and, unfortunately, a family of six who'd just turned the corner onto Front Street. They were all dressed up and talking excitedly to one another. I doubt if they felt the ground or, a moment later, saw the cascade of falling bricks heading straight for them.

"The wand!" Gram shrieked.

Looking back, this whole incident probably took less than three seconds, but at the time, it felt as if everything were happening in slow motion, as if I were running through melted marshmallows.

With what seemed to me like frustrating slowness I pulled the rowan wand out of my sleeve and flicked it toward the falling building, shouting, "Stop!" and willing them to halt in midair. I can honestly say that for that moment, every cell in my brain, every muscle in my body, and every molecule of blood in my veins was focused entirely on those falling bricks, willing them to defy gravity.

It didn't work, of course, at least not perfectly. The building continued to tumble, along with a lot of broken glass, wood, books, metal plumbing, and several stone tabletops from the crumbling chemistry lab. But—and this is a big *but*, since I may not have been perceiving things correctly—they seemed to be falling a lot more slowly than they had been.

At any rate my scream at least alerted the people who'd been walking in the path of the descending rubble. To their great good fortune, they were witches. As soon as they looked up and saw the building coming down, all six of them automatically threw out five fingers while simultaneously ducking out of the way.

From my vantage point the bricks, falling slowly as flower petals on a gentle breeze, changed their trajectory slightly and curved away from the six pedestrians, who were scrambling for shelter like frantic mice. That was the thing: *They* were moving fast, but the bricks were falling very, very slowly. That's what didn't make sense, in the context of what happened next.

After the bricks and assorted debris had all hit the ground in a deafening cloud that surrounded the gaping sinkhole, the people who'd been walking by the school came out of their hiding places under the trees and park benches on the other side of the street. There were two adults and four girls in the group, all of them looking pale and shaky. As I ran up to them to ask if they were all right, I recognized one of the girls.

Becca Fowler. She and all the other females in the group were dressed in what were either floor-length gowns or something like wizards' robes. They were probably on their way to the Meadow, so that Mrs. Fowler could get things ready for the Lammas festival.

"Everyone okay here?" I called out, waving to them.

Becca was brushing furiously at a grass stain on her long skirt. "I'll see that you go to prison for this!" Mrs. Fowler spat, quivering in her long gown like a custard.

"What?" I was stunned. "The building was—"

"You destroyed your own school for the sake of some . . . some *joke!*"

"Joke? No. No, ma'am," I said. "There was a sinkhole. You and your family turned the corner just as—"

"I saw her," Becca chimed in. "She used a *wand.*"

There was a murmur. I looked around. People who lived on the square were starting to come out of their houses to peer at the wreckage on the street.

Mrs. Fowler pointed at me, wild-eyed. "She tried to kill us!" she shouted.

More murmuring.

"Now, wait a second," I said. "How can you possibly say—"

"She used a wand to make the building fall as we were walking by."

"That's not true! I was trying to stop it."

"Well, you weren't very successful, were you?" Mrs. Fowler narrowed her eyes. "You probably stole the wand in the first place."

"I did not!"

"Children do not own or use wands!" she insisted.

"I think she did all right," an old man in the crowd said. "There was a sinkhole, that's for sure. I watched it open up."

"Right. She slowed the fall of the building with that wand," someone else added.

"Good use of magic, if you ask me."

"Oh, really?" Livia Fowler's face was an ugly mask now, her thin red lips forming sharp lines. "Do you know who she is?"

Murmuring speculation. "Cowen" seemed to come up a lot. So did "Agatha Ainsworth" and "crazy". But naturally, Mrs.

Fowler answered her own question. "She is the evil spawn of an evil mother, and possessed of an evil spirit!" she roared, her stentorian voice cutting through all the other sounds on the street.

"Hey, she's the one sent that fireball on Samhain, wasn't she?"

"She most certainly was!" chimed Becca.

"That wasn't me," I said, trying to defend myself, although I doubt if anyone could hear me above all the talk circulating through the crowd.

"I suppose you're going to blame little Eric Shaw for that, too!" Mrs. Fowler gloated.

Low blow. Especially since it was true.

"She was carrying on a blue streak at the hospital, trying to scare everyone to death. She'd say anything, this one, put the blame on anyone except herself."

"That had nothing to do with you, Livia Fowler." I recognized the voice before I spotted Gram making her way through the gathering crowd. "You don't know what you're talking about."

Mrs. Fowler puffed herself up defensively.

"I was there. You weren't." Gram took me by the hand. "As for the building falling, this child saved your miserable neck, you ungrateful . . . *usurper*."

Mrs. Fowler's face scrunched up like a baby about to have a tantrum. "For your information, your precious Hattie Scott declared *herself* incompetent to serve as high priestess!" she shouted, turning to address the crowd. "Moreover, she's been *arrested* for beating her ward, Peter Shaw, while the other Shaw boy is dying from whatever she's been doing to him!"

It was suddenly getting to be too much for me to take. "Take that back, you *bitch*!" I shouted.

There was a collective intake of breath.

"How dare you," Mrs. Fowler seethed, her ample jowls quivering.

Becca came at me like a Mack truck. "You're the bitch!" she snarled, launching herself at me in a flying leap.

I closed my eyes and braced myself for the attack. One second went by, two . . . Carefully I squinted open one eye. Becca was hanging in midair like a stuffed tiger in a taxidermist's. Then slowly she drifted toward the ground, her arms still flung out in front of her, their fingers poised to scratch my eyes out.

I turned toward my great-grandmother. She was standing with her hands on her hips, shaking her head and *tsk*-ing. She had performed the most powerful binding spell I—and probably anyone else—had ever seen, without even throwing out five fingers.

"Awesome," I breathed.

"Minor, very minor," she answered.

The rest of the Fowlers were staring at Becca's slowly descending body in openmouthed wonder as Gram raised her chin slightly and Becca drifted onto her feet. Released from the binding spell, she examined her hands.

"We'll go now," my great-grandmother said.

As we walked back toward the car I heard Becca call out, "She told me she's going to finish the job her mother started!"

"Keep silent," Gram whispered to me.

I obeyed, although I felt as if all the blood in my body had gone into my face.

Two tourists, a couple, gave me an amused look as I got into the Cadillac. "What the heck was that about?" the man asked his companion.

"*Levitation,*" she answered in a *Tales From the Crypt* voice.

"Ooh. Scary. And was there something about a high priestess?"

"I couldn't hear all of it. I thought someone mentioned a magic wand, though."

"You've got to be kidding."

"It's part of the experience. This is 'witch central', after all."

They walked by, laughing.

"Those were *cowen,*" I said quietly. Livia Fowler had allowed total outsiders to watch us.

Back at the Bean mansion, Miss P and Hattie were waiting for us. Each of them was sitting in a straight-backed chair, looking like kids who'd been summoned to the principal's office.

"Oh, dear," Gram said. "Katy, go make some tea."

"I think she should stay," Miss P said quickly. "And tea won't be necessary."

I looked from one to the other. Miss P looked anxious. Hattie's face had no expression at all. Gram nodded subtly. I sat down.

After a long silence, Miss P spoke. "Who besides us knows about the situation with Eric Shaw?" she asked.

"Peter," I said.

"Agnes," Mrs. Ainsworth said.

"We'll have to tell the others before long." She saw me tense and added, "Once we're sure."

"We have to find another way . . ." I began. All three women turned toward me at the same time, with the same *if you say another word I'm going to brain you* expression. I drifted into silence.

"Are you all right, Hattie, dear?" Gram asked.

Hattie gave a dismissive wave of her hand.

"She was held for questioning," Miss P said. "It was a formality that was necessary because of what appeared to be Peter's attempted . . ." She looked at me uncertainly.

"He cut his wrists," Hattie said irritably. "Katy knows that."

I felt my heart clutching.

"And it was my fault," Hattie continued. "This is *all* my fault."

"Now, stop that, Hattie," Gram said. "None of this is anybody's fault."

"No," Hattie said. "It didn't just happen. I should have known. Peter suffered for so long without saying a word . . ." She squeezed her eyes shut and took a deep breath. "I *did* know about what had happened to Eric. Prescott Shaw was full of the Darkness," she recalled bitterly. "It was so thick on him, you could almost smell it. And when he died and that precious baby fell right on top of him to take in that poor fool's dying breath . . ."

With impatient hands she wiped at her eyes. "I knew. But then, when nothing happened . . . of course, why would it? Eric was just an infant. Even the Darkness can't turn a baby evil. They're God's, through and through, till they get smart enough to let things get at them. Least, that's what I thought."

"Hattie . . ."

"And nothing happened. For a long time. He was just a sweet

little baby, that's all." She squeezed her eyes shut and waved her hands in front of her, as if she were trying to erase ten years of memories. "Except sometimes he looked so, so scared. I would hold him close and tell him everything was fine, but he knew. Those little eyes . . . And then it started. Thought it must have been my imagination at first, or something with the light, giving a glint to them. Sometimes they'd stop looking scared, and they'd roll back in his head like he was taking a fit, and when he'd open them again . . . Well, I knew it wasn't him anymore. Eyes like fire. Laughing. . . ." Her voice broke. "Like the devil from Hell . . ."

"Oh, my dear," Gram said, putting her arm around Hattie. "All this time you've borne this burden alone."

Hattie turned away. "I had to, Elizabeth. Sooner or later it would have gotten out, the way it's going to now, and my little boy—"

"That's not going to happen!" I said, a little too loudly. But I didn't care. "We're not going to let anyone hurt him. You're the most powerful witches in Whitfield."

"Which is why we have to consider the whole community," Miss P said softly.

"The Darkness is winning," Hattie said. "Over the years I've seen it get stronger and stronger inside Eric. Your mama, Katy—she saw it right away. Took one look at him across that store, and she knew. It was like a firefight, the energy those two were sending each other."

She shook her head. "When she started walking toward us that day in Wonderland, it was like the air started crackling. I tried to get my boys out of there, away from Agatha, but I couldn't move fast enough. I begged her, please don't, please don't hurt my baby."

She put her hand to her throat. "By the time she got close enough for me to see her face clearly, I saw that she was crying. I said again, 'please, Agatha, I'm your best friend' . . . tears were streaming down her face and she was shaking all over when she reached out for Eric. She said, 'who else is going to do it?' And then she looked me in the eye and said, 'You know.'"

Hattie's eyes looked out, unfocused, remembering. "She tried to take him. Fought me for him. I would have killed her if I could, I'll tell you that, God have mercy. But I was at a disadvantage, holding the baby. And Agatha had power."

Her mouth set into a grim line. "So that was that. She took him out of my arms and threw him against a pile of lumber, and then, while everybody in the store started screaming, she walked away like nothing had happened.

"Except everything happened. Eric didn't die, but Agatha did. Set herself on fire like a damned Buddhist monk. But in the end, she died for nothing."

It was hard for me to breathe. My mother had tried to bring the Darkness into herself by killing Eric and seeing to it that she was the closest person to him when he died.

Gram looked miserable. "How you must hate her," she said quietly.

Hattie looked up, her face riven with tears. "Hate her?" she asked. "How could I hate Agatha? I loved her. Loved her, Elizabeth. She was my sister in every way but blood. Who else would have done what she did?"

We all stared at her, puzzled.

"I *knew*. Don't you see? *I* was the one who should have killed Eric. I was high priestess. It was my duty to the community to keep everyone safe. But I couldn't do it. So I kept it to myself. I kept telling myself that I'd find a way, just like this one is saying now." She motioned toward me with her chin. "But Agatha knew there was no other way."

Her lip trembled. She clenched her jaw tight, still fighting the tears that she couldn't stop. "So Agatha took it on herself to do what had to be done, even though she knew it would cost her her life. She accepted the horror that would have come to Eric sooner or later."

"The burning," Gram whispered.

"There's no worse way to die," Hattie went on, anguished. "She was trying to save Eric from that."

"And save the rest of us from the Darkness," Miss P added.

"Only things didn't work out that clean," Hattie said. "Eric lived, but turned out so brain-damaged that the Darkness couldn't even get hold of his mind. Isn't that something?" She smiled crookedly. "I thought the Lord had given me another chance. If Eric couldn't *think*, then the Darkness couldn't use him." She squeezed her eyes shut, shook her head, then opened them again. "That's the way it's been for ten years. I thought I'd found what I've been praying for since the minute Prescott Shaw died in my house." She stood up and paced around like a nervous cat. "There was just one thing told me that evil was still inside that little boy."

"The drawings," I whispered.

"You know it." She went over to the fireplace and rested both hands on the mantel. "Those pictures—*that* was Eric, trying to tell me he was still fighting in there, warning me— warning us all . . ."

"That ability, his genius—"

"All his," she said. "Even with his mind so messed up, he can draw like Leonardo. The devil himself can't touch that gift." She rested her head on her folded arms. "When we kill him—when *I* kill him—I'm going to kill that, too."

I stood up. "You're not going to kill him, Hattie," I said as calmly as I could. "And you're not going to kill yourself. We're going to find a way out of this."

"*How*?" She glared at me, her eyes like fire.

"Peter . . ." I stumbled. "Peter said he had a plan . . ."

"A plan!" she spat. "What kind of plan does a sixteen-year-old boy come up with?"

"He at least deserves to be listened to, before you light the bonfire!"

"Stop it, both of you!" Gram snapped.

Hattie and I looked at each other, our eyes welling, both our hearts breaking, and then we ran into each other's arms and held on to each other fiercely. "I'm sorry, Hattie," I whispered. "I wouldn't hurt you for anything."

"Hush, child," she said. "I'm half out of my mind just now."

"Still, we'll find a way."

She pushed me gently away from her. "I need to get back to Eric. He's been alone all this time."

"Gracious," Gram said. "The poor thing."

"He's asleep most of the time now," Hattie said dully. "The thing inside him is building its strength. And my baby is dying."

Time seemed to stop for a moment as we all realized how far things had already gone.

"You shouldn't be with him—with *them*—alone," Miss P said. "I'll go with you."

"You?" Gram exclaimed. "A djinn? No, no, Penelope, you're much too valuable. One whiff of what you are, and the Darkness will do anything to infect you." She dabbed her face with her handkerchief. "I'll go. It isn't going to be interested in an old woman with small talents and a short future."

"I will, too," I said. "It already knows me."

"No," Hattie said. "You're too young." Miss P agreed. The two of them were headed toward the door when my great-grandmother spoke.

"I think she should go," she said.

The others turned to face her.

"Peter will talk to her."

"But Peter's in the—"

"Oh, I forgot to tell you. Agnes is bringing him to your house."

"She is?" Hattie asked, confused. "But we just decided to leave a minute ago."

"I know. I only just told Agnes. She's on her way, and Peter's with her." She cast a stern glance at me. "And don't ask," she said. "He's fine."

"But . . ." Hattie shook her head. "How was he released? I never told anyone at the hospital to let him go."

"Well . . . they don't exactly know he's gone yet," Gram said. She smiled sweetly. "Don't worry. Stay here, Penelope."

"But Katy shouldn't . . ."

"No, of course she shouldn't. But she will." The old lady leveled me with her gaze. "Won't you." It was not a question.

"Yes, ma'am," I answered truthfully.

She took a deep, exasperated breath. "That's what I thought," she said. "At least Hattie and I will be with you this time."

Chapter

·

Thirty-six

 ORACLE

When I'd sneaked up to Hattie's rented house at night, it hadn't looked so bad, but up close in the light of day, it was pretty much a wreck. The cement steps were falling apart, the lawn was overgrown, and paint was peeling everywhere. Inside was even worse: Drab, dark, and smelling of stale grease, it looked as if it had been occupied by transients. There was no trace of the vibrant woman who had run Hattie's Kitchen like a great ship.

There was no love here, only fear.

Hattie turned on a wall switch and an overhead light came on, two naked bulbs in a fixture without a shade. It illuminated the pillows of dust gathered at the foot of the stairs.

"Follow me," she said lifelessly as she trudged up to the bedrooms.

I felt myself sweating in the humid, airless hallway. We passed an open door behind which was a room with a dusty computer on a desk with a few books piled beside it. The bed had been hastily covered by a brown blanket. Along the wall were several boxes, never unpacked, and a headboard for the bed, never assembled. It was a room that no one had planned to stay in very long.

Peter's room.

"Eric?" Hattie had stopped at the door at the far end and knocked.

"Maaaaaa," came a sleepy voice.

She walked in. My great-grandmother and I followed her.

The air was thick here, hard to breathe. In one corner, opposite the window, was the straight-backed chair where I'd seen Peter in so many of my dreams, where he'd sat the night I saw him with the Darkness. This was where it spoke to him, where it had flayed the skin off Peter's back. This was where all the secrets had originated.

In the narrow bed occupying the center of the room, with hospital bars enclosing its sides, a ten-year-old boy struggled to sit upright.

"Ma," Eric said faintly, rubbing his eyes and smiling.

"I've got your supper," Hattie said gently, opening up her pocketbook. Inside was a plastic bag with a jar of baby food and a small spoon. "Let's see, what do we have today?" She squinted to read the label. "Turkey with garden vegetables. Sound good?"

She opened the lid with a loud pop that made Eric giggle.

"Yum yum?"

"Yum," he answered, laughing.

I felt my eyes welling. My mind revolved around a single thought: *Not him. Oh God, please, not him.*

How long did the Darkness have to work to get that little

broken body out of this bed, I wondered. Two years? Five? Evil was persistent.

I wiped my face. Well, so was I. It wasn't going to keep this little boy. Not as long as I was alive.

Suddenly Eric noticed me. "Kaaay!" he shouted, spraying baby food all over Hattie. What didn't land on her dribbled down his chin. "Kaaay!" He held out his arms and I ran into them, hugging him.

"Katy," Gram said, her voice cautious. "Maybe you oughtn't . . ."

But I knew I was all right. I knew that as long as I held on to Eric, that connection wouldn't—couldn't—be broken.

I think it was because I loved him. Yes, that was it. I loved him. And he loved me.

"Kaaay?" It was a question, sly and playful. It meant, *Want to see something cool?*

"Uh-*huh*!" I answered emphatically, hanging on to one of his hands while he flapped around his bed with the other. Finally he came up with a crumpled piece of paper under his pillow, along with a blue crayon that had marked his sheet in a number of places. He thrust the drawing at me.

"Great," I said, taking it with one hand. "Let me see that."

The sight sent shivers through me. Because this time it wasn't birds, or sinkholes, or any of Eric's usual subjects. It was a drawing unlike any he'd ever made before: With his customary meticulousness, he had drawn an *island*. It was surrounded by a roiling ocean beneath a lightning-filled sky. On the island was a house engulfed in flames, and beside it lay two charred human bodies, face down and clearly dead. Next to them stood a stick figure with a crude circle for a head and jack-o'-lantern features. It was a child's version of a monster, so out of keeping with the articulate perfection of the rest of the drawing. And it was all in blue, like a scene from a nightmare.

"What is it, Katy?" Gram asked.

I looked from her to Hattie, not knowing what to say, what to think.

"Kaaay?" Eric's eyes were pleading with me.

"Thank you," I whispered, kissing his forehead.

The door opened behind me, and Eric shrieked in delight as Agnes and Peter walked in.

"Hey, buddy," Peter said, heading for Eric. "Ladies." His eyes held mine for a moment. He was so pale that I could see blue veins under his skin. His wrists were bound with thick white bandages. His long fingers trembled as they reached for his brother.

I wanted to run into his arms, to kiss his face, his wounds, to hold him and never let him go. But I stayed where I was while Eric struggled to stand up in his bed, shaking me off to embrace Peter.

Agnes and Gram were talking quietly to each other. Hattie was picking up a pile of Eric's T-shirts that were stacked on a chair. Peter's head was resting alongside his brother's.

So it was that only I saw Eric's eyes begin to roll back in his head and his tongue loll out.

"Eric!" I thrust myself between them, grabbing Eric's hands in my own. "Come back!" I shouted. Peter stepped back, startled. "Eric, listen to me. *You stay here,* understand?"

"Kaaay…"

"I'm here," I said.

"Put him down." Hattie's voice had an edge of hysteria in it. "You don't know what he can do."

"He's here, with me," I said.

His head fell back.

"Don't go," I whispered.

His mouth opened, and a garbled mishmash of sounds spilled out.

The others were all talking at once now, but I couldn't spare them any of my attention. Every fiber of my being was focused on keeping Eric connected to me.

I closed my eyes to go more deeply into that connection. What I saw was a red swirl of torment. Anger and blood, and beyond them a power so profound and ancient that I couldn't begin to assess its depths. Like a distant galaxy seen through a telescope, the Darkness whirled somewhere in those depths.

"Eric," I whispered, willing the boy to me. "Come."

Through the blackness of space, past the image of that nebula of evil, I saw, rising out of the violent red whirlpool, a spark of light. Like the seed of summer born in the cold of midwinter, grew the light emanating from inside Eric—a light that even the Darkness, with all its power, had not been able to extinguish.

"Eric."

It glowed bigger and brighter, until it filled the vista of my consciousness, filled me completely. I opened my eyes. Eric was bathed in light, his face transfigured.

The others stood speechless. Hattie dropped the pile of clothes she was holding. Peter swallowed. The light grew, filling the room.

And then, with the voice of an angel, Eric spoke.

"*Eric,*" he said.

"Eric," I repeated. "Your true name." How hard had it been, I wondered, for him to utter that one word, filled with enough magic to dispel the greatest evil force on earth?

He held his arms out to his brother, and Peter hugged him. "I love you, buddy," he said. "I should never have thought of leaving you," he said hoarsely. "I'm sorry."

Eric kissed him, as somberly as an archbishop. Then he fell back on his bed, curled into a ball, and slept.

We all stood in silence, all of us wanting to ask the same question. I was the one who finally did ask it.

"Why did you do it, Peter?"

He shuffled, blushing, clearing his throat. "He told me . . ."

"He?" Hattie asked archly.

"Eric," Peter whispered. "He said that I was going to be a . . ."

"Go ahead," I prodded.

He sighed. "A great leader," he said. "That there was going to be a crisis in Whitfield, and people would look to me to save them."

"Say *what?*" Hattie looked as if she couldn't even believe what she was hearing.

"And I would be guided by . . . someone."

"Your girlfriend?" Hattie guessed, wagging her head.

"Well . . . yes." He gave me an apologetic look. "He said she'd be a great witch. The most powerful of magicians."

Hattie crossed her arms. "And what exactly was going to happen once you two geniuses took over the world?"

"It wasn't like that, Hattie. He didn't mean we'd—"

"Just spit it out, Peter."

"Well . . ." His voice cracked. "He said we'd fail."

Hattie's eyes narrowed. "Now, let me get this straight. You tried to kill yourself because your little brother, with half a brain and not enough sense to feed himself, and who incidentally just said his name for the first time in his life, said you were going to mess something up sometime in the far distant future?"

"It wasn't Eric. It was the Darkness speaking."

"Oh, excuse me," Hattie said. "It was the Darkness. A voice you can always trust."

Peter's eyes flashed. "Don't you see? It was what was going to happen once the Darkness transferred from Eric to me. That meant that Eric would be dead. I'd have killed him, and corrupted Katy. With the power I'd have, I was going to destroy Whitfield and everyone in it, and it was all going to look like an accident!" He was breathing hard. "That's why I tried to kill myself. To keep that from happening." He glanced at Hattie and the others. "You shouldn't have called the ambulance," he said, his voice ragged. "You shouldn't have saved me."

Hattie strode over to Peter and slapped him hard across his face. "So that's why you cut your wrists?" she shrilled. "Why you broke my heart? Because the Darkness—the *Darkness*, Peter—been telling you to?"

"It wasn't telling me—"

"It's saying you're going to be some big bad boss man, and this girl going to be casting mighty spells to help you. Are you stupid?"

She shoved him backward. "Peter Shaw, you of all people ought to know what the Darkness can do! It can talk in any voice it wants, and it'll say anything it wants you to hear. 'Evil leader,'" she scoffed. "What foolishness!"

"Hattie . . ." It was Agnes, looking worried and thoughtful. "It might have been a true prediction."

"From the Darkness?" She flapped a hand at Agnes. "Mercy, you're as bad as he is."

"It can happen." Agnes looked at the other. "Everything he said."

"Can the Darkness foretell the future?" I asked.

Gram wasn't smiling anymore. "The Darkness can do anything," she said.

Agnes nodded. "Right now, its only restriction is Eric's body. If we can't find a way to take it out of Eric, it will find its way to a stronger body. And a stronger mind. If that happens, I don't know what it will be capable of. Certainly, the scenario that Peter presented would be a possibility."

"But the future can be changed," Gram said. "In this case, it has to be, because it's no longer just Eric. Peter will be affected too. And Katy." She looked at me. "We've always known you would be a great witch, dear. But once you grow into your power, you could use it in destructive ways, if you chose."

"Don't fill the girl's head with nonsense, Elizabeth," Hattie warned. "The last thing we need is for these two fools to be strutting around like barnyard roosters."

"I fear the opposite will happen, Hattie," Agnes said. "If the community finds out about this, no one will ever trust Peter or Katy. They'll certainly never allow either of them to assume any positions of leadership, given this prediction."

"If the community finds out about this, it won't matter," I said flatly. "Because they're still going to burn Eric."

"And maybe the two of us along with him," Peter said.

"What I don't understand is the drawing," Gram said.

"Who are the two figures in it who appear to be dead?"

"And the third," Agnes added. "The monster. Is it the Darkness? Or Peter, after fulfilling the prophecy? And why an island?"

Eric wailed and twisted around in his bed. Hattie ran over to him. "What is it, honey?" she asked, stroking his hair. Sleepy-eyed, his head wagging in a constant figure eight, he slowly pulled himself along the bars of the bed until he was sitting up.

"Baby?" Hattie swept his sweat-soaked hair to the side.

His mouth opened and closed several times. "Kaa . . ." He stumbled. "Kaaay . . ."

"I'm here, Eric," I said, taking his hand. "Go ahead. I'm listening."

"Kaaay . . ." He started to tremble all over.

"Eric?" Hattie was reaching down for him. "Eric?"

"*Ola,*" he breathed, his voice like a feather on the wind. He looked at me. *In* me, deeply, as if to ask, *Do you understand?*

"Ola?" I asked. "Ola'ea?"

"Ola'ea?" Hattie repeated.

Eric patted my hand. Patted it, like an elderly uncle rewarding me for learning my times tables. Then he slumped back onto his pillow.

Hattie and I looked at each other. "Clear out," she said at last. "All of you, let my baby sleep while he can. I'll see you all downstairs in a few minutes."

Hattie came into the living room, where we were all standing in a circle. The naked bulb overhead cast long, ghoulish shadows on the walls. "Well?" she began. "Where do we go from here?"

"We need to get to the Meadow," I said.

The others looked at me as if I were crazy. "For Lammas?" Gram asked.

"That'll be over," I said. "The place will be empty."

"Yes?" Agnes waited.

"We have to open *The Great Book of Secrets*."

Hattie narrowed her eyes. "I've heard enough of this," she said. "Do you know how much effort it would take to retrieve the book?"

"It's a very complex spell," Gram said.

"We need to," I argued. "For Eric. We've got to study the 'Song of Unmaking'."

"Why? We all know what it says!" Hattie put her hands on her hips. "Except for you. You don't know anything. You just think you do."

"I know that Eric said 'Ola'ea'."

"Oh, he did not."

"I think he did, Hattie," Agnes said.

Hattie exhaled noisily. "So? What's the connection?"

Agnes bit her lip. "She wrote the 'Song of Unmaking'. We might know more if we knew the circumstances that prompted her to create the spell."

My heart was racing. Thank God for Agnes. "Yes," I said. "There has to be more to the 'Song of Unmaking' than we've—you've— seen."

Gram clucked. "Burning . . . Such a cruel, crude solution."

"It wasn't Ola'ea's way," Hattie said. "Why would that brilliant witch write a spell—one that had to be *sung*, no less—that just said to get rid of the Darkness' victims by setting them on fire like soulless logs?"

"Precisely. She wouldn't," I said.

Agnes looked at me, frowning.

"It's a long story, but what it comes down to is that Ola'ea wouldn't allow innocent people—and certainly not children—to be burned to death."

We all sat in silence for a moment. Finally Gram spoke. "Well, none of us is getting any younger," she said. "Especially me. Shall we try to open *The Great Book of Secrets*?"

I felt a surge like electricity run through me. "Yes," I whispered.

"Not so fast," Agnes said. "There's a problem."

"Oh?" We all asked in unison.

"To open the book, we'll need all three verses of the spell."

"Huh?" I asked. "Another spell?"

"It requires three stages," my great-grandmother reminded me. "Agnes and I have the words that bring about the first stage. They're embroidered on that hanging over the fireplace."

"Oh. Right."

"And Hattie has the second verse."

"Memorized," Hattie said. "Since I was five years old."

"Well, who else has the third verse?" Gram asked. "Who could we trust to help us open the Book?"

Hattie looked at her watch. "And at this time of night . . ."

"Hold it!" Peter said. Everyone looked up. I think we'd all but forgotten he was even there. He pulled his cell phone out of his pocket and began to click through its applications. "Remember the blanket in the Shaw mansion, Katy?" he asked. "In the bedroom?"

"Gracious!" my great-grandmother exclaimed. "What were the two of you—"

"Yes!" I remembered. "In the compartment under the floorboards."

"Here it is." Looking at the screen, he read, "*The wise and Crafty know rightly where to look . . .*"

"That's it," Agnes said.

"Camera phones," Peter said, tapping the phone with a triumphant grin. "The biggest advance in witchcraft in a thousand years."

Gram dashed over to him and pinched his cheeks. "Darling boy," she said. "You didn't really plan to kill yourself, did you?" she asked softly.

Peter shook his head. "It was just all I could think of to do. I don't have much magic. The Darkness wanted my life. The only way I could keep him from getting it was . . ." He looked down at his bandaged wrists.

"We understand, dear. But you need to stay among us."

"Mrs. Ainsworth . . ." He was frowning in concentration. "My wrists."

"What is it, Peter?"

"They're . . . That is, I can feel . . . " He yanked off the adhesive tape on one arm and began to unravel the gauze.

"Peter!" Hattie shouted. "What in blazes . . ."

As the last of the wrapping fell away, he held out his bare wrist for all of us to see. The wound had healed completely. There was not even a scar to indicate that the skin had ever been broken.

"Good heavens," Gram said.

"What do you mean, 'good heavens'?" Hattie demanded. "You're the one who did it, Elizabeth."

"Did what?" The old woman looked confused. "Do you think I healed the cut on that wrist?"

"And this one," Peter said, displaying his other arm.

"I . . . well, I don't know. I suppose I may have." She raised her eyebrows. "I wasn't conscious of it, though."

"That's all right," Agnes said, putting her arm around her grandmother. "One of the perks of age is that you don't have to remember all your good deeds."

"I suppose," Gram conceded. "That's quite a good job, though. If I do say so myself."

Hattie harrumphed. "Never could toot your own horn worth spit," she said. "I'll go get Eric."

The rest of us looked up in horror. What if Eric became possessed by the Darkness in the Meadow?

"I can't leave him alone again," Hattie explained.

No one moved.

"The doctor gave me a sedative in a filled hypodermic in case he gets too agitated," she added quietly.

I saw Agnes look to her grandmother.

"I'm sure you won't need to use it, dear," Gram said. She always had the right words.

Hattie took the kit, enclosed in a small case, out of her handbag and tucked it into Peter's shirt pocket. "I'll let you know if I need it," she told him.

"Okay," he said. "I'll help you get him ready," The two of them bounded up the squeaky steps.

"To the Meadow, then," Gram said. "Have Penelope meet us," she told Agnes. "She ought to be safe there. And you might perhaps alert a few others, as well." Her gaze drifted up the stairs, where Eric was being dressed. "One never knows when one may be in need of friends."

CHAPTER

·

THIRTY-SEVEN

 THE BOOK OF SECRETS

To avoid notice, Agnes put Gram's Caddy back in the garage and the three of us walked to the Meadow, where we met Peter and Hattie, who carried Eric between them. We all tried to make our way as inconspicuously as possible past the DO NOT ENTER signs posted all around the Wonderland construction site. As it appeared that night, it certainly didn't look much like a sacred sanctuary for witches.

Apparently, work had ceased when the fog began to roll in. Caught off guard as usual, the workmen had simply put down their tools and supplies—even their lunches—and groped their way out of the Meadow, which would lie fallow and unreachable until the fog lifted in a day or two.

It was one of many complaints about the work site. Aside from the on-again, off-again incidence of sinkholes, fires, dead birds that seemingly appeared out of nowhere to litter the place with their ghoulish carcasses, and groundwater leaks that forced the men to work in specially designed rubber gear, the fog—which appeared to cowen to occur at random—was too impenetrable to work in. Just completing the construction, regardless of schedule, was getting to be a real problem, according to local gossip.

But none of that affected us, I told myself as we picked our way through the darkness. The moment we stepped into the fog, the filthy, obstacle-covered floor gave way to green grass on a woodland grave. This was the Meadow as it was in Serenity's time, and had been preserved through magic. It would never change, not for us. Not unless we ourselves changed it through magic.

"It's somewhere around here, isn't it?" Gram asked.

"Five paces from the oak tree, facing the west boulder," Hattie answered impatiently, setting Eric down on a blanket near a moss-covered rock. I helped Hattie get him settled, then gave him a juice box. He was asleep within five minutes.

"Hurry up, Katy," Agnes called. "We don't want this to take forever."

"Oh, dear," Gram said. "I wonder what the others would say? It is supposed to be a community spell, you know. Quite formal."

"Well, it'll have to be informal this time," Miss P said, emerging out of the fog. Mr. Haversall was with her, and Dingo the dog, who went straight to Eric and sat beside him. A few others joined the circle.

Hattie stood beside Miss P. "If anything happens . . ." She looked pointedly at Peter, who nodded and patted the syringe in his shirt pocket.

"It won't," Miss P said reassuringly. "We're in the safest place on the planet."

I wasn't so sure.

"Quickly," Agnes said, calling everyone together. We all held hands. Peter was beside me, and the touch of his hand was like liquid velvet, cool and dry.

"*In the alban field, the circling mists twist low*," Agnes began. My great-grandmother and a couple of the others joined her.

> "*Kith and kin draw the rock on Crafted bow.*
> *Arise, great Arrow, swift as sparrow, sprung from below.*"

We stood in silence for a long time. I wondered if the other people here were making more sense of the words than I did, because I still didn't have the slightest idea what they meant. Actually, I was beginning to think the spell was a dud, when Dingo started barking.

The air in the center of the circle shimmered, as if we were enclosing some powerful heat source. Then the ground began to tremble.

"Oh, man, it's a sinkhole," I whispered, remembering the horrible scene at the school earlier.

"Shh," Peter said.

The air in the circle got thicker and thicker until it looked like gelatin, and the earth swayed in a gentle wave that was nothing like the eruption on the street outside the school. All the trees shimmered so that their leaves turned backward and shone like silver. Then Dingo stopped barking and, staring up at the full moon, pointed his nose straight up and howled.

No, not howled, exactly . . . It was more like singing. It was beautiful. Everything was beautiful then. For a moment—and

I have no idea how long that moment lasted in real time—the whole Meadow seemed to be in sync. The wind, the trees, the rocks and water and grass, the night clouds and the moon. All of it went together perfectly, making its own music. Above it Dingo's voice—and it really was a voice, not a howl—floated like a soloist in front of an orchestra.

The music grew louder as the earth shuddered and trembled, until finally it thrust from its depths a rock the size of a car and four times as tall, black as basalt and pointed near the top like the "arrow" in the conjuring verse.

We all stood there dumbstruck, as into the silence came Hattie's smooth low voice, intoning the second verse of the spell from memory:

> *The kindred wave gathers to loose what is hidden.*
> *Cast line and hook to split the stony mizzen.*
> *One door wakes one thousand more when Craftily bidden.*

Immediately, the huge stone seemed to fly apart with a tremendous noise like the origin of thunder. The rock shimmered and shook, its surface crazing into sinuous lines that made it look like some gigantic, three-dimensional jigsaw puzzle.

And then, with an awesome elegance, the cracks in the rock segmented, the sections flew apart, and the puzzle box opened, revealing a thousand separate closed compartments.

"A botte," I whispered, feeling gooseflesh traveling throughout the length of my body.

"Fantastic," Peter said.

"Peter, now!" It was Hattie, gesturing at him animatedly with her chin.

"What? Oh." Quickly he took his cell phone out of his hip pocket. By its eerie light he read the final verse of the spell.

The wise and Crafty know rightly where to look.
O Word! Spring forth from out thy secret nook.
Ferree Ferraugh diten al blosun na tibuk!

He struggled through the unfamiliar words, and didn't employ a lot of dramatic expression, but it worked.

The drawers and cabinets all shifted around again, forming and reforming into impossible combinations as the shape of the botte changed slightly with each small movement. It was a bizarre display, moving faster and faster until the whole process seemed to be a blur.

While it was in motion, Hattie stepped forward and intoned: "Attend me, ye greater and lesser spirits!" She lifted her arms into the air. "Bring into being the 'Song of Unmaking'!"

And then suddenly, abruptly, absolutely, the botte came to a dead stop.

One drawer, situated in its direct center, snapped open with perfect precision to reveal the only object it contained: An ancient, gilt-edged book bound in frayed leather. There were no words on its cover, only the image of a crescent moon stamped in silver. When struck by the moonlight in the sky above the Meadow, it gleamed with an almost living luster.

"The *Great Book of Secrets*," my great-grandmother said. A responsive murmur rose from everyone assembled. After the wild motion of the botte, the *Great Book of Secrets* exuded a deep gravity, seeming almost to breathe in time to the cosmic music that still permeated the copse where we stood.

Hattie touched the book with the tips of her fingers and spoke: "It is our deepest desire to harm none while protecting our own from the Darkness," she said. "Therefore, with humility and respect, we seek the meaning of the 'Song of Unmaking', and ask to be shown its right use."

The music grew louder as the book opened by itself and its pages turned rapidly, as if blown by a strong wind. When it finally fell still, the music rose all around us, beautiful and hypnotic. Dingo the dog sat up again, reverentially, and crooned his own wild song that went perfectly with the rest of the strange earth-music around us. That was the meaning of harmony, I realized: Everything fitting together, belonging, being exactly where the universe wanted all its pieces.

So it was strange and . . . well, *shocking*, really, when Hattie and Agnes and just about everyone else in the circle started singing this other weird song that didn't fit at all with the earth-music I was hearing.

Dingo didn't like it either. He stopped singing and laid his head down on his paws, but apparently we were the only ones it bothered. Even Peter started to sing the ugly song.

I poked him with my elbow. "What the heck are you singing?" I hissed.

He shrugged. "It's what everybody's taught in kindergarten," he whispered back. "The 'Song of Unmaking' is pretty basic witchcraft."

"But it's . . ." I saw Hattie giving us the stink eye, so I shut up. But there was something jarring about it all. The leaves on the trees turned right-side up again. The air around the botte lost its thick, shimmering quality and, at least for me, the music—the *real* music—diminished to nothing.

Suddenly I wasn't comfortable in that circle, as if my skin were too tight for me. As if, after being in heaven for a few minutes, I'd been tossed into hell. More than anything I wanted to let go of the hands holding mine and run away, breathe some other air, hide. The skin on the back of my neck prickled. I felt *danger*.

I looked over at Eric, but he was still asleep on his blanket, his angelic face undisturbed.

Then what . . .

"What are you doing here?" a woman asked, her clear, loud voice bringing the so-called singing to a halt.

It was Livia Fowler, followed by her daughter, Becca.

"You are no longer high priestess," Mrs. Fowler said to Hattie. "I am. All rituals in the Meadow are conducted by me, exclusively." She turned toward the botte. "And what is this thing?" She scrutinized all of us in the group, one by one. "Well?"

Hattie squared her shoulders. "It is the *Great Book of Secrets*," she said.

"*What?*" I could tell Mrs. Fowler couldn't believe what she was hearing. "Just you? You few? Without informing the rest of the community? Or *me*? Are you mad?"

"We needed to find a spell," Gram offered.

Livia Fowler examined the book. "The 'Song of Unmaking'?" Her eyes narrowed. "Is one of you infected with the Darkness?"

"No, Livia," Gram waffled. "We only wanted—"

"Who is she?" Livia demanded.

"She's not here," Miss P said decisively. And she wasn't lying. Mrs. Fowler had assumed that the witch in question was a woman.

"Then you must bring her," Mrs. Fowler said imperiously. "The rules are clear." She sang the song from the book, using the same cacophonous tune the others had been singing.

> *"Through Love's unbreaking tie*
> *Unmake the Darkness, do not die*
> *No death shall come, good soul, to thee*
> *For by the sacred Fire set thou free."*

When she was done, she pointed a finger at the big oak tree beside the botte, and it burst into flames.

"Oh, dear," Gram murmured, dismayed.

So that was Livia Fowler's talent. She was a firestarter. It figured that her gift would be one of destruction.

"That tree is over four hundred years old," my great-grandmother pointed out indignantly.

"Get the others," Mrs. Fowler ordered.

Becca ran to spread the word that a witch was about to be burned. There were enough telepaths in Whitfield that it wouldn't take long for them to show up, I knew. People were always ready to watch someone getting punished.

"Stop!" I said to Becca as I took the rowan wand from my sleeve and pointed it at her retreating figure. "Right now!"

She fell in a heap.

"Oh, no," I heard my great-grandmother groan.

"I'm sorry, Gram," I said, backing out of the circle. Peter moved with me, step for step. He knew we had to get Eric out of there.

"You're going to be a lot sorrier, missy," Mrs. Fowler said, pulling her own wand out of her sleeve. The few people assembled broke ranks and skittered away in panic. One woman began to sob hysterically. Dingo growled.

"The girl," was all Mrs. Fowler said, smiling maliciously at me. I saw a long blue thread like a visible electric current speeding toward me. The hair on my arms stood on end. I heard Peter shouting my name, slowly—very slowly—but I knew it was too late. Nothing could stop that laser beam of black magic headed for me.

And nothing did. It kept coming until it was an inch away from me, and then, inexplicably, it veered upward and around until it was shooting back the way it had come. It struck Mrs. Fowler in her eyes. She screamed, her hands flying to her face. I saw Agnes turn to look at me incredulously. Of course, it appeared as if I'd deliberately blinded Mrs. Fowler, but I really hadn't done anything. I wouldn't even have known how to do such a reversal.

But who *had* done it? Who had had enough power to turn that beam away? Who would possess enough malice to have it strike Livia's *eyes*?

There were several new voices shouting as a dozen people bounded through the fog into what had been the circle, stopping near the burning oak. Even though she was caught in my binding spell, Becca must have been able to summon her mother's supporters. Two of them were releasing her already, while others tended to Mrs. Fowler, who was still shrieking piteously and in obvious pain.

Aunt Agnes turned to face me, her expression one of utter horror. "Katy!" she shouted.

"I swear, I didn't—"

I turned to look behind me. And I knew who had sent that ray of hatred back toward Livia Fowler to blind her.

"Oh, shit," Peter whispered.

Eric was awake.

CHAPTER

•

THIRTY-EIGHT

 DIES IRAE

A seagull plummeted out of the sky and fell dead directly in front of the botte. Dingo yelped and flew upside down, feet sticking up in the air, and smacked into one of the big trees. He whimpered as he limped into the arms of Mr. Haversall, who looked around in confusion.

"Who's doing this?" he asked.

Mrs. Fowler pointed at Hattie. "She's responsible," she said. "And those two." She meant Peter and me.

"No, it's the little boy," someone whispered in amazement.

Then everyone turned to look at Eric, who was sitting up on the rock like a little prince. His hands were folded in his lap, and a small smile played on his lips. But his eyes. They were like black pools, amused, indifferent, inhumanly intelligent. They never blinked.

"I don't think I like you, Livia," the Darkness said in its clear, emotionless voice.

Mrs. Fowler squealed with fear. We were all afraid by then.

In another moment there was a whooshing sound cutting through the silence. Something had entered the Meadow from the town, something traveling at a tremendous speed.

"Oh, my God," someone said.

It was hard to see what it was at first, but then I noticed the wooden handle and, attached to it, a shiny blade slicing through the air inches over our heads, heading directly toward Livia Fowler.

A dozen people scrambled for their wands, but the thing was moving too fast. Mrs. Fowler's face was frozen in terror as the knife streaked inexorably in her direction. But just before it reached her, one hand in the crowd shot up. With a movement too fast to see, it grabbed the knife by its handle, stopping it in midair.

It was Hattie, the muscles in her forearm straining with tension.

There was a collective sigh as everyone suddenly remembered to breathe. Hattie's eyes were wide with residual fear. "Go," she mouthed.

Peter moved toward Eric, fumbling for the sedative in his pocket.

"Hattie," Eric crooned. "Such an accomplished witch."

"Did you hear that?" Mrs. Fowler shrieked. "That's the Darkness, that boy! And Hattie Scott is his servant!"

Then three things happened:

Mrs. Fowler spewed out a twenty-foot stream of projectile vomit that landed right on top of the *Great Book of Secrets*.

Another bird, bloody and wingless, fell on top of Becca, who screamed.

From the edges of the forest, deer and rabbits emerged,

baring their teeth and growling like predators.

Eric laughed so hard that he had to hold on to the rock he was sitting on to keep his fragile body from falling off.

I shoved Peter toward his brother, and Peter fell on him, sticking the needle into Eric's hip. As the boy lost consciousness, the conjured woodland animals retreated, fading into the fog like creatures of mist.

"It's okay," Peter announced to the crowd. "Everything's fine now."

Mrs. Fowler stood up, her ample torso quivering. "Everything is *not* fine," she rumbled with malefic intensity. "Bring him to me."

Hattie walked up to her. "Please let me take him home," she pleaded. "I will take care of . . . what has to be done."

"Liar! You'll do his bidding!"

"Please," Hattie repeated, broken. "Spare him the fire. I'll take his life."

"No, you won't." Peter said from the rear.

Hattie pushed her way through the people. "Peter, give Eric to me."

"I said no!" He threw out five fingers in an attempt at a binding spell.

Hattie tripped. "Peter . . ."

I took a deep breath. "Get him away from here," I said, moving between Peter and the rest of the witches. "I'll cover you."

"Stop him!" Livia Fowler commanded. A dozen wands snapped into position.

Before I could even think, I flicked my wrist and knocked the wands out of their hands one by one—a temporary solution, but at least enough of one to give Peter a chance to escape with Eric in his arms.

"Katy, you don't know what you're doing!" Hattie shouted, lurching out of Peter's weak binding.

"You're right," I admitted, throwing another binding spell on her that sent her crashing to the ground. "I'm sorry, Hattie."

Mrs. Fowler screamed, the cry of a Valkyrie on the rampage, and produced a wall of flame so close to me that I could smell my hair singeing. "She brought the Darkness into the Meadow!" she accused. "And now she's let it escape!"

I felt the crowd move in one body toward me.

"Put the wand away," Aunt Agnes said to me.

As I backed away, another wall of fire burst behind me. "Okay," I said, putting the wand back into my sleeve. "Okay, okay."

"*Bring her to me*," Mrs. Fowler commanded.

"Burn her!" someone suggested. It sounded like Becca's voice.

Someone pushed me. I fell, feeling my cheek explode against the rocky ground. Dingo whimpered.

"Burn her!" a young man screamed.

"Yes, burn her!"

"*Wait*," came a voice that sounded as if it was inside my own head. "*We've made a mistake.*"

"Oh," someone said. I felt the grip on my clothes loosen. I could stand up. "Yes, a mistake."

"*We'll wait until we're certain.*"

"We *are* certain!" Livia Fowler's voice broke through that other, strangely compelling one, like a chainsaw through butter. "The rules say—"

"We'll WAIT."

The fire crackled. All else was silent.

"All right," Livia said, oddly calm. "We'll wait."

I stood up, looking around, bewildered. Everyone seemed to be sitting and staring quietly ahead as I staggered away from the circle. Everyone except for Miss P, who stood still as a statue, surrounded by an unearthly light. Her eyes, deep as the heart of night itself, glowed an iridescent blue like windows offering a glimpse of a creature of awesome power.

"Thank you, djinn," I whispered, managing a small bow.

She inclined her head slightly, without ever meeting my eyes.

As I backed away into the fog, I saw Mr. Haversall raise one hand, shooting its fingers upward. A bolt of lightning flashed across the night sky, followed by the crash of thunder and a sudden shower of hard rain.

All the fires were extinguished. The big oak smoldered and hissed in the downpour. I nodded to the old man. *A rainmaker,* I thought. *Bringing water, the third harbinger.*

With two fingers he touched the edge of his cap in response. Dingo lay down at his feet. They were all going to wait for an answer.

All Peter and I had to do was to come up with it.

As I bolted out of the Meadow, I felt sick with the realization of how hard that was going to be, especially after I saw that Peter's truck was gone. Where had he taken Eric? I tried to think clearly. Not back to Hattie's, surely. Not after what had just happened. The school, then? Or my great-grandmother's house?

Then it came to me. There was only one place where they could have gone. I finally understood what Peter's "plan" was. It was the same as Hattie's. The same as Henry Shaw's.

I ran back to Gram's and took my bicycle from the garage. With a longing look at the Cadillac, the keys to which were in Agnes' pocketbook, I pedaled out into the pouring rain and didn't stop until I reached the shore of Whitfield Bay, with Shaw Island barely visible in the distance.

CHAPTER

·

THIRTY-NINE

 LADY OF MERCY

One of the rowboats was missing. I tried to remember what condition they'd been in when I first saw them on the last day of school. I looked across the roiling water to Shaw Island. It had seemed so close before, as if you really could walk over to it under the right conditions. Now it was almost invisible in the downpour.

The abandoned boat, so far from shore the last time I'd been here, was practically at the water's edge. Peter must have taken the other. I hoped it had been in better shape than the leaky tub that remained.

Tipping it on its side, I could see through its entire length. I pulled out rocks and pieces of broken glass and several crabs that had nested there. On the sand nearby were a few half-buried strands of rope and some rotted planks.

I looked helplessly at the island. Peter had to have taken Eric there. But how could I follow?

You can only do what you would normally do, Gram had said. *Only more so.*

That was it! Experimentally I concentrated on the broken pieces of wood lying at my feet until they stirred.

"Into the boat," I ordered, and the planks flew into the bottom of the rowboat, arranging themselves into neat rows over the hole.

I took out my wand. "Nails!" Hundreds of rusted nails of every description emerged from the wet sand like midges. I directed them into a formation and sent them hammering into the wood, expelling a few gigantic hand-forged iron monsters from long-sunken ships as I went.

"Rope!" Broken strands from all over the beach, plus an enormous coil buried a hundred feet from where I stood wound around the interior of the rowboat.

Inwardly, I thanked my dad for forcing me to stay holed up in my room without any distractions. The time I'd spent practicing my teleporting skills was paying off.

Within minutes I had what looked like a relatively serviceable vessel. I even managed to scrounge up a couple of oars, but I had no idea whether the boat was seaworthy.

"Well, I don't have to go far," I told myself encouragingly as I slipped the patched rowboat into the water. Instantly the high winds yanked its bow practically out of my hands.

"Okay, Mr. Haversall, that's enough," I said, rowing like crazy just to steer in a straight line in four feet of water. I didn't know how rainmaking worked, but I guessed that, like all magic, once you started something in the natural world, you had to see it through to its natural conclusion. The storm would have to run its course.

But at least now the Meadow wasn't going to burn down. The big oak that Livia Fowler had set on fire might even have survived.

"Power-hungry cow," I said uncharitably. "I wish the djinn had . . . Whoa." A swell lifted me ten feet into the air. My stomach felt as if it had just dropped to my knees. And then it happened again. Lightning spidered across the sky, sending shivers through me. A defunct rowboat was definitely not the place I most wanted to be during an electrical storm, but I was too far from shore to go back now. In fact, to my dismay, it occurred to me that I could no longer even *see* the shore. Or Shaw Island, for that matter. I couldn't see anything at all except for the choppy, swooping waves that threatened to capsize my boat.

I pushed back my sopping hair and tried to wipe the rain out of my eyes. I'd been in worse storms in Florida, even a couple of hurricanes. Although, admittedly, I hadn't been out on the ocean at the time.

Then it came. Lightning, filling the sky with blue light, and revealing Shaw Island off to the left. And one more thing, at my feet:

Water. Quite a bit of it, reaching to the top of my shoes.

Don't panic, don't panic . . .

I hadn't thought to bring a bucket. Bringing in the oars so that they wouldn't drift away, I got on my knees and started bailing water with my cupped hands until my arms felt as if they were falling off. In time, I saw that the bilge level was under control. I was reaching for the oars when I felt my wand slipping out of my sleeve. It fell somewhere on the rope-lined bottom. In the dark I felt around for it, but I couldn't locate it.

Then, during the next illuminating lightning bolt, I saw that it had lodged in the space between two lengths of rope. As I stood up to retrieve it, the boat listed precariously on another swell, but I couldn't risk losing my wand. So I lumbered forward and snatched it up while I was still certain where it was.

That was a mistake. As I was taking the two steps back to my original position behind the oars, another swell lifted the boat, tipping it dangerously at the height of the wave. Windmilling my arms to keep my balance, I couldn't hold on to my wand. It flew out of my hand, tumbling just out of reach toward the sea.

"No!" I shrieked, lurching to grab it as it fell. All I managed to do as the wand vanished under the white-capped waves was to lose my balance. I reeled around for a moment as seawater sloshed over me, until my toe caught under a loose rope and I fell backward, screaming, my head smacking into the wooden stern with a crack.

It was the last thing I heard before I passed out.

Lady of Mercy
Save us from our madness
Let us see the truth
Of our sublime divinity

The voice was faint at first, singing through the thick silence of unconsciousness. *Where . . . how . . . what . . . was I . . . am I . . . ?*

Questions I could not answer.

It took a long time for me to be able to open my eyes, as if there were silver weights on my eyelids. I awoke to a calm silver sea, blinding in its beauty. On it drifted my boat, or what had once been my boat, transformed now into a sleek silver fish complete with scales and a face on its bow like the serene visages on Chinese junks, meant to appease the water gods.

And I was not alone, although I wasn't startled by her presence when I saw her: a beautiful young woman with skin the color of teak and long ropy hair tied at the top of her head so that it hung down her back like a corsair's.

"Ola'ea," I said.

"Shh." She smiled at me through dark elongated eyes. "You must not be so loud here. Too much talk will deafen you to what you need to hear. Learn to be silent," she said. "It will give you courage and power."

"Okay." I spoke as quietly as I could. "Ola'ea?"

"Yes?"

"I'm not dead, am I?"

"No, little one. You are resting."

"Good." I shook myself, trying to get rid of the leaden grogginess that weighed on me so heavily. "I need to reach Peter and Eric. I have to help them."

"The Darkness is stronger than you. Stronger than almost everything."

"I know."

"So you cannot fight it and win."

"I can try," I said. I shifted in my seat. "Will you help me get to the island?"

"Henry Shaw's island?"

"Yes. Where he died."

"He did not die there."

I blinked. "I thought he set himself on fire after being infected by the Darkness."

"That was what he planned. But it was not a good plan. Death is never the answer. There was another way."

"I knew it!"

"Quiet. You know nothing."

"Sorry."

"Still, you have not lost faith. That is why I am here. Your name is Serenity?"

"Katy."

"Oh? Ashamed, or unsure?"

"Huh?"

"Are you ashamed of who you are, or do you still not know your true name?"

"My name is Katy," I said truculently.

"Katy," she repeated. "A safe, harmless, powerless name. Who wouldn't love someone named *Katy*?"

"Ola'ea—"

"Shh."

"It's important."

"That doesn't mean it has to be loud."

"What's the other way to defeat the Darkness? The way you taught Henry Shaw?"

"I did not teach him anything. By the time I arrived on the island, Henry was already near death."

"From burning?"

"From fear, I think. His heart had stopped. I brought him back to the Meadow."

"And he walked into the fire there?"

"Not him. His wife, Zenobia, took his place."

"*What?*" I was outraged. "She would do that for that . . . that creep?"

She shrugged. "Perhaps she knew that it was the Darkness perpetrating such evil, and not her husband."

"But still. She didn't have to *die* for him."

"It was not her dying that saved Henry," she said. "It was her *willingness* to die. A different thing entirely."

I didn't really know what she was talking about, but it didn't seem to be worth pursuing. "Wait a second," I said. "If Henry Shaw didn't die on the island—if there was actually a ritual in the Meadow to get rid of the Darkness in him, and his wife Zenobia took his place in that ritual . . ."

"Yes?"

"Why isn't there any record of that in the *Great Book of Secrets*?" I asked.

"Isn't there?"

"No. There's just the song about the sacred fire. Which is why they think burning people is a good idea."

"Shocking. That isn't even the song."

"It isn't?"

"It's the *spell*. It must be spoken while the 'Song of Unmaking' is sung. Was that not clear?"

I sighed. "Not really."

She shook her head. "I suppose I forgot to write that part down, then."

"Forgot? You just *forgot* to write down something so important?"

"I was rather busy at the time."

"Oh, for heaven's sake," I said disgustedly.

"Transporting an entire village to another plane of existence is not an easy task, whatever you may think in your sixteen-year-old wisdom."

"All right, all right."

"Not to mention holding off the cowen lynch mobs."

"Fine," I said levelly. "I understand. You had your hands full."

There was a long silence. "I suppose I should have written it down," Ola'ea said finally.

"That's okay."

"I think perhaps that was a mistake."

"Hey, I know all about that," I said. "Sometimes I think making mistakes is my calling in life."

She laughed. "You are kind," she said.

"Thanks."

"But loud."

Deflated. "I guess."

"If I could give you any gift, it would be the ability to listen."

I swallowed. "I can listen," I said quietly.

"Good. Practice. You will not be sorry."

"Okay," I said. I lay back in the boat. The sun felt warm on my eyelids. "So did things turn out okay for old Henry?"

"Oh, yes."

"But his wife burned in the fire."

"The sacred fire, yes."

I sat up. "I'm sorry, but that's just not cool. Mrs. Shaw didn't do anything wrong."

"Neither of them did anything wrong."

"But . . . the Darkness . . ."

"There is always the Darkness. The magic lies in being able to walk through the Darkness without being changed by it."

"Without . . . How is that possible?"

"By knowing who you are," Ola'ea said.

"Did Henry Shaw know who he was?"

"He knew he was not the Darkness."

I lay back again. "I'm tired," I said.

"I will sing to you." Ola'ea guided the boat toward a glowing shore.

Lady of Mercy
Save us from . . .

". . . our madness," I finished lazily. "The burning *is* the madness, isn't it?"

"Bad mojo."

"Is that a real word?"

"Not in my language."

"And the song?"

"A translation."

"It sounds familiar, though."

She smiled. "Ah, you have listened. Do you see how valuable silence can be?"

Lady of Mercy

"Is that Olokun? The Lady of Mercy?"

"Olokun, Kwan Yin, Mary, Cybele, Nokomis, Isis, Astarte, Athena, Inanna, Freya, Lakshmi, Amaterasu. She is the Goddess, the Earth, the source of life. The name we use for her does not matter, if we know her true name. What is that name, Serenity?"

"Love," I said.

"Very good. How do you feel?"

"I'm . . . let me see. I'm cold, I think."

"Good. That means you are still alive. Tell me, why would you wish to be alive?"

"Because someone I love needs me," I said.

Ola'ea sighed. "Then you have reached your destination."

"The island? I'm there?"

"Remember the song."

I sang.

> *Lady of Mercy*
> *Save us from our madness*

Oh, so cold.

> *Let us see the truth*

Violent sensations: Horrible pain in my head. Thunder crashing. Rain hitting me like needles. Lightning turning the insides of my eyelids red.

> *Of our sublime divinity*

And cold water, bucketsful.

I opened my eyes, screamed. The rowboat was half submerged, my body almost entirely underwater. When I scrambled to sit up, my foot broke through the rotten floorboards.

"Ola'ea!" I cried as more water gushed in. Memories, or fragments of memories, whizzed through my head. A silver boat, a black woman with hair like a corsair's . . .

A swell picked up the sinking boat and shot it forward

with me inside, still holding on to its sides. I forgot everything about my dream, if that was what it was. All I could think was that I was riding into doom.

Lady of Mercy
Lady of Mercy
Lady of Mercy

With a crash like the crack of a whip the boat collided with a boulder and broke apart, spilling me out along with the ropes and bilge water onto the rocky shallows.

For a while I just lay there, coughing, tasting the sand in my mouth. Lightning forked overhead, illuminating a strange horseshoe-shaped configuration in the distance.

Whitfield Bay.

I'd made it to the island.

Wincing, I got to my feet. Every part of me hurt. One knee and all my knuckles were scraped, and there was a lump the size of a lemon on the back of my head, but I wasn't bleeding badly, and I didn't think any bones were broken. My bare legs under my shorts were covered with goose bumps. I rubbed them to get the blood flowing into them again as I tried to figure out which direction I should take.

There was another flash of lightning, this time fainter and farther away. The storm was finally subsiding. I walked over to the remains of the rowboat. It was in pieces, splintered against an outcropping of big rocks. There was no water around it now, no shoreline for ten feet.

The tide was going out.

I listened. There were no cars on the island, no radios, TVs, computers, no artificial noise at all. The rain was milder now; I could even hear insects in the brush.

And then, with the intensity of a hundred bolts of lightning, a ball of red and yellow flames streaked across the sky and exploded into the trees on the interior of the island. The fourth harbinger, fire.

"Peter," I whispered, already running.

The Darkness had come home.

TRUE NAME

The cabin was already burning when I reached it. Even in the dark I could see that part of the roof had collapsed and most of the windows had blown out.

It was an odd sort of structure. When Peter had mentioned the family "cabin," I figured that the Shaws' idea of a cabin would be a lot different from mine. But this really was little more than a shack, and very, very old, too, judging from the thick, uneven stone walls and squat doorways.

I'd approached the building from the back, and walked around it carefully, feeling my way through the weeds that surrounded the house while trying to avoid the roof slates and broken glass that were still exploding all around me.

"Peter?" I called tentatively. I was sure he was here. I could feel his presence.

And I could feel something else, too.

"Eric?" I asked tentatively.

He was sitting in the crook between two big tree branches,

his useless legs dangling like those of a ventriloquist's dummy. "Kaaay?" he croaked, lifting his arms.

I ran up to him. "Honey, it's going to be all—"

He kicked me in the face. "Surprise!" He burst out laughing. "That was a pretty good imitation of the cretin, don't you think? *Kaaay?*"

I rubbed my cheekbone where his sneaker had connected. It was in almost the same place I'd fallen in the Meadow. I'd have a black eye by tomorrow, for sure. On the bright side, though, it hadn't been a very hard kick. Fortunately, as malevolent and powerful as the Darkness inside him was, it was still restricted by the frailty of Eric's body. The blow hadn't really hurt me. The only real pain was in losing Eric to the monster who had taken over his body and then wanted to destroy it.

"Oh, dear, I'm afraid I haven't been a very gracious host. Let me kiss it and make it better." He showed me his teeth, clacking them in a chomping motion.

"Where's Peter?" I demanded. Eric's gaze slid toward the burning building. As I rushed toward it, Peter emerged from the kitchen entrance, coughing and sweaty. His bare chest was smeared with soot. "Katy," he said. His eyes looked infinitely sad. "Why did you come here?"

"Because I knew this was where you'd be," I said.

He didn't answer, just turned with his hands on his hips to stare at the blaze.

"Maybe I can help you put out the fire," I suggested.

He wiped the back of his hand across his forehead. "I think it's a lost cause. There were some extinguishers in the house, but they weren't much use. I've just been clearing some of the brush away."

"Can I help you with that?"

He shook his head. "There isn't anything more I can do without some kind of tools." He shrugged. "Maybe the rain will put it out."

The fire was already dampening. It looked like smoke was going to be a bigger problem than fire spreading to the greenery. The wild storm had subsided to a steady, cold rain. Peter didn't seem to notice it. Pushing his hair away from his face, he sat down cross-legged on the open ground. "I'd hoped that Eric and I could stay here," he said to no one in particular. He picked up a small stone and tossed it at the fire.

"That was your plan?" I asked.

He grinned. "Yeah. Pretty sketchy, I know."

I swallowed to keep from crying. "Okay," I said, trying not to let my voice reflect the frustration I felt. "We'll go back in the morning. There's got to be some magic—"

"No," he said. His voice was level and weary. "I'm done with magic." He smiled shyly. "I was never very good at it, anyway."

"But Eric . . ."

"Eric's gone," he said, his voice heavy with resignation.

"Excuse me," the boy in the tree declared loudly, waving his hand. "Sitting right here within earshot, in case you didn't notice."

"That's not my brother," Peter said.

I put my head down. "I know."

"But at the same time, it is." His eyes filled.

"I know."

"We can live here . . ." He looked at the smoldering building. ". . . until . . ."

"Okay."

"Not you. Just Eric and me."

"Oh, goodie!" the Darkness exclaimed. "The moron's body will last all of an hour out here in the open." His skinny legs jiggled wildly.

"He wants me to kill him."

"Yes. Then he can move into your body."

"He thinks that if he annoys me enough, I'll off him."

"I guess he comes from a world where that's normal."

"He comes from *this* world, Katy." The corners of his mouth turned down. "We created the Darkness, remember? It's made up of our own evil impulses."

"Well, *we* didn't. Someone else did. That all happened long ago."

"That's what you all say," the demon inside Eric taunted. "If all the evil in the world happened long ago, I wouldn't be here today." He smiled sweetly. "You re-make me every hour, you good people of the earth. I live everywhere at once because of you. In all modesty, I am the greatest entity in the history of the universe, thanks to you and your quietly horrific natures."

The boy sat back in the tree, the ancient, evil intelligence of the Darkness gleaming from behind Eric's eyes. For once it had spoken the truth.

We sat in silence, all three of us, for a long time as the rain slowly put out the fire and the cabin was reduced to a blackened, smoking wreck. I no longer cared that I was soaked and dirty and that half my skin had been scraped off my body. All I was conscious of now was how tired I was. Tired and hopeless and out of ideas.

I remembered Eric's last drawing, showing a monster standing over the bodies of two dead people. I knew now that Peter and I were those people.

The future can be changed, my great-grandmother had said. Our only chance of survival would be to get away from here, but I knew Peter wouldn't be willing to leave his brother. Neither would I, come to think of it.

All three of us had come down a long road that ultimately led nowhere.

"How're you doing?" I asked finally. It seemed weird to be having such a pedestrian conversation under the circumstances, but in the end, there was nothing more to say.

"Oh, just great," Peter said. "Couldn't be better."

"You don't have to be cynical. At least your boat got here in one piece."

Peter snorted. "It stopped being in one piece about five minutes into the storm."

"Oh?" I remembered the violence of that storm. There was no way anyone could make it across that water without a boat. "How'd you get here, then? You didn't swim, did you?"

"No. I doubt if I could have swum it alone, let alone with . . ." He regarded the puppet-boy in the tree. ". . . him." He shook his head. "After the boat broke up, all I could think to do was to tread water with Eric—or whatever that thing is—on my shoulders. He's the one who got us here."

"How?"

"With your precious magic," he said angrily, covering his eyes with one trembling hand. "I wish we'd drowned," he whispered. "In the middle of the ocean, the Darkness couldn't have gone into anyone else. We'd both have disappeared. That was the original plan. Hattie's plan, mine. I should have stayed with it. I tried . . ." He broke down and sobbed. "I tried, but I couldn't. I couldn't kill Eric."

I moved up beside him and kissed him. "You were right," I said as gently as I could. "Death isn't the answer."

"No?" he asked bitterly. "Can you think of another?"

I wanted to say yes, because there was something, *something*, in the back of my mind.

"A song . . ." I said uncertainly.

"The 'Song of Unmaking'?" He jerked his hand away from mine. "We already saw how far that got us."

"The dog," I said, straining to remember. "Even the dog knew it was wrong."

"What are you talking about?" he asked irritably.

Whatever small mental thread I was trying to grab on to slipped away. "I don't know," I said. "There just seemed to be something about remembering who we were and . . . madness."

"Yea, madness!" cheered the voice inside Eric. "Say, guys, I'm hungry. Or rather, *this* is." He grabbed his wrist with his other hand and shook it.

"Save us from our madness," I recalled.

"As if anyone could," Eric said. "Hey, what does this wretched infant eat, anyway? Baby food? Yuck."

"Lady of Mercy . . ."

"Give me pablum or give me death!" Eric shouted.

"That was it. *Lady of Mercy, save us from our madness.* It was a prayer or something."

"Starving here," the Darkness shouted, his voice nasal and trombone-like. "Or do you want this worthless bag of bones to drop dead? Works the same way, you know, stab me or starve me."

"He's not worthless," Peter said hotly. "My brother's been pushed back so far inside that monster that he can't ever come back."

"I don't believe that." I walked toward the boy in the tree. "Eric," I said softly. "Eric, it's Katy. Remember me?"

"Remember me?" he repeated mockingly. "Do you think I'd let that happen again? You just got lucky."

"What's he talking about?"

"Back at your house I summoned Eric by calling his name. He came through the Darkness to answer me."

"I thought you were just waking him up."

"No. A name is a powerful thing. That's why couples have to speak their true names before becoming handfasted. It's like offering your self, your real self."

"That trick only works once, missy." Eric pointed his index finger at me.

Suddenly something slashed across my cheek. I screamed with the pain. When I looked down, there was blood dripping onto my shirt.

"Katy!" Peter shouted, rushing over to me. He touched my face, and his hands came away covered with blood. "Leave her alone," he said, his voice breaking.

"Why should I?" Eric answered. There was a swooping sound, and then something fell at my feet.

It was a bald eagle in the prime of its life, its magnificent eight-foot wings splayed across the sandy soil. I bent over to examine it, but it wasn't wounded. It just seemed to be dying, like the Cory's Shearwaters, for no reason.

"How could you do that?" I whispered.

"Let's hear it for Eric, the mighty hunter," the boy sneered.

Peter stalked toward him.

"Peter, no!" I called. "It's Eric! *Eric!*" I ran up to him. "No matter how far inside he's buried, your brother is somewhere in there."

"How about a little less psychobabble and a little more shut up?" the Darkness said. "Cook the bird. Make yourself useful."

He's tired, I thought. Magic exhausted him as much as physical effort. Once again, Eric's body prevented the Darkness from doing its worst.

"Sweet, Katy. Dear, sweet, stupid Katy," he said.

I sucked in air as the idea struck me full force. I felt as if I'd been slapped across the face. *Who wouldn't love someone named Katy?* I remembered the voice, deep and strange and . . . silver . . .

A safe, harmless, powerless name.

"The true name," I said.

"What? Katy, you're bleeding."

"Shhh. I need to remember something."

"The magic lies in being able to walk through the Darkness without being changed by it."

"How is that possible?"

"By knowing who you are."

I took the boy's hands. He didn't have enough physical strength to break my grip.

Peter tried to stop me. "Katy . . ."

"I am Serenity Ainsworth," I said.

THE SONG OF UNMAKING

Peace fell over me like a cloak. I had spoken the true name.
Not Eric's, but my own. By speaking it, I acknowledged my
entire lineage, my place in the world, and my destiny. My name
was not who I wished to be, but who I really was, whether I
liked what that represented or not. And with it I was calling
forth what Eric really was, beyond the Darkness, beyond even
the brain-damaged child with his broken body. I was calling
to Eric Shaw in his pure, undamaged state, the Eric whom
I knew still existed. "Come to me, Eric," I said, feeling the
compelling power of my voice.

The boy grunted, struggling to snatch his hands away from
mine.

"Walk through the Darkness, Eric. If you know who you
are, it can't harm you."

"Let . . . let go!"

"You are not the Darkness. Speak your name, Eric."

The Darkness screamed, terrified.

Peter came up to us and put his arm around his brother. The boy flailed violently against us, but his muscles, even artificially enabled by magic, were too frail to fight us for long.

"Speak your name."

The creature opened its mouth and exhaled breath so foul that it made me gag. It spit in my face.

"Don't let go, Peter," I said.

The Darkness focused its eyes on me until I felt my skin burning.

"Eric," I said, trying not to respond to the pain. "Say it!" I told Peter. "Say his name."

"Eric . . ." Peter repeated weakly. "I can't do this, Katy."

"You *can*."

"There's blood running down your face." He reached out a hand to touch me.

"Don't let go," I said. "Eric, come to us. We love you. Come toward the love."

My head felt as if it had been split by a cleaver. I almost let go myself, but then I felt Peter's hand over my own, and Eric's little body trembling beneath my fingers. I tried to live within that sensation, making it grow around me like a bubble until there was nothing else in the world except for the love we felt for each other. Us three, and the music from the Meadow. I could hear it again, the same song, the perfect harmony of sounds made by the trees and the wind, of rushing water and the slow turning of the earth. This was the music that Dingo the dog had heard and had added his voice to. It was clear for me now, as pure and strong as the silver light from the moon above.

The rain had stopped.

"*Lady of Mercy*," I sang. "*Save us from our madness . . .*"

"What are you doing now?" Peter asked, bewildered.

"*Let us see the truth . . .*"

Eric thrashed between us.

"*Let us see the truth . . .*" I was forgetting. "*. . . the truth . . .*"

The little body I was holding shuddered, twisting in agony. Tears poured out of my eyes and mingled with the blood from the wound on my cheek, then dropped onto Eric's convulsing chest, over his heart.

"*Let us . . .*"

"Eric," the boy whispered, and a calm fell over us all.

"*Let us see the truth of our sublime divinity,*" I remembered. I remembered everything. "Peter, we need to get him back to the Meadow."

He disengaged from me, his eyes hard. "I won't let my brother burn!" he shouted.

"I know," I said. "I know. Listen to me." I put my hand on his shoulder and looked into his eyes. "I think there's another way." I took a deep breath. This was hard. "I can take his place," I said.

He blinked, confused. "What?"

"It's what saved Henry Shaw. He never killed himself. The witches performed the 'Song of Unmaking', and . . . and his wife walked into the fire."

"His *wife*?"

I nodded. "It was what she wanted."

"How do you know?"

"On the way over here, I had a . . . well, I guess you'd call it a visitation. From Ola'ea. Or her ghost. She told me how Henry Shaw was freed from the Darkness. It was through the 'Song of Unmaking', the real one, the one she taught me. That and Henry's wife, Zenobia."

"So you're saying that someone can die instead of Eric, and the spell would still work?"

"Yes. *I* can."

He sat back. "No, Katy," he said. For the first time in months, I saw Peter's face relax into an expression of perfect peace. "That will be my privilege."

"No, it doesn't work that way."

"Oh, yes it does. You perform the spell. I'll take care of the rest."

"Listen—"

"No, you listen." He held me close. "This is what I've been looking for, praying for. This is how we save Eric. This is how we keep the Darkness' prophecy from coming true. This is the answer, and you know it as well as I do."

"Oh, God, Peter. This wasn't what I wanted."

"It was what *I* wanted. All along." He kissed me, deeply, passionately. "Thank you."

I buried my face in my hands.

"Ap—ap—ap . . ." Eric's eyes fluttered open again, revealing his open, innocent gaze.

"Buddy?" Peter whispered.

The little boy threw his arms around him. He looked at me. "Kaaay?" He cocked his head, puzzled at my misery. I dried my tears with my dirty forearm and tried to smile for him. He crooned sleepily and reached out to touch the cut on my face. It had stopped dripping blood, but it still throbbed painfully. I pulled away from him. "Kaaay," he breathed softly.

I loved him.

"We need to leave now," Peter said, picking Eric up in his arms. "Before the storm picks up again."

"H—how?" I asked, hiccupping. "How'll we get there?"

"Low tide. We'll walk."

"*Walk*? Across the bay? Is that possible?"

"I think so," he said. "Actually, I've never done it. Maybe it'd be best if you stayed here, and—"

"I'm going with you," I said.

"I could call the Coast Guard as soon as—"

"I said I'm going!"

"All right, all right," Peter said placatingly.

I didn't say anything else. If Peter was willing to die, I at least owed him the respect of my silence.

"Now, you stay with us, okay?" Peter charged Eric. "Everything's going to be all right."

Eric nodded broadly. "Hom?"

"That's right, little brother. We're going home."

Home, to the fire that would kill the person I loved most in the world. To save the person *he* loved most.

"Buh," Eric said, waving his arms frantically. It took me a moment to realize he was looking at the dead eagle on the ground.

"Forget about the bird," Peter said. "Katy, try to find something we can tie Eric onto my back with. He may not be able to hold on—" His mouth stopped moving. He was watching the eagle, lying lifeless in the dirt.

In the starless night, it was hard to see clearly, but there was no mistake about it: Its wings were twitching.

"Wind," I said.

Eric screeched with delight as the big bird slowly pulled

itself upright, adjusting its feathers, shaking its head, scratching the ground with its yellow talons.

Peter sucked in his breath. "That's not wind."

The eagle flapped its wings experimentally. Then, with a final glance toward us, it took off in a long, low arc before soaring to the tops of the distant trees.

Gooseflesh covered my arms. "That bird was dead," I said.

"Obviously it wasn't."

Eric clapped his hands. "Buh."

I felt my eyes filling. The eagle had been resurrected by some force beyond my reckoning.

Maybe it was watching over us, too.

One thing I knew, though: Peter wasn't going to die alone. If it came to that—and it probably would—all it would take would be for me to step into the fire with him.

Overhead, the eagle curved in a big loop before disappearing into the sky. *Good-bye,* I thought.

Every day, it seemed, brought another good-bye.

CHAPTER

•

FORTY-TWO

 LEVIATHAN

The shore bordering Shaw Island was a surreal landscape of utter desolation. Gravity had transformed what had been Whitfield Bay only a few hours before into a vast expanse of slimy mud dotted with debris.

The storm had diminished to a cold drizzle. Intermittently, the moon shone through the thick clouds hanging over the night sky to reveal a blanket of discarded objects jutting starkly out of the wasteland. My wrecked boat, resembling the bones of some long-dead sea monster, lay in splinters against the rocks that had destroyed it.

"It's a long way," I said, following Peter into the mud.

"You don't have to go," he reminded me for the fiftieth time. "When I reach your aunt Agnes, she can—"

"I'm coming with you," I groused, also for the fiftieth time. "I just wish I hadn't lost my wand."

"Can it make you fly?" he asked.

"Of course not," I said.

"Then even if you had it, we'd still be standing here up to our asses in mud, wouldn't we?" he said irritably.

My sneakers made a squishy, sucking sound with every step I took. With the additional weight he was carrying, Peter was sinking up to his ankles already. He adjusted Eric on his back—we'd strapped him in place with a network of sticky vines from the island so that he wouldn't fall if he happened to let go of Peter.

"Are you hanging on tight, little brother?" he asked over his shoulder.

"Tiii," Eric answered happily, wrapping his arms closely around Peter's neck.

"Good job. Should we go faster?"

"Go!" Eric shouted, giggling.

"Katy?"

"I'm coming." I was not nearly as cheerful about the prospect as Eric was.

"Got your weapon?"

"Commando One, affirmative," I said, feeling the object in the pocket of my shorts. The "weapon" was actually a vegetable peeler we'd found in the kitchen of the burned cabin. Peter's was a little better, an actual paring knife with a blade about as sharp as the edge of a Frisbee. The sole reason for carrying them at all was so we could cut the vines holding Eric in case something went wrong.

"But only cut if they're strangling him," Peter had said. "We can't afford to lose him out in the bay."

My shoes were filled with gritty slime. I couldn't see where I was going. Then, to make things even worse, the rain was beginning to pick up again. As I wiped it out of my eyes, my fingers strayed to my cheek, where the Darkness had slashed it.

It was still gaping, probably hanging open like a pocket by now. I knew I'd never look the same. Hell, who was I kidding?—how I looked was the least of my problems. I'd be lucky if I didn't die of infection—assuming I failed in my plan to burn at the stake.

But all that was beside the point at the moment. All that mattered now, all we could afford to think about, was that somehow we had to get through this muck to the other side. Whatever happened after that was a universe away.

By the time we were halfway across the bay, the rain was pouring again, coating the sticky mud flat with a filthy soup that skimmed across the surface and washed over us on its way to the ocean. We'd sunk nearly to our knees, and every step had become a monumental effort. Occasionally there would be outcroppings of rock sticking out above the surface where we could pull our legs out of the mud—literally pull them, with our hands—and rest for a few minutes. But mostly it was just a slow, heavy slog in the dark, with only the intermittent light of the moon to tell us we were going in the right direction.

"How much farther do you think it is?" I panted, trying to step as high as I could. My shoes were long gone by then, sucked into the mud so that everything I stepped on came into direct contact with my skin. There were a lot of slippery, squishy things I felt that I was just as happy not having to look at. Once in a while I came across things that hurt. I just tried not to think about those.

"It's not more than half a mile," Peter answered.

"Do you have your shoes?"

"I have one left," he said. "High tops. Harder to lose."

The crud was nearly hip deep on me now, and the rain was coming down harder. "We need oars or something," I said.

"Oars?"

"Or poles. Something to push us along through this muck."

"So? You're the one with the magic," he said. "Make it happen."

"You know perfectly well what I can do and what I can't," I said. To tell the truth, I was beginning to get tired of Peter's anti-magic attitude. I mean, if help is available, why not use it? "Oars!" I commanded defiantly, holding out my hands in expectation. "Oars," I said again.

Nothing. "Er . . . Poles."

I didn't know whether it was because the mud was so thick that even magic couldn't pull anything out of it, or because using a wand had weakened my ability to perform without one, but whatever the reason, nothing happened.

Nothing. If crickets could have lived out here, they'd have been chirping.

"Wand," I said quietly, a little embarrassed. I looked out the corner of my eye. Peter was smiling. "Well, you've got to admit, it would help to have one right about now, wouldn't it?" I pressed.

He turned toward me. "Of course it would help," he said gently. "There's not a single day that I don't wish I had your gifts, Katy."

"I thought you saw the need for magic as a weakness."

"Only for people who don't have it," he said. "I just don't want to be the guy who spends his life wishing he was somebody else. I'm not one of you, Katy. I don't have any special talents.

I'm not a genius at anything, and I've always had to work harder than everyone else to get the same results."

It was awkward. What he said may have been true. It had just never mattered to me, so I assumed it hadn't mattered to him. "Maybe you'll find a special gift later," I said lamely. "People do, sometimes."

"And sometimes there just is no magic," he said. "Sometimes you just have to put one foot in front of the other." He hitched Eric higher on his back and walked on. "Hey, go ahead and summon your wand," he shouted over his shoulder. "You probably just weren't loud enough the first time."

"Okay." I could feel myself blushing. Still, I knew it would make things a lot easier to have a little magic on our side. "Wand!" I called, as loud as I could.

Nothing.

Again: "Wand!"

All I heard was the sound of rain falling. Rain, and the whoosh of a rising wind.

"Wand! Wand!" I felt tears in my eyes. "Wand . . ."

With deliberate slowness, Peter squelched back through the mud to put his arm around me. "The only trouble with magic," he said softly, "is that you can't always count on it."

I wiped my eyes. My dirty hands filled them with grit. "I guess there isn't anything you can really count on," I said.

"Yes, there is," came a voice out of the night, slow and sinister. It gave me chills. "You can count on me."

"Peter, was that . . ."

A cold wind picked up, pelting us with rain. Water sprayed into my eyes and nose and mouth. It was hard to breathe. I staggered against the weight of the moving air.

"Did you really believe I'd allow you to destroy me?" The voice was louder now, recognizable. As the thunder crashed around us, I looked into Eric's now-animated face. He was smiling the empty, soulless grin of a death's head.

"Frankly, I've always felt that three was an unlucky number. One of us doesn't belong here. Does she?"

My blood ran cold.

"How's your belly, dearie?" it asked smoothly.

I doubled over. A sensation like being impaled by a hundred poisoned arrows shot through me. Peter tried to elbow Eric, but I grabbed his arm. "Don't," I warned. I could hear how shaky my voice sounded. "He's . . . he's using me to get to you. He's . . ."

The pain knifed through me again. I threw up, staggered a few steps, then fell face-first into the mud. Black slime oozed into my nose and mouth, and I could taste the briny paste of decayed fish that made up the soil of the seabed. The cut on my cheek filled, pulling the skin under my eye downward.

"Take my hand," Peter said. I tried, but it seemed like every effort I made to extract myself pulled me in deeper. The mud was like quicksand, sucking me under as I struggled to keep breathing.

"Let her go," Eric said. "She can't make it to shore, in any case. Better not waste your strength, Peter."

"Shut *up!*" Peter roared.

"Make me." With that, all manner of debris that had been buried in the seabed flew up into the air—rusted nails, sharp broken shells, splintered pieces of wood—and rained down on me. With a scream I tried to roll out of the path of shrapnel, but every object was trained on me. My hands, which I'd used to protect my face, were cut to ribbons. Then, one by one, I felt my organs puncture: my lungs, my stomach, my kidneys.

"Katy!" Peter lunged toward me, He reached me just as the assault ended. He was crying. He tried to touch me, but I guess there wasn't much left of me that was whole. My face was cut open with a gash that would probably take my whole eye out. My hands, both of them now, were useless. My body . . . well, let's just say that the way it looked, which must have been pretty scary, didn't begin to reveal the extent of the damage.

I tasted blood. I spat. It gushed out of me as if there were a faucet in my mouth. I don't think I'd ever seen so much blood come out of one place.

Eric blinked sleepily, exhausted from his exertion. There was no one but Eric inside him now, at least for the moment. No Darkness.

No more magic.

"I'm sorry," I said to Peter. He was kneeling beside me, and had to lean down to hear what I was saying. It was still raining hard, but I could barely feel it. All I was aware of was a creeping kind of cold. Not a bad sensation, really, sort of like a fog making its way from my hands and feet toward the middle of my body. "I can't seem to move much just now."

"Take it easy," Peter said. He lifted up my head and kissed my mouth. His lips were soft and warm. If I had to die, I thought, I was glad it was with the taste of Peter's kiss on my lips.

"I love you," he said.

"I know." I smiled. "Go ahead," I said. It was easy now. Everything was becoming easy. "I'll catch up."

I meant that to be funny, in a grotesque sort of way, but I

don't think Peter got the joke. He'd always said that my sense of humor was weird.

"Peter . . ." I began, but then I couldn't remember what I was going to say. I could feel myself shutting down. Slowly, gently. Easily.

"Don't you dare," he rasped. "Don't you dare leave me, Katy." He stood up and adjusted Eric on his back. Then, bending his legs, he picked me up and began to walk.

One step, two. Every movement, every instant, was an agony for me. I screamed at first, but even that took too much effort. After a while all I could do was lie back while Peter walked with me in his arms and Eric on his back. Three steps. Four. One foot in front of the other.

My head lolled backward. I had nothing left. Neither did Peter, but he went on anyway.

Five, six, seven . . .

Sometimes there is no magic.

Eight . . . nine . . .

SUMMERLAND

"You see?"

"See what?" The light was blinding bright, golden and welcoming. I tried to shield my eyes, but someone was holding my hand. "Ola'ea?"

"Welcome, my beauty!"

I could see her now. Her hair was white, loose, long.

"Where are we going?" I asked, squinting into the light.

"Why, anywhere you like!"

My heart sank. "I'm dead, then," I said.

"You are with me. Think of it that way."

As my eyes grew accustomed to the light, I saw a crowd of people gathered below us. "This is the Meadow," I said.

Just about every witch in Old Town was there: Dr. Baddely, Mrs. Thwacket, and Mr. Midgen, the school custodian, were all present. Jonathan Carr was standing with his arm around Aunt Agnes. Gram was with the hospital volunteers. Mr. Haversall and Dingo were walking around the perimeter, near Miss P and

Hattie. They were all holding candles. On the other side of the botte, which was still open, stood Livia and Becca Fowler and Mrs. Fowler's followers, grim-faced and eager for bloodletting.

"What are they doing here?" I asked.

"They are waiting for you. They believe they are going to burn the Darkness out of Whitfield."

"All they're going to do is kill Eric," I said dispiritedly. "And probably Peter, too."

"What can I say? They do not know the right song."

I whirled around to face her. "Whose fault is that?" I almost shouted. "You're the one who wrote that stupid spell in the first place. How'd you expect anyone to know what to do with it? You didn't even include the real words!"

She looked hurt. "But the words don't matter," she said sullenly.

"What? What do you mean, *the words don't matter*? It's a *spell*. The words are everything!"

She shook her head. "No, child," she said. "Magic has nothing to do with words. Haven't you figured that out? It is like love, or faith, or anything that matters—saying it does not make it so. The magic lies within. Always."

"So how does it work? The 'Song of Unmaking'?"

She seemed to be practicing spirit tricks, vanishing to a golden point of light and then reappearing. "The Darkness feeds on fear," she explained. "And the living are very fearful— of pain, loss, death—any change at all, really. Unfortunately, all of life is change, nothing *but* change, if you think about it. So they live in constant fear."

That sounded right, as far as it went. "So?"

"So if you can set your fear aside and hear the music of the earth, feel the magic within it . . . If you can become a part of All That Is . . . then anything is possible."

She dimmed until she looked like a real person again, a girl about my age who had hitched a ride on a sailing ship and journeyed, despite being scared to death, to a distant land. "I could not teach the 'Song of Unmaking' because it is true magic. It is not a spell. It is about being a part of the perfection of the universe. The words in the *Great Book of Secrets* are what I spoke as the spell unfolded. It is how I explained to the others what happened."

I turned away.

"What is it?" she asked.

"If that's the only way it works, then it can't be duplicated," I said, crestfallen. "It only worked one time, for Henry Shaw, and that's because you were there to hear the music. Everyone who was infected with the Darkness before and after him ended up being burned to death."

Ola'ea made a little miserable movement. "All they had to do was listen," she said in a small voice. "The music was all around them."

"They couldn't hear it," I said. "They can't hear it now. They won't hear it when Peter walks into the fire. They don't know how."

Ola'ea looked away. We stood in silence for a long time.

"So my friends will die for nothing," I said. "Like I did."

Her eyes grew gentle. "No one dies for nothing," she said softly. "We all sing our little song for just a moment, and then fall silent. But that music echoes. Long after we are gone, the song of our soul moves on to the farthest stars of the Milky Way. That is true for each of us, even if we live only one hour."

I looked down at the people in the Meadow. My family. My friends. I understood now how precious they all were, how valuable. Even people like Becca and her mother, troublesome as they had been, were necessary strands in the fabric of our world. We all learned from one another. We all helped each other to understand ourselves. We all mattered.

Ola'ea and I passed the vigil and moved deeper into the Meadow, toward a cluster of fairy-tale cottages. People dressed like Pilgrims emerged from their squat little doorways.

"Is this the land of the dead?" I asked.

"A morbid appellation," Ola'ea said. "We call it the Summerland." Oddly, these spirits were more solid than the living people carrying candles. Already the Whitfield residents seemed like specters, or dreams, visions that were a little bit less than real.

We stopped, and an old woman made her way through the growing crowd toward us. She looked a little like my great-grandmother. "Ola'ea!" she called, perfectly executing the African stop in the name.

"Dear Serenity, my sister!"

My head snapped in a double take. "Serenity Ainsworth?"

"Look who I have brought you!" Ola'ea shouted.

"Good gracious, it's my namesake," the old woman gushed, hobbling over to me.

"She calls herself Katy," Ola'ea said.

"Nonsense. We heard her speak her name."

"You did?" I asked.

"The truth is all we hear," another woman said.

I knew her, too. "Zenobia," I whispered. "Henry Shaw's wife. You walked through the fire."

She nodded. "I did."

"Was it worth it?" I blurted out before I could stop myself. "I mean . . . was that a mistake?"

Zenobia smiled. "There are no mistakes," she said. "Regret is only for the living."

"But why are you here, child?" Serenity asked. She really was a lot like Gram, down to the doily on her head.

"I failed. I couldn't help Peter. I couldn't help Eric."

There was a lot of whispering among them.

"Oh, stop, all of you," Ola'ea scolded. "The girl was suffering."

I blinked as I began to understand. "Are you saying—can it be—that I'm not really dead?" I asked.

"You shouldn't be," Serenity said, looking sternly toward Ola'ea, who swallowed.

"I took you before your time," Ola'ea explained. "I thought I would be sparing you."

I blinked. "Then you have to send me back," I demanded. "I need to save Eric."

"By doing what?"

"By singing the 'Song of Unmaking'."

"They will kill you first," Ola'ea said.

"Maybe not."

"Of course they will!" she countered. "It would not matter what you did. You were right: Ordinary witches cannot hear the song."

"*I* heard it. I just didn't recognize what it was."

"Well, you would not recognize it if you went back, either. You would not remember this conversation, or the key to the spell, or anything about your time with me here."

"Then you have to help me." I looked around. It was my only chance. "All of you."

"What is it you need, child?" Serenity asked.

I took a deep breath. "The witches in Whitfield are waiting to burn a little boy to death," I said. "Because no one can hear the 'Song of Unmaking'."

"Fools," Ola'ea said. "It is everywhere, all around them! All they ever had to do was listen!"

"Nevertheless, I doubt if we would have heard it ourselves if you hadn't been there to point it out," Serenity observed.

"That's what I'm asking," I said. "Will you come to the ritual? Teach them the song?"

"I have told you, it cannot be taught!"

"It can be *heard*," I said. "Let them hear it. That's all I ask."

"But . . . They can hear it from you."

"They could if they would listen." I looked at my feet. "But they won't. I mean, who am I? Why should they think I know something they don't?"

Serenity looked nonplussed. "Why, because you'd be telling the truth," she said.

Ola'ea shook her head. "You forget, my sister. These people cannot tell truth from lies. They think that because they are witches, they are enlightened beings. But in the end they are all just human."

"In that case, they wouldn't listen to us, either," Serenity said.

"Would you try, though?" I begged. "Please, to save Eric?"

"To save you from your madness," Ola'ea said.

There was a long silence. Then Serenity took my hand. "We will try," she said. "That is all we can do."

"Thank you," I said, feeling the most tremendous relief of my life. "I can go now," I said.

Ola'ea took my elbow. "All right, then, come," she said. "Quickly, before you rot." We took off, moving too fast to see anything. "You realize, of course, you won't remember any of this."

"Yes," I said.

"Not to mention that you may die a horrible death at the hands of those idiots before anyone ever hears the song," she muttered. "And for what? For nothing."

"No one dies for nothing," I reminded her.

She looked into my eyes then, and my heart filled with her sadness and compassion. "We are almost there," she said.

"Good."

"By the way, what was said in the Meadow was true. None of this has been a mistake."

"I know." I held out my hand in farewell.

"Try to listen," she said as she fell away like a veil into the wind.

I felt something brush against my lips. A kiss. From Ola'ea? I wondered. No, of course not. What had given me that idea? It was Peter. Who else would kiss me with such tenderness, such perfect, healing love?

I opened my eyes. Eric's face—Eric's, not Peter's—was poised above mine.

I shivered involuntarily when I thought that I might be looking straight at the Darkness. Then I saw that the eyes were really Eric's, happy, open, guileless. It was Eric who had kissed me, I realized. That was a first. I tried to smile at him, but I don't know if I succeeded or not.

The second thing I saw was Peter's arm wrapped around me. Overhead, the moon shone full. The rain had stopped. In the distance, the horseshoe cliffs of Whitfield Bay stood out in silhouette against the white moon, and beyond them, the dark shape of Shaw Island.

"We made it," I said. At least that had been my intention. My throat was so parched and dry that my words just sounded like mush.

As soon as I spoke, though, I felt Peter's knees jerk upward beneath me. "Did she . . . you . . ." he stammered.

"Kaaay," Eric crooned sweetly. He kissed me again. I smiled.

Peter's face, tearstained and filthy, came into view as he craned his head over his arm. He stared at me, blinking incredulously, for a long time. Finally I reached up to touch his mouth.

"Sometimes you don't need magic," I said. I'd literally come back from the dead to tell him that, even though all that came out was "Some." I tried again. "Love," I managed. He could figure out the rest.

Peter's eyes flooded. He held me against him so closely that I felt as if we were melting together into one person. For as long as I could, I let myself be where I was, next to him in that moment and nowhere else, with nothing else in my mind, feeling his strong body beneath his clothes, taking in his heat, his scent, his aliveness.

I was happy. For the first time in my life, I wanted nothing more than I already had.

Then he pulled away from me, holding me at arm's length, his expression a mask of amazement. "Your face," he whispered.

Oh. That. But then, did I expect that he wouldn't notice that I'd been torn to pieces? "That bad, huh?" I raised my hand to my face.

Then I saw it: my *hands*. The thumb had nearly been cut off one of them. But it wasn't cut anymore. It looked as if it had never been injured. I held up the other hand then, the one that had been flayed to bare flesh. It was clean. Unmarked. I moved my fingers. The moon gave me a good light. The wound was gone, healed without a trace. "Just like your wrists, Peter," I said, astonished. But Peter was still staring at my face. I reached up to touch it. The skin was smooth and warm, as if it had never been marred.

How could that be? I wondered. My face had been scraped against rocks, kicked, slashed open, packed with mud and pebbles, and smashed by falling debris.

"My eye?"

"It looks fine. Can you see?"

I nodded.

Then we both looked at Eric. He patted my cheek.

"Mrs. Ainsworth didn't heal my wrists," Peter said, dazed. "It was my brother."

"And the eagle on the island. That was Eric, too."

Peter bit his lip. "Katy, when we got to shore, you had no heartbeat."

"I know." I was going to try to explain. *No, it wasn't a miracle, it was Ola'ea's ghost who took me to the Land of the Dead by mistake, and then . . .*

But of course that wasn't possible, I realized. I must have been in some sort of demented dream that, even now, was falling away.

"We have to get to the Meadow," I said.

Eric touched my face, and I felt the peace of eternity wash over me. Everything about this moment was right. Right, and inevitable, and perfect. This was how real magic worked, I now knew, when all the parts of the universe worked together perfectly, at the perfect time.

"You're a healer, Eric," I said. I turned toward Peter. "More than a healer. He's stronger than death. Stronger than the Darkness."

We looked at one another, we three who we knew now stood at the center of the magic.

Let us see the truth
Of our sublime divinity

All of it was perfect. No matter what happened to any of us from now on, we would always know who we were.

"Let's go," Peter said.

CHAPTER
·
FORTY-FOUR

 BALEFIRE

They were waiting, their candles making dots of light, hanging in the night like accusations.

We walked in silence. Finally, as I began to make out the first faces in the moonlight, I asked in a small voice, "Are you scared?"

He squeezed my hand. "Yes," he said.

"Do you think maybe they'll spare . . ." I was going to say *us*, but I didn't want an argument now. ". . . you?"

"No," he said. "How could they? But they'll spare Eric. They'll have to."

If the Lady of Mercy really can save us from our madness, I thought.

As we approached, I got a look at the faces of our friends. None of these people wanted to see Eric killed. I'd even have bet that every one of them, except maybe for the Fowlers, would have traded places with Eric if they could have.

At least we had that alternative, I told myself. Someone

would be able to take Eric's place. Peter thought he would be the one, but I would make sure it was me.

It was Eric himself who told us when to begin. I hadn't even known where we were going, and I doubted if Peter knew, either. But Eric started fidgeting and kicking his legs just about where Mr. Haversall was standing.

The old man took an uncertain step backward. I didn't blame him. The last time anyone had seen Eric, he was sending knives flying through the air.

Well, the ones who wanted retribution for that were going to get it. But Mr. Haversall wasn't one of those. He was a little disconcerted at the attention Eric was giving him, but he didn't walk away from us.

Trying to be unobtrusive about it, I checked out Eric's face. I thought I was sufficiently acquainted with the Darkness to be able to recognize it in Eric's eyes. It hadn't appeared since the three of us had made it back to Whitfield, but you never knew. Just because the real Eric had come through didn't mean the Darkness was gone. Not by any means. Until his talent as a healer emerged, the Darkness had been growing steadily stronger in him.

I wondered if his gift had actually been helped in some way by the Darkness itself—strengthened, somehow, by having to push through that cloud of evil inside him. It made sense, in a way. Steel that's been welded is stronger than newly forged metal. It was just a thought. I would never know for sure, unless Eric learned to talk.

But I'd be gone by then. Everything seemed to come around to that: Life was short. It would be shorter for Peter and me than most, but it was never long enough for any of us. Perhaps one day, in the Summerland, where only the truth is heard, I would learn the secret of Eric's great gift.

Which, incidentally, Mr. Haversall knew nothing about as Eric waved his arms at him frantically.

"I think he wants to touch you," Peter said. "To find out what's wrong."

"With me?"

"With your body," Peter said.

"Shoot, practically everything," Mr. Haversall said. He looked inquiringly at his dog. "What do you say, Dingo? Should I let the doctor here have a look at me?"

Dingo sat down with a dignified nod of his head.

"Well, all right," he said with a sigh. "I'm an old man. I've lived my life." He swallowed, then stepped forward bravely into Eric's embrace.

"Oo," Eric cooed, slapping Mr. Haversall in the center of his chest.

The old man winced, but stuck out his chin, prepared for another onslaught.

There was none. Dingo barked once.

"Is that it?"

"I guess so," Peter said.

"Well, that wasn't so bad," Mr. Haversall admitted. "To tell the truth, my chest feels like a hundred-pound weight's been lifted off it." He bent down and patted Dingo on the head. "But you knew that would happen all along, didn't you, fella?"

"Woof," Dingo said.

Eric's next stop was in front of Gram. "Mmm," Eric said, taking her gnarled hands in his.

"Land sakes!" she exclaimed as her swollen knuckles shrank before her eyes. "Look at this!" She opened and closed her fists. She swiveled her neck, swung her hips from side to side, and hitched up her dress to show her shapely knees.

"Grandmother!" Agnes whispered.

"My arthritis! It's gone!"

Then an odd thing happened. People began to emerge from behind the trees and rocks, looking curiously at Eric. Some of them looked astonished, hopeful. Others had closed, careful faces, their bodies hidden behind crossed arms and tightly held children. Around Livia Fowler was a group of young men. I recognized some of them from school. They must have been the ones I'd heard about, the ones Gram said were just some sports team. From the arrogant looks on their faces, though, I kind of doubted that.

Boldly, a young man wearing a cast on his leg—I think he was Gram's mailman—limped up to Eric with a what-have-I-got-to-lose attitude. He left with his crutches under his arm.

After that, a crowd began to form around Eric.

"Get away!" a woman called, her voice shrill and cutting. "Get away from him. Now!" Livia Fowler pushed her way to the front of the assembly. Defiantly, she took a gaudy brooch from the front of her gown and raked the pin across her hand. Her face never registered the slightest discomfort as the blood welled and spilled across her fingers.

"Heal that," she demanded, thrusting her hand at Eric.

He touched her with infinite gentleness. The wound healed perfectly.

"It's the Devil," she hissed.

"It's Eric, Mrs. Fowler," Peter corrected.

"A trick to win us over to the Darkness. We know how you work."

"Hey, he *helped* you!" I put in. "Which is more than I would have done, considering you scratched yourself just to see what would happen."

"Katy, please," Peter said.

There appeared at his side a small boy with dirty hands and matted hair. His lips were blue. Aside from that, everything about him was gray, from his gray face to his gray ragged clothes. Eric reached out for him.

"No!" a woman screamed, rushing through the crowd. "Don't you touch him!"

Eric's hand remained poised in the air as the woman grabbed the child by the collar of his shirt and dragged him back among the onlookers, who slowly slid back to widen the circle around the three of us. There was an odd silence as people decided whether or not to allow Eric to help them.

Then the boy with the blue lips broke free and ran back into the circle, wheezing and panting, his arms outstretched. He touched Eric as if he were playing a desperate game of tag.

Instantly his face transformed. The gray cheeks grew pink, the blue lips reddened. The line of his mouth softened, and the pinched look of his eyes vanished, replaced by a clear green-blue gaze.

He smiled once, briefly, then ran back. On the way he tripped on a stone and lay sprawled and surprised on the ground, his scraped knee reddening before him.

His mother let out a blood-curdling cry that caused the little boy to look up in alarm. "See what they've done!" she shrieked. "My boy! They've killed my boy!"

The boy tried to scramble to his feet, but the crowd—led, not surprisingly, by Mrs. Fowler's cadre of young thugs—closed around him.

"Nothing's wrong with the boy," I heard Gram shout as loud as she could, but I doubt if anyone heard her.

Suddenly the air seemed charged with danger and terror as the little boy cried out in panic. The crowd murmured, its collective voice rising and falling, occasionally bursting with hysteria, but always with an undertone of suspicion and fear. Once merely curious, they had turned into a swarm.

"Now!" Livia Fowler screamed. "Now!"

And the swarm came for us.

Livia's vanguard appeared at the front of the crowd, moving purposefully. Three of them grabbed Peter and Eric and me, while others acted immediately to subdue anyone who might have objected, strong-arming Hattie and Agnes and Jonathan, and taking wands from the others.

This was all planned, I realized. Orchestrated down to the last detail.

Mrs. Ainsworth screamed as two burly boys threw a cloth over Miss P's head and carried her out of the Meadow.

"Djinn!" I shouted. "You can make them stop! You can—"

"She can't work unless her mind is clear," Peter said. "They're going to make sure she can't think straight."

In response, the men holding us yanked our arms behind our backs. Eric whimpered in terror as they wrenched him from Peter's arms.

"She trained them," I said quietly, wishing it weren't true. Wishing that everything that was happening wasn't real.

A separate group of Livia's boys scurried behind the trees, emerging with armloads of wood. It was dry, despite hours of torrential rain. The wood had been kept dry. And I knew why.

Three tall stakes were placed into the ground. The holes for them had already been dug. The three of us were dragged over to them.

"Kaaay!" Eric sobbed. "Kaaay!"

"It's okay, Eric," I said, although I could feel my heart breaking. This wasn't how things were supposed to happen.

And yet it was the way it *had* happened, again and again. Through the centuries, people as innocent as we were, as young as Eric, had been put to death with the explicit consent of righteous people who thought they were acting for the good of humanity. Those smirking thugs who were tossing the firewood at our feet were all calling themselves agents of God, or warriors in a good cause, or the swords of justice. Every one of them.

"No!" Peter shouted. "Not them! Katy doesn't have anything to do with this!"

The saddest thing about human beings, I realized, was that no matter what terrible things we did, what horrors we committed, none of us ever thought of ourselves as evil.

"Please!" Peter begged, even though I think from the way he was standing that one of his legs might have been broken. "I can take Eric's place! Just me, not them! Listen to me!"

Listen. That was a joke. These people weren't going to listen to anything. They'd already made up their minds about what they wanted to hear. I should have known better than to think the truth would matter to them.

"Through love's unbreaking tie," Mrs. Fowler warbled. *"Unmake the Darkness, do not die . . ."*

The wrong song. Again. Dingo started barking, evading kicks from all directions. As Livia sang, if you could call it that, her boys stacked firewood hip deep all around us.

For the first time ever, I hoped that the Darkness would make an appearance. It would at least give us a chance to get out of there.

But Eric only looked up at me with his trusting eyes and smiled as he sank into the ropes that bound him, blinking away his tears.

Livia sang louder and more horribly as she drew a binding circle around us with her wand. A magic circle that no one could enter or leave. The three of us were truly alone now.

"No death shall come, good soul, to thee . . ."

Who was she kidding, I thought. Plenty of death was going to come. Just like it always did.

Tears filled my eyes. Nobody ever learned anything.

"Bring the torches!" Livia commanded. She hadn't even finished the song.

It was crazy. If this were anywhere else, the police would have been all over the place. You didn't burn people at the stake anymore. But this wasn't anywhere in the world. This was the Meadow. To anyone passing on the street, this would look like nothing more than an empty construction site.

Mrs. Fowler's boys rushed up with torches and stood around us in formation. Also part of the plan, I guessed, to make the spectacle as entertaining as possible for her audience.

Tomorrow they would all shake their heads and say how sorry they were that those three young people had to die, as if they had played no part in it. As if by doing nothing, they had not given permission.

I knew why Eric was not manifesting the Darkness. He didn't have to. It was all around us.

Black smoke curled up from the torches slowly, like fog. Like evil.

"Katy." It was Peter. He was straining to hold his hand out from beneath the ropes that bound his wrists. Quietly he asked, "Will you be handfasted to me?"

I wasn't expecting that. Being burned at the stake can wreak havoc on your love life. But that was Peter. He always knew what was really important.

I smiled. "Okay," I said.

He spoke first, words of sanity in a world gone mad long ago. "I, Peter Prescott Shaw, declare my love for thee, and offer thee my heart for a year and a day, that thou may love me as well."

It was my turn. It was so hard to breathe. The wood at our feet hadn't yet been lit, but the heat from the torches was warm enough to make me sweat, a hint of the agony to come. But that was later, I told myself. Another time, a universe away. For now, there was only Peter and Eric and me, and what we had together.

"I, Serenity Katherine Ainsworth, declare my love for thee, and offer thee my heart for a . . ." I pressed my lips together. "Forever," I said. "I love you, Peter."

"I love you, Katy."

Forever.

CHAPTER

•

FORTY-FIVE

 EXALTATION

"Light the fire," Livia ordered.

I wished I could have held him then, held both of them, through the coming ordeal.

Eric started to cry. There was nothing I could do to comfort him, nothing at all. Against my will, a lightning bolt of fear shot through me. I swallowed and stood up as straight as I could, but my body was trembling like a leaf in the wind as the first tendrils of hot smoke snaked into my lungs.

"Sing, Katy," Peter said.

"What?" I looked around wildly. "Now?" Who would hear me now? The trees weren't singing. The wind wasn't blowing. There was no music. Not anywhere. "I can't even hear the song," I said.

"That doesn't mean it's not there," Peter said.

I was shaking like crazy. "It doesn't?"

"Just listen," he said.

"Do you hear it?"

He smiled. "No, but you will."

Listen.

All right. Maybe it was somewhere beyond my hearing. Somewhere.

I began to sing.

"Lady of Mercy . . ."

My voice quavered pitifully, and was all but lost in the cacophony that filled the meadow.

"Save us from our madness . . ."

Only Dingo heard me. Softly, sitting respectfully in front of us, he began to howl. One of Mrs. Fowler's boys kicked him. Dingo yelped and scurried away, limping.

I coughed, choking. *"Let us see the truth . . ."*

I sobbed. I couldn't. Just couldn't.

Then, from far away, I heard Dingo singing again, giving me the melody.

"Of our sublime divinity," I croaked. *"Lady of Mercy, save us—"*

FROM OUR MADNESS!

It came like cannon fire from everywhere at once: the music, sudden, unexpected, magnificent. And at that moment, I remembered.

"They've come," I whispered as the spirits from the Summerland rushed around us. The trees bent double and the wind began to sing along with the ghosts who had come to keep their promise. Together, their music was as loud as the birth of a planet, and as perfect as the formation of a flower. It was a force of nature, stronger than a hurricane or a tsunami.

Livia Fowler was blithering around trying to control things, issuing commands that no one heeded, chattering like a magpie while her followers stood dumbstruck, blinking at the awesome power that had been unleashed around them. Her army—a puny bunch of adolescent boys, I saw now, willing to sell their souls for a few moments of false authority—were quaking and looking for places to hide, behaving like the cowards they really were.

Hattie pushed past them and stood before the fire that contained Peter and Eric and me, raised her arms in the manner of the high priestess, and spoke the words of Ola'ea's spell:

Love's unbreaking tie
Unmake the Darkness, do not die
No death shall come, good souls, to thee
For by the sacred fire set thou free.

A brilliant blue light suddenly surrounded us. The fire around us leaped up, twenty feet tall. I screamed reflexively before I realized that the fire was no longer hot. The ropes binding us fell away. I reached out my hand to touch the flames, blue and cool and comforting as a mother's arms.

The sacred fire.

My hair stood on end as every cell in my body was infused with the magic of that fire. I felt new, washed clean, as if for this one moment, and never again in my human life, I was utterly free of evil.

This was how Eric must feel all the time, I realized. He never mistook himself for the Darkness, even when it controlled his body . . . even though everyone else did.

The music grew louder as the spirits settled among the living, hundreds now, filling the whole Meadow with an eldritch glow. I saw Serenity Ainsworth among them, and her daughters. Henry Shaw's wife Zenobia's eyes met mine, and I understood at last why she had willingly gone into the fire for someone she might have hated. "It was not her dying that saved Henry; it was her willingness to die," Ola'ea had said. Zenobia had given her husband her *life*—all that was good and true within her. She, too, had stood in this fire and felt the balm of forgiveness coat her like honey.

Ola'ea was there as well, dressed like an African queen. There was Dorothea Lyttel and her family, and Constance Ainsworth, who was burned in 1929. With them stood all of the witches who'd been tortured and murdered by the evil that they themselves had been accused of harboring.

There were generations of them, the spirits of the families of Whitfield who had seen the Darkness and had come to show us where it truly lived.

To save us from our madness.

I saw my grandparents, young and vibrant, and beyond them, my mother, Agatha, smiling at me with my own green eyes, bright now in the waning moonlight.

Maybe, in some way, I had helped to make up for her crime—a crime she had never considered even to be a crime. She had thought that by killing Eric those years ago, she was eradicating evil. Instead, without knowing, she had perpetrated it. She had fed the Darkness that was already living inside her, as it lived in all of us.

What I'd learned from the Darkness was that it wasn't really necessary for it to possess anyone in the way it possessed Eric. That was just a catalyst, a way to bring the Darkness that was buried deep in the hearts of good people to the surface. Because inside the best of us, I knew, was enough evil to destroy the world. And we didn't even know it, because evil was so easy. All it took was the willingness to forget who we can be. What, when it matters, we really are.

I held out my hand to my mother, and she reached out to me. On opposite sides of the living blue fire, our palms touched. I felt her love move through the fire and into my heart. My eyes welled with tears, blurring my vision, but that last image of her, happy, peaceful, her face shining with love for me, would stay in my heart forever.

Eric, who had watched the drama unfold around us as if it were a stage play, now began to tremble and cry in pain.

"It's all right," I said. "This is a magic fire. This is—"

With a roar of rage and anguish, something stretched out of Eric like bubble gum, forming a series of hellish faces as it threw itself against the impenetrable blue barrier of the sacred fire.

It was a red devil with horns. It was the face in the fire that had chased Peter and me through the Shaw mansion, the ventriloquist's dummy face of Eric as he tortured his brother. Against the barrier pressed an ever-changing stream of faces, those who had been possessed by the Darkness, and those who had killed them. Now, at last, we were able to see the true face of evil:

It looked just like us.

Eric himself, the real Eric, was limp, his eyes rolled back in his head, his mouth open as the thing inside him struggled against the forces that were drawing it out. I knew that it wouldn't do any good to call him now. What was going on was beyond anything any of us could do. So I just held on to Eric with one hand and Peter with the other, and tried to tell them with my heart that I loved them.

Then there was an explosion of golden light, a column so bright that I was nearly blinded by it. It was the same light I'd seen when I was flying to the Summerland with Ola'ea. Could it have been Olokun, I wondered? The Lady of Mercy?

"The name we use for her does not matter," Ola'ea had said, "if we know her true name."

Yes, I remembered. Her true name: Love. That was the spell, the only real magic there was.

The Darkness swirled around the inside of our blue globe, faster and faster, until its changing faces were no longer discernable and they all blended together into what looked like smoke. Then, with a wail of sorrow that captured all the suffering in the world since the beginning of time, it moved upward, congealing into a cone that shot out of the fire, shattered the magic circle as if it were a dome of glass, and flew into the night.

The blue fire vanished. As Eric collapsed, Hattie ran toward us and caught him. "My baby," she said, cradling him in her arms.

Eric squirmed away from her just long enough to embrace Peter's broken leg.

"Thanks, buddy," Peter said, handing him back to Hattie.

He smiled at her. "Mama." He touched her face. "Mama."

I could only stare stupidly at my own hands and feet, marveling that we'd all come out of this mess alive. After a while, Peter touched my hand with a trembling tentativeness. "Did you mean the words of the handfasting?" he asked.

I buried my face in his chest. "You don't have to ask," I said.

Below us, Livia Fowler bustled up to Hattie. "I appreciate your concern, Mrs. Scott," she said, "But really, you had no right to take over the ritual. As reigning high priestess—"

"Oh, shut up, Livia," Hattie said wearily.

The look on Mrs. Fowler's face was enough to make anyone laugh out loud. "Can you believe her?" I muttered.

"Now, now, we mustn't be uncharitable, dear." My great-grandmother was climbing over the mound of firewood at my feet, clutching a blanket. "Here, put this over your shoulders," she said.

"I was almost burned at the stake, Gram," I said crankily. "I'm not *cold*."

"She's grateful," Peter said, draping the thing over me. "It's easier this way," he whispered. I knew he was right.

"Where's Miss P?" I asked.

"Agnes has her. We're all fine. Just be careful of the crush of people. Everyone will be leaving, you know."

"As if nothing's happened?" I asked hotly.

She sighed. "As if we were always good people," she said, patting my hand. "Give them that much, Katy."

I strained my eyes to see through the smoke that still lay thick across the Meadow. The first signs of dawn were appearing in the sky, streaks of light that dulled the once-bright light of the full moon. The woods were full of animals, deer and rabbits and birds, that had sensed the change in the air.

It was a new day.

We were headed out of the Meadow with Hattie when Eric began to wave his arms agitatedly.

"What is it, honey?" she asked.

"Maybe he's telling you to stay," someone said behind them. It was Becca Fowler.

"Is there something you want?" Hattie asked coldly.

Becca shook her head.

Hattie sniffed and turned away.

Tentatively Becca reached her hand toward Eric, then withdrew it quickly, unsure. Annoyed, Hattie swivelled her head around, making a sound of impatient disgust.

Eric responded by blowing bubbles through his lips. Then, showing all his crooked teeth in a big smile, he reached out to the girl, his straight arms waving urgently, wanting to touch her.

"Becca! You get away from there, now!" Livia Fowler called.

Becca took a step backward, her eyes downcast.

"Come on, baby," Hattie said to Eric. With more vigor than was necessary, she swung him away from Becca.

"Becca!"

"Go to your mama," Hattie spat.

But Becca didn't go. Ignoring her mother, she held out her arms to Eric, her hands cupped, her head bowed. Even from where I was standing, I could see that it was supplication.

Gently, perhaps sensing her need, Eric placed both his hands on hers.

She looked up, astonished, relieved, smiling.

I didn't know what had been wrong with Becca. Sometimes people have pain you can't see.

Afterward, she walked slowly to her mother and held her, just held her. Mrs. Fowler looked suddenly smaller than I'd ever seen her. She cried as she held Becca, hanging on to her daughter as if her life depended on it.

You didn't always need to use magic. Even Eric's nuclear-strength healing couldn't hold a candle to the miracles that were all around us every day. And, riddled with the Darkness as we all were, I knew that we fit into the magic, too.

Let us see the truth
Of our sublime divinity.

Nothing less.

Livia and Becca Fowler walked up to Hattie together. "I want you to see something," Mrs. Fowler said. She didn't speak the way she normally did, with that loud, imperious voice that made you want to punch her. She was humble. Her shoulders hunched forward. Her hands, I saw, were wrinkled and trembling, claws on her wide pigeon body.

Hattie nodded, circumspect. She didn't have my great-grandmother's grace, but she wasn't cruel. She knew when someone was apologizing, even if they didn't use the right words.

She handed Eric over to me, and then followed Mrs. Fowler to the botte containing the *Great Book of Secrets*. As they approached, Livia waved her wand over it in an arc, removing the barrier she had constructed to keep the rain—and any of us—away from it. Gently she closed the book, then opened its front cover. There was a piece of parchment inside, carefully preserved over centuries.

"This belongs to you," she said, giving it to Hattie. "I found it last night, when I put the protective spell around the botte." Hattie peered at the document, squinting as she tried to read the unfamiliar handwriting.

Unable to contain her curiosity, Gram leaned over Hattie's shoulder to read it along with her. "Why, it's . . ."

"It's the deed to the Meadow," Livia said. "Serenity Ainsworth signed it over to your ancestor Ola'ea Olokun in 1728, two years before she died. It was witnessed by Henry Shaw . . . and Veronica Fowler, from my family."

Hattie staggered backward, leaning heavily on Gram and Peter, who had come over to help. "The *deed*," Hattie said, dazed. "Do you think . . ."

"We'll see that it stands up in court," Agnes said.

"But . . . does this mean . . ." It was almost too good to be true. "Wonderland . . ."

Gram snatched the deed from her and held it aloft. "To *hell* with Wonderland!" she shouted, and a cheer went up that resounded through the entire Meadow.

We were all so busy hugging and whooping that no one seemed to notice the tall elderly man who had come into the crowd and was talking intently to Hattie. I wouldn't have paid any attention to him at all if Gram hadn't staggered back and clutched my hand.

"What is it?" I asked, alarmed. "Gram, are you okay?"

She waved the nearly three-hundred-year-old deed in front of her face like one of her handkerchiefs. "Good heavens," she whispered. "It's Jeremiah Shaw."

I think you could have heard my gasp in Rhode Island. Jeremiah Shaw, a witch! My gaze drifted over to Peter, who stood silently, polite but alert as the old man strode over to him. "Peter Shaw, isn't it?" he asked, holding out his hand.

Peter shook it. "Yes, sir."

"Are you the one who burned down my house?"

"It was my house, sir," Peter answered without a moment's hesitation.

Jeremiah chuckled. "That depends on which house you're talking about. I believe there were two."

Damn. I'd forgotten about the cabin.

"Mr. Shaw's going to rebuild the restaurant," Hattie said excitedly, taking Eric out of my arms. "For free."

I was ready to whoop again, but Peter's expression never changed. "What are you getting out of it?" he asked Mr. Shaw.

Jeremiah's smile faded. "Is that any of your business?"

"I believe it is," Peter said. "Hattie Scott is my guardian. My family," he said pointedly.

The old man put his hands in his pockets. "Well, if you must know, I'm trying to avoid a long series of lawsuits and countersuits," he said. "I don't want to spend the rest of my life in court."

"Me neither," Hattie said gently. "It's the best thing all around, Peter." She squeezed his shoulder before being swallowed by a happy mob of well-wishers.

Jeremiah looked Peter up and down, assessing him with

narrowed, farseeing eyes. "I'd like you to come visit me sometime," he said.

Peter frowned. "Why?" It was bald, aggressive, and rude. But honest.

Jeremiah put his hands in his pockets. The two of them, both tall and thin, with long fingers and aristocratic noses, stared silently at each other. They might have been mirror images of one another, separated only by years.

"Because I want to get to know you."

They continued to stare at one another for an embarrassingly long time, although neither of them looked the least bit uncomfortable. Finally Peter nodded curtly.

"Tomorrow, then," Jeremiah said. "Ten o'clock. My office."

"Ten o'clock," Peter repeated.

Jeremiah smiled. "Thinking about college, Peter?"

"Yes, sir."

"What interests you?"

"A lot of things."

"Money?"

Peter reddened. "I beg your pardon?"

"I said, 'money'. Are you interested in money?"

Peter looked at the old man. It was uncanny. They had the same eyes, piercing, intelligent, with a trace of humor and more than a little caution. "Not much," Peter said.

The old man grinned. "We'll see," he said.

Before turning and walking away, he reached into his pocket, pulled out a quarter, and flipped it into the air. The coin spun so fast that it made a sound like music. Then, as it slowed, it descended, gleaming, glinting yellow. Shiny.

Peter caught it. "It's gold," he said, following Jeremiah's retreating figure with his eyes.

There was just one more thing to do. Peter and I carried Eric over to the ancient oak that stood beside the botte. The rain had put out the fire that Mrs. Fowler had started, but it had come too late. The tree was burned beyond redemption. It had been old when the Meadow had first been created as a sanctuary for our people. Now it was a charred wreck, stinking and limbless.

From a high branch one leaf fell. It was shriveled and dry, as dead as the tree on which it had grown. It floated lazily on the early morning breeze, catching the thin sunlight as it made its way down fifty feet of desolation to land, curled and papery, into Eric Shaw's hand.

He looked at it for a moment, cooing softly in amazement as it plumped and grew green, it veins stiff with water, while those of us with him stood open-jawed at what was happening behind him: The tree was coming back to life, shedding its blackened bark, growing new branches, sprouting a crown of green leaves and young acorns.

The breeze picked up, filling the air with the scent of green. All through the Meadow, the spirits of the Summerland stirred. Serenity Ainsworth passed by me, and Zenobia, and Ola'ea. They were no more than a fragrance now, a vague memory. The dead cannot stay with us for long. They cannot bear our sorrow.

"Thank you," I said as they rustled through the new green leaves of the living oak. I doubted if any of us—even me—would remember that they were ever here. But in the distance, far away, I could hear the sound of water and wind and the turning of the earth, and the sun shone warm on my face as I listened to the great song, and knew that I would never, never be alone again.

EPILOGUE

 WITNESS

Concentric circles.

In the midst of one world lies another, a mystic sanctuary where witches live as if they were mere humans. They celebrate the rare triumph of good over evil, congratulating themselves on their integrity and goodwill.

The revelers feast, unaware of all the circles around them. They are noisy, happy, lighthearted, satisfied. There is the sound of laughter. Talking. Music. The occasional snap of a party favor, the pop of a champagne cork.

Then, outside, the chirp of crickets, the songs of nightbirds. Voiceless creatures moving delicately through the woods. A snapped branch. The whistle of the wind. The rush of moving water. The deep, terrifying call of the sea.

Beyond that, wrapped in the conjured fog, the spirits of the Summerland arise, come to remember the agony and joy of life. Quiet stirrings, the longings of stilled hearts made uneasy through memory. On this night, the dead cannot rest. On this night, they watch.

Above them, above it all, too far for the living to notice, too silent even for the dead to hear, curls a presence like black smoke against the black of night, invisible, inexorable, certain.

The Darkness.

Apart from the lands of the living and the dead, in the realm of deepest magic, it circles like a bird of prey, waiting, waiting . . .

Suddenly, in the center of the circle, something glimmers. A gold coin, turning, spinning, flashing prettily, seductively, fulfilling a prophecy that none of the witches remembers. Gold and power, and utter destruction.

Delicious.

The Darkness shivers.

Patient.

Waiting . . .

Waiting . . .

ACKNOWLEDGMENTS

I am indebted to so many people for their support, encouragement, and assistance in the creation of this work: among them my agent Lucienne Diver and my editor Alexandra Penfold, for guiding me through the peculiarities and difficulties of this new genre . . . my stalwart readers Pam Williamson, Lynne Carrera, and Shay Miller, who vetted each page as soon as it was written and cheered me through the hard parts . . . my son Devin Murphy, for keeping me abreast of trends in fashion, speech, music, and electronics . . . Lady Liadan, who graciously supplied the three-part spell used in the book . . . Tim Fox and Michael Belletti of Fox Optical in Bethlehem, Pennsylvania, for providing me with gorgeous new glasses when mine broke so that I could finish my story . . . and BFF Michele Horon, who spent many tortured hours agonizing over the plot with me.

I also need to thank my last corporate boss who, by firing me on a whim, convinced me to go back to writing, which, for all its heartbreak, is a lot more fun than actually working.

Blessings on them all.

Mischief abounds at the Ainsworth School and evil is lurking. When the three most popular girls at school fall mysteriously ill, Katy is wrongfully accused. Desperate to clear her name, she finds herself battling all odds to harness her growing magical skill to dispel the Darkness once more.

PRINT AND EBOOK EDITIONS AVAILABLE.

I probably went to the only school in the country with a rule against practicing witchcraft.

That wasn't really as crazy as it sounded. The Massachusetts town where I lived was sort of known for its rumored history of magical residents. Some said it was even more haunted by witches than Salem, our famous neighbor. The story went that while the Pilgrims in Salem were burning innocent women at the stake, the real witches went to Whitfield and vanished into a fog.

Of course, that wasn't entirely true. Nobody had actually been burned at the stake in Salem. Oh, there had been plenty of murders, jailings, and torture of women who hadn't done much more than piss off their neighbors. Lots of widows had their property stolen, and one guy got crushed to death. But the burnings were pretty much left to the Europeans. The part of the story that *was* true was the part about the real witches going to Whitfield.

I knew because I was the descendant of one of those witches.

A lot of us were, although we kept quiet about it. That was because even there, in the town where at least half the population were witches, we had to live among *cowen*, aka non-magical people. Actually, we thought of ourselves as *talented*—we could all do different things—rather than *magical*. But that wouldn't have mattered to cowen. They had a nice tradition of destroying anything they couldn't understand. Look at Salem.

At school there were two kinds of students, the Muffies and the witches. Muffies were the kinds of girls you'd find at every boarding school in the northeast: fashionable, promiscuous, and clueless. Okay, that wasn't fair. There were plenty of cowen kids at Ainsworth School who weren't Muffies. Half of them weren't even girls. But those non-Muffies generally left us alone. It was the Muffies who were always making life difficult.

They sneered at us. They called us names. (Yeah, these were the same people who were legally named Bitsy, Binky, and Buffy). "Geek" was probably the most popular name for us, since it was pretty much true, at least from their point of view. We generally didn't have problems with drugs, alcoholism, reckless driving, kleptomania, credit card debt, or STDs. To be fair, we did sometimes have issues with ghosts, apparitions, disappearing, transmogrification, rainmaking, telepathy, demon rampages, telekinesis, and raising the dead. And maybe a few more things.

Hence the injunction against performing witchcraft at Ainsworth. This rule had been in place ever since my ancestor Serenity Ainsworth had founded the school. (I liked to think that one of her pupils had given some Puritan Muffy a pig nose in a catfight.)

The Muffies didn't know about this rule. They didn't know

that Whitfield was the biggest and oldest community of witches in the United States, or that the geeks at Ainsworth School could summon enough power to make a hydrogen bomb seem like a fart in a bathtub if we wanted to. They thought that Whitfield was an ordinary place and that Ainsworth was an ordinary school.

Or did they?

I'd often wondered if they knew. . . . I mean, how could they *not* know? On every major witch holiday the Meadow—that was a big field in the middle of Old Town—filled up with fog so dense that you couldn't see through it. It was the same fog that saved the witches from being grabbed by the Puritans back in the day. When the fog appeared, the witches all tumbled into it like lemmings, but cowen couldn't—physically *couldn't*—enter. And that was only one of the weird shenanigans that went on there. Even the dumbest Muffies must have had an inkling once in a while that Whitfield, Massachusetts, was a little different from wherever they called home.

At least that was my theory about how the whole mess started. With a jealous Muffy.

And an idiot who should have known better than to forget the no-witchcraft rule, since it was her relative who'd made it in the first place.

Right. It was me. But in all fairness I had a good reason. I was protecting my friend Verity from Summer Hayworth, the most evil of the evil Muffies at Ainsworth. More accurately, I was protecting her boyfriend, Cheswick, from expulsion, and possibly arrest, for what he was about to do to Summer in Verity's defense.

I could still see it—Summer, who had the taste level of a dung beetle, laughing when Verity opened her locker and found a stuffed witch doll hanging by its neck. The doll had been made to look like Verity, with striped stockings and red hair. Its eyes had been removed and replaced by Xs, and someone had sewn a red tongue hanging out the side of its mouth.

There was no doubt about who'd done it. Even though none of them had classes near Verity's locker, Summer and her three main cohorts—A. J. Nakamura, Tiffany Rothstein, and Suzy Dusset—just *happened* to be hanging around the area. Aside from Verity, me, and our boyfriends, Cheswick and Peter, the evil Muffies were the only people within a hundred feet of the locker in question. As for the witch doll itself, well, it had "evil Muffy" stamped all over it. A.J. was an artist, and the tongue definitely looked like her work, but the idea had to have been Summer's because nobody else in the school could possibly have been so crass.

If it had been my locker, I wouldn't have thought much about it. The witch doll was actually kind of cute, X-ed out eyes and all. But Verity was, well, sensitive. More to the point, she was a QMS—a quivering mass of sensitivity—of the highest order. She got emotional if someone swatted a fly or squashed a mosquito. She went into coughing fits if anyone in the room was wearing perfume. She was a vegan, of course, and only wore plastic shoes. Frankly, she wasn't the most fun person to party with, but that wasn't the point.

The point was, she was from a very old witch family, and being outed by Muffies in high school was, for Verity, pretty much on a par with being ravaged by wild dogs. She went all pale and started shaking so hard that Cheswick had to hold her up. Her eyes filled with tears. Her nose ran. Her fingertips turned blue.

"She needs something to drink," Cheswick said. He was looking at me, but Summer answered:

"What would she like? Bat's blood?"

"Shut up, Summer," I said.

"You going to make me, or are you just going to turn me into a frog?"

"I'd turn you into a jerk, except someone must have beat me to it," I said. Peter poked me in the arm. He thought I asked for trouble. Not true. I never had confrontations with horrible people if I could help it. Peter was just more of a "go with the flow" kind of person than I was.

Tiffany almost laughed at my little comeback, but she checked herself. Summer had no sense of humor, especially about herself. A.J. and Suzy just stared, as bored and clueless as ever.

"Let's get out of here," Peter said.

"Yeah," Cheswick agreed, slamming Verity's locker with a little more force than necessary.

"Oh, yeah. Go with your cool boyfriend," Summer said. A.J. and Suzy smiled. Cheswick, who looked like a dandelion puff and was the all-school champion in Lord of the Rings trivia, was not considered cool, even by the geeks.

I think this, more than Summer's offending Verity, was what set him off. Before any of us knew what was happening, Cheswick hurled Verity at Peter like he was passing a football, and threw five fingers at Summer.

The Muffies laughed at that, which showed how dumb they really were. When witches did that—flicked their fingers at someone—it was like aiming a wand at them. And when the witch was as pissed off as Cheswick was, the result usually wasn't good.

"Cheswick!" I whispered, but it was too late to stop him. All I could do at that point was try to weaken his spell by throwing out one of my own to cross his.

"Stink!" I shouted. Don't ask me why I chose that one. It was probably at the core of what I felt about Summer and the skank girls. Anyway, at that moment A. J. Nakamura, Japanese-American princess that she was, let loose with this tremendous salami-scented belch. Tiffany sniffed at her armpits, and then gagged. Suzy Dusset grabbed her belly and headed for the bathroom, sounding like a Formula One race car the whole way.

"What the hell do you think . . . ," Summer began, then stopped to sniff the air she had just fouled with her breath. The rest of us shrank backward. Verity started to retch. Summer narrowed her eyes at me. "You'll be sorry," she said. Then she smiled at Peter and made the *Call me* gesture with her fingers. That was how crusty she was.

"Er . . . you wouldn't happen to have some air freshener in your locker, would you?" I asked Verity.

Cheswick led her away. Figuring that Verity didn't need a repeat of what had just gone on, I opened the locker and took out the doll.

"I don't think you should be touching that," Peter said.

"Hey, somebody has to get rid of it."

He sighed. "Okay, but why does that person always have to be you?"

"It's just better if we avoid complication," I said. "Look, I'm not doing anything wrong, okay?"

"Exactly what *are* you doing, Katy?" a pleasant voice behind me asked. It was Miss P, the assistant principal.

"Oh, no," Peter muttered.

"Move along, Peter," Miss P said, her eyes never leaving mine. "Is that your locker?"

Quickly I stashed the doll behind my back. "Miss P, I can explain."

"I don't think so," she said in a tone she might have used to discuss the weather. "I saw you using special ability on those girls." "Special ability" was code for "witchcraft."

"Then you know I didn't—" I thrust out my arms, having forgotten about the doll, whose head bobbed in mute accusation.

"I'll take that, please."

Abashed, I handed it to her as I watched Peter recede into the distance, shaking his head.

"Do you have a minute?" Miss P said cheerfully. That was code for "Bend over and kiss your butt good-bye."

Did you love this book?

Want to get access to
the hottest books for free?

Log on to simonandschuster.com/pulseit

to find out how to join,

get access to cool sweepstakes,

and hear about your favorite authors!

Become part of Pulse IT and tell us what you think!

Margaret K.
McElderry Books   SIMON & SCHUSTER BFYR

CAROL LYNCH WILLIAMS

In one moment it can all be gone,
but it can take forever to find out why. . . .

★"Williams's decision to wait until the end to divulge the cause of Lizzie's misery is a gamble, but one that works."—*Publishers Weekly*, starred review for *Glimpse*

★"Exceptional."—*Kirkus Reviews*, starred review for *Waiting*

★"Inspirational."—*Publishers Weekly*, starred review for *Waiting*

★"Gut-wrenching."—*SLJ*, starred review for *Waiting*

PRINT AND EBOOK EDITIONS AVAILABLE

SIMON & SCHUSTER BFYR

TEEN.SimonandSchuster.com

A sacred oath,
a fallen angel,
a forbidden love

YOU WON'T BE ABLE TO
KEEP IT *HUSH, HUSH.*

EBOOK EDITIONS ALSO AVAILABLE

SIMON & SCHUSTER BFYR · TEEN.SimonandSchuster.com

WHAT IF YOU KNEW EXACTLY WHEN YOU WOULD DIE?

THE CHEMICAL GARDEN TRILOGY

WITHER

LAUREN DESTEFANO

THE CHEMICAL GARDEN TRILOGY

FEVER

THE CHEMICAL GARDEN TRILOGY

LAUREN DESTEFANO

Rhine Ellery's time may be running out, but her fight can outlast her fate.

EBOOK EDITIONS ALSO AVAILABLE

SIMON & SCHUSTER BFYR

TEEN.SimonandSchuster.com